"You're in the tow

Mindy handed her the key. "If you don't mind waiting just a moment, Kevin will take your suitcases up for you."

"That's not necessary," a male voice coming from behind Amanda said. "I'll take care of Ms. Stockenberg's luggage."

No, Amanda thought. *It can't be!*

She slowly turned around. "Hello, Dane."

Although a decade had passed, he looked just the same. But better, she thought. His shaggy dark hair was still in need of a haircut, and his eyes, nearly as dark as his hair, were far from calm, but the emotions swirling in their midnight depths were too complex for Amanda to decipher. A five-o'clock shadow did nothing to detract from his good looks; the dark stubble only added to his appeal. His jeans, white T-shirt and black leather jacket were distractingly sexy.

"Hello, princess." His full, sensual mouth curved in a smile. "Welcome to Smugglers' Inn."

FINDING HER HERO

NEW YORK TIMES BESTSELLING AUTHOR

JoAnn Ross

AND

Michelle Major

**Previously published as *It Happened One Week*
and *Romancing the Wallflower***

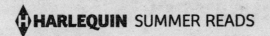

HARLEQUIN SUMMER READS

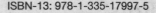

HARLEQUIN® SUMMER READS

ISBN-13: 978-1-335-17997-5

Recycling programs for this product may not exist in your area.

Finding Her Hero
Copyright © 2020 by Harlequin Books S.A.

It Happened One Week
First published in 1996. This edition published in 2020.
Copyright © 1996 by Joann Ross

Romancing the Wallflower
First published in 2017. This edition published in 2020.
Copyright © 2017 by Michelle Major

This edition published by arrangement with Harlequin Books S.A.

For questions and comments about the quality of this book, please contact us at CustomerService@Harlequin.com.

Harlequin Enterprises ULC
22 Adelaide St. West, 40th Floor
Toronto, Ontario M5H 4E3, Canada
www.Harlequin.com

Printed in U.S.A.

CONTENTS

JoAnn Ross is the *New York Times* bestselling author of over one hundred novels and has been published in twenty-six countries. Her books have been Doubleday, Rhapsody, Literary Guild and Mystery Guild book club selections. A member of the Romance Writers of America Honor Roll of bestselling authors, she's won several awards, including the *RT Book Reviews* Career Achievement Award and RWA Pro Mentor of the Year. Currently writing her Honeymoon Harbor series, set on Washington State's Olympic Peninsula, JoAnn lives with her high school sweetheart, whom she married twice, in her beloved Pacific Northwest.

Books by JoAnn Ross

HQN Books

Once Upon a Wedding (novella)
Herons Landing
Home to Honeymoon Harbor (novella)
Snowfall on Lighthouse Lane

Visit the Author Profile page at
Harlequin.com for more titles.

IT HAPPENED ONE WEEK

JoAnn Ross

To Dianne Moggy—who provided the inspiration.

Prologue

Satan's Cove

The letters had been painstakingly carved into the shifting silver sands. Although she could see them from the top of the jagged cliff overlooking the Pacific Ocean, fifteen-year-old Amanda Stockenberg could not make out the message.

As she descended the stone steps to the beach, slowly at first, then faster, until she was nearly running, the words became clearer.

Dane loves Amanda.

Despite the fact that she'd spent most of last night crying, Amanda began to weep.

He was waiting for her in their secret, private place. Just as he'd promised. Just as she'd hoped.

Smugglers' Cave, carved by aeons of wind and ocean

out of the rocky seaside cliffs, had long been rumored to be one of the local sites where pirates had once hidden stolen booty before moving it inland.

Amanda wasn't interested in the legends about the pirates' nefarious behavior. And despite the violence that supposedly occurred here, to her, Smugglers' Cave was the most romantic place on earth.

It was here, on a star-spangled July Fourth night, while the glare of fireworks lit up the night sky, that Dane first kissed her. Then kissed her again. And again. Until she thought she'd literally melt from ecstasy.

"I thought you wouldn't come," she cried, flinging herself dramatically into his strong dark arms. Her avid mouth captured his. The kiss was hot and long and bittersweet.

"I told you I would," he reminded her, after they finally came up for air.

"I know." Her hands were linked together around his neck. Her young, lithe body was pressed against his so tightly that it would have been impossible for the morning ocean breeze to come between them. "But I was so afraid you'd be mad at me."

"Mad?" Dane looked honestly surprised by the idea. "Why would I be mad at you?"

"For leaving." Just thinking about her imminent departure caused the moisture in Amanda's sea blue eyes to overflow.

"You don't have any choice, sweetheart." With more tenderness than she would have imagined possible, he brushed her tears away with his fingertips. "We've both known that from the beginning."

"That doesn't make it any less awful!" she wailed.

"No." Despite his brave words, Dane's dark eyes were

every bit as bleak as hers as he traced her trembling, downturned pink lips with a tear-dampened finger. "It doesn't."

The tender touch left behind a taste of salt born of her overwhelming sorrow. "We could run away," she said desperately, grabbing his hand and holding it tightly between both of hers. "Just you and I. Somewhere no one could ever find us. To Wyoming. Or Florida."

"Don't think I haven't been tempted." His lips curved at the idea, but even as distressed as she was, Amanda noticed that the smile didn't reach his eyes. "But running away is never the answer, princess."

She was too desperate, too unhappy, to listen to reason. "But—"

"We can't." His tone, while gentle, was firm. "As attractive as the idea admittedly is, it's wrong."

"How can love be wrong?"

Dane sighed, looking far older, far more world-weary than his nineteen years. "You're only fifteen years old—"

"I'll be sixteen next week."

"I know." This time the reluctant smile turned his eyes to the hue of rich, warm chocolate. "But you still have your entire life ahead of you, honey. I'm not going to be responsible for ruining it."

"But you wouldn't!" she cried on a wail that scattered a trio of sea gulls. "You'd make it better. Perfect, even."

As much as she'd first resisted joining her family for this annual summer vacation on the Oregon coast, the moment she'd first seen Smugglers' Inn's sexy young bellhop, lifeguard, and all-around handyman, Amanda had changed her mind.

Over the past four glorious weeks, her life had been

focused on Dane Cutter. He was all she wanted. All she would ever want. She'd love him, Amanda vowed, forever.

But now, she didn't want to waste time talking. Not when their time together was coming to an end, like sands falling through some hateful hourglass. Rising on her toes, she pressed her lips against his once more.

The morning mist swirled around them; overhead, sea gulls squawked stridently as they circled, searching for mussels in the foaming surge. Caught up in emotions every bit as strong—and as old—as the forces that had formed the craggy coastline, neither Dane nor Amanda heard them.

The ocean's roar became a distant buzz in Amanda's ears. For this glorious suspended moment, time ceased to have meaning. The hungry kiss could have lasted a minute, an hour, an eternity.

Finally, the blare of a car horn managed to infiltrate its way into Amanda's consciousness. She tried to ignore it, but it was soon followed by the sound of an irritated male voice cutting through the fog.

Dane dragged his mouth from hers. "Your father's calling." He skimmed his lips up her cheeks, which were damp again from the cold ocean mist and her tears.

"I know." She swiped at the tears with the backs of her trembling hands, looking, Dane thought, more like an injured child than the almost-grown-up woman she insisted that she was. Unwilling, unable to leave, she twined her arms around his neck again and clung.

For not the first time since her arrival in Satan's Cove, Dane found himself sorely tested. For not the first time, he reminded himself that she was far too young for the thoughts he kept having, the feelings he kept experiencing. But even as his mind struggled to hold on to that crucial fact—like a drowning man clinging to a piece of driftwood in a storm-tossed sea—his body was literally aching for fulfillment.

Dane was not inexperienced. He'd discovered, since losing his virginity to a sexy blond Miss Depoe Bay the summer of his sixteenth year, that sex was easy to come by. Especially during vacation season, when the beaches were filled with beautiful girls looking for a summer fling.

But he'd never wanted a girl as he wanted Amanda. What was worse, he'd never *needed* a girl as he needed Amanda. Accustomed to keeping a tight rein on his emotions, Dane wasn't at all comfortable with the effect Amanda Stockenberg had had on him from the beginning.

Finally, although it was nearly the hardest thing he'd ever had to do—second only to refusing her ongoing, seductive pleas to make love these past weeks—Dane gently, patiently, unfastened Amanda's hold on him.

"You have to go," he said again, prying her hands from around his neck. He kissed her fingers one at a time. "But it's not over, princess. Not unless you want it to be."

Distraught as she was, Amanda failed to hear the question—and the uncharacteristic lack of assurance—in his guarded tone.

"Never!" she swore with all the fervor of a young woman in the throes of her first grand love. "I promise."

Her father called out again. The van's horn blared. Once. Twice. A third time.

Giving Dane one last desperate kiss, Amanda spun

around, sobbing loudly as she ran up the rock stairs. She did not—could not—look back.

He stood there all alone, hands shoved deep into the pockets of his jeans, and watched her leave, resisting the urge to call out to her. He heard the van drive off, taking her far away from Satan's Cove. Away from him.

Dane stayed on the windswept beach for a long, silent time, watching as the relentless ebb and flow of the tide slowly, inexorably, washed away the love letter he'd written in the drifting silver sand.

Chapter 1

Portland, Oregon
Ten years later

"This can't be happening. Not to me. Not now!" Amanda Stockenberg stared in disbelief at the television screen where towering red-and-orange flames were engulfing the Mariner Seaside Golf Resort and Conference Center located on the Oregon coast.

"It *is* lousy timing," her administrative assistant, Susan Chin, agreed glumly. It had been Susan who'd alerted Amanda to the disaster, after hearing a news bulletin on the radio.

"That has to be the understatement of the millennium," Amanda muttered as she opened a new roll of antacids.

Hoping for the best, but fearing the worst, she'd left a meeting and run down the hall to the conference room.

Now, as the two women stood transfixed in front of the television, watching the thick streams of water prove ineffectual at combating the massive blaze, Amanda could see her entire career going up in smoke right along with the five-star resort.

She groaned as the hungry flames devoured the lovely cedar-shake shingled roof. The scene shifted as the cameras cut away to show the crews of helmeted firemen valiantly fighting the fire. From the grim expressions on their soot-stained faces, she sensed that they knew their efforts to be a lost cause.

And speaking of lost causes...

"It's obvious we're going to have to find a new site for the corporate challenge," she said, cringing when what was left of the wooden roof caved in with a deafening roar. Water from the fire hoses hit the flames, turned to steam and mixed with the clouds of thick gray smoke.

"I'd say that's a given," Susan agreed glumly. "Unless you want to have the group camping out on the beach. Which, now that I think about it, isn't such a bad idea. After all, the entire idea of this coming week is to present the creative teams with challenges to overcome."

"Getting any of the managers of *this* company to work together as a team is going to be challenge enough." Amanda sank into a chair, put her elbows on the long rectangular mahogany conference table and began rubbing at her temples, where a headache had begun to pound. "Without tossing in sleeping in tents on wet sand and bathing out of buckets."

Advertising had been a cutthroat, shark-eat-shark business since the first Babylonian entrepreneur had gotten the bright idea to chisel the name of his company onto a stone tablet. Competition was always fierce, and everyone knew that the battle went not only to the most creative, but to the most ruthless.

Even so, Amanda felt the employees of Janzen, Lawton and Young took the idea of healthy competition to unattractive and often unprofitable extremes. Apparently, Ernst Janzen, senior partner of the company that had recently purchased Amanda's advertising agency, seemed to share her feelings. Which was why the idea of corporate-management teams was born in the first place.

In theory, the concept of art, copy and marketing working together on each step of a project seemed ideal. With everyone marching in unison toward the same finish line, the firm would undoubtedly regain superiority over its competitors.

That was the plan. It was, Amanda had agreed, when she'd first heard of it, extremely logical. Unfortunately, there was little about advertising that was the least bit logical.

The agency that had hired her directly after her graduation from UCLA, Connally Creative Concepts, or C.C.C., had made a name for itself by creating witty, appealing and totally original advertising that persuaded and made the sale through its ability to charm the prospect.

Although its location in Portland, Oregon, was admittedly a long way from Madison Avenue, some of the best copywriters and art directors in the country had been more than willing to leave Manhattan and take pay cuts in order to work long hours under the tutelage of Patrick Connally. C.C.C. had been like a family, Patrick Connally playing the role of father to everyone who came for inspiration and guidance.

Unfortunately, two years ago Patrick Connally had

died of a heart attack at the age of seventy-five, after a heated game of tennis. His widow, eager to retire to Sun City, Arizona, had sold the agency to another company. Eight months after that, the new owner merged the united agencies with yet a third creative shop.

Unsurprisingly, such multiple mergers in such a short span of time resulted in the dismissal of several longtime employees as executives trimmed excess staff. A mood of anxiety settled over the offices and morale plummeted as everyone held their collective breath, waiting to see who was going to be "downsized" next.

After the initial purge, things had seemed to be settling down until the advertising wars kicked up again. A six-month battle that played out daily in the newspapers and on the internet had resulted in an unfriendly takeover by the international mega-agency of Janzen, Lawton and Young, and those employees who'd been breathing at last, found their livelihoods once again in jeopardy.

Janzen, Lawton and Young had long had a reputation for the most artless and offensive commercials to run in America. But it also boasted the highest profits in the business. In order to keep profits up to the promised levels, a new wave of massive staff cuts had hit the agency.

Morale plummeted to new lows.

Unsurprisingly, the same creative people who had once been responsible for some of the most innovative— and effective—advertising in the business, turned on one another.

A recent case in point was today's client meeting. The creative group had been assigned to propose a new concept for a popular line of gourmet ice cream. From day one, the members of the recently established team had been at each other's throats like a pack of out-of-control pit bulls.

"I can't believe you seriously expect me to be a part of this presentation," Marvin Kenyon, the head copywriter, had complained after viewing the animated sequence proposed by award-winning art director Julian Palmer.

"It's a team effort," Amanda reminded him mildly. "And you *are* a valuable member of the team."

The copywriter, who'd won his share of awards himself, folded his arms over the front of his blue oxford-cloth shirt and said, "I categorically refuse to share blame for something as sophomoric and static as that animation sequence."

"Sophomoric?" Julian Palmer rose to his full height of five feet five inches tall. What he lacked in stature, he more than made up for in ego. "Static? Since when are you an expert on visuals?"

"I know enough to see that if we present your idea, we'll blow the account for sure," Marvin retorted. "Hell, a baboon with a fistful of crayons could undoubtedly create a more visually appealing storyboard."

Julian arched an eyebrow as he adjusted the already perfect Windsor knot in his Italian-silk tie. "This from a man who creates—" he waved the printed sheets Marvin had handed out when he'd first arrived in the presentation room like a battle flag "—mindless drivel?"

"Drivel?" Marvin was on his feet in a shot, hands folded into fists as he came around the long, polished mahogany table.

"Marvin," Amanda protested, "please sit down. Julian didn't mean it, did you, Julian?"

"I never say anything I don't mean," the artistic director replied. "But in this case, I may have been mistaken."

"There, see?" Amanda soothed, feeling as if she were refereeing a fight between two toddlers in a kindergarten sandbox. "Julian admits he was mistaken, Marvin. Perhaps you can amend your comment about his work."

"I *was* wrong to call it drivel," Julian agreed. "That's too kind a description for such cliché-ridden rubbish."

"That does it!" Marvin, infamous for his quicksilver temper, was around the table like a shot. He'd grabbed hold of his team member's chalk-gray vest and for a moment Amanda feared that the two men were actually going to come to blows, when the conference-room door opened and the client arrived with Don Patterson, the marketing manager, on his heels.

"Am I interrupting something?" the longtime client, a man in his mid-fifties whose addiction to ice cream had made him a very wealthy man, asked.

"Only a momentary creative difference of opinion," Amanda said quickly. "Good afternoon, Mr. Carpenter. It's nice to see you again."

"It's always a pleasure to see you again, Ms. Stockenberg." The portly entrepreneur took her outstretched hand in his. His blue eyes warmed momentarily as they swept over her appreciatively. "I'm looking forward to today's presentation," he said as his gaze moved to the uncovered storyboard.

Wide brow furrowed, he crossed the room and began studying it for a long silent time. Since it was too late to begin the presentation as planned, the team members refrained from speaking as he took in the proposed campaign. Amanda didn't know about the others, but she would have found it impossible to say a word, holding her breath as she was.

When Fred Carpenter finally did speak, his words

were not encouraging. "You people have serviced my account for five years. I've dropped a bundle into your coffers. And this is as good as you can come up with? A cow wearing a beret?"

"Let me explain the animation," Julian said quickly. Too quickly, Amanda thought with an inner sigh. He was making the fatal mistake of any presenter: appearing desperate.

"Don't worry, the art can be rethought," Marvin interjected as Julian picked up the laser pen to better illustrate the sequence. "Besides, it's the words that'll sell your new, improved, French vanilla flavor, anyway." He paused, as if half expecting a drumroll to announce his message. "A taste of Paris in every spoonful."

"That's it?" the snack-food executive asked.

"Well, it's just the beginning," Marvin assured him. Moisture was beading up on his upper lip, his forehead. Another rule broken, Amanda thought, remembering what Patrick Connally had taught her about never letting the client—or the competition—see you sweat. "See, the way I envision the concept—"

"It's drivel," Julian said again. "But the team can fix that, Fred. Now, if we could just get back to the art."

"It's not drivel," Marvin exploded.

"Marvin," Amanda warned softly.

"I've seen cleverer copy written on rolls of novelty toilet paper," the art director sniffed.

"And I've seen better art scrawled on the sides of buildings down at the docks!"

Amanda turned toward the client who appeared less than amused by the escalating argument. "As you can see, Mr. Carpenter, your campaign has created a lot of in-house excitement," she said, trying desperately to salvage the multimillion-dollar account.

"Obviously the wrong kind," Carpenter said. "Look, I haven't liked how all these mergers resulted in my account being put into the hands of the same agency that handles my competitors. It looks to me as if you guys have been instructed by your new bosses to soften your approach—"

"The hell we have," both Julian and Marvin protested in unison, agreeing for once. Amanda tried telling herself she should be grateful for small favors.

"Then you've lost your edge," the self-proclaimed king of ice cream decided.

"That's really not the case, Fred," Don Patterson, the marketing member of the team, finally interjected. A man prone to wearing loud ties and plaid sport jackets, he was nevertheless very good at his job. "Perhaps if Julian and Marvin went back to the drawing board—"

"There's no point. We've had five great years working together, you fellows have helped make Sweet Indulgence the second-bestselling ice cream in the country. But, the team over at Chiat/Day assures me that they can get me to number one. So, I think I'm going to give them a try."

He turned toward Amanda, who could literally feel the color draining from her face. "I'm sorry, Ms. Stockenberg. You're a nice, pretty lady and I'd like to keep my account here if for no other reason than to have an excuse to keep seeing you. But business is business."

"I understand." With effort, Amanda managed a smile and refrained from strangling the two ego-driven creative members of the ill-suited team. "But Don does have a point. Perhaps if you'd allow us a few days to come up with another concept—"

"Sorry." He shook his head. "But things haven't been the same around here since all the mergers." His round face looked as unhappy as hers. "But if you'd like," he said, brightening somewhat, "I'll mention you to the fellows at Chiat/Day. Perhaps there's a spot opening up over there."

"That's very kind of you. But I'm quite happy where I am."

It was what she'd been telling herself over and over again lately, Amanda thought now, as she dragged her mind from the disastrous meeting to the disaster currently being played out on the television screen.

"You know," Susan said, "this entire challenge week isn't really your problem. Officially, it's Greg's."

"I know." Amanda sighed and began chewing on another Tums.

Greg Parsons was her immediate supervisor and, as creative director, he was the man Ernst Janzen had hand-selected for the job of instituting the team concept. The man who had moved into the executive suite was as different from Patrick Connally as night from day. Rather than encouraging the cooperative atmosphere that had once thrived under the founder of C.C.C., Greg ruled the agency by intimidation and fear.

From his first day on the job, he'd set unrealistic profit targets. This focus on profits diverted attention from what had always been the agency's forte—making clients feel they were getting superior service.

Apparently believing that internal competition was the lifeblood of success, he instigated political maneuvering among his top people, pitting one against the other as they jockeyed for key appointments.

Although such intrigue usually occurred behind the scenes, one of the more visible changes in policy was the conference table at which Amanda was sitting. When she'd first come to work here, the room had boasted a giant round table, the better, her former boss had declared, to create the feeling of democracy. Now, five days a week, the staff sat around this oblong table while Parsons claimed the power position at the head.

Although it might not seem like such a big thing, along with all the other changes that had taken place, it was additional proof that C.C.C. had lost the family feeling that had been so comfortable and inspirational to both employees and clients.

Desperate to salvage his foundering career, Parsons had come up with the idea of taking the teams to a resort, where, utilizing a number of outward-bound-type game-playing procedures he'd gleaned from his latest management-training course, the various independent-minded individuals would meld into one forceful creative entity.

"The problem is," Amanda said, "like it or not, my fortunes are tied to Greg."

"Lucky him. Since without you to run interference and do all his detail work, he'd undoubtedly have been out on his Armani rear a very long time ago," Susan said.

"That's not very nice."

"Granted. But it's true."

Amanda couldn't argue with her assistant's pithy analysis. From the time of Greg's arrival from the Dallas office three months ago, she'd wondered, on more than one occasion, exactly how the man had managed to win the corporate plum of creative director. It certainly hadn't been on merit.

Then, six weeks after he'd moved into the expensively redecorated executive office, the question was answered when Susan returned from a long lunch with the other administrative assistants where she'd learned that Greg just happened to be married to Ernst Janzen's granddaughter. Which, Amanda had agreed, explained everything.

It was bad enough that Greg was frightfully incompetent. Even worse was the way he saw himself as a modern-day Napoleon—part dictator, part Don Juan. And although she'd deftly dealt with his less-than-subtle passes, her refusal had earned Amanda her superior's antipathy. He rode her constantly, belittling her work even as he routinely took credit for her ideas in upper-level corporate meetings.

It was no secret that the man was unhappy in Portland. He constantly berated the entire West Coast as hopelessly provincial. It was also common knowledge that he had his eye on a superior prize—that of national creative director and vice president. Along with the requisite increase in salary and numerous perks, the coveted slot also came with a corner-window penthouse office on Manhattan's famed Madison Avenue.

"I still don't see why you put up with the man," Susan said, her acid tone breaking into Amanda's thoughts.

"It's simple. I want his job."

"It should have been yours in the first place."

Once again, Amanda couldn't argue with the truth. While she hadn't specifically been promised the creative director's spot when she was first hired, there'd been every indication that Patrick Connally considered her on the fast track to success.

She'd worked hard for the past four years, forgoing any social life, giving most of her time and energy to the company.

The sacrifices had paid off; there had been a time, not so long ago, when the job of creative director had looked like a lock. Until Greg Parsons arrived on the scene.

"Blood's thicker than water. And unfortunately, Greg happens to be married to Mr. Janzen's granddaughter."

"Talk about sleeping your way to the top," Susan muttered.

"Unfortunately, family ties seem to have gotten Greg this far." Amanda frowned up at the oil portrait of the new creative director hanging on the wall. The ornate, gilt-framed painting featured Parsons in one of his dress-for-success chalk-striped suits, holding a cigar.

"But," she continued, "after the problems he's had instituting the team concept, he's stalled in the water."

Susan arched a jet eyebrow. "Are you saying you think he's on the way out?"

"Unfortunately, I don't think—unless Jessica Janzen Parsons wises up and divorces him—there's any chance of that. So, I've come up with a plan to get the guy out of my life—and out of town—once and for all."

"Please tell me it involves tar and feathers."

"Not quite." Actually, although she'd never admit it, Amanda found the idea of running Parsons out of town on a rail—like in the good old days of the Wild West—eminently appealing.

"Actually, it's simple. Or at least it was," she amended with another bleak glance toward the television screen. "Until the resort went up in smoke."

"Let me guess. You were going to lure the bastard out onto the cliff behind the resort late one night, hit him in the head with his precious new PING nine iron, then shove him into the ocean. Where, with any luck, he'd be eaten by killer sharks."

Despite all her problems, Amanda smiled. "As attractive as that scenario may be, the sharks would probably spare him because of professional courtesy. Besides, I've come to the conclusion that the easiest way to get Greg out of my hair is to give him what he most wants."

"Don't tell me that you're going to go to bed with him?"

"Of course not." Amanda literally shuddered at the unpalatable idea. "Actually, I've decided to get him promoted."

A slow, understanding grin had Susan's crimson lips curving. "To Manhattan."

Amanda returned the smile with a cocky, confident grin of her own. "To Manhattan."

Amanda couldn't deny that losing the conference-center resort to fire was a setback. After all, without someplace to hold the corporate challenge, Greg couldn't prove that his idea had merit. Which in turn would keep him here in Portland indefinitely.

But it wasn't the first challenge she'd overcome in her rise up the advertising corporate ladder. Amanda doubted it would be her last.

A part of her hated the idea of Greg Parsons getting any more credit, when in reality, if the upcoming week proved a success, it would be her doing. A stronger part of her just wanted him gone. She would swallow her pride, along with her ego, if it meant getting the obnoxious man out of her life.

Now all she had to do was find some other location for the challenge. Which wasn't going to be easy, considering this was the high tourist season on the Oregon coast.

Could she do it? Amanda asked herself as she pointed the remote toward the television and darkened the screen.

You bet.

Satan's Cove

"We've got a problem."

Dane Cutter stopped in the act of nailing down cedar shingles and glanced over the steep edge of the roof. "So why don't you tell me something I don't know?"

He'd been the proud owner of Smugglers' Inn for two months. Well, if you wanted to get technical, he and the bank actually owned the century-old landmark building. Since he'd signed the final papers, Dane doubted a single day had gone by that he hadn't had to overcome some new catastrophe.

Having paid for an extensive professional inspection of the building that, because of competition from larger, fancier resorts catering to the corporate trade, had fallen into disrepair during his time away from Satan's Cove, Dane knew the problems he was taking on. And although they were considerable, he'd foolishly expected to have some time to do all the necessary renovations.

Thus far, he'd tackled the inn's ancient plumbing and electrical systems, evicted countless field mice and killed more spiders than he cared to think about.

He'd also replaced the ancient gas oven, replastered the algae-filled swimming pool, and was in the process of replacing the shingles that had blown away during last night's storm.

The next thing on his lengthy list—barring any further emergencies—was replacing the ancient gas heater, after which he planned to resand and seal the oak floors in the public rooms, then resurface the tennis court.

Since reopening last week, he'd reassured himself at least daily that it was just as well potential guests weren't exactly beating down his door. Although he admittedly needed all the bookings he could get to make the hefty mortgage payments, he also needed time to restore the inn to its former glory.

Reva Carlson grinned up at him. "Technically it's a bit of good news and some bad news. I suppose it's all in how you look at it."

"Why don't you give me the good news first?"

The way things had been going, after the storm and the burst pipe that had left the inn without water for twenty-four hours, Dane figured he could use a little boost. Hell, what he needed was a miracle. But he was willing to settle for whatever he could get.

"Okay." Reva's grin widened. "It looks as if we're going to meet this month's mortgage payment, after all."

"We got a booking?" If he'd had his choice, he would have kept the inn closed until all the needed repairs could be done. Unfortunately, his cash flow being what it was, he'd been forced to open for limited occupancy.

"We've sold out the entire place," Reva revealed proudly.

She was right. This was definitely a case of good and bad news. "Not including the tower room?" The last he'd looked into the hexagonal-shaped room that boasted a bird's-eye view of the Pacific Ocean, the wallpaper had been peeling off the walls.

"Of course not. You're good, boss, but you're not exactly a miracle worker. However, every other room, every bed, every last nook and cranny of Smugglers' Inn is going to be taken over by some Portland ad agency for an entire week."

Dane rapidly went over a mental list of repairs he'd have to accomplish in order to accommodate such a crowd.

"So, when are these ad people scheduled to arrive, anyway?"

"You could at least pretend to be pleased," she complained. "Besides, it's not that bad. We've plenty of time to get ready."

"What, exactly, do you consider plenty of time?"

"Three days."

"Three days?" He dragged his hand through his hair.

"Well, technically four. Including this one."

It was already four in the afternoon. "Damn it, Reva—"

"You're the one who's been bitching about needing bookings," she reminded Dane. "Well, now you've got some. Or would you rather me call the woman back and tell her that we're full?"

Reminding himself that the difficult could be accomplished immediately, while the impossible might take a bit longer, he said, "You did good, lady."

Another thought, beyond the necessary repairs, occurred to him. "You'd better warn Mom." He'd taken his mother out of a forced retirement and put her back in the remodeled kitchen, where she had happily begun stocking the pantry and whipping up recipes that rivaled those of any five-star resort in the country.

"I already did," she assured him, reminding him why he'd hired the former night manager away from the world-famous Whitfield Palace hotel chain. "Which reminds me, she told me to tell you that you'll have to drive into town for supplies."

"Tell her to make out a list and I'll do it as soon as I finish with the roof."

Dane returned to his hammering. And even as he wondered exactly how he was going to get everything done in time for the arrival of all those guests, he allowed himself to believe that things around Smugglers' Inn were definitely beginning to look up.

Chapter 2

Portland

"You were right about every motel, hotel, resort and cottage up and down the coast being booked to the rafters," Susan reported to Amanda. "Every place with the exception of Smugglers' Inn, which, I'll have to admit, made me a little nervous. But the woman from the Satan's Cove visitors' bureau assured me that it's listed on the historical register."

"It is," Amanda murmured, thinking back to that wonderful summer she'd spent at Satan's Cove.

The memory was, as always, bittersweet—part pleasure and part pain. She'd never been happier than she'd been that summer of her first love. Nor more heartbroken than on the day she'd driven away from Smugglers' Inn—and Dane Cutter—back to Los Angeles with her family.

He'd promised to write; and trusting him implicitly, Amanda had believed him. For the first two weeks after arriving home, she'd waited for a letter assuring her that she was not alone in her feelings—that the kisses they'd shared, along with the desperate promises, had been more than just a summer romance.

When three weeks passed without so much as a single postcard, Amanda had screwed up enough nerve to telephone Dane at the inn. But the woman working the desk informed her that he'd left Satan's Cove to return to college. No, the woman had insisted, in a bored tone, he hadn't left any forwarding address.

She'd thought about asking to talk to his mother, who'd been the inn's cook. But youthful pride kept her from inquiring further. So, believing she'd simply been one more conquest for a drop-dead-gorgeous college boy who already had more than his share of girls throwing themselves at him, Amanda tried to write the intense, short-lived romance off to experience.

And mostly, she'd been successful. But there were still times, when she would least expect it, that she'd think back on that summer with a mixture of wistfulness and embarrassment.

"I'm surprised they could take us," she said now, recalling the inn's popularity. Her father had had to book their rooms six months in advance. "They must have had a huge cancellation."

"According to the reservations clerk, the place has been closed for several years," Susan revealed. "Apparently it's recently changed hands. This is the new owner's first season."

"I'm not sure I like the sound of that," Amanda muttered. Even in an industry built on ego and turf, the agency had become a nest of political intrigue and back-biting. The corporate team challenge week was going to be tough enough without them having to serve as some novice innkeeper's shakedown summer season.

"You can always call Popular Surplus and order up the tents."

Despite her concerns, Amanda laughed. The truth was, she really didn't have any other choice. She could put twenty people—none of whom got along very well in the best of circumstances—into tents on the beach, eating hot dogs cooked over an open fire, or she could trust the new owner of Smugglers' Inn to know what he or she was doing.

After all, how bad could it be? The landmark inn, located on one of the most scenic stretches of Pacific Coast, was pretty and cozy and wonderfully comfortable. She thought back on the lovely flower-sprigged wallpaper in the tower room she'd slept in that long-ago summer, remembered the dazzling sunsets from the high arched windows, recalled in vivid detail the romance of the crackling fires the staff built each evening in the stone fireplace large enough for a grown man to stand in.

"Smugglers' Inn will be perfect," she said firmly, as if saying the words out loud could make them true. "I don't know why I didn't think of it in the first place."

"Probably because you've had a few other things on your mind," Susan said, proving herself to be a master of understatement. "And although I have no doubt you can pull this thing off, I'm glad I'll be holding down the fort here while you lead the troops in their wilderness experience."

That said, she left Amanda to worry that this time she'd actually bitten off more than she could chew.

Never having been one to limit herself to a normal, eight-hour work schedule, Amanda remained at her desk long into the night, fine-tuning all the minuscule details that would ensure the challenge week would be a success.

But as hard as she tried to keep her mind on business, she could not keep her unruly thoughts from drifting back to the summer of her fifteenth year.

She'd fallen in love with Dane the first time she'd seen him. And although her parents had tried to convince her otherwise, she knew now, as she'd known then, that her feelings had been more than mere puppy love.

It had, admittedly, taken Dane time to realize they were a perfect match. But Amanda had steadfastly refused to give up her quest. She pursued him incessantly, with all the fervor of a teenager in the throes of a first grand love.

Everywhere Dane went, Amanda went there, as well, smiling up at him with a coy Lolita smile overbrimming with sensual invitation. After discovering that one of his duties was teaching a class in kayaking, despite her distaste for early morning awakenings, she showed up on the beach at six-thirty for lessons. Although the rest of the class was sensibly attired for the foggy sea air in jeans and sweatshirts, she'd chosen to wear a hot-pink bikini that barely covered the essentials.

And that was just the beginning. During Dane's life-guarding stint each afternoon, she lounged poolside, wearing another impossibly scant bikini, her golden skin glowing with fragrant coconut oil. Grateful for child-hood diving lessons, she would occasionally lithely rise from the lounge to treat him to swan dives designed to show off her budding female figure.

She tormented him endlessly, pretending to need his assistance on everything from a flat bicycle tire to fastening her life jacket before going out on a sight-seeing boat excursion.

Adding local color to the inn's reputation had been the legend—invented by a former owner—that it was haunted by a woman who'd thrown herself off the widow's walk after her fiancé's ship was sunk by pirates off the rocky shoals. One night, Amanda showed up at Dane's room, insisting that she'd seen the ghost.

It would have taken a male with inhuman strength to resist her continual seduction attempts. And, as Dane later confessed, he was, after all, only human.

Which was why, seven days after Amanda Stockenberg's arrival at Smugglers' Inn, Dane Cutter succumbed to the inevitable. However, even as they spent the star-spangled nights driving each other insane, Dane had steadfastly refused to make love to her.

"I may be too damn weak where you're concerned, princess," he'd groaned during one excruciatingly long petting session, "but I'm not reckless enough to have sex with a minor girl."

She'd sworn that no one would ever know, promised that she'd never—ever—do anything to get him in trouble. But on this point, Dane had proved frustratingly intractable.

And although, as the years passed, Amanda begrudgingly admitted that he'd done the right and noble thing, there were still times, such as tonight, when she was sitting all alone in the dark, that she'd think back over the bliss she'd experienced in Dane Cutter's strong young arms and wish, with all her heart, that he hadn't proved so strong.

Satan's Cove

The day before the group was due to arrive at Smugglers' Inn, Dane was beginning to think they just might make it.

The roof was now rainproof, the windows sparkled like diamonds, and every room in the place—with the exception of the tower room, which he'd written off as impossible to prepare in such short time—was white-glove clean. And although the aroma of fresh paint lingered, leaving the windows open another twenty-four hours should take care of that little problem.

His mother had definitely gone all out in the kitchen. The huge commercial refrigerator was stuffed with food and every shelf in the pantry was full. Kettles had been bubbling away on the new eight-burner stove nearly around the clock for the past two and a half days, creating mouth-watering scents.

Using the hefty deposit Reva had insisted upon, he'd hired additional staff and although the kids were as green as spring grass, they were bright, seemingly hardworking and unrelentingly cheerful.

He was passing the antique registration desk on his way to the parlor, planning to clean the oversize chandelier, when the sound of a stressed-out voice garnered his instant attention.

"I'm sorry, ma'am," Mindy Taylor, the nineteen-year-old cheerleader, premed student and local beauty queen he'd hired, said in an obviously frustrated voice. "But—"

She sighed and held the receiver a little away from her ear, indicating that it was not the first time she'd heard the argument being offered on the other end of the line.

"Yes, I can appreciate that," Mindy agreed, rolling

her expressive eyes toward the knotty-pine ceiling. "But I'm afraid it's impossible. No, it's not booked, but—"

Dane heard the renewed argument, although he couldn't make out the words.

"It's a woman from that Portland advertising agency." Mindy covered the mouthpiece with her hand to talk to Dane. "She's insisting on the tower room, even though I told her that it wasn't available."

Dane held out his hand. "Let me talk to her."

"That's okay." Perfect white teeth that Dane knew had cost her parents a fortune in orthodontia flashed in the dazzling smile that had earned Mindy the Miss Satan's Cove title two years running. As this year's Miss Oregon, she'd be competing in the national pageant, which made her a local celebrity.

"It'll be good practice for Atlantic City. I need to work on my patience," she admitted. "Sometimes I think if I'm asked one more stupid question by one more judge I'm going to scream.

"I understand your feelings," Mindy soothed into the receiver as she tried yet again. "But you see, Ms. Stockenberg, Smugglers' Inn has been closed for the past few years, and—"

"Wait a minute," Dane interrupted. "Did you say Stockenberg?"

The name hit him directly in the gut, reminding him of the time he'd been standing behind the plate and his cousin Danny had accidentally slammed a baseball bat into his solar plexus.

"Excuse me, but could you hold a moment, please?" Mindy put her hand over the mouthpiece again and nodded. "That's right."

"Not Amanda Stockenberg?" It couldn't be, Dane told himself, even as a nagging intuition told him it was true.

"That's her." Mindy appeared surprised Dane knew the name. "The guest list the agency sent along with their deposit lists her as an assistant creative director.

"I put her in the cliff room, but she's insisting on being moved to the tower. Something about it having sentimental meaning. I explained that it was impossible, but—"

"Let her have it."

"What?" Eyes the color of a sun-brightened sea widened to the size of sand dollars.

"I said, book Ms. Stockenberg into the tower room." His tone was uncharacteristically sharp and impatient.

Mindy was not easily cowed. Especially by a man she'd been able to talk into playing Barbie dolls back in his teenage baby-sitting days, when their mothers had worked together at this very same inn. "But, Dane, it's a terrible mess."

She wasn't telling him anything he didn't already know. "Don't worry," he said, softening his voice and his expression. "I'll take care of it."

Mindy eyed him with overt curiosity. Then, as the voice on the other end of the phone began talking again, she returned her attention to the conversation.

"It seems I was mistaken, Ms. Stockenberg," she said cheerfully, switching gears with a dexterity that had Dane thinking she'd ace her Miss America interview. "As it happens, the tower room is available after all. Yes, that is fortunate, isn't it?"

She turned to the new computer Dane was still paying for. Her rosy fingernails tapped on the keys, changing

Amanda Stockenberg from the cliff room to the tower suite.

"It's all taken care of," she assured Dane after she'd hung up. Her expressive eyes held little seeds of worry. "It's none of my business, but I sure hope you know what you're doing."

"If I knew what I was doing, I wouldn't have bought the inn in the first place." His crooked grin belied his complaint. After years of traveling the world for the Whitfield Palace hotel chain, there was no place he'd rather be. And nothing he'd rather be doing. "If you see Reva, tell her I had to run into town for some wallpaper."

"Ms. Stockenberg mentioned little blue flowers," Mindy said helpfully.

"I remember."

And damn it, that was precisely the problem, Dane told himself two hours later as he drove back to Smugglers' Inn from the hardware store in Satan's Cove with the newly purchased wallpaper. He remembered too much about Amanda Stockenberg's long-ago visit to Satan's Cove.

The only daughter of a wealthy Los Angeles attorney and his socialite wife, Amanda had come to the Oregon coast with her family for a month-long vacation.

Pampered and amazingly sheltered for a modern teenager, she'd obviously never met anyone like him. Unfortunately, during his years working at Smugglers' Inn—part-time while in high school, then summers and vacations to put himself through college—Dane had run across too many rich girls who considered him along the same lines as a summer trophy.

Dane's own father, scion of a famous Southern department-store family, had been a masculine version of those girls. Rich and spoiled, he'd had no qualms about taking what he wanted, then moving on after the annual Labor Day clambake, leaving behind a young, pregnant waitress.

Although Mary Cutter—a quiet, gentle woman who'd gone on to be a cook at the inn—had brought Dane up not to be bitter about his father's abandonment, he'd decided early on that it was better to stick with your own kind.

Which was why he'd always avoided the temptation of shiny blond hair and long, tanned legs. Until Amanda Stockenberg arrived on the scene.

She pursued him endlessly, with the single-mindedness of a rich, pretty girl accustomed to getting her own way. She was part siren, part innocent; he found both fascinating.

When she showed up at his door in the middle of the night during a thunderstorm, swearing she'd seen the ghost reputed to haunt the inn, Dane took one look at her—backlit by flashes of lightning, clad in a shorty nightgown—and all his intentions to resist temptation flew right out the window.

Being male and all too human, he allowed her into his room.

"That was your first mistake," he muttered now, at the memory of the sweet lips that had kissed him senseless. His second mistake, and the one that had cost him dearly, had been letting Amanda Stockenberg into his heart.

They did not make love—she was, after all, too young. And even if he'd wanted to—which, Lord help him, he did—he knew that by legal standards Amanda was jailbait. And from the no-holds-barred conversation Stockenberg had with Dane when even he could no longer ignore his daughter's outrageously flirtatious behavior, Dane knew the attorney would not be averse to filing statutory rape charges on any boy who dared take Amanda to bed.

Dane's mother, remembering her own youthful summer romance, had worried about his succumbing to his raging hormones and blowing his chances at finishing college.

"Don't worry, Mom," he'd assured her with the cocky grin that had coaxed more than one local beauty into intimacy. "I won't risk prison for a roll in the hay with a summer girl."

With that intent firmly stated, he'd managed to resist Amanda's pleas to consummate their young love. But drawn to her in ways he could not understand, Dane had spent the next three weeks sneaking off to clandestine trysts.

Dane and Amanda exchanged long slow kisses in the cave on the beach, forbidden caresses in the boathouse, passionate promises in the woods at the top of the cliff overlooking the sea, and on one memorable, thrilling, and terrifying occasion, while her parents slept in the room below them, they'd made out in Amanda's beloved tower room with its canopied bed and flower-sprigged walls.

Although he'd tried like hell to forget her, on more than one occasion over the past years, Dane had been annoyed to discover that her image had remained emblazoned on his mind, as bright and vivid—and, damn it, as seductive—as it had been a decade ago.

"It's been ten years," he reminded himself gruffly as he carried the rolls of paper and buckets of paste up the narrow, curving staircase to the tower room.

And, damn it, he'd dreamed about her over each of those ten years. More times than he could count, more than he'd admit. Even to himself.

"Hell, she's probably married."

It took no imagination at all to envision some man—a rich, suave guy with manicured fingernails and smooth palms that had never known the handle of a hammer, a man from her own social set—snapping Amanda up right after her debut.

Did girls still have formal debuts? Dane wondered, remembering a few he'd worked as a waiter during college—formal affairs in gilded hotel ballrooms where lovely rich girls donned long elbow-length gloves, their grandmothers' pearls and fancy white dresses that cost nearly as much as a semester's tuition, and waltzed with their fathers. He'd have to ask Mindy. The daughter of a local fisherman, she'd certainly met her share of society girls at various beauty pageants. On more than one occasion she'd complained to Dane that those rich girls only entered as a lark. Their futures, unlike hers, didn't depend on their winning the scholarship money. The fact that Amanda still had the same name as she had that long-ago summer meant nothing, Dane considered, returning his thoughts to Amanda Stockenberg's marital status. Married women often kept their maiden names for professional reasons.

His jaw clenched at the idea of Amanda married to some Yuppie who drove a BMW, preferred estate-bottled wine to beer, bought his clothes from Brooks Brothers, golfed eighteen holes on Saturday and sailed in yachting regattas on Sundays.

As he'd shopped for the damn wallpaper, Dane had hoped that he'd exaggerated the condition of the tower room when he'd measured the walls after Amanda's telephone call. Unfortunately, as he entered it now, he realized that it was even worse.

He wasn't fixing it up for sentimental reasons, Dane assured himself firmly. He was only going to the extra trouble because he didn't want Amanda to think him unsuccessful.

He pulled the peeling paper from the walls, revealing wallboard stained from the formerly leaky roof. Water stains also blotched the ceiling, like brown inkblots in a Rorschach test. The pine-plank floor was badly in need of refinishing, but a coat of paste wax and some judiciously placed rugs would cover the worst of the damage.

A sensible man would simply turn around and walk out, close the door behind him and tell the lady, when she arrived, that the clerk had made a mistake; the tower room wasn't available.

For not the first time since he'd gotten the idea to buy Smugglers' Inn, Dane reminded himself that a sensible man would have stayed in his executive suite at the New Orleans home office of the Whitfield Palace hotel chain and continued to collect his six-figure salary and requisite perks.

I'll bet the husband plays polo. The thought had him snapping the plumb line with more force than necessary, sending blue chalk flying. Dane had not forgotten Amanda's father's boastful remarks about the polo ponies he kept stabled at his weekend house in Santa Barbara.

What the hell was he doing? Dane asked himself as he rolled the paper out onto a board placed atop a pair of sawhorses and cut the first piece. Why torture himself with old memories?

He slapped the paste onto the back of the flowered paper and tried not to remember a time when this room had smelled like the gardenia cologne Amanda had worn that summer.

When something was over and done with, you forgot it and moved on.

Wasn't that exactly what she had done?

After promising him "forever," Amanda Stockenberg had walked out of his life without so much as a backward glance.

And ten years later, as he climbed the ladder and positioned the strip of paper against the too-heavy blue chalk line, Dane was still trying to convince himself that it was only his pride—not his heart—that had been wounded.

Although many things in Amanda's life had changed over the past ten years, Smugglers' Inn was not one of them. Perched on the edge of the cliff overlooking the Pacific Ocean, the building's lit windows glowed a warm welcome.

"Well, we're here, folks," the driver of the charter bus announced with a vast amount of cheer, considering the less-than-ideal circumstances of the trip. A halfhearted round of applause rippled down the rows.

"It's about time," Greg Parsons complained. He speared Amanda a sharp look. "You realize that we've already lost the entire first day of the challenge."

Having been forced to put up with her supervisor's sarcasm for the past hour, Amanda was in no mood to turn the other cheek.

"That landslide wasn't my fault, Greg." They'd been stuck on the bus in the pouring rain for five long, frustrating hours while highway crews cleared away the rock and mud from the road.

"If we'd only left thirty minutes earlier—"

"We could have ended up beneath all that mud."

Deciding that discretion was the better part of valor, Amanda did not point out that the original delay had been caused by Kelli Kyle. The auburn-haired public-relations manager had arrived at the company parking lot twenty-five minutes after the time the bus had been scheduled to depart.

Watercooler rumors had Kelli doing a lot more for Greg than plotting PR strategy; but Amanda's working relationship with Greg was bad enough without her attacking his girlfriend.

She reached into her purse, took out a half-empty roll of antacids and popped two of the tablets into her mouth. Her stomach had been churning for the past twenty miles and a headache was threatening.

Which wasn't unusual when she was forced to spend the entire day with Greg Parsons. Amanda couldn't think of a single person—with the possible exception of Kelli Kyle—who liked the man.

The first thing he'd done upon his arrival in Portland was to prohibit staffers from decorating their office walls and cubicles with the crazy posters and wacky decorations that were a commonplace part of the creative environment at other agencies. When a memo had been sent out two months ago, forbidding employees even to drink coffee at their desks, Amanda had feared an out-and-out rebellion.

The hand grenade he kept on his desk and daily memos from *The Art of War* also had not endeared him to his fellow workers.

"Let's just hope we have better luck with this inn you've booked us into," he muttered, scooping up his crocodile attaché case and marching down the aisle. "Because so far, the corporate challenge is turning out to be an unmitigated disaster."

Unwilling to agree, Amanda didn't answer. The welcoming warmth of the fire crackling in the large stone fireplace soothed the jangled nerves of the challenge-week participants, as did the glasses of hot coffee, cider and wine served on a myrtle-wood tray by a handsome young man who vaguely reminded Amanda of Dane Cutter.

The young girl working behind the front desk was as pretty as the waiter was handsome. She was also, Amanda noticed, amazingly efficient. Within minutes, and without the Miss America smile fading for a moment, Mindy Taylor had registered the cranky, chilled guests into their rooms, handed out the keys and assigned bellmen to carry the luggage upstairs.

Finally it was Amanda's turn. "Good evening, Ms. Stockenberg," Mindy greeted Amanda with the same unfailing cheer she had the others. "Welcome to Smugglers' Inn."

"It's a relief to be here."

The smile warmed. "I heard about your troubles getting here from Portland." She tapped briskly on the computer as she talked. "I'm sure the rest of your week will go more smoothly."

"I hope so." It sure couldn't get any worse.

"You're in the tower room, as requested." Mindy handed her the antique brass key. "If you don't mind waiting just a moment, Kevin will be back and will take your suitcases up for you."

"That's not necessary," a male voice coming from behind Amanda said. "I'll take care of Ms. Stockenberg's luggage."

No, Amanda thought. *It couldn't be!*

She slowly turned around, taking time to school her expression to one of polite surprise. "Hello, Dane."

Although a decade had passed, he looked just the same. But better, she decided on second thought. Dark and rugged, and so very dangerous. The kind of boy— no, he was a man now, she reminded herself—that fathers of daughters stayed awake nights worrying about.

His shaggy dark hair was still in need of a haircut, and his eyes, nearly as dark as his hair, were far from calm, but the emotions swirling in their midnight depths were too complex for Amanda to decipher. A five-o'clock shadow did nothing to detract from his good looks; the dark stubble only added to his appeal.

His jeans, white T-shirt and black leather jacket were distractingly sexy. They also made her worry that standards might have slipped at the inn since the last time she'd visited.

"Hello, princess." His full, sensual mouth curved in a smile that let her know the intimacy implied by the long-ago nickname was intentional. "Welcome to Smugglers' Inn." His gaze swept over her. "You're looking more lovely than ever."

Actually, she looked like hell. To begin with, she was too damn thin. Her oval face was pale and drawn. Her beige linen slacks and ivory top, which he suspected probably cost as much as the inn's new water heater, looked as if she'd slept in them; her hair was wet from her dash from the bus, there were blue shadows beneath her eyes, and sometime during the long trip from Portland, she'd chewed off her lipstick.

Dane knew he was in deep, deep trouble when he still found her the most desirable woman he'd ever seen.

Amanda struggled to keep Dane from realizing that he'd shaken her. All it had taken was his calling her that ridiculous name to cause a painful fluttering in her heart.

How could she have thought that she'd gotten over him? Dane Cutter was not a man women got over. Not in this lifetime. Her hand closed tightly around the key.

"Thank you. It's a relief to finally be here. Is the dining room closed yet? I know we're late, but—"

"We kept it open when it was obvious you'd gotten held up. Or, if you'd prefer, there's room service."

The idea of a long bath and a sandwich and cup of tea sent up to her room sounded delightful. "That's good news." The first in a very long and very trying day.

"We try to make our guests as comfortable as possible."

He scooped up both her cases, deftly tucked them under his arm and took her briefcase from her hand. It was biscuit-hued cowhide, as smooth as a baby's bottom, with her initials in gold near the handle. "Nice luggage."

She'd received the Louis Vuitton luggage from her parents as a graduation present. Her mother had been given a similar set from her parents when she'd married. And her mother before her. It was, in a way, a family tradition. So why did she suddenly feel a need to apologize?

"It's very functional."

His only response to her defensive tone was a shrug. "So I've heard." He did not mention that he'd bought a similar set for his mother, as a bon voyage gift for the Alaskan cruise he'd booked her on last summer. "If you're all checked in, I'll show you to your room."

"I remember the way." It had been enough of a shock to discover Dane still working at the inn. Amanda didn't believe she could handle being alone in the cozy confines of the tower room with him. Not with the memory of their last night together still painfully vivid in her mind.

"I've no doubt you do." Ignoring the clenching of his stomach, Dane flashed her a maddening grin, letting her know that they were both on the same wavelength. The devil could probably take smiling lessons from Dane Cutter. "But someone needs to carry your luggage up and Jimmy and Kevin are tied up with other guests."

"There's no hurry." Her answering smile was as polite as it was feigned. Although she'd never considered herself a violent person, after the way Dane had treated her, dumping her without a single word of explanation, like he undoubtedly did the rest of his summer girls, her hands practically itched with the need to slap his face. "I'll just go on up and they can bring my bags to the tower whenever they're free."

"I have a feeling that might be a while." He nodded his head toward the doorway, declaring the subject closed.

Not wanting to create a scene in front of the avidly interested young clerk, Amanda tossed her damp head and marched out of the room.

This was a mistake, she told herself as she stood beside Dane in the antique elevator slowly creaking its way up to the third floor. The next few days were the most important in her life. Her entire career, everything she'd worked so hard to achieve, depended on the corporate challenge week being a success. She couldn't allow herself to be distracted.

Unfortunately, Smugglers' Inn, she was discovering too late, held far too many distracting memories.

"I'm surprised to find you working here," she murmured, trying to ignore the familiar scent of soap emanating from his dark skin.

He chuckled—a low, rich tone that crept under her skin and caused her blood to thrum. "So am I." He put the bags on the floor, leaned against the back wall and stuck his hands in his pockets. "Continually."

Amanda thought about all the plans Dane had shared with her that summer. About how he was going to get out of this isolated small coastal town, how he planned to make his mark on the world, how he was going to be rich by his thirtieth birthday.

She did some rapid calculations and determined him to be twenty-nine. Obviously, if his unpretentious clothing and the fact that he was still carrying bags for guests at the inn were any indication, if Dane hoped to achieve even one of those goals, he'd have to win the lottery.

"Looks as if you've done all right for yourself." His measuring glance swept over her. "Assistant creative director for one of the top advertising firms in the country. I'm impressed."

"Thank you."

"Tell me, do you have a window office?"

"Actually, I do." Realizing that he was daring to mock her success, she tossed up her chin. "Overlooking the river."

"Must be nice. And a corporate credit card, too, I'll bet."

"Of course." She'd been thrilled the first time she'd

flashed the green American Express card granted only to upper-level management personnel in an expensive Manhattan restaurant. It had seemed, at the time, an important rite of passage. Having been born into wealth, Amanda wanted—needed—to achieve success on her own.

"High-backed swivel desk chair?"

Two could play this game. "Italian cream leather."

She refused to admit she'd bought the extravagant piece of office furniture for herself with last year's Christmas bonus.

Of course, the minute Greg Parsons had caught sight of it, after returning from a holiday vacation to Barbados, he'd rushed out and bought himself a larger, higher model. In jet leather. With mahogany trim.

Dane whistled appreciatively. "Yes, sir, you've definitely come a long way. Especially for a lady who once professed a desire to raise five kids in a house surrounded by a white picket fence, and spend summers putting up berries and long dark winters making more babies in front of a crackling fire."

How dare he throw those youthful fantasies back into her face! Didn't he realize that it had been *him* she'd fantasized about making love to, *his* babies she'd wanted?

After she'd been forced to accept the fact that her dreams of marrying Dane Cutter were only that—stupid, romantic teenage daydreams—she'd gone on to find a new direction for her life. A direction that was, admittedly, heavily influenced by her father's lofty expectations for his only child.

"People grow up," she said. "Goals change."

"True enough," he agreed easily, thinking how his own life had taken a 180-degree turn lately. "Speaking of changes, you've changed your scent." It surrounded them in the enclosed space, more complex than the cologne that had haunted his dreams last night. More sensual.

"Have I?" she asked with feigned uninterest. "I don't remember."

"Your old cologne was sweet. And innocent." He leaned forward, drinking it in. "This makes a man think of deep, slow kisses." His breath was warm on her neck. "And hot sex on a steamy summer night."

His words, his deep voice, the closeness of his body to hers, all conspired to make her knees weak. Amanda considered backing away, then realized there was nowhere to go.

"I didn't come here to rehash the past, Dane." Her headache was building to monumental proportions. "This trip to Satan's Cove is strictly business."

"Yeah, I seem to recall Reva saying something about corporate game-playing stunts."

Her remarkable eyes were as blue as a sunlit sea. A careless man could drown in those wide eyes. Having succumbed to Amanda Stockenberg's siren call once before, Dane had no intention of making that mistake again. Although he knew that to touch her would be dangerous, he couldn't resist reaching out to rub the pads of his thumbs against her temples.

Amanda froze at his touch. "What do you think you're doing?"

Her voice might have turned as chilly as the rain falling outside, but her flesh was warming in a way he remembered all too well. "Helping you get rid of that headache before you rub a hole in your head."

He stroked small, concentric circles that did absolutely nothing to soothe. One hand roamed down the side of her face, her neck, before massaging her knotted shoulder muscle.

His hand was rough with calluses upon calluses, hinting at a life of hard, physical work rather than the one spent behind a wide executive desk he'd once yearned for. It crossed Amanda's mind that in a way, she was living the successful, high-powered life Dane had planned for himself. Which made her wonder if he was living out her old, discarded dreams.

Was he married? Did he have children? The idea of any other woman carrying Dane Cutter's baby caused a flicker of something deep inside Amanda that felt uncomfortably like envy.

"You sure are tense, princess." His clever fingers loosened the knot even as they tangled her nerves.

She knew she should insist he stop, but his touch *was* working wonders on her shoulder. "Knotted muscles and the occasional headache come with the territory. And don't call me *princess*."

Dane knew the truth of her first statement all too well. It was one of several reasons he'd bailed out of corporate life.

"How about the occasional ulcer?" He plucked the roll of antacids from her hand, forestalling her from popping another tablet into her mouth.

"I don't have an ulcer."

"I suppose you have a doctor's confirmation of that?"

She tossed her head, then wished she hadn't when the headache stabbed like a stiletto behind her eyes. "Of course."

She was a liar. But a lovely one. Dane suspected that it had been a very long time since Amanda had taken time to visit a doctor. Her clothes, her title, her luggage, the window office with the high-backed Italian-leather chair, all pointed to the fact that the lady was definitely on the fast track up the advertising corporate ladder.

Her too-thin face and the circles beneath her eyes were additional proof of too many hours spent hunkered over advertising copy and campaign jingles. He wondered if she realized she was approaching a very slippery slope.

He was looking at her that way again. Hard and deep. Just when Amanda thought Dane was going to say something profound, the elevator lurched to a sudden stop.

"Third floor, ladies' lingerie," he said cheerfully. "Do you still wear that sexy underwear?"

She wondered if he flirted like this with all the female guests, then wondered how, if he did, he managed to keep his job. Surely some women might complain to the management that the inn's sexy bellhop brought new meaning to the slogan Service With a Smile.

"My underwear is none of your business." Head high, she stepped out of the elevator and headed toward the stairway at the end of the hall, leaving him to follow with the bags.

"I seem to remember a time when you felt differently."

"I felt differently about a lot of things back then. After all, I was only fifteen." The censorious look she flashed back over her shoulder refused to acknowledge his steadfast refusal to carry their teenage affair to its natural conclusion.

"I recall mentioning your tender age on more than one occasion," he said mildly. "But you kept insisting that you were all grown-up."

Not grown-up enough to hold his attention, Amanda

thought grimly. As she climbed the stairs to the tower room, she decided she'd made a major mistake in coming to Smugglers' Inn.

Her focus had been clear from the beginning. Pull off the corporate challenge week, get the obnoxious Greg Parsons promoted out of her life, then move upward into his position, which should have been hers in the first place.

Awakening old hurts and reliving old memories definitely hadn't been part of the plan.

And neither had Dane Cutter.

Chapter 3

The first time Amanda had seen the tower room, she'd been entranced. Ten years hadn't lessened its appeal.

Delicate forget-me-nots bloomed on the walls, the high ceiling was a pale powder blue that had always reminded her of a clear summer sky. More blue flowers decorated the ribbon-edged curtains that were pulled back from the sparkling window and matched the thick comforter.

"The bed's different," she murmured.

"Unfortunately, during the time the inn was closed, it became a termite condo and had to go."

"That's too bad." She'd loved the romantic canopy. "But this is nice, too." She ran her hand over one of the pine-log posts that had been sanded to a satin finish.

"I'm glad you approve."

He'd taken the bed from his own room this morning.

Now, watching her stroke the wooden post with her slender fingers, Dane felt a slow, deep ache stir inside him.

"I'd suggest not getting too near the woodwork," he warned. "The paint's still a bit sticky."

That explained the white specks on his jeans. A pang of sadness for lost opportunities and abandoned dreams sliced through Amanda.

"Well, thank you for carrying up my bags." Her smile was bright and impersonal as she reached into her purse.

An icy anger rose inside him at the sight of those folded green bills. "Keep your money."

All right, so this meeting was uncomfortable. But he didn't have to get so nasty about it. "Fine." Amanda met his strangely blistering look with a level one of her own. "You realize, I suppose, that I'm going to be here at the inn for a week."

"So?" His tone was as falsely indifferent as hers.

"So, it would seem inevitable that we'd run into each other from time to time."

"Makes sense to me."

It was obvious Dane had no intention of helping her out with this necessary conversation. "This is an important time for me," she said, trying again. "I can't afford any distractions."

"Are you saying I'm a distraction?" As if to underscore her words, he reached out and touched the ends of her hair. "You've dyed your hair," he murmured distractedly.

"Any man who touches me when I don't want him to is a distraction," she retorted, unnerved at how strongly the seemingly harmless touch affected her. "And I didn't dye it. It got darker all on its own."

"It was the color of corn silk that summer." He laced

his fingers through the dark gold hair that curved beneath her chin. "Now it's the color of caramel." He held a few strands up to the light. "Laced with melted butter."

The way he was looking at her, the way he kept touching her, caused old seductive memories to come barreling back to batter at Amanda's emotions.

"Food analogies are always so romantic."

"You want romance, princess?" His eyes darkened to obsidian as he moved even closer to her.

As she tried to retreat, Amanda was blocked by the edge of the mattress pressing against the backs of her knees. Unwilling desire mingled with a long-smoldering resentment she'd thought she'd been able to put behind her.

"Damn it, Dane." She put both hands on his shoulders and shoved, but she might as well have been trying to move a mountain. He didn't budge. "I told you not to call me *princess.*"

"Fine. Since it's obvious that you've grown up, how about *contessa?*"

It suited her, Dane decided. *Princess* had been her father's name for a spoiled young girl. *Contessa* brought to mind a regal woman very much in charge of her life, as Amanda appeared to be.

The temper she'd kept on a taut leash during a very vexing day broke free. "You know, you really have a lot of nerve." Her voice trembled, which made her all the more angry. She did not want to reveal vulnerability where this man was concerned. "Behaving this way after what you did!"

"What I did?" His own temper, worn to a frazzle from overwork, lack of sleep, and the knowledge that Amanda was returning to Satan's Cove after all these years, rose to engulf hers. "What the hell did I do? Except spend an entire month taking cold showers after some teenage tease kept heating me up?"

"Tease?"

That did it! She struck out at him, aiming for his shoulder, but hitting his upper arm instead. When her fist impacted with a muscle that felt like a boulder, the shock ran all the way up her arm.

"I loved you, damn it! Which just goes to show how stupid a naive, fifteen-year-old girl can be."

What was even more stupid was having wasted so much time thinking about this man. And wondering what she might have done to make things turn out differently.

His answering curse was short and rude. "You were too self-centered that summer to even know the meaning of the word *love*." Impatience shimmered through him. "Face it, contessa, you thought you'd get your kicks practicing your feminine wiles on some small-town hick before taking your newly honed skills back to the big city."

He would have her, Dane decided recklessly. Before she left Smugglers' Inn. And this time, when she drove away from Satan's Cove, he'd keep something of Amanda for himself. And in turn, leave her with something to remember on lonely rainy nights.

"I loved you," she repeated through clenched teeth. She'd never spoken truer words. "But unfortunately, I was stupid enough to give my heart away to someone who only considered me a summer fling."

Thank heavens she'd only given her heart. Because if she'd given her body to this man, she feared she never would have gotten over him.

Which she had.

Absolutely. Completely.

The hell she had.

The way he was looking at her, as if he couldn't decide whether to strangle her or ravish her, made Amanda's heart pound.

"You were a lot more than a summer fling." His fingers tightened painfully on her shoulders. His rough voice vibrated through her, causing an ache only he had ever been able to instill. "When I went back to college, I couldn't stop thinking about you. I thought about you during the day, when I was supposed to be studying. I thought about you at night, after work, when I was supposed to be sleeping. And all the time in between."

It was the lie, more than anything, that hurt. All right, so she'd misinterpreted their romance that long-ago summer. Amanda was willing to be honest with herself. Why couldn't he be equally truthful?

"It would have been nice," she suggested in a tone as icy as winter sleet, "if during all that time you were allegedly thinking of me, you thought to pick up a pen and write me a letter. An email. Hell, one of those postcards with the lighthouse on it they sell on the revolving rack downstairs next to the registration desk would have been better than nothing."

"I did write to you." He was leaning over her, his eyes so dark she could only see her reflection. "I wrote you a letter the day you left. And the next day. And for days after that. Until it finally got through my thick head that you weren't going to answer."

The accusation literally rocked her. The anger in his gritty voice and on his face told Amanda that Dane was telling the truth. "What letters? I didn't get any letters."

"That's impossible." His gaze raked over her snow-white face, seeking the truth. Comprehension, when it dawned, was staggering. "Hell. Your parents got to them first."

"Apparently so." She thought about what such well-meaning parental subterfuge had cost her. What it had, perhaps, cost Dane. Cost them both.

"You know, *you* could always have written to *me,*" Dane said.

"I wanted to. But I couldn't get up the nerve."

He arched a challenging eyebrow. But as she watched reluctant amusement replace the fury in his eyes, Amanda was able to breathe again.

"This from a girl nervy enough to wear a polka-dot bikini horseback riding just to get my attention?" The ploy had worked. The memory of that cute little skimpily clad butt bouncing up and down in that leather saddle had tortured Dane's sleep.

The shared memory brought a reluctant smile from Amanda. She'd paid for that little stunt. If Dane's mother hadn't given her that soothing salve for the chafed skin on the insides of her legs, she wouldn't have been able to walk for a week.

"It was different once I got back home," she admitted now. "I kept thinking about all the older girls who worked at the inn, and went to college with you, and I couldn't imagine why you'd bother carrying a torch for a girl who'd only just gotten her braces off two weeks before coming to Satan's Cove."

Damn. He should have realized she might think that. But at the time, he'd been dazzled by the breezy self-confidence he'd assumed had been bred into Amanda from generations of family wealth.

Oh, he'd known she was too immature—her passionate suggestion that they run away together had been proof of that. But it had never occurred to him that she wasn't as self-assured as she'd seemed. She had, after all, captured the attention of every male in Satan's Cove between the ages of thirteen and ninety. She'd also succeeded in wrapping him—a guy with no intention of letting any woman sidetrack his plan for wealth and success—around her little finger.

Looking down at her now, Dane wondered how much of the girl remained beneath the slick professional veneer Amanda had acquired during the intervening years.

"I did work up my nerve to call you once," she said quietly. "But you'd already gone back to school and the woman who answered the phone here said she didn't have your forwarding address."

"You could have asked my mother."

Her weary shrug told him that she'd considered that idea and rejected it.

Dane wondered what would have happened if his letters had been delivered. Would his life have turned out differently if he'd gotten her call?

Never one to look back, Dane turned his thoughts to the future. The immediate future. Like the next week.

"It appears we have some unfinished business." His hand slipped beneath her hair to cup the back of her neck.

"Dane—" She pressed her palm against his shirt and encountered a wall of muscle every bit as hard as it had been when he was nineteen. There was, she decided recklessly, definitely something to be said for a life of physical work.

"All this heat can't be coming from me." His fingers massaged her neck in a way that was anything but soothing as his lips scorched a trail up her cheek. "The sparks are still there, contessa." His breath was warm against her skin. "You can't deny it."

No, she couldn't. Her entire body was becoming hot and quivery. "Please." Her voice was a throaty shimmer of sound. "I can't concentrate when you're doing that."

"Then don't concentrate." His mouth skimmed along her jaw; Amanda instinctively tilted her head back. "Just feel." When his tongue touched the hollow of her throat, her pulse jumped. "Go with the flow."

"I can't," she complained weakly, even as her rebellious fingers gathered up a handful of white cotton T-shirt. "This week is important to me."

"I remember a time when you said *I* was important to you." The light abrasion of his evening beard scraped seductively against her cheek as his hands skimmed down her sides.

"That was then." She drew in a sharp breath as his palms brushed against her breasts and set them to tingling. In all her twenty-five years Dane was the only man who could touch off the fires of passion smoldering deep inside her. He was the only man who could make her want. And, she reminded herself, he'd been the only man who'd ever made her cry. "This is now."

"It doesn't feel so different." He drew her to him. "*You* don't feel so different."

He wanted her. Too much for comfort. Too much for safety. The way she was literally melting against him made Dane ache in ways he'd forgotten he could ache.

"This has been a long time coming, Amanda." His hands settled low on her hips. "We need to get it out of our systems. Once and for all."

She could feel every hard male part of him through

her clothes. He was fully, thrillingly aroused. Even as she tried to warn herself against succumbing to such blatant masculinity, Amanda linked her fingers around his neck and leaned into him.

"I don't know about *your* system," she said breathlessly, as his tongue skimmed up her neck, "but mine's doing just fine."

"Liar." His lips brushed against hers. Teasing, testing, tormenting.

Desire throbbed and pooled between her thighs. Flames were flicking hotly through her veins. She'd never wanted a man the way she wanted Dane Cutter right now. Worse yet, she'd never *needed* a man the way she needed him at this moment.

Which was why she had to back away from temptation. When, and if, she did make love to Dane, she wanted to make certain she knew exactly what she was doing. And why.

She needed to be certain that the desire coursing through her veins was not simply a knee-jerk response to the only man who'd ever made her burn. She had to convince herself that she wasn't succumbing to the seduction of the romantic setting, old memories, and sensual fantasies.

After suffering the resultant pain from her impulsive, teenage behavior, Amanda had acquired a need for an orderly, controlled life. Unfortunately, there was nothing orderly or controlled about the way Dane Cutter made her feel.

"I need to think," she protested weakly. "It's been a long and frustrating day and I'm exhausted, Dane."

"Fine." He'd give her that. There would, Dane told

himself, be other times. "But before I go, let me give you something to think about."

Amanda knew what was coming. Knew she should resist. Even as she warned herself to back away now, before she got in over her head, another voice in the back of her mind pointed out that this was her chance to prove she was no longer a foolish young girl who could lose her heart over a simple kiss.

Since the second option seemed the more logical, Amanda went with it. She stood there, her palms pressed against his chest, as he slowly, deliberately, lowered his mouth to hers.

It was definitely not what she'd been expecting.

The first time he'd kissed her, that long-ago night when she'd come to his room, clad in her sexiest nightie, Dane had been frustrated and angry—angry at her for having teased him unmercifully, angry at himself for not being able to resist.

His mouth had swooped down, causing their teeth to clang painfully together as he ground his lips against hers. He'd used his mouth and his tongue as a weapon and she'd found it shocking and thrilling at the same time.

Later, as the days went by, Dane had grown more and more sexually frustrated, and it had showed. Although his kisses were no longer tinged with anger, they were riddled with a hot, desperate hunger that equaled her own.

Although the attraction was still there a decade later, it was more than apparent to Amanda that the years had mellowed Dane, taught him patience. And finesse.

He cupped her face in his hands and she trembled.

He touched his mouth to hers and she sighed.

With a rigid control that cost him dearly, Dane forced himself to take his time, coaxing her into the mists by skimming kisses from one side of her full, generous mouth to the other.

"Dane—"

Ignoring her faint protest, he caught her bottom lip in his teeth and tugged, causing a slow, almost-languid ache.

Prepared for passion, she had no defenses against this exquisite, dreamy pleasure. Amanda twined her arms tighter around his neck and allowed herself to sink into his kiss.

"Oh, Dane…"

"Lord, I like the way you say my name." His breath was like a summer breeze against her parted lips. "Say it again."

At this suspended moment in time, unable to deny Dane anything, Amanda softly obliged.

"Your voice reminds me of warm honey." He soothed the flesh his teeth had bruised with his tongue. "Sweet and thick and warm."

He angled his head and continued making love to her with his mouth. The tip of his tongue slipped silkily between her lips, then withdrew. Then dipped in again, deeper this time, only to withdraw once more.

Every sense was heightened. Every nerve ending in her body hummed.

His clever, wicked tongue repeated that glorious movement again and again, each time delving deeper, seducing hers into a slow, sensual dance. The rest of the world drifted away. Until there was only Dane. And the pure pleasure of his mouth.

Damn. This wasn't going the way he'd planned. The

rich, warm taste of her was causing an ache in his loins far worse than the teenage horniness he'd suffered the last time he'd been with Amanda like this. Sweat broke out on his forehead as he felt the soft swell of her belly pressing against his erection.

Her throaty moans were driving him crazy and if she didn't stop grinding against him that way, stoking fires that were already close to burning out of control, he was going to throw her down on that bed and rip away those travel-rumpled clothes.

He imagined sliding his tongue down her throat, over her breasts, swirling around the hard little nipples that were pressing against his chest, before cutting a wet swath down her slick, quivering stomach, making her writhe with need; then lower still, until he was sliding it between her legs, gathering up the sweet taste—

"Hell."

Jerking his mind back from that perilous precipice, Dane literally pushed himself away from her. For his sake, not hers.

It had happened again! Ten minutes alone with Amanda and he'd nearly lost it. What was it about this woman? Even at nineteen he'd been far from inexperienced. Yet all it had taken then—and, apparently, all it took even now—was a taste of her succulent lips, the feel of her hot, feminine body pressed against his, to bring him to the brink of exploding.

Her head still spinning, her body pulsing, Amanda stared at Dane and watched as his rugged face closed up.

He jammed his hands into the pockets of his jeans with such force that her eyes were drawn to the brusque movement. Heaven help her, the sight of that bulge pressing against the faded denim caused something like an ocean swell to rise up from her most feminine core.

Realizing what she was staring at, Dane again cursed his lack of control. "I'm not going to apologize." His voice was distant, and amazingly cold for a man who, only moments earlier, had nearly caused them both to go up in flames.

"I wouldn't ask you to." She dragged her hair back from her temples, appalled by the discovery that her hands were shaking. "I'm no longer a teenager, Dane. You don't have to worry about my father showing up at the door with a shotgun."

Dane almost laughed. He wondered what she'd say if he told her that he found the idea of an irate father far less threatening than what he was currently feeling.

"You're tired." And she had been for some time, if the circles beneath her eyes were any indication. "We'll talk tomorrow. After you've had some rest."

"There's no need to—"

"I said, we'll talk tomorrow."

Amanda stiffened, unaccustomed to taking such sharp, direct orders from any man. Before she could argue, he said, "Just dial three for room service. The cook will fix anything you'd like. Within reason."

With that, he was gone. Leaving Amanda confused. And wanting.

As he descended the narrow, curving stairway, Dane assured himself that his only problem was he'd been taken by surprise. Initially, he hadn't expected Amanda to show up from the shadows of the past. Then, when she had arrived, he certainly hadn't expected such a knee-jerk, gut-wrenching physical reaction.

By tomorrow morning, Dane vowed, he'd have control of his body.

What was worrying the hell out of him was the problem he feared he was going to have gaining control over his heart.

Chapter 4

Amanda was not in a good mood the following morning, as she went downstairs to prepare for the kickoff meeting. Her headache had returned with a vengeance and her stomach was tied up in knots. She'd spent the night tossing and turning, reliving old memories of her days—and nights—at Smugglers' Inn.

And then, when she had finally fallen asleep shortly before dawn, her dreams had been filled with the man who had, impossibly, become an even better kisser. The sensual dreams had resulted in her waking up with an unhealthy curiosity about all the women with whom Dane had spent the past ten years practicing his kissing technique.

After a false turn, she found the conference room Susan had reserved. Ten years ago, the room had been a sleeping porch. The oversize green screens had been

replaced with glass, protecting occupants from the un-
predictable coastal weather without taking away from
the dazzling view, which, at the moment, was draped
in a soft silver mist.

It was absolutely lovely. Greg would find nothing to
complain about here. The only problem would be keeping people's minds off the scenery and focused on the
challenge.

Drawn by the pull of the past, she walked over to the
wall of windows and gazed out, trying to catch a glimpse
of the cave where she and Dane had shared such bliss.

Both relieved and disappointed to see the fog blocked
the view of that stretch of beach, she turned her back on
the sea and crossed the room to a pine sideboard where
urns of coffee and hot water for tea had been placed. Beside the urn were baskets of breakfast breads, and white
platters of fresh fruit.

Amanda poured herself a cup of coffee and placed
some strawberries onto a small plate. When the fragrant
lure proved impossible to resist, she plucked a blueberry
muffin from one of the baskets, then set to work unpacking the boxes of supplies.

As she separated T-shirts bearing the team challenge
logo into red and blue stacks, Amanda wondered what
Dane was doing.

Although she remembered him to have been an early
riser, she doubted he'd have arrived at the inn. Not after
the late hours he'd worked yesterday. Which was just as
well, since she still hadn't sorted out her feelings. All
the agonizing she'd done during the long and sleepless
night had only confused her more.

Last night, alone with him in the tower room that had
been filled with bittersweet memories, it had felt as if

no time at all had passed since that night they'd lain in each other's arms, driving each other to painful distraction, whispering tender words of love, vowing desperate promises.

This morning, Amanda was trying to convince herself that stress, exhaustion and the surprise of seeing Dane again had been responsible for her having responded so quickly and so strongly to him. To his touch. His kiss.

Memories of that enticing kiss flooded back, warming her to the core. "You have to stop this," she scolded herself aloud.

It was imperative that she concentrate on the difficult week ahead. If she allowed her thoughts to drift constantly to Dane Cutter, she'd never pull off a successful challenge. And without a successful challenge, not only would she lose her chance for promotion, she could end up being stuck with Greg Parsons for a very long time.

"And that," she muttered, "is not an option."

"Excuse me?"

Having believed herself to be alone, Amanda spun around and saw a woman standing in the doorway. She was casually dressed in navy shorts, a white polo shirt and white sneakers. If it hadn't been for her name, written in red script above her breast, Amanda would have taken her for a guest.

"I was just talking to myself," she said with embarrassment.

"I do that all the time." The woman's smile was as warm and friendly as Mindy Taylor's had been last night. "Sometimes I even answer myself back, which was beginning to worry me, until Dane said that the time to worry was if I began ignoring myself."

She crossed the room and held out her hand. "I'm Reva Carlson. And you must be Amanda Stockenberg."

Having observed the frenzied activity that had gone into preparing the tower room, then hearing how Dane had insisted on carrying Amanda's bags last night, Reva was more than a little interested in this particular guest. As was every other employee of Smugglers' Inn.

"You're the conference manager Susan spoke with," Amanda remembered.

"Among other things. The management structure around this place tends to be a bit loose."

"Oh?" Amanda wasn't certain she liked the sound of that. One of the advantages of the Mariner Seaside Golf Resort and Conference Center had been an assistant manager whose sole function had been to tend to the group's every need.

"Everyone's trained to fill in wherever they're needed, to allow for optimum service," Reva revealed the management style Dane had introduced. "Although I'm embarrassed to admit that I've been barred from the kitchen after last week's fire."

"Fire?" After having watched her first choice of resort go up in flames, Amanda definitely didn't like hearing that.

"Oh, it wasn't really that big a deal." The shoulders of the white knit shirt rose and fell in a careless shrug. "I was merely trying my hand at pears flambé. When I poured just a smidgen too much brandy into the pans, things got a little hot for a time." Her smile widened. "By the time the fire department showed up, Dane had things under control."

When even the sound of his name caused a hitch

in her breathing, Amanda knew she was in deep, deep trouble. "Dane was working in the kitchen?"

"Sure." Another shrug. "I told you, we're pretty loose around here. And Dane's amazingly handy at everything. He shot the pan with the fire extinguisher, and that was that. But in the meantime, I've been banned from any further cooking experiments, though Mary did promise to let me frost a birthday cake for one of our guests tomorrow."

"Mary?" At the familiar name, Amanda stopped trying to picture Dane in an apron, comfortable in a kitchen. "Mary Cutter?"

"That's right." Reva tilted her head. "Sounds as if you know her."

"I used to." Amanda couldn't quite stop the soft sigh. "I came here with my parents on a vacation ten years ago."

"Mindy mentioned something about that." Reva's friendly gaze turned speculative. "I guess Dane must have been working here at the time, too." Her voice went up on the end of the sentence, turning it into a question.

It was Amanda's turn to shrug. "I suppose. It was a long time ago, and there was quite a large staff, so it's hard to remember everyone."

From the knowing expression in the convention manager's eyes, Amanda had the feeling she wasn't fooling her for a moment. "I do remember his mother made the best peach pie I've ever tasted." She also, Amanda had discovered this morning, baked dynamite blueberry muffins.

"Mary's peach pie wins the blue ribbon at the county fair every year." Returning to her work mode, Reva glanced around the room. "Do you have everything you need?"

"I think so." Amanda's gaze took another slow sweep around the room, trying to seek out any lapses Greg might catch.

"If you think of anything—anything at all—don't hesitate to call on any of us. I have to run into town on some errands, but Dane's around here somewhere."

"I'm sure we'll be fine," Amanda said quickly. Too quickly, she realized, as Reva's gaze narrowed ever so slightly.

"Well, good luck." Reva turned to leave. "With everything."

Matters taken care of to her satisfaction, Reva Carlson returned to her own work, leaving Amanda with the feeling that the woman's parting comment had little to do with the upcoming challenge exercises.

After she finished unpacking the boxes, Amanda headed down the hall to the kitchen, to thank Mary Cutter for the superb Continental breakfast, when she heard her name being called.

Believing it to be someone from the agency, she turned, surprised to see two familiar faces.

"Miss Minnie? Miss Pearl?" The elderly sisters had been guests the last time Amanda had stayed at the inn.

"Hello, dear," one of them—Minnie or Pearl, Amanda couldn't remember which was which—said. Her rosy face was as round as a harvest moon and wreathed in a smile. "We heard you'd come back. It's lovely to see you again."

"It's nice to see you, too. It's also a surprise."

"I don't know why it should be," the other sister

said. "With the exception of the three years the inn was closed—"

"A terrible shame," the other interrupted. "As I was telling Dane just yesterday—"

"Sister!" A scowl darkened a sharp, hatchet face. "I was speaking."

"I'm sorry, sister." There was a brief nod of a lavender head that had been permed into corkscrews; the pastel hue complemented the woman's pink complexion. "I was just pointing out to Amanda how sad it was that such a lovely inn had been allowed to fall into disrepair."

"You'd never know that to look at it now," Amanda said.

"That's because Dane has been working around the clock," the thinner of the two sisters huffed. It was more than a little obvious she resented having her story sidetracked. "As I was saying, with the exception of those three unfortunate years, we have been visiting Smugglers' Inn for the last sixty-four years."

"I believe it's only been sixty-three, sister."

A forceful chin thrust out. "It's sixty-four."

"Are you sure?"

"Of course. I remember everything that happened that year," the other snapped with the certainty of a woman who'd spent forty-five years as the research librarian for the Klamath County Library in southern Oregon.

The term *sibling rivalry* could have been invented to define Minnie and Pearl Davenport. Recalling all too well how these arguments could go on all day, Amanda repeated how nice it was to see the women again and escaped into the kitchen.

This room, too, was as she remembered it—warm and cheerful and immensely inviting. Fragrant, mouth-watering steam rose from the pots bubbling away on the gleaming stove; more copper pots hung from a ceiling rack and the windowsill was home to a row of clay pots filled with fresh green herbs.

An enormous refrigerator that hadn't been there the last time Amanda had sneaked into the kitchen for a heart-to-heart talk with Mary Cutter was open.

"Hello?"

A dark head popped out from behind the stainless-steel door. "Amanda, hello!" Dane's mother's expression was warm and welcoming. She closed the refrigerator and opened her arms. "I was hoping you'd get a chance to escape those boring old business meetings and visit with an old friend."

As she hugged the woman, Amanda realized that Mary Cutter had, indeed, become a friend that summer. Even though, looking back on it, she realized how concerned Mary had been for Dane. As she would have been, Amanda admitted now, if some sex-crazed, under-age teenage girl had been chasing after her son.

"They're not that bad." Amanda felt duty-bound to defend the group.

"Oh?" Releasing her, Mary went over to the stove and poured two cups of coffee. She put them on the table, and gestured for Amanda to sit down. "Then why do you have those dark circles beneath your eyes?"

Amanda unconsciously lifted her fingers to the blue shadows she thought she'd managed to conceal success-fully this morning. It was bad enough having to deal with Dane and their past, which now seemed to be unset-tled. By the time the corporate challenge week was over, she'd undoubtedly be buying concealer by the carton.

"I've been working long hours lately."

"You're not sleeping very well, either, I'd suspect. And you have a headache."

"It's not that bad," Amanda lied as Mary reached out and rubbed at the lines carving furrows between her eyes.

The older woman's touch was gentle and more maternal than any Amanda had ever received from her own mother. Then again, the Stockenbergs never had been touchers. The Cutters—mother and son—definitely were.

Mary's smile didn't fade, but the way she was looking at her, hard and deep, made Amanda want to change the subject. "I just ran into Miss Minnie and Miss Pearl," she said. "But I couldn't remember which was which."

"Minnie is the one with white hair and an attitude. Pearl has lavender hair and hides Hershey's Kisses all over the inn."

"Why would she do that?"

"Because the poor dear has an enormous sweet tooth. And Minnie has her on a diet that would starve a gerbil." Mary flashed a quick grin that was remarkably like her son's, although it didn't have the capability to affect Amanda in such a devastating manner. "I feel so sorry for Pearl. She's been sneaking in here for snacks ever since they arrived last week."

"Well, I can certainly understand that. I had a muffin that was just short of heaven."

"I'm so pleased you enjoyed it." Mary's eyes skimmed over Amanda judiciously. "You're a bit thin, dear. We'll have to see what we can do about fattening you up a little."

"A woman can never be too thin," Amanda said, quoting one of her sleek mother's favorite axioms.

"Want to bet?" a deep voice asked from the doorway.

Amanda tamped down the little burst of pleasure brought about by the sight of Dane, clad again in jeans. Today's shirt was faded chambray; his shoes were high-topped sneakers.

Mary greeted him with a smile. "Good morning, darling."

"Morning." He crossed the room on a long, easy stride and kissed his mother's cheek. "Do I smell sugar cookies?"

"It's my new cologne," Mary said with a laugh. "The saleswoman said it has vanilla in it." She shook her head in mock regret. "She also said men would find it impossible to resist. I'm afraid I was oversold."

"Never met a man yet who didn't like sugar cookies," Dane said agreeably. His grin slipped a notch as his attention turned to Amanda. "Good morning."

Amanda had watched the way he brushed his finger down his mother's cheek in a casual, intimate gesture that was as natural to him as breathing. Once again she was reminded how different the Cutters were from the Stockenbergs. It would be wise to keep those differences in mind over the next several days.

"Good morning." Her tone was friendly, but cool. She could have been speaking to a stranger at a bus stop.

"Sleep well?" His tone was as studiously casual as hers.

"Like a baby," she lied. She pushed herself up from the table. "Well, I really do have to get back to work. I just wanted to stop in and say hi," she told Mary. "And to thank you for the lovely breakfast."

"It's been lovely seeing you again, dear." Dane's mother took Amanda's hand in both of hers. "I realize you're going to be extremely busy, but I hope you can find time to visit again."

"I'd like that." It was the truth.

Without another word to Dane, Amanda placed her cup on the counter, then left the kitchen.

"Well, she certainly has grown up to be a lovely young lady," Mary said.

"Really?" Dane's answering shrug was forced. "I didn't notice."

Mary poured another cup of coffee and placed it in front of him. "Reva says she has a very responsible position at that advertising agency."

This earned little more than a grunt.

"I couldn't help noticing she's not wearing any ring on her left hand."

Dane's face shuttered. "No offense, Mom, but I really don't want to talk about Amanda."

"Of course, dear," Mary replied smoothly. But as she turned to the stove and poured pancake batter into an iron skillet, Mary Cutter was smiling.

Despite instructions that they were to meet at eight o'clock sharp, the team members straggled into the conference room. By the time everyone had gotten coffee, fruit and pastries and taken their seats, it was twenty-eight minutes past the time the kickoff had been scheduled to begin.

"Well, this is certainly getting off to a dandy start," muttered Greg, who was sitting beside Amanda at the pine trestle table at the front of the room. "Didn't you send out my memo letting the troops know I expected them to be prompt?"

"Of course." Amanda refrained from pointing out that

if one wanted troops to follow orders, it was helpful if they respected their commanding officer. "We arrived awfully late last night," she said, seeking some excuse for the tardy team members. "Everyone was probably a little tired this morning."

His only response to her efforts was a muttered curse that did not give Amanda a great deal of encouragement.

Greg stood and began to outline the week's activities, striding back and forth at the front of the room like General Patton addressing the soldiers of the Third Army. He was waving his laser pointer at the detailed flowchart as if it were Patton's famed riding crop. The troops seemed uniformly unimpressed by all the red, blue and yellow rectangles.

As he set about explaining the need for consistent process and implementation, even Amanda's mind began to wander, which was why she didn't hear the door open at the back of the room.

"I'm sorry to interrupt," one of last night's bellmen, who bore an amazing resemblance to Brad Pitt, said. "But Ms. Stockenberg has a phone call."

"Take a message," Greg snapped before Amanda could answer.

"He says it's urgent."

"I'd better take it," Amanda said.

"Just make it quick. I intend to get on schedule."

"I'll be right back." Amanda resisted the urge to salute.

The news was not good. "But you have to come," she insisted when the caller, the man she'd hired to conduct the physical adventure portion of the weekend, explained his predicament. "I understand you've broken your leg. But surely you can at least sit on the beach and instruct—"

She was cut off by a flurry of denial on the other end of the line. "Oh. In traction? I'm so sorry to hear that." She reached into her pocket, pulled out the antacids she was never without and popped one into her mouth.

"Well, of course you need to rest. And get well soon." She dragged her hand through her hair. "There's no need to apologize. You didn't fall off that motorcycle on purpose."

She hung up the phone with a bit more force than necessary. "Damn."

"Got a problem?"

Amanda spun around and glared up at Dane. "I'm getting a little tired of the way you have of sneaking up on people."

"Sorry." The dancing light in his eyes said otherwise.

"No." She sighed and shook her head. "I'm the one who should apologize for snapping at you. It's just that I really need this week to go well, and before we can even get started on the kayak race, my adventure expert ends up in the hospital."

"That *is* a tough break."

She could hear the amusement in his voice. "Don't you dare laugh at me."

"I wouldn't think of it." He reached out and rubbed at the parallel lines his mother had smoothed earlier. "I don't suppose a hotshot businesswoman—with her own window office and fancy Italian-leather chair—would need any advice?"

The soothing touch felt too good. Too right. Amanda backed away. "At this point, I'd take advice from the devil himself." Realizing how snippy she sounded, she felt obliged to apologize yet again.

"Don't worry about it. People say things they don't mean under stress." Which he knew only too well. Dane had found it enlightening that the temper he'd developed while working for the Whitfield Palace hotel chain seemed to have vanished when he'd bought the inn, despite all the problems refurbishing it had entailed. "How about me?"

"How about you, what?"

"How about me subbing for your kayak guy?"

Remembering how he'd taught her to paddle that double kayak so many years ago, Amanda knew it was the perfect solution. Except for one thing.

"Don't you have work to do?"

Dane shrugged. "It'll keep."

"I wouldn't want you to get in trouble."

"Why don't you let me worry about that, contessa? Besides, we all kind of pitch in where needed around here."

That was exactly what Reva had told her. And Amanda was grateful enough not to contest that ridiculous name. "Thank you. I really appreciate your help."

"Hey, that's what we're here for." He grinned and skimmed a dark finger down the slope of her nose. "Service With a Smile, that's the motto at Smugglers' Inn."

The knot of tension in her stomach unwound. It was impossible to worry when he was smiling at her that way. It was nearly impossible to remember that the man represented a dangerous distraction.

Relieved that she'd overcome the first hurdle of the week, and putting aside the nagging little problem of what she was going to do about the rest of the scheduled adventure exercises, Amanda returned to the conference room and began handing out the challenge-team shirts.

"What the hell are these?" Don Patterson, the marketing manager, asked.

"They're to denote the different teams," Amanda explained. "Reds versus blues."

"Like shirts versus skins," Marvin Kenyon, who'd played some high school basketball, said.

"Exactly."

"I wouldn't mind playing shirts and skins with Kelli," Peter Wanger from the computer-support division said with a leer directed toward the public-relations manager, who was provocatively dressed in a pair of tight white jeans and a thin red top. The scoop neck barely concealed voluptuous breasts that, if they hadn't been surgically enhanced, could undoubtedly qualify as natural wonders of the world.

"Watch it, Peter," Amanda warned. "Or you'll have to watch that video on sexual harassment in the workplace again."

"Oh, Peter was just joking," Kelli said quickly, sending a perky cheerleader smile his way. "It doesn't bother me, Amanda."

That might be. But it did bother Greg. Amanda watched her superior's jaw clench. "Amanda's right," he growled. If looks could kill, Peter would be drawn and quartered, then buried six feet under the sand. "Just because we're not in the office doesn't mean that I'll stand for inappropriate behavior."

It sounded good. But everyone in the room knew that what was really happening was that Greg had just stamped his own personal No Trespassing sign on Kelli Kyle's wondrous chest.

"Talk about inappropriate," Laura Quinlan muttered as Amanda handed her a red T-shirt. "My kid's Barbie doll has tops larger than that bimbo's."

At thirty-six, Laura was a displaced homemaker who'd recently been hired as a junior copywriter. Amanda knew she was struggling to raise two children on her own after her physician husband had left her for his office assistant—a young woman who, if Laura could be believed, could be Kelli Kyle's evil twin.

Secretly agreeing about the inappropriateness of Kelli's attire, but not wanting to take sides, Amanda didn't answer.

"I can't wear this color," Nadine Roberts complained when Amanda handed her one of the red shirts. "I had my colors done and I'm a summer."

"This week you're an autumn." Amanda tossed a blue shirt to Julian Palmer.

"You certainly chose a graphically unsatisfying design," he complained.

"We should have come to you for help," she said, soothing the art director's easily ruffled feathers. Personally, she thought the white Team Challenge script just dandy. "But I knew how overworked you've been with the Uncle Paul's potato chip account, and didn't want to add any more pressure."

"The man's an idiot," Julian grumbled. "Insisting on those claymation dancing barbecue chips."

"It worked for the raisin growers," Kelli reminded everyone cheerfully. Despite all the rumors that had circulated since the woman's arrival two weeks ago, no one could accuse her of not being unrelentingly upbeat.

Amanda had been surprised to discover that beneath that bubbly-cheerleader personality and bimbo clothing,

Kelli possessed a steel-trap mind when it came to her work. Which made it even more surprising that she'd stoop to having an affair with a man like Greg.

Not that there was actually any proof, other than gossip, that they were sleeping together, she reminded herself. However, given Greg's Lothario tendencies, along with all the time the pair spent together in his office with the door closed, Amanda certainly wouldn't have bet against the possibility.

Julian stiffened and shot Kelli a look that suggested her IQ was on a level with Uncle Paul's. "Potato chips," he said, "are not raisins."

No one in the room dared challenge that proclamation.

"Wait a damn minute," Marvin Kenyon complained when Amanda handed him a blue shirt. "I categorically refuse to be on *his* team." He jerked a thumb in Julian's direction.

Amanda opened her mouth to answer, but Greg beat her to the punch. "You'll be on whatever team I tell you you're on," he barked from the front of the room. "In case I haven't made myself clear, people, challenge week isn't about choice. It's about competition. Teamwork.

"And effective immediately, you are all going to work together as teams. Or at the end of the week, I'll start handing out pink slips. Do I make myself clear?"

He was answered by a low, obviously unhappy mumble.

Smooth move, Greg, Amanda thought.

The worst problem with mergers was their effect on the employees. Even more so in advertising, where people were the agency's only real assets.

The rash of changeovers had caused dislocation, disaffection, underperformance and just plain fear. Which explained why more and more accounts were leaving the agency with each passing day. It was, after all, difficult to be creative when you thought you were going to be fired.

There were times, and this was definitely one of them, when Amanda wished she'd stuck to her youthful dreams of creating a family rather than an ad for a new, improved detergent or a toothpaste that supposedly would make the high school football quarterback ask the class wallflower to the prom.

When the idea of home and children once again brought Dane to the forefront of her mind, she shook off the thought and led the group out of the room, down to the beach where the first challenge activity was scheduled to take place.

Chapter 5

"Oh, my God," Laura said as the group reached the beach and found Dane waiting. "I think I'm in love."

While Greg had been harassing the troops and Amanda had been handing out T-shirts, Dane had changed into a black neoprene body glove. The suit somehow seemed to reveal more of him than if he were stark-naked.

His arms, his powerful legs, his chest, looked as if they had been chiseled from marble. No, Amanda decided, marble was too cold. Dane could have been hewn from one of the centuries-old redwoods found in an old-growth forest.

"That man is, without a doubt, the most drop-dead-gorgeous male I've ever seen in my life." Kelli was staring at Dane the way a religious zealot might stare at her god. "Oh, I do believe I'm going to enjoy this week."

"We're not here to enjoy ourselves," Greg ground out.

"It's not a damn holiday." He turned his sharp gaze on Amanda. "That's the guy you hired to lead the adventure exercises?"

Call her petty, but Amanda found watching Greg literally seething with masculine jealousy more than a little enjoyable. Less enjoyable was the realization that Kelli's and Laura's lustful looks and comments had triggered a bit of her own jealousy.

"Not exactly."

Blond brows came crashing down. "What does that mean?"

"I'll explain later." She cast a significant glance down at her watch. "You're the one who wanted to stay on schedule, Greg. Come with me and I'll introduce you."

The introductions were over quickly, neither man seeming to find much to like about the other.

"The plan," Amanda explained to Dane, "as it was originally laid out to me, works like a relay race. Team members pair up, two to a kayak, paddle out to the lighthouse, circle it, then return back to the beach where the next group takes their places in the kayak and follows the same course. The best combined times for the two out of three heats is declared the winner."

Dane nodded. "Sounds easy enough."

"Easy for you to say. You haven't seen this group in action."

Seeing her worried expression and remembering what she'd told him about this week being vastly important to her, Dane understood her concern.

"Don't worry, Ms. Stockenberg," he said in his best businesslike tone, the one that had served him well for all those years in the big city, "before the week's over, you'll have turned your group into a lean, mean, advertising machine."

"That's the point," Greg Parsons snapped.

Amanda, who'd detected the sarcasm in Dane's tone, didn't respond. Instead, she introduced Dane to the others, then stood back and ceded control to the man she hoped could pull it off.

He didn't raise his voice above his usual conversational tone, but as he began to explain the basics of kayaking, Amanda noticed that a hush settled over the suddenly attentive group. Even the men were hanging on every word.

It was more than the fact that he was a stunningly good-looking male specimen. As amazing as it seemed for a man who'd been content to stay in the same job he'd had in high school, Dane Cutter definitely displayed leadership potential, making Amanda wonder yet again what had happened to sidetrack all his lofty career goals.

Perhaps, she considered, once this week was over and she'd earned the position of Northwest creative director, she'd offer Dane a job in management. After all, if he actually managed to pull this disparate, backbiting group into cohesive teams, helping him escape a dead-end life in Satan's Cove would be the least she could do.

Then again, she reminded herself firmly when she realized she was thinking too much like her autocratic father, there was no reason for Dane to be ashamed of having chosen a life of manual labor. It was, she admitted reluctantly, more honest than advertising.

Dane gave the teams a brief spiel about the versatility of kayaks, demonstrated forward and bracing strokes, explaining how the foot-operated rudder would help steer in crosswinds or rough seas, and skimmed over the wood-paddles-versus-fiberglass argument.

Amanda was not surprised to discover that despite the introduction of high-tech models, Dane remained an advocate of wood. The fact that he obviously felt strongly about a century-old inn proved he was a traditionalist at heart.

When he asked for questions, Kelli's hand shot up. "Shouldn't we be wearing wet suits like yours?" she asked.

"It's not really necessary," Dane assured her, making Amanda extremely relieved. She figured the sight of Kelli Kyle in a neoprene body glove could easily cause at least two heart attacks.

"But what if we get wet?"

"One can only hope," Peter murmured, earning laughter from several of the men and another sharp glare from Greg. At the same time, Amanda worried that Kelli in a wet T-shirt could be even more distracting than Kelli in a snug neoprene suit.

"Hopefully that won't prove a problem," Dane said with an answering smile.

"I've seen kayaking on the Discovery channel." This from Nadine Roberts. "And they always tip over."

"That technique is called an Eskimo roll. And you don't have to worry about learning it for this exercise," Dane told her.

"What if we don't intend to learn it? What if we roll anyway?" An auditor in the accounting department, Nadine was not accustomed to letting things slide.

"Never happen." Dane's grin was quick and reassuring. "You're thinking of the Inuit cruiser style, which is designed for speed and minimum wind interference.

You'll be in double touring kayaks, which are extremely stable. Think of them as floating minivans."

"My minivan is a lot bigger," Laura argued.

"People," Greg interjected sharply, "we're wasting valuable time here." He turned toward Dane. "As fascinating as all this might be," he said, his sarcastic tone indicating otherwise, "we don't have all day. So, if you're through with the instructions, Cutter, it's time to get this show on the road."

"It's your show," Dane said agreeably. But Amanda could see a simmering irritation in his dark eyes. "I'll need a volunteer for a demonstration." His seemingly casual gaze moved over the group before landing on Amanda. "Ms. Stockenberg," he said, "how about helping me with a little show-and-tell?"

Every head on the beach had turned toward her. Knowing that refusal would garner unwanted interest, Amanda shrugged. "Fine."

She took the orange life jacket Dane held out to her and put it on over her challenge T-shirt.

"Need any help with that?" he asked, reminding her of the time she'd pretended to need him to fasten the ties for her.

"I'm fine, thank you."

"Actually," he murmured, for her ears only, "you're a helluva lot better than fine, contessa."

Her temper flared, predictably. Remembering where she was, Amanda tamped it down.

"You'll need this." He handed her a helmet not unlike the one she wore when rollerblading or biking. "There are a lot of rocks around the lighthouse."

"I thought you said there's no risk of capsizing," she argued as she nevertheless put the white helmet on.

"Good point. But it never hurts to be prepared."

Good point, she echoed mentally as she watched him drag the kayak toward the water. If she'd been prepared to discover Dane still working here, she wouldn't be suffering from these unsettling feelings.

Within minutes of being afloat, she began to remember the rhythm he'd so patiently taught her that long-ago summer. Holding the blade of the wooden paddle close to her chest, her hands a bit more than shoulders' width apart, she plunged the blade in cleanly, close to the hull, pulling back with her lower hand, using torso rotation rather than arm strength, punching forward with her upper hand at the same time. When the blade of the paddle reached her hip, she snapped it out of the water and stroked on the other side.

Stab, pull, snap. Stab, pull, snap. Behind her, she could feel Dane moving in concert. *Stab, pull, snap.* "Not bad," Dane said. "For someone who probably considers the rowing machine at the gym roughing it."

Since his remark hit close to the truth, Amanda opted not to take offense. "I can't believe it's coming back so fast." *Stab, pull, snap. Left, right, left, right.* Although the touring kayak was built for stability, not speed, they were skimming through the surf toward the lighthouse. "I suppose it's like riding a bicycle."

"Or kissing," Dane suggested. *Stab, pull, snap.* The paddles continued to swish through the water. "We always did that well together, too. Ten years ago. And again, last night."

His words stopped her cold. "I don't want to talk about last night." Unnerved, she forgot to pull the paddle out until it had drifted beyond her hip. When she did, she caused the boat to veer off course.

The brisk professional ad executive was back. Dane was tempted to flip the kayak just to teach her a lesson. And to cool himself off. Didn't she know what she'd done to him last night? Didn't she realize how all it had taken was the taste of those succulent lips and the feel of that soft body against his to cause time to go spinning backward and make him feel like a horny, sex-starved teenager again?

"Tough," he deftly corrected, setting them straight again. Didn't she know that showing up this morning in that soft cotton T-shirt and those shorts that made her legs look as if they went all the way up to her neck was like waving a red flag in front of a very frustrated bull?

When he felt his hand tighten in a death grip on the smooth wooden shaft, he flexed his fingers, restraining the urge to put them around her shoulders to shake her.

"Because I have no intention of spending the next five nights lying awake, thinking about might-have-beens."

His tone was gruff, but Amanda was no longer an easily cowed fifteen-year-old girl. She began to shoot him a glare over her shoulder, but the lethal look in his eyes had her missing yet another stroke.

"You agreed to teach the kayaking just to get me alone with you, didn't you?"

"I could see from that schedule you and Mr. Slick have devised for the week that having you to myself for any decent length of time was going to be difficult, if not impossible," he agreed without displaying an iota of guilt about utilizing such subterfuge. "Fortunately, I've always prided myself on managing the impossible. Like resisting making love to a painfully desirable teenager."

"Dane..." Words deserted her as something far more dangerous than anger rose in those dark eyes.

They were behind the lighthouse now, out of view of the challenge-team members waiting for them back on the beach.

Dane stopped stroking and laid his paddle across the kayak. "I've thought about you, Amanda. I've remembered how you felt in my arms, how you tasted, how my body would ache all night after I'd have to send you back to your room."

"Don't blame me. *You're* the one who didn't want to make love."

"Wrong. What I wanted to do and what I knew I had to do were two entirely different things, contessa. But just because I was trying to do the honorable thing—not to mention staying out of jail—doesn't mean that I haven't imagined how things might have been different. If we'd met at another time."

"It wouldn't be the same." It was what she'd been telling herself for years. "That summer was something apart, Dane. Something that belongs in its own time and its own place. It doesn't even seem real anymore. And it certainly doesn't fit in our real lives."

She wasn't saying anything Dane hadn't told himself innumerable times. The problem was, he hadn't bought the argument then. And he wasn't buying it now.

"Are you saying you haven't thought about me?"

"That's exactly what I'm saying." It was the first and only lie she'd ever told him.

"Never?"

"Never."

He considered that for a moment. "All right. Let's fast-forward to the present. Tell me you didn't feel anything last night, and I'll never mention it again."

"I didn't mean for that to…" She shook her head. "It just happened," she said weakly.

"Tell me."

She swallowed and looked away, pretending sudden interest in a trio of dolphins riding the surf on the horizon. There was a tug-of-war going on inside her. Pulling her emotionally toward Dane, pushing her away. Pulling and pushing. As it had done all during the long and lonely night.

"Tell me you haven't thought about how it could be," he continued in a low, deep voice that crept beneath her skin and warmed her blood. "Tell me you haven't imagined me touching you. You touching me. All over. Tell me that you don't want me."

Amanda knew that the easy thing, the safe thing, would be to assure him that the kiss they'd shared had been merely pleasant. But certainly nothing to lose sleep over. Unable to lie, she did the only thing she could think of. She hedged.

"You're certainly not lacking in ego." She tried a laugh that failed. Miserably.

"Tell me." His soft, gently insistent tone, touched with a subtle trace of male arrogance, was, in its own way, more forceful than the loudest shout. Once again Amanda wondered why Dane was wasting such talents here, at a small inn in a small coastal town, miles from civilization.

"I can't." She closed her eyes and shook her head.

Dane let out a long relieved breath that Amanda, caught up in the grips of her own turmoiled emotions, did not hear. So he'd been right. She wanted him, even as she didn't want to want him. He knew the feeling all too well.

"Have dinner with me tonight."

Was there anyone in the world who could resist that deep velvet voice? She certainly couldn't.

"I can't." Her voice shimmered with very real regret. "Greg and I have to go over today's results at dinner. And try to come up with substitutes for the bike race, backpacking trip and rock climb, now that we've lost our adventure leader."

"That's no problem. I'll do it."

The part of her who was desperate for the challenge week to be a success wanted to jump at his offer. Another, even stronger part of her, the part she feared was still a little bit in love with Dane, could not put his job in jeopardy on her account.

"I can't let you do that."

"I told you, it's no big deal."

"You won't think so if you lose your job."

Dane shrugged. "Jobs are easy to come by." His smile, while warm, was unthreatening. "Now, dinner with a beautiful woman, that's well worth throwing caution to the wind for.

"I'm volunteering for purely selfish reasons, Amanda. If I help out with the rest of the challenge week, you won't have to spend so much of your evenings with that cretin you're working so hard to get promoted back East, so I can be with you."

Her eyes widened. "How did you know I was trying to get Greg promoted to Manhattan?"

Amanda desperately hoped that he hadn't overheard any of the team members discussing such a possibility. She hadn't wanted anyone but Susan to know about her plan to win Greg Parsons's job. The job, she reminded herself, that should have been hers.

He watched the fear leap into her eyes and wondered if she realized that the goal she was chasing was not only illusive, but not worth the struggle.

"Don't worry. It was just a wild shot in the dark." He wanted to touch her—not sexually, just a hand to her cheek, or her hair, to soothe her obviously jangled nerves. "It's you city folks who are big on corporate intrigue. Out here in the boonies, we tend to spend more time trying to decide whether to take our naps before dinner or afterward."

Amanda still hadn't gotten a handle on Dane. But she knew he wasn't the country bumpkin he was pretending to be.

"I'd love to have you take over leading the corporate challenge. Of course, the agency will insist on paying you."

The figure she offered would pay for the new furnace the inn needed if he wanted to stay open year-round. Pride had Dane momentarily tempted to turn it down. He remembered just in time that the money would not come out of Amanda's pocket, but from the corporate checkbook of a very profitable advertising agency.

"That sounds more than reasonable. It's a deal."

"Believe me, Dane, you're saving my life."

He watched the worry lines ease from her forehead and wished that all her problems could be so simple to solve. He also wondered how bad those headaches would become, and how many cases of antacids she'd have to chew her way through before she realized that advertising wasn't real life.

"So, now that we've solved that problem, what about dinner?"

"I honestly can't."

She paused, running through a mental schedule. Now that they didn't have to come up with new activities, she and Greg didn't have all that much to cover. Besides, he'd undoubtedly want to get away early in order to sneak off to Kelli's room. Which, she'd noticed, conveniently adjoined his.

"How about dessert? We have to get together," he reminded, "so you can fill me in on the rest of the activities the leader you originally hired had planned for the week."

Telling herself that she'd just have to keep things on a strictly business level, Amanda said, "With your mother in the kitchen, how can I turn down dessert?"

"Terrific." His smile was quick and warmed her to the core. "I'll meet you down by the boathouse."

The boathouse had been one of their secret meeting places. Amanda knew that to be alone with Dane in a place that harbored so many romantic memories was both foolhardy and dangerous.

"Something wrong with the dining room?"

"It's too public."

"That's the idea."

"Ah, but I was under the impression that part of the corporate challenge agenda was to keep the teams off guard. So you can observe how they respond to unexpected trials."

Amanda vaguely wondered how Dane knew so much about corporate game-playing strategy. "So?"

"So, if we go over the events you have planned in any of the public rooms, some of the team members might overhear us."

He had, she admitted reluctantly, a good point.

"There's always my room," he suggested when she didn't immediately answer.

"No," she answered quickly. Too quickly, Dane thought with an inward smile. It was obvious that they were both thinking about the first time she'd shown up at his door.

"Okay, how about the tower room?"

Not on a bet. "The boathouse will be fine."

"It's a date."

"It's not a date." Amanda felt it important to clarify that point up front. "It's a business meeting."

Dane shrugged. "Whatever." Matters settled to his satisfaction, he resumed paddling.

As Amanda had suspected, other than complain about the outcome of the first challenge event, Greg was not inclined to linger over dinner. Forgoing appetizers, he got right to the point of their meeting as he bolted through the main course.

"Today was an unmitigated disaster." His tone was thick with accusation.

"It wasn't all that bad," she murmured, not quite truthfully. The race hadn't been as successful as she'd hoped.

Unsurprisingly, Julian and Marvin had not meshed. They never managed to get their stroking rhythm in sync, and although each continued to blame the other loudly, their kayak had gotten so out of control that it had rammed into the one piloted by Laura and Don at the far turn around the lighthouse. Fortunately, Dane was proved right about the stability of the craft. But although neither kayak overturned, once the four were back on the beach, the three men almost came to blows.

Needless to say, Greg's subsequent cursing and shout-ing only caused the friction level to rise even higher. The only thing that had stopped the altercation from turning into a full-fledged brawl was Dane's quiet intervention. Amanda had not been able to hear what he was saying, but his words, whatever they were, obviously did the trick. Although their boatmanship didn't improve much during the second heat, the combatants behaved like kit-tens for the remainder of the afternoon.

"It was a disaster," Greg repeated. He pushed his plate away and took a swig from the drink he was never with-out. "I don't have to tell you that your career is on the line here, Amanda."

She refused to let him see how desperately she wanted the week to be successful. If he knew how important it was to her, he might try to sabotage her participation.

"If I remember correctly, this entire scheme was *your* idea."

"True." He turned down a second cup of coffee from a hovering waitress, and declined dessert. "But my job's not in jeopardy so long as *I'm* the one who eats a family holiday dinner with Ernst Janzen every Christmas." He placed his napkin on the table and rose.

"Make it work, Amanda," he warned, jabbing a fin-ger toward her. "Or you'll be out on the street. And your assistant will be pounding the pavement, looking for a new job right along with you."

She felt the blood literally drain from her face. It was just an idle threat. He couldn't mean it, she assured her-self. But she *knew* he did.

It was one thing to blow her plans for advancement. She was also willing to risk her own career. But to be suddenly responsible for Susan's job, six months before her assistant's planned wedding, was more pressure than Amanda needed.

"I expect tomorrow's exercise to be a model of efficiency and collaboration," he said. "Or you can call Susan and instruct her to start packing both your things into boxes."

With that threat ringing in her ears, he turned on his heel and left the dining room.

The long day, preceded by a sleepless night, had left Amanda exhausted. Her dinner with Greg had left her depressed. And although she'd been secretly looking forward to being alone with Dane, now that the time had arrived, Amanda realized she was more than a little nervous.

Butterflies—no, make that giant condors—were flapping their wings in her stomach and she'd second-guessed her agreement to meet with him at least a dozen times during dinner.

Admittedly stalling, she was lingering over dinner when Mary appeared beside the table, a small pink bakery box in her hand.

"How was your meal?"

Amanda smiled, grateful for the interruption that would keep her from having to decide whether or not to stand Dane up again. Which would be difficult, since they were scheduled to spend the remainder of the week working on the challenge together.

"Absolutely delicious." The salmon pasta in white-wine sauce had practically melted in her mouth. "I'll probably gain ten pounds before the week is over."

"From what Dane tells me, with the week you have planned, you'll undoubtedly work off any extra calories."

Mary held out the box. "I thought you and Dane might enjoy some carrot cake."

For ten years Amanda had been searching for a carrot cake as rich and sweet as Mary Cutter's. For ten years she'd been constantly disappointed.

"Make that twelve pounds," she complained weakly, eyeing the box with culinary lust.

Mary's look of satisfaction was a carbon copy of her son's. Although not as direct as Dane, in her own way, Mary Cutter could be a velvet bulldozer. "As I said before, a few extra pounds couldn't hurt, dear."

Running her hand down Amanda's hair in another of those maternal gestures Amanda had never received from her own mother, Mary returned to the kitchen, leaving Amanda with two pieces of carrot cake and a date for which she was already late.

She was on her way across the front parlor when someone called her name. Turning, she viewed the gorgeous young woman who'd been on duty last night, standing behind the desk.

"Yes?"

"I hate to ask, especially since you're a paying guest and all, but would you mind doing me a favor?" Mindy Taylor asked.

"If I can."

"Could you tell Dane that the furnace guy promised to begin work on Friday?"

Two things crossed Amanda's mind at nearly the same time. The first being that her meeting with Dane seemed to be common knowledge. The second being the fact that along with his other duties, Dane appeared to be in charge of maintenance.

"If I see him," she hedged.

"Great." Mindy flashed her dazzling Miss Satan's Cove smile. "Isn't it great how things work out?"

"What things?"

"Well, if the Mariner resort hadn't burned down, your advertising agency wouldn't have come here in the first place. Then, if your adventure leader hadn't spun out on his Harley on that rain-slick curve, you wouldn't have needed to hire Dane to fill in, and the inn would have to close after Labor Day."

Last night, Amanda had been impressed with Mindy's seeming combination of intelligence and beauty. Tonight she wondered if she'd made a mistake in judgment.

"I don't understand what hiring Dane to lead the challenge week has to do with Smugglers' Inn being able to remain open after Labor Day."

"Without a new furnace, we would have had to shut down for the winter."

"But what does that have to do with Dane?"

It was Mindy's turn to look at Amanda as if she was lacking in some necessary intelligence. "Because he's using the check from your agency to buy the new furnace."

"But why would Dane…" Comprehension suddenly hit like a bolt of lightning from a clear blue summer sky. "Dane's the new owner of Smugglers' Inn."

"Lock, stock and brand-new gas furnace," Mindy cheerfully confirmed.

Chapter 6

A full moon was floating in an unusually clear night sky, lighting Amanda's way to the boathouse. At any other time she might have paused to enjoy the silvery white path on the moon-gilded waters of the Pacific Ocean, or stopped to gaze up at the millions of stars sparkling overhead like loose diamonds scattered across a black velvet jeweler's cloth.

But her mind was not on the dazzling bright moon, nor the silvery water, nor the stars. Amanda was on her way to the boathouse to kill Dane Cutter.

He was waiting for her, just as he'd promised. Just as he had so many years ago. Unaware of the pique simmering through her, Dane greeted her with a smile that under any other conditions she would have found devastatingly attractive.

"I was getting worried about you."

She glared up at him, a slender, furious warrior with right on her side. "I got held up."

"So I see." Lines crinkled at the corners of his smiling eyes. "I hope that's Mom's carrot cake."

She'd forgotten she was still carrying the pink box. "It is." She handed it to him. Then reached back and slammed her fist into his stomach.

He doubled over with a grunt of surprise, dropping the cake box. "Damn it, Amanda!"

He gingerly straightened. She was standing, legs braced, as if intending to pound him again. He waited until he was sure his voice would be steady.

"You get one free shot, contessa. That's it. Try another cheap stunt like that and I'll have no choice but to slug you back."

"You wouldn't dare!" He might be a liar, but the man she'd fallen in love with ten years ago would never strike a woman. Then again, she reminded herself, apparently there was a lot she didn't know about the man Dane Cutter had become.

"I wouldn't risk putting it to the test." His dark eyes were hard. Implacable.

Dane saw her hand move to her stomach and damned himself for having caused another flare-up of her obviously touchy nerves.

But damn it, he hadn't started this. His plans for the evening had been to start out with some slow, deep kisses. After that, he'd intended to play things by ear, although if they ended up in bed, he certainly wasn't going to complain.

The worst-possible-case scenario was that they might waste valuable time together actually talking about her damn challenge-week events. One thing he hadn't planned on was having a fist slammed into his gut.

"You know, you really ought to see a doctor about that."

She frowned, momentarily thrown off track. "About what?"

"You could have an ulcer."

Following his gaze, she realized that the way her hand was pressed against the front of her blouse was a sure giveaway that she wasn't as much in control as she was trying to appear. "I don't have an ulcer."

"You sure? They can treat them with antibiotics, so—"

"I said, I don't have any damn ulcer."

Dane shrugged. "Fine. Then I'd suggest you work on your attitude."

"My attitude?" Her hands settled on her hips. "How dare you question *my* attitude. After what you've done!"

"What, exactly, have I done? Other than to offer to pull your fat out of the fire? Corporately speaking, that is."

Physically, she didn't appear to have an ounce of fat on her—one of the things he was hoping his mother's cooking could change. Amanda's society mother had been wrong; there was such a thing as a woman being too thin.

"That wasn't exactly the act of pure selflessness you made it out to be at the time," she countered with a toss of her head. "Not when you consider the new furnace for the inn. Which is scheduled to be installed Friday, by the way."

"Ah." It finally made sense. "Who told you?"

Amanda didn't know which made her more angry.

That Dane had lied to her in the first place, or that he appeared so cavalier at having gotten caught.

"That doesn't matter," she said between clenched teeth. "What matters is that you lied to me."

Now that he knew what all the storm and fury was about, Dane found himself enjoying the murder in her eyes. It spoke of a passion he had every intention of experiencing before this week was over.

"I'd never lie to you, Amanda."

She folded her arms and shot him a disbelieving look. "I don't recall you telling me that you were the new owner of Smugglers' Inn."

"I don't recall you asking."

Frustrated and furious, Amanda let out a huff of breath. "It's not the sort of question one asks a person one believes to be a bellman."

Her words were dripping icicles. Although hauteur was not her usual style, having been on the receiving end of her mother's cool conceit for all of her twenty-five years, Amanda had learned, on rare occasions, to wield the icy weapon herself. Tonight was one of those occasions.

Dane revealed no sign of having been fatally wounded. "You know, that snotty attitude doesn't suit you, contessa." Ignoring her warning glare, he reached out and stroked her hair. "It's too remote." Stroked her cheek. "Too passionless." Stroked the side of her neck. "Too untouchable."

That was precisely the point, damn it! Unfortunately, it wasn't working. Seemingly undeterred by her fury, he was jangling her nerves, weakening her defenses. Reminding herself that she was no longer a naive, hopelessly romantic young fifteen-year-old, Amanda moved away from his beguiling touch.

"You let me think you were still just an employee." Although his touch had regrettably cooled her ire, the thought that he might have been laughing at her still stung.

Just an employee. He wondered if she knew how much like her rich, snobbish mother those words sounded. "I suppose I did." Until now, Dane hadn't realized that he'd been testing her. But, he admitted, that was exactly what he'd been doing.

"Does it really make that much of a difference? Whether I work at the inn? Or own it?" Her answer was suddenly uncomfortably important.

Amanda had worked long enough in the advertising jungle to recognize a verbal trap when she spotted one. "That's not the point," she insisted, sidestepping the issue for the moment.

He lifted an eyebrow. "May I ask what the point is, then? As you see it?"

"You were pretending to be something you weren't."

"We all pretend to be something—or someone—we aren't from time to time."

Like that long-ago summer when she'd pretended to be the Lolita of Satan's Cove. She hadn't fooled Dane then. And she didn't now. Although he had no doubt that she was more than capable of doing her job, he also knew that she wasn't the brisk, efficient advertising automaton she tried so hard to appear.

"I don't." She jutted her chin forward in a way that inexplicably made Dane want to kiss her. Then again, he'd been wanting to kiss her all day long.

Thinking how ridiculous their entire situation was turning out to be, Dane threw back his head and laughed.

"I hadn't realized I'd said anything humorous," she said stiffly.

Her vulnerability, which she was trying so hard to conceal, made him want to take her into his arms. "I'm sorry." He wiped the grin from his face. "I guess you've spent so many years perfecting your career-woman act that you've forgotten that it really isn't you."

His accusation hit like the sucker punch she'd slammed into his stomach. The familiar headache came crashing back. "It isn't an act."

"Of course, it is." As he watched the sheen of hurt, followed by a shadow of pain, move across her eyes, Dane damned himself for putting them there. Laying aside his romantic plans, he began massaging her throbbing temples, as he had last night.

"I don't want you to touch me," she complained.

"Sure you do. The problem is you don't want to *want* me to touch you." His fingertips were making circles against her skin. Igniting licks of fire, burning away the pain. "Would it make you feel any better if I promised not to seduce you tonight?"

"As if you could," she muttered, trying to ignore the delicious heat that his caresses were creating.

Dane didn't answer. They both knew there was no need.

He abandoned his sensual attack on her headache, sliding his hands down her neck, over her shoulders, and down her arms. Amanda did not resist as he linked their fingers together.

"For the record, I think you're intelligent, creative,

and ambitious. You believe you think you know what you want—"

"I do know," she insisted.

"And you're not going to stop until you get it," he said, ignoring her firmly stated correction. "Whatever the cost."

"I have every intention of becoming Northwest regional creative director of Janzen, Lawton and Young." Determination burned in her eyes and had her unconsciously lifting her chin. "Once I get rid of Greg Parsons, just watch me go."

He smiled at that, because tonight, despite the change in plans, was not a night for arguing. "Believe me, I have no intention of taking my eyes off you."

Alerted by the huskiness in his tone, Amanda blew out a breath. "Am I going to have trouble with you?"

His answer was a slow masculine grin. "I certainly hope so." He moved closer. "Lots and lots of it."

She pulled a hand free and pressed it against his shoulder. "Damn it, Dane—"

He touched a finger against her mouth, cutting off her weak protest. "If you can forget what we had together, Amanda, you're a helluva lot stronger person than I am."

With effort, she resisted the urge to draw that long finger into her mouth. "It's over. And has been for years."

"That's what you think." He lifted the hand he was still holding and pressed his lips against her knuckles. Their eyes met over their linked hands—his, hot and determined; hers, soft and wary. "It's just beginning, Amanda. And we both know it."

Those words, so quietly spoken, could have been a promise or a threat. Needing time to think, not to mention space in which to breathe, Amanda tugged her hand free and backed away. Both physically and emotionally.

"I only came down here to discuss the challenge."

Frustration rose; Dane controlled it. For now. "You're the boss," he said agreeably.

"Not yet," Amanda corrected. "But I will be." Because her unpleasant conversation with Greg was still in her mind, her shoulders slumped. "If I'm not fired first."

He wondered if she had any idea how vulnerable she could appear and decided that bringing it up now, after what even he would have to admit had not been the most successful of days, would serve no purpose.

Dane wanted to put his arm around her, to soothe more than seduce, but knew that if he allowed himself to touch her again, all his good intentions would fly right out the window. That being the case, he slipped his hands into the pockets of his jeans to keep them out of trouble.

"I can't see that happening."

"Believe me, it's a distinct possibility." She hadn't thought so, before today. Oh, she'd considered herself so clever with her little plan to get Greg promoted. Caught up in the logistics of getting the horrid man out of Portland, she hadn't given enough thought to the inescapable fact that half the challenge team actively disliked the other half. "After what happened today."

She dragged her hand through her hair. "Speaking of which, I suppose I ought to thank you."

"And here I thought you wanted to knock my block off."

"I did. Still do," she admitted. "But, as angry as I am at you for not being entirely honest with me, I can't overlook the fact that you were probably the only thing standing between me and the unemployment line today."

She sighed and shook her head as she stared out over the gilded sea. "From the way Julian, Marvin, Don, and Greg were behaving, you'd think we'd all come here to play war games."

"Business is probably as close to war as most people get," Dane said. "Other than marriage."

His grim tone suggested he was speaking from experience. A thought suddenly occurred to her. "You're not married, are you?"

Dane swore. Annoyance flickered in his dark eyes, and drew his lips into a hard line. "Do you honestly believe that if I had a wife, I'd be planning to take you to bed?"

"Planning is a long way from doing." As she'd learned, only too well. She'd had such plans for this week!

"That may be true for some people. But I've developed a reputation for being tenacious." He cupped her chin between his fingers, holding her gaze to his. "I'm going to have you, contessa. And you're going to love it."

The last time she'd allowed him to bait her, she'd ended up kissing him as if there were no tomorrow. Afraid that the next time she wouldn't be able to stop with a mere kiss, Amanda jerked her head back, folded her arms across her chest and reminded herself that it was important at least to pretend to remain cool.

"You may be accustomed to women succumbing to your seduction techniques, Dane. But I have no intention of joining the hordes. I'm also a tougher case than you're obviously accustomed to."

"Victories are always more satisfying when they don't come easily. And you haven't answered my question."

Discounting his arrogant male statement about taking her to bed, despite the fact that he was also confusing, beguiling, and distracting her, Amanda sensed that Dane was a caring, compassionate individual. And although he had misled her, she knew, from past experiences, that he was also an honorable man. Most men would have taken what she was literally throwing at him ten years ago without a backward glance when the summer was over. But Dane was not most men.

"I suppose I can't imagine you committing adultery."

"Well, I suppose that's a start. Perhaps I ought to have someone write a reference letter. How about my mother? She'd love an opportunity to sing my praises."

"That's not the way I remember it."

"Ten years ago she was a single mother concerned her son was about to repeat her own romantic mistake." Because he could not continue to stand this close to Amanda without touching, he reached out and twined a strand of her hair around his finger.

"These days, she's a mother who's begun to worry that her son isn't ever going to provide her with the grandchildren she's so eager to spoil."

That was yet another difference between the Stockenbergs and the Cutters. Amanda's mother refused even to discuss the possibility of becoming a grandmother anytime in this century. While her father had warned her on more than one occasion of the dangers of falling prey to the infamous "baby track" that would hinder her success.

"How do you feel about that?" she asked.

"Actually, I think it's a pretty good idea. With the right woman, of course."

She couldn't help thinking of a time when she'd dreamed of having children with this man. She also had no intention of asking Dane what type of woman fit his criteria. Deciding that the conversation was drifting into dangerous territory, she opted to change the subject.

"May I ask a question?"

"Shoot."

"What did you say to Greg and the others today? To stop them from brawling on the beach?"

Dane shrugged. "Not that much. I merely pointed out to Parsons that he had too much riding on this week to risk getting into a fistfight with his employees."

That was why Greg had marched away, steam practically coming from his ears, Amanda decided. "But what about Julian and Marvin? They were at each other's throats after that disastrous first heat, but by the end of the day they were behaving as if they were candidates for the Kayaking Olympic Team."

Dane knew he was treading in dangerous waters again. He didn't want to lie to Amanda. But if he told her the truth about his conversation with the art director and head copywriter, she'd undoubtedly want to slug him again.

She'd also be furious that he'd interfered, little mind the fact that she'd needed some help at the time. Especially since her egocentric supervisor was obviously not only a bully, but an incompetent idiot to boot.

"I said pretty much the same thing to them I did to Parsons." He forced himself to meet her lovely, serious eyes. "I suggested this week was going to be long and tough enough to get through without complicating things with useless feuds.

"I also mentioned that since management, in its own ignorance, tended to take things like this ridiculous corporate challenge week seriously, it made sense to save their differences for the creative arena where it mattered, bury their individual hatchets and cooperate by trying to win the thing together."

"I'm impressed."

"It's not that big a deal."

It was the truth, so far as it went. What he'd failed to mention was that he'd also told the two combatants that if they didn't shape up and do their best to make this week a success, he'd throw them both off the cliff. Then drown them.

Although they'd resorted to bluster, from the uneasiness in their eyes, he realized that they'd half believed he might actually do it. And, although he wasn't violent, such behavior was undeniably tempting. If it helped Amanda.

Watching her today, seeing how seriously she took her work, understanding how important it was to her that she pull off this week, Dane knew that in order to get what *he* wanted, he would have to see that Amanda got what *she* wanted. And what she wanted, it seemed, was Greg Parsons's job. That being the case, he intended to move heaven and earth—and a portion of the Oregon coast, if necessary—to ensure her success.

"Believe me, Dane, it was a very big deal." Thinking back on what he'd done for her—for no other reason than that he'd wanted to help—Amanda felt guilty. "I'm sorry I hit you."

Her hand was on his arm. Dane covered it with his. "You were right. I haven't exactly been the most forthright guy in the world the past couple of days. But I never meant to hurt you. Or to make you feel I was having fun at your expense."

His hand was darker than hers. Larger. And warmer. When she began imagining it moving over her body, touching her in places that were aching for just such a sensual touch, Amanda knew that no matter how hard she tried to deny it, Dane was right. Before this week was over, they would become lovers.

That idea was thrilling and terrifying at the same time.

"There's something I don't understand," she murmured.

"What's that?"

"What made you decide to buy the inn? After swearing that you couldn't wait to get away from Satan's Cove, I'm surprised to find you still here."

"Not still."

"Pardon me?"

"I said, I'm not still here. I'm back."

"Oh." That made a bit more sense, she supposed. "What did you do in between?"

Dane took encouragement from the fact that she cared about how he'd spent his life during those intervening years. "A little of this. A little of that."

"That's not very enlightening."

"I suppose not." He gave her a long look. "I guess I just can't figure out why you'd care. Since you've already said you haven't thought about me since that summer."

"I may have thought of you," she admitted, realizing that there was no way she'd be able to keep up the subterfuge. "From time to time."

Dane didn't answer. He just stood there, looking down at her, a frustratingly inscrutable look on his face, as the tension grew thicker and thicker between them.

"All right!" She threw up her hands in surrender. "I lied. I thought about you a lot, Dane. More than I should have. More than I wanted.

"Every man I've ever gone out with, I've ended up

comparing to you. Once I dated a man for six months because, believe it or not, if I closed my eyes, his voice reminded me of yours.

"I go to work, and if I'm not careful, my mind will drift and I'll think of you and wonder where you are, and what you're doing. And at night—" On a roll now, she began to pace. "At night I'll lie in bed, and you'll be lying there beside me, kissing me, touching me, loving me.

"And then I'll wake up, and realize it was only a dream. But it doesn't seem like a dream, damn it. It seems real! And then, last night, I was tired and cranky, and worried, and all of a sudden I heard this voice I've dreamed about time and time again, and I turned around and there you were, and this time you weren't a dream.

"You were real. Wonderfully, marvelously real! And it was all I could do not to throw myself in your arms and beg you to make love to me—with me—for the rest of my life!

"So, there." She stopped in front of him, close enough that he could see the sheen of tears in her expressive blue eyes. "Now you know. Is that what you wanted to hear me say? Is your almighty male ego satisfied now?"

She was trembling. Once again the need to comfort warred with the desire to seduce. Once again comfort won out. "Yes. It's what I wanted to hear."

He put his hands on her shoulders and drew her to him. And although she remained stiff, she wasn't exactly resisting, either.

He cupped her chin again. "But only because it's a relief to know that I wasn't the only one feeling that way."

Amanda read the truth in his warm, loving gaze and felt even more like weeping. Her emotions were in a turmoil. She couldn't think straight. She could only feel.

She wrapped her arms around his waist and clung. "Really?"

"Really." His smile was that crooked, boyish one that had once possessed the power to make her young heart turn somersaults. It still did.

"And if you think it's dumb dating a guy for six months because he sounds like someone else, how about marrying someone because she has the same laugh as a girl you once loved?"

"You didn't!"

"Guilty." His grin turned sheepish. "I was young and determined to get you out of my system when I met Denise."

Denise. Dane had been married to a woman named Denise. A woman with her laugh. Amanda hated her. "What happened?"

"It's a long story."

"I'm not in any hurry to be anywhere." On the contrary, a very strong part of Amanda wished she could stop time and make this night last forever.

There'd been a moment, during her passionate speech about how many times she'd thought of him over the intervening years, that Dane had thought perhaps tonight would turn out to be the night he finally made love to Amanda. Now that he'd made the mistake of bringing up his ex-wife, he knew he'd have to remain patient a bit longer.

Reminding himself that Amanda was worth waiting for, Dane took her hand and led her over to a rowboat tied to the pier.

"We may as well get reasonably comfortable," he said. "Because this is going to take a while."

Chapter 7

Dane's fingers curved around her waist as he lifted her easily into the boat. Amanda sat down on the bench seat, leaned back against the bow and waited.

Dane sat down beside her. When he began talking, his words were slow and measured.

"I liked Denise from the moment I met her. Along with the all-important fact that she had your laugh, she was also beautiful and smart and sexy. And the only woman I'd ever met who was every bit as driven to succeed as I was."

"She sounds like an absolute paragon."

Dane would have had to be deaf not to hear the female jealousy in Amanda's dry tone. He chuckled as he put his arm around her shoulder, encouraged when she did not pull away.

"Unfortunately, except for our work, we didn't have a single solitary thing in common. Six months later, when neither of us had much to laugh about, we decided to call it quits before our disastrous marriage ruined a very good working relationship."

"I can't imagine working with an ex-husband."

Dane shrugged. "It hadn't been a typical marriage from the beginning. I'd married her to get over you and she married me on the rebound after her divorce from a miserable first marriage. Right before the split, I was promoted into a position that involved a lot of traveling. After a time, it was as if our marriage had never happened and we found we could be friends again. Two years ago, I introduced her to an old college friend of mine who's a stockbroker in San Francisco. They clicked right off the bat, got married, and I got a note from her last week announcing her pregnancy. So things worked out for the best."

"You said you were young?"

Dane sighed. Although he'd overcome any regrets he'd once harbored over his marriage, revealing such irresponsible behavior to the one woman he wanted to impress was proving more than a little embarrassing.

"I graduated from University of Oregon the summer after I met you," he said. "Mom was there, of course, along with Denise—who was my supervisor during my apprentice program at Whitfield. We went out to dinner, then after I took Mom back to her hotel, Denise invited me out for a drink to celebrate.

"One toast led to another, and another, and a few more, then we bought a bottle of champagne—a magnum—and the next thing I remember we were waking up in a motel room in Reno, Nevada.

"Denise couldn't remember much of anything, either, but the signed certificate from a justice of the peace on the dresser spoke for itself, so after several cups of strong coffee and a great many aspirin, we figured, since we'd always gotten along so well at the office, we might as well try to make a go of it."

Amanda didn't know which part of the story—so unlike the Dane she'd known who'd driven her crazy with his self-control—she found most amazing. "You actually married your boss?"

This time his grin was more than a little sheepish. "Women aren't the only ones who can sleep their way to the top of the company."

Since she knew he was joking, Amanda overlooked his blatantly chauvinistic remark. "She must have been older."

"About twelve years. But that didn't have anything to do with the breakup. We were just mismatched from the get-go."

In all his travels around the world, Dane had met a great many chic women, but none of them had oozed sophistication like his former wife. Denise preferred Placido Domingo to Garth Brooks, champagne cocktails at the symphony to hot dogs at the ballpark, and given the choice between spending an afternoon at a stuffy art museum with her uptown friends or fly-fishing on a crystal-clear Oregon river, she'd choose Jackson Pollack over rainbow trout any day.

Dane had often thought, over these past months since his return to Satan's Cove, that if he and Denise hadn't broken up that first year, they definitely would have divorced over his need to leave the city for this wildly beautiful, remote stretch of Oregon coast. Since there could have been children involved by this point, he was grateful they'd cut their losses early.

So stunned was Amanda by the story of Dane's marriage, it took a while for something else he'd said to sink in.

"You said she was your supervisor at Whitfield. Whitfield as in the Whitfield Palace hotel chain? 'When Deluxe Will No Longer Do'?" she asked, quoting the world-famous slogan. "*That's* where you were working?"

"I was in the intern program at Whitfield while I was in college and they hired me full-time after graduation."

This was more like it. This fit the burning need Dane had professed to escape Satan's Cove. This was the man, when she'd daydreamed about Dane, she'd imagined him to be. "What did you do there?"

"A bit of everything. Whitfield makes its managerial prospects start at the bottom and work in all the different departments. I was assigned to the custodial department my sophomore year at U of O, worked my way up to housekeeping my junior year, reservations my senior year, then spent the summer after graduation in the kitchen."

"That's the summer you were married." Even knowing that it hadn't worked out, Amanda realized that she hated the idea of any other woman sharing Dane's life. Let alone his bed.

It should have been her, Amanda thought with a surprisingly furious burst of passion. It could have been her, if her parents hadn't manipulated things to keep them apart. Or if her feelings hadn't been so wounded and his pride so stiff.

Unaware of her thoughts, Dane nodded. "That's it. By Christmas I was on my way to being single again."

Denise's petition for divorce—they'd agreed she'd be the one to file—had arrived at his office on December

23. He'd spent the next two days in Satan's Cove with his mother.

The morning after Christmas, he was on a plane to Paris. And after that Milan. Then Zurich. And on and on until he was spending so much of his life at 30,000 feet, he'd often joked—not quite humorously—that he should just give the postal service his airline schedule.

"And then you began traveling." Amanda recalled the earlier condensed version. "Still for Whitfield?"

"When Denise and I split, I'd just gotten promoted to assistant director of guest relations, working out of the New Orleans headquarters. Essentially, it was my job to visit each hotel at least twice a year and pull a surprise inspection."

"You must have been popular," Amanda said dryly.

"I like to think I bent over backward to be fair. But I will admit to being tough. After all, guests pay big bucks to stay at a Whitfield Palace. It's important they feel they're getting their money's worth."

"I stayed at the Park Avenue Whitfield last month," Amanda revealed, "on a trip back to Manhattan. The New York agency handles their advertising account." With luck and Dane's help, Greg Parsons would soon be transferring to those renowned Madison Avenue offices. "It really was like being in a palace."

Although she'd grown up with wealth, Amanda hadn't been able to keep from staring at the sea of marble underfoot or the gleaming crystal chandeliers overhead. She'd had the impression that at any minute, a princess would suddenly appear from behind one of the gilded pillars.

"That's the point," Dane said.

"True." Whoever had named the worldwide hotel chain had definitely hit the nail right on the head.

Amanda also remembered something else about her stay at the flagship hotel. Her room, furnished with genuine antiques and boasting a view of the leafy environs of Central Park, had been comfortably spacious. And the marble bathrooms had an amazing selection of French milled perfumed soaps, shampoos and lotions. In addition, the staff had been more than accommodating. Still, even with all that, Amanda had felt vaguely uncomfortable during her three-day stay.

"You know," she said thoughtfully, "as luxurious as the Park Avenue Whitfield is, I like what you've done with Smugglers' Inn better. It's more comfortable. Cozier."

His slow, devastating grin reached his eyes. "That's the point." Dane was undeniably pleased that she understood instinctively the mood he'd wanted to create. "I'm also glad you approve."

"I really do." He was looking at her as if he wanted to kiss her again. Her heart leaped into her throat. Then slowly settled again. "It's lovely, Dane. You should be very proud."

The sea breeze fanned her hair, causing it to waft across her cheek. Dane reached out to brush it away and ended up grabbing a handful. "Speaking of lovely…"

He pulled her closer with a gentle tug on her hair.

"It's too soon," she protested softly.

Personally, Dane thought it was about ten years too late. "Just a kiss." His mouth was a whisper from hers. "One simple kiss, Amanda. What could it hurt?"

She could feel herself succumbing to the temptation in his dark eyes, to the promise of his silky breath against her lips, to the magic in the fingers that had slipped beneath her hair to gently massage the nape of her neck.

A simple kiss. What could it hurt?

"Just a kiss," she whispered in a soft, unsteady breath. Her lips parted of their own volition, her eyes fluttered shut in anticipation of the feel of his mouth on hers. "You have to promise."

He slid the fingers of his free hand down the side of her face. "I promise." He bent his head and very slowly, very carefully, closed the distance.

The stirring started, slow and deep. And sweet. So achingly, wonderfully sweet.

There was moonlight, slanting over the sea, turning it to silver. And a breeze, feathering her hair, whispering over her skin, carrying with it the salt-tinged scent of the sea. Somewhere in the distance a foghorn sounded; the incoming tide flowed over the rocks and lapped against the sides of the boat that was rocking ever so gently on the soft swells.

His lips remained night-cool and firm while hers heated, then softened. Amanda's hand floated upward, to rest against the side of his face as Dane drew her deeper and deeper into a delicious languor that clouded her mind even as it warmed her body to a radiant glow.

Although sorely tempted, Dane proved himself a man of his word, touching only her hair and the back of her neck. With scintillating slowness, and using only his mouth, he drew out every ounce of pleasure.

A soft moan slipped from between Amanda's heated lips. No man—no man except Dane—had ever been able to make her burn with only a kiss. He whispered words against her mouth and made her tremble. He murmured promises and made her ache.

Dane had spent most of the day hoping that he'd over-reacted to last night's encounter. A man accustomed to thinking with his head, rather than his heart—or that other vital part of his anatomy that was now throbbing painfully—he'd attempted to make sense out of a situation he was discovering defied logic.

Despite all the intervening years, despite all the women he'd bedded since that bittersweet summer, Dane found himself as inexplicably drawn to Amanda as ever.

The first time they'd been together like this, his desire had been that of a boy. Last night, and even more so now, as he shaped her lips to his, forcing himself to sample their sweet taste slowly, tenderly, Dane knew that this desire was born from the age-old need of a man for his mate.

Because he could feel himself rapidly approaching that dangerous, razor-thin line between giving and taking, Dane lifted his head. Then waited for Amanda to open her eyes.

Those wide eyes he'd never been able to put out of his mind were clouded with unmistakable desire as she stared up at him in the moonlight.

He could have her, Dane knew. Right here, he could draw her into his arms and crush her mouth to his until she was senseless, until she couldn't speak, couldn't think, couldn't breathe. And couldn't run away.

Although he'd never considered himself a masochist, Dane fantasized about the way her body would feel next to his, beneath his, on top of his. He wanted her in every way possible.

The problem was, Dane realized with a stunned sense of awareness, he also wanted her forever.

She murmured a faint, inarticulate protest as he

brushed one last quick kiss against her parted lips, then stood.

"Just a kiss," he reminded her, holding out his hand to help her to her feet.

Amanda needed all the assistance she could get. Her mind was still spinning from that devastating, heart-swelling kiss and she wasn't certain if her legs would hold her. She wanted Dane. Desperately. Worse yet, she needed him. Absolutely. For not the first time in her life, Amanda found herself damning his iron control.

"This is getting impossible," Amanda said.

Watching the myriad emotions storm in her eyes—desire, confusion, frustration—Dane vowed that there would be a time when he would take more. But for to-night, that kiss would have to be enough.

"What's that?" he asked mildly.

"You. Me. And what's happening between us. I had my life planned. I knew what I wanted. But ever since I arrived back in Satan's Cove, I can't understand what I'm feeling."

Sympathy stirred as the hair she'd ruffled with un-steady fingers fell back into place. "I think the prob-lem is that you understand exactly what you're feeling."

"All right," she said on a frustrated sigh. "You're right. I do know. But you have to understand that I'm not that silly teenager who threw herself at you ten years ago, Dane. I've worked hard to get where I am. My en-tire life, from the day I chose a major in college, has re-volved around advertising."

Personally, Dane thought that was about the saddest thing he'd ever heard, but not wanting to get into an ar-gument over the art and artifice of the advertising mar-ketplace, he kept silent.

"I've given up so many things, made so many sacrifices, not to mention plans—"

"They say life is what happens when you're making plans," he interjected quietly.

Amanda stared up at him and shook her head. "Yes. Well."

She, who'd always been so smug about her ease with words, could not think of a single thing to say. Still unnerved by the kiss they'd shared, and uneasy at the way he was looking down at her, so calm, so comfortable with who he was and where he was, Amanda dragged her gaze back out to sea. A boat drifted by on the horizon, the running lights looking like fallen stars on the gleaming black water.

They stood there, side by side, looking at the ocean, all too aware of the closeness of the other.

"Damn it," she said with a sudden burst of frustration. "You, of all people, should understand. You obviously didn't succeed at Whitfield because you married your supervisor. You had to have worked hard."

"Sixteen to eighteen hours a day," he agreed. "Which is one of the reasons I quit."

"Yet I'll bet there are still days when you put in that many hours."

"Sure." Dane thought about the hours he'd spent fixing up the tower room. Just for her. He'd told himself at the time that the work had been done out of ego, because he wanted her to see what a success he'd made of the place. But now Dane suspected that his motives had been far more personal.

"But I said long hours were *one* of the reasons I quit Whitfield," he reminded her. "There were others."

"Such as?" Amanda was genuinely interested in

whatever roads Dane had taken that had led him all over the world before returning to Satan's Cove.

"I wasn't overly fond of corporate structure." That was the truth. "And corporate structure wasn't overly fond of me."

That was a major understatement. Fortunately, he'd been successful enough that the guys in the pin-striped suits in the executive towers had overlooked his independent streak. Most of the time.

Granted, he'd thoroughly enjoyed the work in the beginning. Especially the travel. For a young man who'd grown up in an isolated coastal town of less than two hundred people, his early years at the hotel chain had been an exhilarating, eye-opening experience.

But newness faded over time and the day he'd realized he was close to suffocating in the luxurious eighteenth-floor corner window suite of the glass tower that dominated New Orleans's central business district, he'd turned in his resignation.

Eve Whitfield Deveraux—who'd inherited control of the hotel chain from her father—had asked him to reconsider. Having married a maverick herself, the hotel CEO appreciated having someone she could always count on to tell her the truth. There were already too many sycophants around her, she'd told him on more than one occasion. What she needed was a few more rebels like Dane Cutter.

As much as he'd genuinely liked her, Dane couldn't stay. So he'd cashed in his stock options and his IRA, closed his money-market and checking accounts, and returned home.

Dane realized that while his mind had been drifting, Amanda had been quietly waiting for him to continue.

"Besides," he said, "working long hours these days is a helluva lot different. Because Smugglers' Inn is mine. It's not some trendy real-estate investment I plan to sell to some foreign development company in a few years for a quick profit.

"I've put more than money into the place, though to be truthful, it's just about cleaned out my bank account, which is the only reason I decided to take that money from your agency.

"But I don't really mind the broken heaters and clogged pipes and leaky roofs, because I'm building something here, Amanda. I'm building a home. For myself and my family.

"Because as much of a rush as it admittedly was at first, flying all over the world, staying in presidential suites, having everyone snap to attention the moment my car pulled up in front of a Whitfield Palace hotel, the novelty eventually wore off.

"That was when I realized that what I truly wanted, more than money, or power, or prestige, was someone to come home to at the end of the day.

"Someone to walk along the beach with in the twilight of our years. Someone who'll love me as much as I'll love her—and our children, if we're lucky enough to have them."

He'd definitely been on a roll. It was, Dane considered as he felt himself finally running down, probably the longest speech he'd ever given. And, he thought, perhaps his most important.

Amanda didn't speak for a long time. Dane's fervent declaration, while sounding well-thought-out, had definitely taken her by surprise. Since arriving at Smugglers' Inn, she'd been trying to make the various aspects of Dane mesh in her mind.

The young man she'd first fallen in love with had been the most driven individual she'd ever met. And that included her father, who was certainly no slouch when it came to workaholic, success-at-all-cost strategies.

Remembering all Dane's lofty dreams and plans and ambitions, when she'd mistakenly believed he'd never left Satan's Cove, she hadn't been able to understand how he could have failed so miserably in achieving his goals.

Then she'd discovered he actually owned the landmark inn. And, as lovely as it admittedly was, she couldn't help wondering how many people could so easily turn their back on power and prestige.

"That picture you're painting sounds lovely."

"You almost sound as if you mean that."

He wondered if she realized it was almost the exact same picture she'd painted for him so many years ago. It was, Dane considered, ironic that after all these years apart they were back here in Satan's Cove, still attracted to one another, but still at cross purposes. It was almost as if they'd entered a parallel universe, where everything—including their individual dreams and aspirations—was reversed.

"Of course I mean it. I also admire you for knowing yourself well enough to know what's right for you."

"I think I hear a *but* in there."

"No." She shook her head. "Perhaps a little envy."

"I don't know why. Seems to me you're in the catbird seat, contessa. All you have to do is get Parsons out of your way and you're definitely back on the fast track."

"So why does it feel as if the lights at the end of the tunnel belong to an oncoming train?" She was not accustomed to revealing weakness. Not to anyone. But tonight, alone at the edge of the world with Dane, it somehow seemed right.

"Because you're tired." Dane couldn't resist touching her. "Because change is always disruptive," he murmured as he began kneading her tense, rocklike shoulders. "And with the takeovers and mergers, you've been going through a lot of changes lately.

"Not to mention the fact that Parsons is the kind of jerk who'd stress out Deepak Chopra. And along with trying to juggle this stupid corporate challenge week, you're being forced to confront feelings you thought you'd put behind you long ago."

His talented fingers massaged deeply, smoothing out the knots. "If I were a better man, I'd leave you alone and take a bit of the pressure off. But I don't think I'm going to be able to do that, Amanda."

She knew that. Just as she knew that deep down inside, she didn't really want Dane to give up on her.

"I just need a little more time." She was looking up at him, her eyes eloquently pleading her case. When she allowed her gaze to drift down to his mouth—which she could still taste—Amanda was hit with an arousal more primal and powerful than anything she'd ever known.

She imagined those firmly cut lips everywhere on her body, taking her to some dark and dangerous place she'd only ever dreamed about. "To think things through."

It wasn't the answer he wanted. Unfortunately, it *was* the answer he'd been expecting.

Dane's response was to cup the back of her head in his hand and hold her to a long, deep kiss that revealed both his hunger and his frustration. And, although she was too caught up in the fire of the moment to recognize it, his love.

"Think fast," he said after the heated kiss finally ended. Still too aroused to speak, Amanda could only nod.

Chapter 8

Amanda was more than a little relieved when the next day began a great deal more smoothly than the previous day's kayak races. When team members woke to a cool, drizzling rain streaming down the windows that necessitated putting off the bike race until afternoon, she was prepared to switch gears.

Taking the indoor equipment from her store of supplies, she divided the teams into subgroups and put everyone to work building a helicopter from pieces of scrap paper, cardboard, rubber bands and Popsicle sticks. Although speed was of the essence, it was also important that the constructed vehicle manage some form of brief flight.

"I still don't get the point of this," Laura complained as yet another attempt fatally spiraled nosefirst into the rug.

"You're blending science and art," Amanda explained

patiently yet again. "Advertising is a subtle, ever-changing art that defies formularization."

"That's what it used to be," Luke Cahill muttered as he cut a tail rotor from a piece of scarlet construction paper. "Until the invasion of the MBA's." A rumpled, casual man in his mid-thirties, he possessed the unique ability to pen a catchy tune and link it with an appealing advertising idea.

Amanda had always considered Luke to be the most easygoing person working at the agency. She realized the recent stress had gotten to him, as well, when he glared over at Don Patterson, the financially oriented marketing manager, who stopped remeasuring the length of the cardboard helicopter body to glare back.

"However much you artsy types would like to spend the day playing in your creative sandboxes, advertising is a business," Don countered. "I, for one, am glad to see this agency finally being run as a profit-making enterprise."

"You won't *have* any profits if the product suffers," Luke snapped back. "Advertising is more than numbers. It's our native form of American anthology."

"He's right," Marvin Kenyon said. "Advertising—and life—would be a helluva lot easier if it could be treated like science—A plus B equals C—but it can't.

"Life is about change, damn it. And advertising reflects that. The best advertising, the kind we *used* to do for C.C.C., can even act as an agent for change."

Greg, who was sitting off to the side, watching the group, applauded, somehow managing to make the sound of two hands coming together seem mocking.

"Nice little speech, Kenyon." He poured himself a drink—his second of the morning—and took a sip. "But if you're not part of the solution you're part of the problem. If you can't get with the program, perhaps you don't belong in advertising."

"Not belong?" This from Julian. "You *do* realize that you're talking to a man who has twenty-nine years' experience creating witty, appealing, and totally original advertising that makes the sale through its ability to charm prospective buyers?"

As she heard the art director stand up for the head copywriter, Amanda felt a surge of excitement. As foolish as these games had seemed at first, something was happening.

Until the pressures brought about by first the mergers, then the takeover, C.C.C. had been viewed throughout the advertising world as a flourishing shop.

Unfortunately, because of the political machinations that were part and parcel of becoming a bigger agency, Marvin and Julian had started sniping at each other, causing morale to tailspin as sharply and destructively as Laura's failed helicopter model.

But now, thanks to Greg's threat, Julian had just felt the need to stand up for his former creative partner. And although she wondered if they'd ever regain the sense of "family" that had been the hallmark of Connally Creative Concepts, Amanda hoped such behavior was a sign that the creative members of the agency would resume encouraging each other, spurring their colleagues to even greater achievements, as they'd done in the past.

"We can't ignore the fact that we're in a service business," she said. "Unfortunately, no matter how creative our advertising is, if we don't possess the organization to effectively service our clients, we'll fail."

"That's what I've been trying to say," Don insisted.

"On the other hand," Amanda said, seeking a middle ground, "we could have the best media buying and billing system in the world but if creativity suffers because everyone's getting mired down in details, we won't have any clients to bill. And no profits. Which, of course, eventually would mean no salaries."

She reached out and picked up the helicopter the blue team had just finished and held it above her head. When she had their undivided attention, she let it go. The copter took off on a sure, albeit short flight, ending atop a bookcase.

"That was teamwork, ladies and gentlemen," she said with a quick, pleased grin. "Science and creativity, meshing into one efficient, artistic entity."

Dane had slipped into the back of the room during the beginning of the argument. He'd convinced himself that Amanda wasn't really happy in her work; that deep down inside, where it really counted, she was still the young girl who wanted to have babies and make a comfortable home for her family.

Now, having observed the way she'd deftly turned the discussion around, he was forced to admit that perhaps Amanda really did belong exactly where she was.

It was not a very satisfying thought.

Her spirits buoyed by the successful helicopter project, Amanda found herself thoroughly enjoying the excellent lunch of grilled sockeye salmon on fettucini, black bean salad, and fresh-baked sourdough bread, the kind that always reminded her of San Francisco's famed Fisherman's Wharf. Dessert was a blackberry cobbler topped with ice cream. The berries, Mary told the appreciative guests, had been picked from the bushes growing behind the inn; the ice cream, which was almost unbearably rich with the unmistakable taste of real vanilla beans, was homemade.

"It's a good thing I'm only spending a week here," Amanda said when she stopped by the kitchen to thank Dane's mother again for helping make the week a success.

"Oh?" With lunch successfully behind her, Mary had moved on to preparing dinner and was slicing mushrooms with a blindingly fast, deft stroke that Amanda envied, even as she knew she'd undoubtedly cut her fingers off if she ever dared attempt to duplicate it. "And why is that, dear?"

"Because I'd probably gain a hundred pounds in the first month." She still couldn't believe she'd eaten that cobbler.

"Oh, you'd work it all off," Mary assured her easily. "There's enough to do around here that burning calories definitely isn't a problem."

"I suppose you're right." Amanda had awakened this morning to the sound of hammering. Although the sun was just barely up, when she'd looked out her window she'd seen Dane repairing the split-rail fence that framed the front lawn and gardens. "Dane certainly seems to be enjoying it, though."

"He's happy as a clam."

"It's nice he's found his niche."

"It's always nice to know what you want out of life," Mary agreed easily. "Even nicer if you can figure out a way to get it."

"You must have been proud of him, though. When he was working for the Whitfield Palace hotel chain."

Amanda had the feeling that if she'd made the life-style reversal Dane had chosen, her father would have accused her of dropping out. Amanda's father remained vigilant for any sign that his daughter might be inclined to waver from the straight-and-narrow path he'd chosen for her—the one that led directly to an executive suite in some Fortune 500 company.

Never having been granted a son, Gordon Stockenberg had put all his paternal dreams and ambitions onto Amanda's shoulders. And except for that one summer, when she'd fallen in love with a boy her father had found totally unsuitable, she'd never let him down.

"I'd be proud of Dane whatever he chose to do." Mary piled the mushrooms onto a platter and moved on to dicing shallots. "But I have to admit that I'm pleased he's come home. Not only do I enjoy working with my son, it was obvious that once he became a vice president at Whitfield, he began feeling horribly constrained, and—"

"Vice president?"

"Why, yes." Mary looked up, seeming surprised that Amanda hadn't known.

"Dane was actually a vice president at Whitfield Palace hotels?" After last night's conversation, she'd realized he'd been important. But a vice president?

"He was in charge of international operations," Mary divulged. "The youngest vice president in the history of the hotel chain. He was only in the job for a year, and Mrs. Deveraux—she's the CEO of Whitfield—wanted him to stay on, especially now that she and her husband have begun a family and she's cut back on her own travel, but Dane has always known his own mind."

Once again Amanda thought of her boastful words about her window office and her lovely, expensive Italian-leather chair. Unfortunately, as much as she wanted to be irritated at Dane for having let her make a fool of herself, she reluctantly admitted that it hadn't really been his doing. She'd been so eager to prove how important she was....

A vice president. Of International Operations, no less. She groaned.

"Are you all right, dear?"

Amanda blinked. "Fine," she said, not quite truthfully. She took out her roll of antacids. Then, on second thought, she shook two aspirin from the bottle she kept in her purse.

Mary was looking at Amanda with concern as she handed Amanda a glass of water for the aspirin. "You look pale."

"I'm just a little tired." And confused. Not only did she not really know Dane, Amanda was beginning to wonder if she even knew herself.

"You're working very hard." The stainless-steel blade resumed flashing in the stuttering coastal sunlight coming in through the kitchen windows. "Dane told me how important this week is to you."

"It is." Amanda reminded herself exactly how important. Her entire career—her life—depended on the challenge week's being a success.

"He also told me you're very good at motivating people."

"Dane said that?" Praise from Dane Cutter shouldn't mean so much to her. It shouldn't. But, it did.

"I believe his exact words were, barring plague or pestilence, you'll have your promotion by the end of the week."

"I hope he's right."

Mary's smile was warm and generous. "Oh, Dane is always right about these things, Amanda. He's got a sixth sense for business and if he says you're going to win your creative director's slot, you can count on it happening."

It was what she wanted, damn it. What she'd worked for. So why, Amanda wondered as she left the kitchen to meet the members of the team, who were gathering in the parking lot for their afternoon bicycle race, did the idea leave her feeling strangely depressed?

The mountain bikes, like the team-challenge T-shirts and accompanying slickers, were red and blue.

"At least they look sturdy," Julian decided, studying the knobby fat tires.

"And heavy," Kelli said skeptically. "What's wrong with a nice, lightweight ten-speed?"

"Kelli has a point, Amanda," Peter interjected with what Amanda supposed was another attempt to make points with the sexy public-relations manager. "Why can't we just use racing bikes?"

"In the first place, you're not going to be sticking to the asphalt." Amanda handed everyone a laminated map of the course. "You'll need a sturdy bike for all the detours over gravel and dirt roads and creekbeds."

When that description earned a collective groan, Amanda took some encouragement from the fact that everyone seemed to share the same reservations. That, in its own way, was progress.

"Think of it as touring new ground," she suggested optimistically.

"That's definitely pushing a metaphor," Marvin complained over the laughter of the others.

Amanda's grin was quick and confident. "That's why I leave the copywriting to you."

She went on to explain the rules, which involved the riders leaving the parking lot at timed intervals, following the trail marked on the maps, then returning to the inn, hopefully in time for dinner. She would ride along as an observer and, if necessary, a referee. Once everyone was back, the collective times would determine which team had won.

"Any questions?" she asked when she was finished.

"I have one." Laura was adjusting the chin strap on her helmet with the air of someone who'd done this before. "Since it's obvious you can't be at every checkpoint, how are you going to ensure some people don't skip a segment?"

"Are you accusing people of not being honest?" Don complained.

"You're in advertising marketing, Don," Luke reminded. "I'd say a lack of forthrightness goes with the territory."

When everyone laughed, Amanda experienced another surge of optimism. Only two days ago, such a comment would have started a fight. Things were definitely looking up!

"Not that I don't trust everyone implicitly," Amanda said, "but now that you bring it up, there will be referees at all the checkpoints to stamp the appropriate section of your map." She had arranged with Dane to hire some of his off-duty employees.

"Is Mindy going to be one of those referees?" Peter asked hopefully.

"Mindy Taylor will be working the second segment," Amanda revealed.

"There go our chances," Don grumbled as he pulled on a pair of leather bicycle gloves. "Because with Miss America working the second checkpoint, Peter will never get to number three."

There was more laughter, and some good-natured teasing, along with the expected complaints from Peter, which only earned him hoots from his fellow teammates and the opposing team.

"Well," Amanda said, glancing down at her stopwatch, "if everyone's ready, we'll send off the first team."

"Oh, look!" Kelli exclaimed, pointing toward the inn. "Here comes Dane." Amanda found the public-relations manager's smile far too welcoming. "Hey, coach," Kelli called out, "any last advice?"

Since the course was easily followed and everyone knew how to ride a bike, Amanda had decided it wouldn't be necessary for Dane to come along. He was, however, scheduled to lead the upcoming backpacking trip and rock-climbing expedition.

"Just one." He rocked back on his heels and observed the assembled teams with mild amusement. "Watch out for logging trucks."

Marvin frowned. "I didn't realize they were logging this part of the coast."

"Well, they are. And those drivers aren't accustomed to sharing the back roads. Stay out of their way. Or die."

With that ominous warning ringing in everyone's ears, the teams pedaled out of the parking lot.

She was going to die. As she braked to a wobbly stop outside the inn, Amanda wondered if she'd ever recover the feeling in her bottom again.

"You made good time," Dane greeted her. He was up on a ladder, painting the rain gutter. He was wearing cutoff jeans and a white T-shirt. "Considering all the extra miles Kelli said you put in riding back and forth between teams."

"You'd think adults could conduct a simple bike race without trying to sabotage one another, wouldn't you?" Amanda frowned as she remembered the fishing line members of the blue team had strung across a particularly rocky stretch of path.

"You wanted them working together," he reminded her. "Sounds as if that's exactly what they were doing."

"I wanted them to cooperate," she muttered. "Not re-enact Desert Storm." The red team had, naturally, sought to retaliate. "Thanks for the suggestion to take along the extra tire tubes. I still haven't figured out where they got those carpet tacks."

"I've got a pretty good guess." Dane had found evidence of someone having been in the workshop.

"Well, other than a few bumps and bruises, at least no one got hurt," Amanda said with a long-suffering sigh. "You were also right about those trucks, by the way. They're scary."

"Like bull elk on amphetamines." As he watched her gingerly climb off the bike, Dane wiped his hand over his mouth to hide his smile. "You look a little stiff."

How was it that she had no feeling at all in her rear, yet her legs were aching all the way to the bone? "That's an understatement." She glared at the now muddy mountain bike that had seemed such a nifty idea when the original challenge coach, who'd conveniently managed to avoid taking part in the week's activities, had first suggested it. "I swear that seat was invented by the Marquis de Sade."

"If you're sore, I can give you a massage. To get the kinks out," he said innocently when she shot him a stern look. "I've got pretty good hands. If I do say so myself."

He flexed his fingers as he grinned down at her from his perch on the ladder.

Amanda had firsthand knowledge of exactly how good those hands were. Which was why there was absolutely no way she was going to take Dane up on his offer.

"Thanks, anyway. But I think I'll just take a long soak in a hot bath." Suddenly uncomfortably aware of how dirty and sweaty she must look, she was anxious to escape.

"Suit yourself." He flashed her another of those devastating smiles, then returned to his painting.

She was halfway up the steps when he called out to her.

"Yes?" She half turned and looked up at him. He was so damn sexy, with that tight, sweat-stained T-shirt and those snug jeans that cupped his sex so enticingly. He reminded her of the young Brando, in *A Streetcar Named Desire.* Rough and dangerous and ready as hell.

It crossed Amanda's mind that if Eve Deveraux had ever seen her vice president of international operations looking like this, she probably would have offered to triple his salary, just to keep him around to improve the scenery.

"If you change your mind, just let me know."

"Thank you." Her answering smile was falsely sweet. "But I believe that just might be pushing your hospitality to the limit."

"We aim to please." The devilish grin brightened his dark eyes. "Service With a Smile. That's our motto here at Smugglers' Inn."

She might be confused. But she wasn't foolish enough to even attempt to touch that line. Without another word, she escaped into the inn.

Enjoying the mental image of Amanda up to her neck in frothy white bubbles, Dane was whistling as he returned to work.

Chapter 9

After a long soak and a brief nap, Amanda felt like a new woman. During her time in the claw-footed bathtub, she'd made an important decision. The next time Dane tried to seduce her, she was going to let him.

Having already spent too much time thinking of him, she'd come to the logical conclusion that part of her problem regarding Dane was the fact that they'd never made love.

Tonight, Amanda vowed as she rose from the perfumed water, toweled off and began dusting fragrant talcum powder over every inch of her body, she was going to remedy that nagging problem.

She dressed carefully for dinner, in an outfit she'd providentially thrown into her suitcase at the last minute—a broomstick gauze skirt that flowed in swirls the color of a summer sunrise, and a matching scoop-necked top with crisscross lacing up the front. The bright hues brought out the heightened color in her cheeks.

She paused in front of the mirror, studying her reflection judiciously. Her freshly washed hair curved beneath her chin, framing her face in gleaming dark gold. Anticipation brightened her eyes, while the fullness of the skirt and blouse suggested more curves than she currently possessed.

"You'll do," she decided with a slow smile ripe with feminine intent. Spritzing herself one last time with scent, she left the tower room, heading downstairs to dinner. And to Dane.

He wasn't there! Amanda forced a smile and attempted to make small talk with the other people at her table as the evening droned on and on. On some level she noted that her meal of shrimp Provençal and tomato, mushroom and basil salad was excellent, but the food Mary Cutter had obviously labored over tasted like ashes in Amanda's mouth.

She wasn't the only person inwardly seething. Greg, who was seated at the neighboring table, did not even bother to conceal his irritation at the fact that Kelli was also absent from the dining room. He snapped at his table companions, glared at the room in general and ordered one Scotch after another.

Finally, obviously fed up, Miss Minnie marched up to the table and insisted that he display more consideration.

"This is, after all," she declared with all the haughty bearing of a forceful woman accustomed to controlling those around her, "supposed to be a civilized dining room."

Greg looked up at her through increasingly bleary eyes. "In case it's escaped your notice," he said, the alcohol causing him to slur his words, "the firm of Janzen, Lawton and Young happens to have booked every room in this inn, with the exception of the suite occupied by you and your sister."

His jaw was jutted out; his red-veined eyes were narrowed and unpleasant. "That being the case, if you have a problem with my drinking, I would suggest that you just hustle your skinny rear end upstairs and order room service."

A hush fell over the dining room. Shocked to silence for what Amanda suspected was the first time in her life, Miss Minnie clasped a blue-veined hand to the front of her dove-brown silk dress.

Out of the corner of her eye, Amanda saw Mary emerging from the kitchen at the same time Mindy was entering from the lobby. Feeling somehow to blame—she was responsible for the horrid man having come to Smugglers' Inn, after all—Amanda jumped to her feet and went over to Greg's table.

"You owe Miss Minnie an apology, Greg," she said sternly. She bestowed her most conciliatory smile upon the elderly woman. "It's been a long day. Everyone's tired. And out of sorts."

"Don't apologize for me, Amanda," Greg growled, continuing to eye the elderly woman with overt contempt.

"But—"

"He's right," Miss Minnie agreed in a voice that could have slashed through steel. "There's no point in trying to defend such uncouth behavior. It would be like putting a top hat and tails on an orangutan and attempting to teach him how to waltz." She lifted her white head and marched from the room.

A moment later, Miss Pearl, who'd been observing the altercation from across the room, hurried after her sister, pausing briefly to place a plump hand on Amanda's arm.

"Don't worry, dear," she said. "My sister actually enjoys these little tiffs." Dimples deepened in her pink cheeks. "She insists it keeps her blood flowing." With that encouragement ringing in Amanda's ears, she left the room.

Perhaps Miss Minnie found such altercations beneficial, but this one had sent Amanda's blood pressure soaring. "That was," she said, biting her words off one at a time, "unconscionable behavior."

"Don't take that holier-than-thou tone with me, Amanda," Greg warned. "Because, in case it's escaped that empty blond head of yours, I can fire you. Like that." He attempted to snap his fingers, but managed only a dull rubbing sound that still managed to get his point across. Loud and clear.

"You're representing the agency, Greg. It seems you could try not to be such a bastard. At least in public."

"It's not *me* you need to worry about, sweetheart," he drawled as he twisted his glass on the tablecloth. "We both know that what's got you so uptight tonight is that our host is off providing personal service to the missing member of our challenge team."

No. As furious as she'd been at Dane, Amanda couldn't believe that the reason he hadn't come to dinner was because he preferred being with Kelli Kyle. Her eyes unwillingly whipped over to Laura—who was Kelli's roommate. When Laura blushed and pretended a sudden interest in the tablecloth, Amanda realized that about this, at least, Greg wasn't lying.

"You're wrong," she managed to say with a composure she was a very long way from feeling. "But there's nothing so unusual about that, is there? Since I can't think of a single thing you've been right about since you arrived in Portland.

"You're stupid, Greg. And mean-spirited. Not to mention lazy. And one of these days, Ernst Janzen is going to realize that nepotism isn't worth letting some incompetent bully destroy his empire."

Amazingly, the knot in her stomach loosened. She might have lost her job, but she'd finally gotten out feelings she'd been keeping bottled up inside her for too long.

When the other diners in the room broke out in a thundering ovation, she realized she'd been speaking for everyone. Everyone except, perhaps, the missing Kelli.

"And now, if you'll excuse me," she said, lifting her head, "I've another matter to take care of."

As fate would have it, Amanda passed Kelli coming into the inn as she was coming out.

"Hi, Amanda," Kelli said with her trademark perky smile. "Isn't it a lovely evening?"

Amanda was not inclined to bother with pleasantries. "Where's Dane?"

The smile faded and for a suspended moment, Kelli appeared tempted to lie. Then, with a shrug of her shoulders, she said, "On the beach."

Amanda nodded. "Thank you."

"Anytime."

Intent on getting some answers from Dane, as she marched away, Amanda didn't notice Kelli's intense, thoughtful look.

She found Dane at the cave. The place where those long-ago pirates had allegedly stashed their treasure. The place she'd always thought of as *their secret sanctuary.* He'd lit a fire and was sitting on a piece of driftwood beside it, drinking a beer. The lipstick on the mouth of the empty bottle beside the log told its own story.

"Hello, contessa." His smile was as warm as any he'd ever shared with her. "I've been waiting for you."

As confused as Amanda had been about everything else, the one thing she'd thought she could believe for certain was that Dane was an honorable man. To discover otherwise was proving terribly painful.

"Why don't you tell that to someone stupid enough to believe you." She'd tried for frost and ended up with heat. Instead of ice coating her words, a hot temper made them tremble.

Amanda's bright gauze skirt was almost transparent in the firelight. Dane found it difficult to concentrate on her anger when his attention was drawn to her long, firm legs.

He slowly stood. "I think I'm missing something here."

"I can't imagine what." Amanda sent him a searing look. "Unless it's your scorecard." When he gave her another blank look, she twined her fingers together to keep from hitting him as she'd done the other night. "To keep track of all your women."

"What women? I don't—"

"Don't lie to me!" When he reached out for her, she gave him a shove. "I passed Kelli on the way down here." Her voice rose, shaky but determined. "She told me where to find you."

"I see." He nodded.

She'd hoped he would explain. On her way down the steps to the beach, she'd prayed that he would have some logical reason for being alone on a moonlit beach, or worse yet, in this cozy cave, with a woman like Kelli Kyle.

Her imagination had tossed up scenario after scenario—perhaps the faucet was dripping in Kelli's bathroom, or perhaps her shutters had banged during last night's brief storm. Perhaps...

Perhaps she'd decided that Dane would make a better lover than Greg Parsons.

Ignoring the anger that was surrounding Amanda like a force field, Dane put his hands on her shoulders. "I can explain."

"That's not necessary." She shrugged off his touch and turned away. "Since it's all perfectly clear. 'Service With a Smile.' Isn't that what you said?"

He spun her around. "Don't push it, Amanda."

Threats glittered in his dark gaze, frightening her. Thrilling her. "And don't *you* touch *me.*"

She was still gorgeous. Still stubborn. And so damn wrong. "I'll touch you whenever I want."

"Not after you've been with her. But don't worry, Dane, I understand thoroughly. Kelli was just a fling for you. Like you would have been for me."

Temper, need, desire, surged through him. "You still know what buttons to push, don't you, sweetheart?"

Before she could answer, his head swooped down. Unlike the other times he'd kissed her over the past few days, this time Dane wasn't patient.

His mouth crushed hers with none of his usual tenderness. The hard, savage pressure of his lips and teeth grinding against hers was not a kiss at all, but a branding.

Fear battered, pleasure surged. She tried to shake her

head, to deny both emotions, but his hand cupped the back of her head, holding her to the irresistible assault.

All the passions Amanda had suppressed, all the longings she'd locked away, burst free in a blazing explosion that turned her avid lips as hungry as his, had her tongue tangling with his, and had her grabbing handfuls of his silky hair as she gave herself up to the dark. To the heat. To Dane.

He pulled back, viewed himself in her passion-clouded eyes, then took her mouth again.

This time Amanda dived into the kiss, matching his speed, his power. She'd never known it was possible to feel so much from only a kiss. She'd never known it was possible to need so much from a man.

Having surrendered to the primitive urges coursing through her blood, she clung to Dane as she went under for the third time, dragging him down with her.

Somehow—later she would realize that she had no memory of it happening—they were on their knees on the blanket he'd laid on the sand when he'd first arrived at the cave, and his hand was beneath her skirt while she was fumbling desperately with the zipper at the front of his jeans.

Despite the danger of discovery—or perhaps, she would consider later, because of it—as those clever, wicked fingers slipped beneath the high-cut elastic leg of her panties, seeking out the moist warmth pooling between her legs, Amanda wanted Dane. Desperately.

There were no soft words. No tender touches. His hands were rough and greedy. And wonderful. As they moved over her body, creating enervating heat, Amanda gasped in painful pleasure, reveling in their strength, even as she demanded more.

A fever rose, rushing through her blood with a heat that had nothing to do with flames from the nearby fire. Her need was rich and ripe and deep, causing her to tear at his clothing as he was tearing at hers. She wanted—needed—the feel of flesh against flesh. Her skin was already hot and damp. And aching.

There was a wildness in Dane that thrilled her. A violence that staggered Amanda even as she strained for more. This was what she'd wanted. This mindless passion that she'd known, instinctively, only he could create.

She hadn't wanted gentle. Or tender. What she'd sought, what she'd been waiting for all of her life, was this heat. This madness. This glory.

Dane Cutter knew secrets—dark and dangerous secrets. Tonight, Amanda swore, he would teach them to her.

She was naked beneath him, her body bombarded by sensations her dazed mind could not fully comprehend. When his harshly curved lips closed over her breast, she locked her fists in his jet hair and pressed him even closer.

She said his name, over and over. Demands ripped from her throat. "Take me," she gasped, arching her hips upward as something dark and damning curled painfully inside her. "Now. Before I go mad."

She was wet and hot. Her flesh glowed in the flickering orange light from the flames. She looked utterly arousing.

She was not the only one about to go mad. His long fingers urgently stroked that aching, swollen bud between her quivering thighs with wicked expertise. Within seconds she was racked by a series of violent shudders that left her breathless.

Trembling, she stared up at Dane, momentarily stunned into silence, but before she could recover, his hands had grasped her hips, lifting her against his mouth. He feasted greedily on the still-tingling flesh. She was pulsing all over, inside and out. Amanda clung to Dane, unable to do anything else as he brought her to another hammering climax.

Her body was slick and pliant. His was furnace-hot. Dane wanted Amanda with a desperation like nothing he'd ever known. There was no thought of control now. For either of them.

Hunger had them rolling off the blanket and onto the sand, hands grasping, legs entwined, control abandoned. As the blood fired in his veins and hammered in his head, Dane covered her mouth with his and plunged into her, swallowing her ragged cry.

For a suspended moment as he encountered the unexpected barrier, Dane turned rigid, his burning mind struggling to make sense of the stunning message riveting upward from his pounding loins. But before he could fully decode it, a red haze moved over his eyes and he was moving against her, burying himself deep within her heat.

Sensations crashed into passion, passion into love, with each driving stroke. It was more than Amanda could have imagined, more than she'd ever dreamed. The pain she'd expected never came. Instead, there was only glorious heat and dazzling pleasure.

She wrapped her legs around Dane's lean hips, pressed her mouth against his and hung on for dear life.

Just when she thought she couldn't take any more, he was flooding into her. Then entire worlds exploded.

Her mind was numb, her body spent. She lay in his

arms, her hair splayed over his chest, her lips pressed over his heart, which seemed to be beating in rhythm with her own.

Although the stinging pulsating had begun to diminish, Amanda's entire body remained devastatingly sensitized. His hand, resting lightly at the base of her spine, seemed to be causing her body to glow from inside with a steady, radiant heat.

"Why the hell didn't you tell me?" Emotions churned uncomfortably inside Dane. Of all the stupid mistakes he'd made concerning this woman, this one definitely took the cake.

Amanda knew there was no point in pretending ignorance. She knew exactly what he was talking about. Besides, she'd made her decision and had no intention of apologizing for it.

"I didn't think it mattered." She closed her eyes and wished that this conversation could have waited until she was ready to return to the real world. And her real life.

"She didn't think it mattered." He grabbed hold of her hair—not gently—and lifted her composed gaze to his. "My God, Amanda, I practically raped you."

The fire was burning down, but there was still enough light for her to see the guilt in his dark eyes.

"It wasn't anything near rape." Amanda refused to let Dane take away what he'd given her. Refused to let him reject what she'd given him.

"I sure as hell didn't use any finesse."

"I know." She stretched, enjoying the feel of his muscular legs against her thighs. "And it was wonderful." Actually, it was better than wonderful. But there were not enough words in all the world to describe what she was feeling.

"I was too damn rough." His dark eyes, already laced with chagrin, turned bleak with self-disgust. He frowned as he viewed the bruises already beginning to form on her arms, her hips, her thighs.

He brushed his knuckles over the tops of her breasts, which were also marred with angry smudges. "A woman's first time should be special." He touched the tip of his tongue to a nipple and heard her sigh.

"It *was* special." She lifted her hands to comb them through his hair, but a lovely lethargy had settled over her, infusing her limbs, and she dropped them back to her sides. "The most special thing that ever happened to me."

Her softly spoken words could not quite expunge his feelings of guilt. "It was too fast."

She laughed at that. The rich, satisfied sound of a woman in love. "Don't worry," she murmured against his neck as she pressed her body against his, rekindling cooling sparks. "We can do it again." She ran her tongue in a provocative swath down his neck. "And this time, you can take all night."

It was an offer he was not about to refuse. But having already screwed up what should have been one of the most memorable occasions of her life, Dane intended to do things right.

Wanting to set a more romantic stage—and on a practical level, wanting to wash off the sand he feared was embedded in every pore—he suggested moving to the house. To his room.

Amanda immediately agreed. "But I'd rather we make love in the tower room." Her smile, as she refastened the lacy bra he'd ripped off her, was as warm as any a woman had ever shared with any man. "It already has warm memories for me. I love the idea of making more."

He suddenly realized that he definitely wasn't pleased by the thought that she'd soon be leaving Satan's Cove. Whatever they did together tonight in the refurbished tower room would simply become another memory that she'd look back on with fondness over the coming years.

"Dane?" She witnessed the shadow moving across his eyes, watched his lips pull into a taut line. "Did I say something wrong? If I'm pushing you—"

"No." Her hands had begun to flutter like frightened birds. He caught them by the wrists, lifted them to his mouth and kissed them. "I want you, Amanda. I have from the moment you walked in the door. The problem is, I don't know what you want."

"I want you." The answer was echoed in the sweet warmth of her smile.

Dane couldn't help himself. He had to ask. "For how long?"

He could not have said anything worse. Amanda flinched inwardly even as she vowed not to let him see he'd scored such a direct hit. Obviously, she considered, now that he'd discovered she'd been a virgin, he was concerned she'd take what had happened between them, what was about to happen again, too seriously.

He'd already professed the belief that he should have done more—as if such a thing was humanly possible— to make her first lovemaking experience special. Now, it appeared he was afraid of becoming trapped in a permanent relationship he hadn't initially bargained for.

"If you're asking if I'm going to call my father and have him show up in Satan's Cove with a shotgun, you don't have to worry, Dane." She withdrew her hands from his and backed away, just a little.

As he watched her trying to relace the blouse he'd torn open, Dane experienced another pang of regret for having treated her so roughly.

"Just because I chose to make love with you, doesn't mean that I'm foolish enough to get all misty-eyed and start smelling orange blossoms and hearing Lohengrin." Her voice was remarkably calm, given the fact that she was trembling inside.

Once again he found himself missing the young girl who wanted nothing more from life than to spend her days and nights making babies with him. On the heels of that thought came another.

"Hell." This time he dragged both hands through his hair. "I didn't use anything."

He'd put the condoms in his pocket before coming down here, but then he'd gotten sidetracked by Kelli Kyle. Then, when Amanda had arrived, she'd been so busy spitting fire at him and had made him so angry, he'd completely forgotten about protection.

Smooth move, Cutter, he blasted himself. Even in his horny, hormone-driven teenage days, he'd never behaved so irresponsibly.

He looked so furious at himself, so frustrated by the situation, that Amanda wrapped her arms around his waist and pressed a brief kiss against his scowling mouth. "It's okay. It's a safe time of the month for me."

He'd heard that one before. "You know what they call people who use the rhythm method of family planning, don't you?"

She tilted her head back and looked up at him. "What?"

"Parents." He shook his head again, thinking that

tonight was turning out to be just one disaster after another. "I'm sorry."

"I do wish you'd stop saying that," she said on a soft sigh. "Truly, Dane, it would take a miracle to get me pregnant tonight. And besides, it was only one time."

Dane wondered how many pregnant women had ended up reciting that old lament. "Things aren't the same as they were that summer, Amanda. There's a lot more to be worried about than pregnancy, as serious as that is."

His expression was so somber, Amanda almost laughed. "I don't need a lecture, Dane. I know the risks. But I also know you. And trust you."

"Sure. That's why you went ballistic when you realized I'd been drinking beer out here with Parsons's PR manager."

She'd been hoping that wouldn't come up. She still couldn't believe that she'd behaved like a teenager who'd just caught her date necking with another girl in the parking lot outside the senior prom.

"I *was* jealous," she admitted reluctantly.

"Join the club." He smiled and ran the back of his hand down the side of her face in a slow, tender sweep. "When Jimmy was adjusting your bike pedals today, I just about saw red."

The Brad Pitt look-alike had been unusually attentive. At the time, Amanda had been flattered by his obvious admiration. Especially when the inn was overrun with young girls who could compete with Mindy for her Miss Satan's Cove crown.

"You're kidding."

"I'd already decided that if he touched your leg one more time, I'd fire him."

Amanda laughed at that, finding Dane's confession surprising and wonderful. "I suppose having a crush on an older woman is natural at nineteen."

"I wouldn't know." He gathered her close and kissed her smiling mouth. Lightly. Tenderly. Sweetly. As he'd planned to do all along. "When *I* was nineteen I was so bewitched by a sexy young siren, I wouldn't have thought of looking at anyone else."

It was exactly what she'd been hoping he'd say. Rising up on her toes, she twined her arms around his neck and clung.

"By the way," Dane said when the long, heartfelt kiss finally ended, "I had a life-insurance physical when I bought this place. You don't have to worry about any diseases."

"I wasn't worried." She watched him carefully put out the fire. When he crouched down, his jeans pulled tight against his thighs, making her all too aware of how wonderful those strong, firm legs had felt entwined with hers. "May I ask one question without sounding like a jealous bitch?"

"You could never sound like a bitch." Satisfied with his efforts, he stood again. "But shoot."

"What *was* Kelli doing down here?"

Dane shrugged. "Damned if I know." Seeing the disbelief on her face, he mistook it for another stab of feminine pique. "But if she was trying to lure me into her bed, she sure had a funny way of going about it."

"Oh?" Amanda believed that was exactly what Kelli had had in mind. Obviously she'd tired of Greg and was looking for some way to pass the time until returning to Portland. What better diversion than a man for whom the word *hunk* had been invented?

"She spent the entire time it took her to drink that beer talking about you," he revealed.

"Me?" That was a surprise. "Why on earth would she be interested in me? And what did she say?"

"It was more what she wanted me to say." He rubbed his chin thoughtfully. The conversation had seemed strange at the time. Looking back, it didn't make any more sense.

Unless, of course, Greg was using her to pump him to discover any flaws he might use against Amanda in their corporate warfare. "She asked a lot of questions about how I thought you were conducting the challenge week. If you'd mentioned your feelings about the value of the games. And whether or not you had discussed individual team members with me."

"That doesn't make any sense," Amanda mused. "Perhaps Greg's using her as a spy. To discover my weak points. And to find out if I'm trying to unseat him."

"That'd be my guess." Even as Dane agreed, he thought that although the explanation made sense, it hadn't seemed to fit Kelli Kyle's probing questions. Putting the nagging little problem away for now, he ran his hands through Amanda's tousled hair, dislodging silvery grains of sand.

"Are we through talking about business?"

"Absolutely." She beamed up at him. "Are you going to make love to me again?"

"Absolutely." And, after a long interlude spent beneath the shower in the bath adjoining the tower room, that's exactly what Dane did.

With a restraint that she never would have guessed possible, he kept the pace slow and this time when he took her, the ride was slow and long and heartbreakingly gentle. But no less dizzying.

Amanda had mistakenly believed that in that whirlwind mating in the cave, Dane had taught her everything he knew about love. Before the sun rose the following morning, she realized that she'd been wrong.

Her first heady experience, as dizzying as it had proved to be, had only been a prelude to the most glorious night any woman could have known.

A night she knew she would remember for the rest of her life.

Chapter 10

It was the coo of a pigeon sitting on her windowsill that woke her. Amanda stretched luxuriously and felt her lips curve into a slow, satisfied smile. For the first time in her life she knew exactly how Scarlett had felt the morning after Rhett had carried her up all those stairs.

Although she felt a pang of regret to find herself alone in bed, she decided that Dane must have slipped away to prevent gossip. Not that anyone would actually come all the way up here to the tower room. But it was thoughtful of him all the same.

It certainly wouldn't help matters to have the team members gossiping about her and Dane sleeping together. Not that either of them had gotten much sleep.

Besides, they both had a busy day today. Amanda was taking the team out on a deep-sea fishing trip, while Dane caught up on some much-needed grounds work.

She climbed out of the high log bed, aware of an unfamiliar stiffness. *To think you've wasted all that time on the stair stepper,* she scolded herself lightly. *When there are far better ways to work out.*

Perhaps, she considered with an inward grin, she should take Dane back to Portland with her at the end of the challenge. *Maybe, with the raise that comes with the creative director's slot, I could hire him to be my personal trainer.* And dear Lord, how *personal* he'd been!

Even as she found the idea more than a little appealing, it brought home, all too clearly, that their time together was coming to an end. If everything went according to plan, in two short days she'd be getting back on that bus and returning to Portland, where hopefully she'd move into Greg's office. While Dane would stay here, in Satan's Cove, living the bucolic life of a coastal innkeeper.

The thought of losing him, just when she'd found him again, was not a pleasant one. But unwilling to spoil what brief time they had left together, Amanda decided to take yet another page out of Scarlett O'Hara's story and think about that tomorrow.

She went into the adjoining bathroom, which was now overbrimming with memories of the long hot shower they'd taken together last night.

This morning, as she stood beneath the streaming water, she wondered if she'd ever be able to take a shower again without remembering the feel of Dane's strong, sure hands on her body, or the taste of his lips on hers, or the dazzling, dizzying way his mouth had felt when he'd knelt before her and treated her to lovemaking so sublime she'd actually wept.

When memories began flooding her mind and stimulating her body yet again, Amanda decided it was time to get to work. She turned off the water and slipped into the plush white robe—reminiscent of those favored by the Whitfield Palace hotels—hanging on the back of the door.

She found Dane pouring coffee. The scent of the rich dark brew, along with the aroma of Mary Cutter's freshly baked croissants, drew her like a magnet.

"You weren't kidding about special service."

"With a smile." He handed her a cup of steaming coffee, but before she could drink it, he bent his head and kissed her. "I knew it."

"What?" How was it that he could set her head spinning with a single kiss? Although she doubted they'd had more than three hours' sleep, Amanda had never felt more alive.

"That you'd be drop-dead gorgeous in the morning." His eyes took a slow tour of her, from her wet caramel-colored hair down to her toes, painted the soft pink of the inside of a seashell. Beads of water glistened on the flesh framed by the lapels of the bulky white robe. Dane was struck with an urge to lick them away.

"Flatterer." She laughed and dragged a hand through her damp hair. "And if you don't stop looking at me that way, I'll miss the fishing boat."

"If you've ever smelled a fishing boat, you'd know that would be no great loss." His own smile faded. "I've been thinking about the final challenge event."

Amanda nodded. It had been on her mind, as well. "The cliff climb."

"You realize there isn't much room for error in rock climbing."

"I know." She sat down at the skirted table and tore

off a piece of croissant. It was as flaky as expected, layered with the sweet taste of butter. "I trust you to keep things safe."

"I'm not in the survival business." He sat down as well, close enough that their knees were touching.

"I know that, too." After last night, Amanda couldn't find it in her to worry about anything. "But so far, you've done a wonderful job."

"You haven't been so bad, yourself, sweetheart. The way you've kept those team members from going for one another's throats would probably earn you a top-level job in the diplomatic corps, if you ever decide to give up advertising."

She wondered what he'd say if he knew she thought about exactly that on an almost daily basis lately. One of the things that had drawn her to advertising in the first place was that it was a service business, a business that prospered or failed on how it served its clients.

With all the recent megamergers, there seemed to be very little benefit to clients. In fact, more than one old-time C.C.C. client had proclaimed to be upset by a supposed conflict of interest now that the same huge agency was also handling their competitors' advertising.

"You know," she murmured, "a lot of people—mostly those in New York—used to consider C.C.C. old-fashioned. And perhaps it was." Which was, she'd often thought lately, one of the things she'd loved about Connally Creative Concepts. "But it was still an agency where clients' desires were catered to.

"These days, it seems that if you can't win new accounts by being creative, you buy them by gobbling up other, more innovative shops. But the forced combination inevitably fails to create a stronger agency."

"Instead of getting the best of both worlds, you get the worst of each," Dane guessed.

"Exactly." Amanda nodded. "Creativity becomes the last item on the agenda. And, although I hate to admit it, the advertising coming out of Janzen, Lawton and Young these days shows it. In the pursuit of profits, our clients have become an afterthought. They're getting lost in the shuffle."

"It's not just happening in advertising," Dane observed. "The workplace, in general, has become increasingly impersonal."

Which was another of the reasons he'd left the world of big business. Although, under Eve Whitfield Deveraux's guidance, the Whitfield Palace hotel chain routinely topped all the Best 100 Corporations to Work For lists, it was, and always would be, a profit-driven business.

"Every day I arrive at my office, hoping to rediscover the business I used to work in." Amanda had been so busy trying to keep things on an even keel at work, she hadn't realized exactly how much she'd missed the often-frantic, always-stimulating atmosphere of C.C.C. "But I can't. Because it's disappeared beneath a flood of memos and dress codes and constantly changing managerial guidelines."

She sighed again. "Would you mind if we tabled this discussion for some other time?" The depressing topic was threatening to cast a pall over her previously blissful mood.

"Sure." It was none of his business anyway, Dane told himself again. What Amanda chose to do with her life was no one's concern but her own. Knowing that he was utterly hooked on this woman who'd stolen his heart so long ago, Dane only wished that were true.

"May I ask you something?"

There was something in his low tone that set off warnings inside Amanda. She slowly lowered her cup to the flowered tablecloth. "Of course."

"Why me? And why now?"

Good question. She wondered what he'd say if she just said it right out: *Because I think—no, I know—that I love you.*

She put her cup down and stared out at the tall windows at the sea, which was draped in its usual silvery cloak of early morning mist.

"When I was a girl, I was a romantic."

"I remember." All too well.

"I believed that someday a handsome prince would come riding up on his white steed and carry me off to his palace, where we'd live happily ever after." Dane had had a Harley in those days instead of a white horse, but he'd fit the romantic fantasy as if it had been created with him in mind. He still did.

"Sounds nice," Dane agreed. "For a fairy tale." Speaking of fairy tales, he wondered what would happen if, now that he finally had her back again, he just kept Amanda locked away up here in the tower room, like Rapunzel.

"For a fairy tale," she agreed. "I also was brought up to believe that lovemaking was something to be saved for the man I married."

"A not-unreasonable expectation." Dane considered it ironic that he might have Gordon Stockenberg to thank for last night.

"No. But not entirely practical, either." She ran her

fingernail around the rim of the coffee cup, uncomfortable with this discussion. Although they'd been as intimate as two people could be, she was discovering that revealing the secrets of her heart was a great deal more difficult than revealing her body.

"If we'd made love that summer, I probably would have found it easier to have casual sex with guys I dated in college. Like so many of my friends.

"But you'd made such a big deal of it, I guess I wanted to wait until I met someone I could at least believe myself to be in love with as much as I'd been in love with you."

Which had never happened.

"Then, after I graduated, I was so busy concentrating on my work, that whenever I did meet a man who seemed like he might be a candidate, he'd usually get tired of waiting around and find some more willing woman."

"Or a less choosy one."

She smiled at that suggestion. "Anyway, after a time, sex just didn't seem that important anymore."

"You *have* been working too hard."

Amanda laughed even as she considered that now that she'd experienced Dane's magnificent lovemaking, sex had taken on an entirely new perspective.

"Anyway," she said with a shrug designed to conceal her tumultuous feelings, "perhaps it was old unresolved feelings reasserting themselves, but being back here again with you, making love to you, just felt so natural. So right."

"I know the feeling." He covered her free hand with his, lacing their fingers together. "You realize, of course, that you could have saved me a great many cold showers if you'd just admitted to wanting me that first night?"

The way his thumb was brushing tantalizingly against the palm of her hand was creating another slow burn deep inside Amanda. "Better late than never."

"Speaking of being late…" He lifted her hand to his lips and pressed a kiss against the skin his thumb had left tingling. "How much time do we have before you're due at the dock?"

She glanced over at the clock on the pine bedside table and sighed. "Not enough."

"I was afraid of that." He ran the back of his hand down her cheek. "How would you like to go into town with me tonight?"

The opportunity to be alone with Dane, away from the prying eyes of the others, sounded sublime. "I'd love to."

"Great. Davey Jones's Locker probably isn't what you're used to—I mean, the tablecloths are white butcher paper instead of damask and the wine list isn't anything to boast about. But the food's pretty good. And the lighting's dark enough that we can neck in the back booth between courses."

Her smile lit her face. "It sounds absolutely perfect."

Other than the fact that the sea had turned rough and choppy by midafternoon, and Dane had been right about the smell of fish permeating every inch of the chartered fishing boat, the derby turned out better than Amanda had honestly expected.

The teams seemed to be meshing more with each passing day, and at the same time the competitive viciousness displayed on the bike race had abated somewhat. At least, she considered, as the boat chugged its way into the Satan's Cove harbor, no one had thrown anyone overboard.

As team members stood in line to have their catch weighed and measured, Amanda noticed that Kelli was missing. She found her in the restroom of the charter office, splashing water on her face. Her complexion was as green as the linoleum floor.

"Whoever thought up this stupid challenge week should be keelhauled," the public-relations manager moaned.

Since the week had been Greg's idea, Amanda didn't answer. "I guess the Dramamine didn't work." Prepared for seasickness among the group, Amanda had given Kelli the tablets shortly after the boat left the dock, when it became obvious that the woman was not a natural-born sailor.

"Actually, it helped a lot with the seasickness. I think it was the smell of the fish that finally got to me." She pressed a hand against her stomach. "I'm never going to be able to eat salmon or calamari again."

"I'm sorry," Amanda said, realizing she actually meant it. "Is there anything I can do?"

"No." Kelli shook her head, then cringed, as if wishing she hadn't done so. "I just want to get back to the inn, go to bed, pull the covers over my head and if not die, at least sleep until morning."

"That sounds like a good idea. I'll ask Mary Cutter to fix a tray for you to eat in your room."

If possible, Kelli's complexion turned an even sicklier hue of green. "I don't think I could keep down a thing."

"You need something in your stomach. Just something light. Some crackers. And a little broth, perhaps."

Although obviously quite ill, Kelli managed a smile. "You know, everything I've been told about you suggests you're a dynamite advertising executive. Yet, sometimes, like during that stupid helicopter session, you seem to be a born diplomat."

"Thank you." Amanda was surprised to receive praise from someone so close to her nemesis.

"You don't have to thank me for telling the truth," Kelli said. "But there's another side to you, as well. A softer, nurturing side. So, what about children?"

The question had come from left field. "What about them?"

"Do you intend to have any?"

"I suppose. Someday."

"But not anytime soon?"

"Getting pregnant certainly isn't on this week's agenda," Amanda said honestly.

For some reason she could not discern, Kelli seemed to be mulling that over. Amanda waited patiently to see what the woman was up to.

"You don't like me much, do you?" Kelli asked finally.

"I don't really know you."

"True. And spoken like a true diplomat. By the way, Dane was a perfect gentleman last night."

"I can't imagine Dane being anything but a gentleman."

"What I mean is—"

"I know what you mean." Amanda didn't want to talk about Dane. Not with this woman.

Kelli reached into her canvas tote, pulled out a compact and began applying rose blush to her too-pale cheeks. "You love Dane, don't you?"

"I really don't believe my feelings are anyone's business but my own."

"Of course not," Kelli said quickly. A bit too quickly, Amanda thought. "I was just thinking that advertising is a very unstable business, and if you were to get involved with our sexy innkeeper, then have to move back East—"

"I doubt there's much possibility of that. Besides, as exciting as New York admittedly is, I'm comfortable where I am."

Kelli dropped the blush back into the bag and pulled out a black-and-gold lipstick case. "Even with Greg as creative director?"

She'd definitely hit the bull's-eye with that question.

"Greg Parsons isn't Patrick Connally," Amanda said truthfully. "And his management style is a great deal different." Sort of like the difference between Genghis Khan and Ghandi. "But, as we've pointed out over these past days, advertising is all about change."

"Yes, it is, isn't it?" Kelli looked at Amanda in the mirror. Her gaze was long and deep. Finally, she returned to her primping. After applying a fuchsia lipstick that added much-needed color to her lips, she said, "I suppose we may as well join the others."

As they left the restroom together, Amanda couldn't help thinking that their brief conversation wasn't exactly like two women sharing confidences. It had strangely seemed more like an interview. Deciding that she was reading too much into the incident, she began anticipating the evening ahead.

Amanda hadn't been so nervous since the summer of her fifteenth year. She bathed in scented water that left her skin as smooth as silk, brushed her newly washed hair until it shone like gold and applied her makeup with unusual care. Then she stood in front of the closet, wondering what she could wear for what was, essentially, her first real date with Dane.

She'd only brought one dress, and she'd already worn it last night. Besides, somehow, the front ties had gotten torn in their frantic struggle to undress. And although she had no doubt that the patrons of Davey Jones's Locker wouldn't complain about her showing up with the front of her blouse slit down to her navel, she figured such sexy attire would be overkill for Satan's Cove.

Although she'd been underage, hence too young to go into the bar/restaurant the last time she'd visited the coastal town, from the outside, the building definitely did not seem to be the kind of place where one dressed for dinner.

With that in mind, she finally decided on a pair of black jeans and a long-sleeved white blouse cut in the classic style of a man's shirt. Some gold studs at her ears, a gold watch, and a pair of black cowboy boots completed her ensemble.

"Well, you're not exactly Cinderella," she murmured, observing her reflection in the antique full-length mirror. "But you'll do."

So as not to encourage unwanted gossip, she'd agreed to meet Dane in the former carriage house that had been turned into a garage. As she entered the wooden building, his eyes darkened with masculine approval.

"You look absolutely gorgeous, contessa."

She was vastly relieved he hadn't seen her when she'd arrived from the boat, smelling of fish, her face pink from the sun, her nose peeling like an eleven-year-old tomboy's and her hair a wild tangle.

"I hope this is appropriate." She ran her hands down the front of her jeans. "I thought I'd leave my tiara at home tonight."

"All the better to mingle with your subjects," he agreed, thinking that although she'd cleaned up beautifully, he still kind of liked the way she'd looked when she'd returned from the fishing derby today.

He'd been in the garden, tying up his mother's prized tomato plants, when he'd seen her trying to sneak into the lodge, her complexion kissed by the sun and her tangled hair reminding him of the way it looked when she first woke up this morning after a night of passionate lovemaking.

"I got to thinking," he said, "that perhaps, after a day on a fishing boat, taking you out for seafood wasn't the best idea I've ever had."

"Don't worry about me." Her smile was quick and warm and reminded him of the one he'd fallen for when he was nineteen. "I've got a stomach like a rock. And I adore seafood."

"Terrific. Iris has a way with fried oysters you won't believe."

"I love fried oysters." She batted her lashes in the way Scarlett O'Hara had made famous and a fifteen-year-old girl had once perfected. "They're rumored to be an aphrodisiac, you know."

"So I've heard. But with you providing the inspiration, contessa, the last thing I need is an aphrodisiac."

He drew her into his arms and gave her a long deep kiss that left her breathless. And even as he claimed her mouth with his, Dane knew that it was Amanda who was claiming him. Mind, heart and soul.

Satan's Cove was laid out in a crescent, following the curving shoreline. As Dane drove down the narrow main street, Amanda was surprised and pleased that the town hadn't changed during the decade she'd been away.

"It's as if it's frozen in time," she murmured as they drove past the cluster of buildings that billed themselves as the Sportsman's Lodge, and the white Cape Cod–style Gray Whale Mercantile. "Well, almost," she amended as she viewed a window sign on another building that advertised crystals and palm readings. A For Rent sign hung in a second-story window above the New Age shop.

"Nothing stays the same." Dane said what Amanda had already discovered the hard way at C.C.C. "But change has been slow to come to this part of the coast."

"I'm glad," she decided.

"Of course, there was a time when Satan's Cove was a boomtown. But that was before the fire."

"Fire?"

"Didn't you learn the town's history when you were here before?"

"I was a little preoccupied that summer," she reminded. "Trying to seduce the sexiest boy on the Pacific seaboard. Visiting dull old museums was not exactly high on my list of fun things to do."

Since he'd had far better places to escape with her than the town museum, Dane decided he was in no position to criticize.

"With the exception of Smugglers' Inn, which was located too far away, most of the town burned down in the early nineteen-thirties. Including the old Victorian whorehouse down by the docks. Well, needless to say, without that brothel, the fishermen all moved to Tillamook, Seaside and Astoria."

"Amazing what the loss of entrepreneurs can do to a local economy," she drawled sapiently. "So what happened? Didn't the women come back after the town was rebuilt?"

"By the time the city fathers got around to rebuilding in the mid-thirties, the prohibitionists had joined forces with some radical religious reformers who passed an ordinance forbidding the rebuilding of any houses of ill repute.

"After World War II, alcohol returned without a battle. And so did sex. But these days it's free." He flashed her a grin. "Or so I'm told."

Even though she knew their time was coming to an end, his flippant statement caused a stab of purely feminine jealousy. Amanda hated the idea of Dane making love to any other woman. But short of tying him up and taking him back to Portland with her, she couldn't think of a way to keep the man all to herself.

She was wondering about the logistics of maintaining a commuter relationship—after all, Portland was only a few hours' drive from Satan's Cove—when he pulled up in front of Davey Jones's Locker.

From the outside, the weathered, silvery gray building did not look at all promising. Once inside, however, after her eyes adjusted to the dim light, Amanda found it rustically appealing.

Fish, caught in local waters, had been mounted on the knotty-pine-paneled walls, yellow sawdust had been sprinkled over the plank floor and behind an L-shaped bar was a smoky mirror and rows of bottles.

"Dane!" A woman who seemed vaguely familiar,

wearing a striped cotton-knit top and a pair of cuffed white shorts, stopped on her way by with a tray of pilsner glasses filled with draft beer. Her voluptuous breasts turned the red and white stripes into wavy lines. "I was wondering what it would take to get you away from that work in progress."

She flashed Dane a smile that belonged in a tooth-paste commercial and her emerald eyes gleamed with a feminine welcome Amanda found far too sexy for comfort. Then her eyes skimmed over Amanda with unconcealed interest.

"Just grab any old table, you two," she said with an airy wave of her hand. "As soon as I deliver these, I'll come take your drink order."

With that, she was dashing across the room to where a group of men were playing a game of pool on a green-felt-topped table. The seductive movement of her hips in those tight white shorts was nothing short of riveting.

"Old friend?" Amanda asked as she slipped into a booth at the back of the room.

"Iris and I dated a bit in high school," Dane revealed easily. "And when I first returned to town. But nothing ever came of it. We decided not to risk a great friendship by introducing romance into the relationship."

Relief was instantaneous. "She really is stunning." Now that she knew the woman wasn't a threat, Amanda could afford to be generous.

"She is that," Dane agreed easily. "I've seen grown men walk into walls when Iris walks by. But, of course, that could be because they've had too much to drink."

Or it could be because the woman had a body any *Playboy* centerfold would envy. That idea brought up Dane's contention that she was too thin, which in turn had Amanda comparing herself with the voluptuous Iris, who was headed back their way, order pad in hand. The outcome wasn't even close.

"Hi," she greeted Amanda with a smile every bit as warm as the one she'd bestowed upon Dane. "It's good to see you again."

Amanda looked at the stunning redhead in confusion. "I'm sorry, but—"

"That's okay," Iris interrupted good-naturedly. "It's been a long time. I was waiting tables at Smugglers' Inn the summer you came for a vacation with your parents."

Memories flooded back. "Of course, I remember you." She also recalled, all too clearly, how jealous she'd been of the sexy redheaded waitress who spent far too much time in the kitchen with Dane. "How are you?"

"I'm doing okay. Actually, since I bought this place with the settlement money from my divorce, I'm doing great." She laughed, pushing back a froth of copper hair. "I think I've found my place, which is kind of amazing when you think how badly I wanted to escape this town back in my wild teenage days."

She grinned over at Dane. "Can you believe it, sugar? Here we are, two hotshot kids who couldn't wait to get out of Satan's Cove, back home again, happy as a pair of clams."

"Iris was making a pretty good living acting in Hollywood," Dane revealed.

"Really?" Although she'd grown up in Los Angeles, the only actors she'd ever met were all the wannabes waiting tables at her favorite restaurants. "That must have been exciting."

"In the beginning, I felt just like Buddy Ebsen. You know—" she elaborated at Amanda's confused look

"—'The Beverly Hillbillies.' Movie stars, swimming pools... Lord, I was in hog heaven. I married the first guy I met when I got off the bus—an out-of-work actor. That lasted until I caught him rehearsing bedroom scenes with a waitress from Hamburger Hamlet. In our bed.

"My second marriage was to a director, who promised to make me a star. And I'll have to admit, he was doing his best to keep his promise, but I was getting tired of being the girl who was always murdered by some crazed psycho. There's only so much you can do creatively with a bloodcurdling scream.

"Besides, after a time, a girl gets a little tired of her husband wearing her underwear, if you know what I mean."

"I can see where that might be a bit disconcerting," Amanda agreed. She'd never met anyone as open and outgoing as Iris. She decided it was no wonder the woman had chosen to leave the art and artifice of Hollywood.

"After my second divorce, I got fed up with the entire Hollywood scene and realized, just like Dorothy, that there's no place like home."

"I just realized," Amanda said, "I've seen one of your films."

"You're kidding!"

"No. I went to a Halloween party a few years ago and the host screened *Nightstalker*."

"You've got a good eye," Iris said. "I think I lasted about three scenes in that one."

"But they were pivotal," Amanda said earnestly, remembering how Iris's character—a hooker with a heart of gold—had grabbed her killer's mask off, enabling a street person rifling through a nearby Dumpster to get a glimpse of his scarred face. Which in turn, eventually resulted in the man's capture.

"I knew I liked you." Iris flashed a grin Dane's way. "If I were you, I'd try to hold on to this one."

"Thanks for the advice." Dane didn't add that that was exactly what he intended to do.

Chapter 11

Although the ambience was definitely not that of a five-star restaurant, and the food was not covered in velvety sauce or garnished with the trendy miniature vegetable-of-the-week, Amanda couldn't remember when she'd enjoyed a meal more.

There was one small glitch—when Julian, Marvin, and Luke Cahill had unexpectedly shown up. Fortunately, they appeared no more pleased to see her than she was to see them, and after a few stiltedly exchanged words, settled into a booth across the room.

Amanda wondered what the three were doing together. They could be plotting strategy, were it not for the fact that Marvin and Julian were on the blue team and Luke was on the red.

As much as she had riding on the corporate challenge, for this one night Amanda refused to think about her plan for success. After all, here she was, on her first real date with the man she'd always loved, and she wasn't going to spoil things trying to figure out this latest bit of corporate intrigue.

Instead, she took a sip of the house white wine, smiled enticingly over the heavy rim of the glass, and allowed herself to relax fully for the first time since arriving in Satan's Cove.

It was late when they returned to the inn. The moon and stars that had been so vivid the other night were hidden by a thick cloud of fog.

Someone—undoubtedly Mindy—had left a lamp in the downstairs reception parlor on; it glowed a warm welcome. The lights in the upstairs windows were off, revealing that the other guests had gone to bed.

Amanda didn't invite Dane up to her room. There was no need. Both of them knew how the night would end.

The elevator was cranking its way up to the third floor when Dane turned and took her in his arms. "I'd say tonight went pretty well," he murmured against her cheek. "For a first date."

"Better than well." She sighed her pleasure as she wrapped her arms around his waist. "I can't remember when I've enjoyed myself more."

"I'm glad." His lips skimmed up to create sparks at her temple. Dane didn't add that he'd worried she'd find Davey Jones's Locker too plebeian for her city tastes.

"And just think—" she leaned back a bit, sensual amusement gleaming in her eyes "—the night's still young."

Actually, that wasn't really the case. But Dane wasn't about to argue. After all the sleep he'd lost fixing up the inn, he wasn't about to complain about losing a bit more if it meant making love again to Amanda.

Lowering his head, he touched his lips to hers. At first briefly. Then, as he drew her closer, the kiss, while remaining tender, grew deeper. More intimate. More weakening.

Her limbs grew heavy, her head light. Amanda clung to him, wanting more. She'd never known an elevator ride to take so long.

The cage door finally opened. Hand in hand, they walked to the stairwell at the end of the hallway. It was like moving in a dream. A dream Amanda wished would never end.

They'd no sooner entered the tower room than Dane pulled her close and kissed her again. Not with the slow self-control of a man who knew how to draw out every last ounce of pleasure, but with the impatient demand of a lover who realized that this stolen time together was rapidly coming to an end.

With a strength and ease that once again bespoke the life of hard, physical work he'd chosen over shuffling papers, Dane scooped her up in his arms and carried her across the plank floor to the bed, which had been turned down during their absence. A mint, formed in the unmistakable shape of the inn, had been left on the pillow. Dane brushed it onto the floor with an impatient hand and began unbuttoning Amanda's blouse.

"No." It took an effort—her bones had turned to syrup—but she managed to lift her hands to his.

"No?" Disbelief sharpened his tone, darkened his eyes.

She laid a calming hand against his cheek and felt the tensed muscle beneath her fingertips. "It's my turn." Unconsciously, she skimmed her tongue over her lips, enjoying the clinging taste of him. "To make love to you."

It was at that moment, when every atom in his body was aching to take Amanda—and take her now—that Dane realized he could deny this woman nothing.

His answering smile was slow and warm and devilishly sexy. "I'm all yours, contessa." He'd never, in all his twenty-nine years, spoken truer words.

He rolled over onto his back, spread out his arms and waited.

Never having undressed a man—last night's frantic coupling in the cave didn't really count, since Amanda still couldn't remember how they'd ended up naked—she was more than a little nervous. But, remembering how his bare torso had gleamed like bronze in the firelight, she decided to begin with his shirt.

With hands that were not as steady as she would have liked, she tackled the buttons one by one. She'd known he was strong—his chest was rock hard and wonderfully muscled. But it was his inner strength that continued to arouse her. Just as it was his loyalty, integrity and steely self-confidence that Amanda had fallen in love with.

When she reached his belt, she had two choices—to unfasten his jeans or tug the shirt free. Unreasonably drawn to the enticing swell beneath the crisp indigo denim of the jeans that had become his dress slacks when he'd changed lifestyles, Amanda stuck to her vow to keep things slow.

Dane was moderately disappointed when she took the easy way out and pulled his shirt free of his waistband—until she folded back the plaid cotton and pressed her silky lips against his bare chest. Her mouth felt like a hot brand against his flesh, burning her claim on him, just as she'd done so many years ago.

"I'm not very experienced." Her lips skimmed down the narrow arrowing of ebony chest hair, leaving sparks. "You'll have to tell me what you like." Retracing the trail her mouth had blazed, she flicked her tongue over a dark nipple. The wet heat caused a smoldering deep in his loins, which threatened to burst into a wildfire.

"That's a dandy start," he managed in a husky voice roughened with hunger.

"How about this?" She bestowed light, lazy kisses back down his chest, over his stomach.

"Even better," he groaned, when she dipped her tongue into his navel. His erection stirred, pushing painfully against the hard denim barrier. Realizing that it was important to cede control to Amanda, Dane ignored the ache and concentrated on the pleasure.

He could have cursed when she suddenly abandoned her seduction efforts. Relief flooded through him as he realized she was only stopping long enough to take off his shoes and socks.

For a woman who a little more than twenty-four hours ago had been a virgin, Amanda was definitely making up for lost time.

"I've never noticed a man's feet before," she murmured, running her hands over his. "Who could have guessed that a foot could be so sexy?"

He began to laugh at that outrageous idea, but when she touched her lips to his arch, lightning forked through him, turning the laugh into a choked sound of need.

"Lord, Amanda—" He reached for her, but she deftly avoided his hands.

She touched her mouth to his ankle, felt the thundering of his pulse and imagined she could taste the heat of his blood beneath her lips.

Realizing that she was on the verge of losing control of her emotions, Amanda shifted positions, to lie beside him. She returned her mouth to his face, kissing her way along his rigid jaw as her hands explored his torso, exploiting weaknesses he'd never known he possessed.

She left him long enough to light the fire he'd laid while she'd been out on the fishing boat. Then she proceeded to undress. She took as much time with her buttons as she had with his. By the time the white shirt finally fluttered to the floor, Dane had to press his lips together to keep his tongue from hanging out. As he observed her creamy breasts, unbearably enticing beneath the ivory lace bra, Dane discovered that ten years hadn't lessened his reaction to the sexy lingerie that had driven a sex-crazed nineteen-year-old to distraction.

She sat down in the wing chair beside the bed, stuck out a leg and invited him to pull off the glove-soft cowboy boot. Dane obliged her willingly. The left boot, then the right, dropped to the floor.

The jeans were even tougher to get off than the boots. "I should have thought this through better," she muttered as she tugged the black denim over her hips, irritated she'd lost the sensual rhythm she'd tried so hard to maintain.

"You certainly don't have to apologize, contessa." The sexy way she was wiggling her hips as she struggled to pull the tight jeans down her legs had Dane feeling as if he was about to explode. "Because it definitely works for me."

Their gazes touched. His eyes were dark with desire,

but tinged with a tender amusement that eased her embarrassment.

She had to sit down in the chair again to drag the jeans over her feet, but then she was standing beside the bed, clad only in the lacy bra and panties. The soft shadow beneath the skimpy lace triangle between her thighs had Dane literally biting the inside of his cheek.

"Don't stop now."

Thrilled by the heat flashing in his midnight-dark eyes, along with the hunger in his ragged tone, Amanda leaned forward, unfastened the back hooks of the bra, then held it against her chest for a suspended moment. With her eyes still on his, she smiled seductively.

As she raised her hands to comb them through her hair in a languid gesture, the lace bra fell away.

Unbearably aroused, Dane drank in the sight of her creamy breasts. While not voluptuous, they were smooth and firm. He remembered, all too well, how perfectly they had fit in his hands. In his mouth.

Watching him watch her, Amanda experienced a rush of power—followed by a wave of weakness. Although far more nervous now than when she'd begun the impromptu striptease, Amanda was determined to see it through. She hooked her fingers in the low-cut waistband, drawing the lace over her hips and down her legs.

"You are absolutely gorgeous." The truth of his words was echoed in his rough voice.

"And you're overdressed." Returning to the bed, she knelt over him, struggling with his belt buckle for a few frustrating seconds that seemed like an eternity.

Success! She dragged his jeans and white cotton briefs down his legs, then kissed her way up again.

"You're killing me," he moaned as her hand encircled his erection.

"Now you know how I felt." His sex was smooth and hot. "Last night." She lowered her head, and her hair fell over his hips like a gleaming antique-gold curtain as she swirled her seductive tongue over him.

Curses, pleas, or promises, Dane wasn't sure which, were torn from his throat. For the first time in his life, he understood what it was to be completely vulnerable.

She touched. He burned.

She tasted. He ached.

Amanda straddled Dane, taking him deep inside her, imprisoning him willingly, wonderfully, in her warmth.

Their eyes locked, exchanging erotic messages, intimate promises that neither had dared put into words.

Then, because they could wait no longer, she began to move, quickly and agilely, rocking against him, driving him—driving herself—toward that final glorious crest.

Although their time together was drawing to an end, neither Amanda nor Dane brought up the subject of what would happen once the challenge week ended. By unspoken mutual agreement, they ignored the inevitable, intent on capturing whatever pleasure they could. Whenever they could.

On the overnight backpacking trip, while the others tossed and turned, unaccustomed to sleeping on the ground, Dane slipped into Amanda's tent. Their lovemaking, while necessarily silent, was even more thrilling because of the risk of discovery. And when she couldn't remain quiet at the shattering moment of climax, Dane covered her mouth with his, smothering her ecstatic cry.

Time passed as if on wings. On the day before she

was scheduled to leave, while Dane was on the beach, preparing for the final event of the challenge week—the cliff climb—Amanda was alone in her room, her eyes swollen from the tears she'd shed after he'd left her bed.

The knock on her door had her wiping her damp cheeks. "Yes?"

"Amanda?" It was Kelli. "May I speak with you?"

Although they hadn't exchanged more than a few words since the fishing-boat incident, Amanda had gotten the impression that Kelli had been watching her every move, which had only increased her suspicions that the public-relations manager was spying for Greg.

"Just a minute." She ran into the adjoining bathroom, splashed some cold water on her face and pulled a brush through her hair. Then she opened the door.

"I'm sorry to bother you, but…" Kelli's voice drifted off as she observed Amanda's red-rimmed eyes. "Is something wrong?"

"No." When Kelli arched an eyebrow at the obvious lie, Amanda said, "It's personal."

Kelli's expression revealed understanding. "Love can be a real bitch, can't it?"

"Is it that obvious?" Amanda thought she and Dane had been so careful.

"Not to everyone," Kelli assured her.

Amanda decided it was time to get their cards on the table. "That's probably because not everyone has been watching me as closely as you."

If she'd expected Kelli to be embarrassed, Amanda would have been disappointed.

"That's true. But none of the others were sent here from Manhattan to evaluate the office."

"So you *are* a company spy?"

"*Spy* is such a negative word, don't you think?" Kelli suggested mildly. "I prefer to think of myself as a troubleshooter."

"Then you ought to shoot Greg Parsons," Amanda couldn't resist muttering.

"I've considered that. But my recommendation is going to be to fire him, instead."

"You're kidding!" Amanda could have been no more surprised than if Kelli had told her that Martians had just purchased the agency. "But he's family."

"Not for long," Kelli revealed. "It seems his wife has gotten tired of his philandering and is about to file for divorce. Obviously, Mr. Janzen isn't eager to employ the man who's broken his granddaughter's heart."

"It probably helps that he's incompetent to boot."

"That is a plus," Kelli agreed. "Which is, of course, where you come in." She paused a beat. For effect, Amanda thought. "You're the obvious choice to replace Greg as regional creative director."

"I'd hoped that was the case."

"I've already informed the partners that you'd be terrific at the job. But after receiving my daily emails, they've instructed me to offer you another position.

"You also know that all the recent mergers and downsizing has created a great deal of anxiety."

"Of course."

"Your Portland office is not unique. Janzen, Lawton and Young has been experiencing the same problems with all its new worldwide acquisitions. Which is why the partners have come up with the idea of creating the post of ombudsman. Which is where you come in.

"If you decide to accept the position, you'll achieve upper-management status and be required to travel between offices, creating the same good feeling and teamsmanship you've managed with this group."

"I'd rather have a root canal than repeat this challenge week."

Kelli grinned. "After that fishing trip, I'm in your corner on that one. Actually, the partners think the challenge week was overrated and undereffective. They believe that you could achieve the same results simply by visiting each office and employing your diplomatic skills to assure the employees that the mergers are in everyone's best interests."

"Even if I don't believe they are?" Amanda dared to ask.

"You're in advertising," Kelli reminded her with one of her perky trademark smiles. "Surely you're not averse to putting a positive spin on things. As you've done to get Marvin and Julian working together this week. You weren't lying when you stressed how important it was for the creative people and the accounting people to work together, were you?"

"Of course not, but—"

"Take some time to think it over," Kelli suggested. She went on to offer a salary that was more than double what Amanda was currently making. "Of course, you'll have a very generous expense account. Since image is important in advertising, all upper-level employees travel first class."

"It sounds tempting," Amanda admitted. She thought about what her father would say when she called him with the news.

"Believe me, you'll earn every penny."

"If I decide not to accept—"

"The job of creative director for the Northwest region is still yours."

"How much time do I have?"

"The partners would like your answer by the end of next week. Sooner if possible."

With that, Kelli flashed another self-assured grin and turned to leave. She was in the doorway when she looked back. "I'd appreciate you not saying anything about this to Greg."

"Of course not," Amanda murmured, still a bit stunned by the out-of-the-blue offer. It was more than she'd dared hope for. More than she'd dreamed of. So why wasn't she ecstatic?

Chapter 12

The rock cliffs towered above the beach, looking cold and gray and forbidding.

"Who'll take care of my kids when I die?" Laura asked, her lack of enthusiasm obvious.

"No one's going to die," Dane assured her.

"This isn't fair to the women," Nadine complained. "I've seen rock climbers on the Discovery channel, and they're mostly all men."

"It's true that some climbing—like overhangs—requires strength in the shoulders and arms. But the fact that women aren't usually as strong in those areas isn't as important as you'd think," Dane said. "Since women tend to be smaller than men, they don't need as much strength. In fact, on the average, smaller people have a better strength-to-weight ratio, which is what's important in climbing."

"That's easy for you to say," Nadine muttered, casting a disparaging glance at Dane's muscular arms.

"It's true. Climbing is done primarily with the legs and feet because they're stronger. You can stand for hours at a time on your feet, but even the strongest man can only hang from his arms for a few minutes. The most essential element of climbing is balance."

While the group eyed the cliff with overt suspicion, Dane explained the basics of rock climbing. "One of the most important things to remember," he told the team members, "is that although the tendency is to look up for handholds, you should keep your hands below your shoulders and look down for footholds.

"Balance climbing, which is what you'll be doing, is like climbing stairs, although today you'll be climbing more sideways than vertically. You find a place for your foot, settle into a rest step, then make a shift of your hips and move on to the next step, always striving to keep your body poised over one foot.

"You can pause, or rest supported by both feet. You can also lift your body up with both legs, but never advance a foot to the next hold until you're in balance over the resting foot."

"What about ropes?" Laura, still unconvinced, asked.

"There's an old adage—'It's not the fall that hurts, it's the sudden stop.' If a rope stops a fall too fast, you can end up with a broken body. Or, a rope can pull loose and let you continue to fall. So, although you'll be equipped with a rope harness, since there are plenty of ledges and handholds, you shouldn't need to use the rope on this climb."

"We're not going to rappel?" Luke asked.

"Not today." Dane's assurance drew murmurs of relief.

After more explanation of terms and techniques, Dane climbed up the side of the cliff to set the woven climbing rope while the others watched.

"He makes it look so easy," Laura said.

"Kobe Bryant makes hoops look easy, too," Luke added. "But I wouldn't be stupid enough to play one-on-one with the guy."

"It's tricky," Kelli allowed. "But this cliff is only a grade one."

"What does that mean?" Julian asked. "And how do you know so much about it?"

"I've been climbing since my teens," she answered the second question first. "As for the rating, climbs are divided into grades from one to six. A grade one, like this one, will only have one to two pitches. A grade six, like some of the routes on El Capitan, can have more than thirty pitches."

"Terrific," Julian muttered. "The red team's brought in a ringer."

"I've already decided to take myself off the team," Kelli revealed, as Dane came back down the rocks with a deft skill that Amanda admired, even as her heart leaped to her throat.

"That's not necessary," Marvin said. "I've been climbing since college. And while I haven't done El Capitan, I think I can do my bit for the blue team."

With the competitive balance restored, the final challenge event began. To everyone's surprise, the climb went amazingly well. Even Laura, who'd sworn that she wouldn't be able to get past the first rest stop, managed to make her way to the top, then back down again.

The final participant was Julian, who was making record time when, eager to reach the top of the cliff, he leaned too far into the slope, pushing his feet outward, causing him to slip. Sensing he was about to slide, he grabbed for a handhold, causing a small avalanche of pebbles.

Everyone watching from below breathed a united sigh of relief as the rope looped around his waist held.

"There's a ledge six inches to the left of you," Dane called out. "Just stay calm. You can reach it with no trouble."

Dangling against the cliff, Julian managed to edge his left foot sideways until it was safely on the ledge.

"That's it," Dane said encouragingly. "Now, put the heel of your right foot on that outcropping just below where it is now."

Although he was trembling visibly, Julian did as instructed.

"It's going to be okay," Dane assured Amanda and the others. "He's not in any danger." He lifted his cupped hands again. "Now, all you have to do is come back down the way you went up and you're home free."

Later, Amanda would decide that the next moment was when Julian made his mistake. He looked down, viewed the gathered team members far below, realized exactly how close he'd come to falling—and literally froze.

Dane was the first to realize what had happened. He cursed.

"I'd better go bring him down."

"No," Marvin said. "He's my teammate. I can talk him the rest of the way up."

"It's just a game," Amanda protested. "Winning isn't worth risking anyone's life."

"I know that." Marvin gently pried her fingers off his arm. "But there's more at risk than winning, Amanda. Julian will never forgive himself if he gives up now."

That said, he repeated the ascent path he'd worked out the first time he'd scaled the cliff. Within minutes he was perched on a rock horn beside the art director and although it wasn't possible to hear what they were saying, it was obvious the two men were engaged in serious conversation.

When Julian looked down again, Amanda drew in a sharp breath, afraid that he'd panic and lose his balance again. But instead, he turned his attention back to the rock wall and began slowly but surely moving upward, with Marvin right behind him, offering words of encouragement and pointing out possible paths.

When Julian reached the top of the cliff, cheers rang out from the team members below.

"Talk about teamwork," Kelli murmured to Amanda. "You've definitely pulled it off, Amanda. I hope you're seriously considering the partners' offer."

"How could I not?" Amanda answered.

As Julian and Marvin made their way back down the cliff, Dane came over to stand beside Amanda. "I couldn't help overhearing Kelli. Congratulations. You'll be great."

She looked up at him with confusion. "You know?"

It was Dane's turn to be confused. "Know what? I assumed you'd been offered Parsons's job."

"I was." She glanced around, not wanting the others to hear. "But it's turned out to be a bit more complicated."

She didn't want to discuss the amazing offer with Dane until they were alone and she could attempt to discern how he felt about her possibly moving to New York.

If he asked her to stay, she would. Already having missed one opportunity with this man, she was not about to blow another.

Something was wrong. Dane felt it deep in his gut. He was going to lose her again.

The ride back to the inn was a boisterous one. Although the blue team had won the week's event on points, even their opponents were fired up by Julian and Marvin's cooperative team effort. By the time the van pulled into the parking lot of the inn, everyone had decided to go into Satan's Cove to celebrate having ended the week on such a high note.

"Are you sure you don't want to come with us?" Kelli asked an hour later, after the trophies had been handed out.

"It's been a long day," Amanda demurred. "I have a lot to think about. I think I'll just stay here."

"If you're sure."

"I'm sure."

Kelli glanced at Dane, who'd come into the room during the awards ceremony, then back at Amanda. "It's a fabulous offer, Amanda."

"I know."

"But then again, men like Dane Cutter don't come into a girl's life every day."

"I know that, too." She'd had two chances with Dane. How many more would she be lucky enough to be given?

"Well, I don't envy you your choice, but good luck." Kelli left the room to join the others, who were gathering in the reception foyer for their trip to town.

Unbearably nervous, Amanda stood rooted to the spot as Dane walked toward her.

"Your hands are cold," he said as he took both of them in his.

"It's the weather." Rain streaked down the windows, echoing her mood. "It'll be good when you get the new furnace installed."

"Yes." It wasn't the chill outside that had turned her fingers to ice, but a nervousness inside, Dane decided.

"Would you like to talk about it?" he asked quietly.

Amanda swallowed past the lump in her throat. "Actually," she said, her voice little more than a whisper, "I would. But first I'd like to make love with you."

Dane needed no second invitation.

Alone in the tower room, Dane and Amanda undressed each other slowly, drawing out this suspended time together with slow hands and tender touches.

The candles she'd lit when they'd first entered the room burned low as they moved together, flowing so effortlessly across the bed, they could have been making love in an enchanted world beneath the sea.

Whispered words of love mingled with the sound of rain falling on the slate roof; soft caresses grew more urgent, then turned gentle again as they moved from patience to urgency, returning to tenderness, before continuing on to madness. All night long.

The candles stuttered out. The rain stopped, the moon began to set. And despite their unspoken efforts to stop time, morning dawned. Gray and gloomy.

Amanda lay in Dane's arms, feeling more loved than she'd ever felt in her life. And more miserable.

"Are you ready to talk about it?" he asked quietly.

As his thumb brushed away the errant tear trailing down her cheek, she squeezed her eyes tight and helplessly shook her head.

"We have to, Amanda." His voice was as calm and self-controlled as it had been ten years ago, making her feel like a foolish, lovestruck fifteen-year-old all over again. "We can't put it off any longer."

"I know."

With a long sigh, she hitched herself up in bed. Dane wondered if she realized how beautiful she was, with her face, flushed from making love, framed by that tousled dark gold cloud of hair. Her eyes were wide and laced with more pain than a woman who'd spent the night making mad, passionate love should be feeling. She dragged her hand through her hair. "I don't know where to start."

He sat up as well and put his arm around her shoulder. "How about at the beginning?"

This wasn't going to be good. Dane's mind whirled with possibilities, trying to get ahead of the conversation so he could supply an argument to any reason she might try to give for leaving.

"Kelli *is* a company spy. But not for Greg."

"She works for the home office." All the pieces of the puzzle that had been nagging at him finally fell into place.

"Yes."

"When did you find out?"

"Right before the rock climb. She told me Greg was going to be fired. And that his job was mine, if I wanted it."

"Which you do." Dane decided there were worse things than commuter marriages. Portland wasn't that far away, and if her job made her happy…

"I thought I did." Her fingers, plucking at the sheets, revealed her nervousness. Dane waited.

"She offered me another position."

"Oh?" His heart pounded hard and painfully in his chest. "In Portland?"

Her words clogged her throat. Amanda could only shake her head.

"The job's in Manhattan," Dane guessed flatly.

"Yes." She shook her head again. "No."

"Which is it? Yes? Or no?" An impatience he'd tried to control made his tone gruff.

"My office would be in Manhattan. But I'd be traveling most of the time. In an ombudsman position."

It made sense. Having watched her in action, Dane knew she'd be a natural. And Lord knows, if the lack of morale the employees of the former C.C.C. agency had displayed when they'd first arrived at Smugglers' Inn was indicative of that of the international firm's other acquisitions, they were in desperate need of an effective ombudsman.

"That's quite an offer."

"Yes." Her voice lacked the enthusiasm he would have expected. "I think I could be good at it."

"I know you'd be great." It was, unfortunately, the absolute truth.

"And the salary and benefits are generous."

When she related them to Dane, he whistled. "That would definitely put you in the big leagues." Which was where her father had always intended her to be.

"I've dreamed of ending up on Madison Avenue, of course," Amanda admitted. "But I never thought my chance would come this soon. My parents would probably be proud of me," she murmured, echoing his thoughts.

"They'd undoubtedly be proud of you whatever you did." It wasn't exactly the truth. But it should be.

Her crooked, wobbly smile revealed they were thinking the same thing.

"When do you have to give the partners your answer?"

"By the end of next week." *Tell me not to go,* she begged him silently.

Dane wanted to tell her to turn the offer down. He wanted to insist she stay here, with him, to make a home during the day and babies at night, as they'd planned so many years ago.

But, just as he'd had to do what was right for him, Dane knew that Amanda could do no less for herself.

"It's a terrific opportunity," he forced himself to say now. "I'm sure you'll make the right choice."

Because he feared he was going to cry, Dane drew her back into his arms, covered her mouth with his, and took her one last time with a power and a glory that left them both breathless.

Not wanting to watch Amanda walk out of his life for a second time, later that morning Dane went down to the beach, seeking peace.

In the distance, he heard the bus taking the corporate team—and Amanda—away.

He knew that Eve Deveraux would be happy to give him a job at the Park Avenue Whitfield Palace. But, although it would allow him to be with Amanda, Dane was honest enough with himself to admit that there was no way he could return to the rat race of the city.

During his last years at Whitfield, he'd become driven and impatient. He hadn't liked that hard-edged individual, his mother definitely hadn't, and he knew damn well that Amanda wouldn't, either. Which made his choice to go to Manhattan no choice at all.

He saw the words written in the sand from the top of the cliff, but the mist kept him from being able to read them.

As he climbed down the stone steps, the words became clearer.

Amanda loves Dane.

"I love you." The soft, familiar voice echoed her written words. Dane turned and saw Amanda standing there, looking like his every dream come true.

"We found something together the other night in the cave, Dane. Something that's far more valuable to me than any alleged pirate's treasure. I want to stay. Here, in Satan's Cove with you." Her heart was shining in her eyes. "If you'll have me."

As much as he wanted to shout out *Yes!*, Dane knew they'd never be happy if she felt her decision was a sacrifice.

"What about New York?"

"It's a great place to visit."

"But you wouldn't want to live there."

"Not on a bet."

He felt a rush of relieved breath leave his lungs. "What about the job of creative director?"

"You're not going to make this easy for me, are you?" she asked with a soft smile.

"I don't think a decision this important *should* be easy."

"True." She sighed, not having wanted to get into the logistics of her decision right now. "The problem is, if I move into Greg's job, I'd still be working for a huge agency. Which wasn't why I got into advertising in the first place.

"After you left the room this morning, I had some visitors. Marvin, Julian, and Luke. They've been as unhappy as I have with the profit craze that's taken over the industry lately. They also decided Satan's Cove was a perfect place to open a shop.

"They've arranged to lease the offices above the crystal store and asked me to join them." Her smile was beatific, reminding Dane of how she looked after they'd made love.

"As much as I love the idea of you staying here, with me," Dane said, "I have to point out there aren't many prospective accounts in Satan's Cove, sweetheart."

"They've already contacted former clients who are unhappy with the way things have been going, and want to sign on. A lot of our business can be done by phone and email, with the occasional trip into the city.... And speaking of local clients, I thought you might consider redoing your brochure."

"What's wrong with my brochure?"

"It's lovely. But it could use some fine-tuning. Why don't I give you a private presentation later?" She'd also come up with a nifty idea for Davey Jones's Locker she intended to run by Iris.

Putting advertising aside for now, Amanda twined her arms around Dane's neck and pressed her smiling lips to his.

As they sealed the deal with a kiss, the last of the fog burned off.

Amanda loves Dane.

The brilliant sun turned the love letter she'd written in the sand to a gleaming gold nearly as bright as Dane and Amanda's future.

* * * * *

Michelle Major grew up in Ohio but dreamed of living in the mountains. Soon after graduating with a degree in journalism, she pointed her car west and settled in Colorado. Her life and house are filled with one great husband, two beautiful kids, a few furry pets and several well-behaved reptiles. She's grateful to have found her passion writing stories with happy endings. Michelle loves to hear from her readers at michellemajor.com.

Books by Michelle Major

Harlequin Special Edition

Maggie & Griffin
Falling for the Wrong Brother
Second Chance in Stonecreek
A Stonecreek Christmas Reunion

Crimson, Colorado
Anything for His Baby
A Baby and a Betrothal
Always the Best Man
Christmas on Crimson Mountain
Romancing the Wallflower
Sleigh Bells in Crimson
Coming Home to Crimson

The Fortunes of Texas: Rambling Rose
Fortune's Fresh Start

The Fortunes of Texas: The Secret Fortunes
A Fortune in Waiting

Visit the Author Profile page at
Harlequin.com for more titles.

ROMANCING THE WALLFLOWER

Michelle Major

To all my favorite Broadmoor Elementary teachers.
Thanks for everything you do for our kids.

Chapter 1

"Stop staring at the hottie brewmaster's butt."

Erin MacDonald choked on the gulp of strawberry daiquiri she'd just swallowed. "I'm not staring at anyone's butt," she said as she grabbed a wad of napkins and dabbed at her chin and shirtfront. "And don't talk so loud."

Melody Cross, one of the second-grade teachers at Crimson Elementary, snorted. "It's a crowded bar on a busy Thursday night. No one can hear me."

But Melody had the kind of booming voice that could quiet a room full of squirming eight-year-olds the afternoon before summer break. The tall table they stood at was a good five feet from the bar, but Erin swore she saw the man's broad shoulders stiffen.

"Want me to take a picture of him?" Suzie Vitale, her fellow kindergarten teacher, offered with a tipsy smile. "It lasts longer."

Before Erin could stop her, the curvy blonde aimed her phone at the backside of the gorgeous guy who not only worked the bar but also owned Elevation Brewery. The brewpub had opened a little over a year ago and had become a popular hangout for both locals and tourists in the quaint mountain town of Crimson, Colorado.

Erin had noticed David McCay, the brewery's owner, the first time she'd stepped into the nouveau rustic— and very on-trend for Colorado—space. He was tall and lean, with dark blond hair that curled around the collars of the flannel shirts he favored. David McCay was as handsome as a movie star and built like he spent endless hours tossing huge sacks of barley—or whatever it was beer brewers did.

Erin, who was built like she spent her days sitting cross-legged on a reading rug, had surreptitiously watched him each time she came into the bar with friends or coworkers for a random happy hour or birthday celebration. He was often tending bar or sometimes she'd spot him coming out from the back, wearing the heavy rubber boots and backward ball cap that she'd quickly learned were his uniform when actually brewing beer.

Colorado was known for its craft brews, and the fact that Elevation had made a name for itself so quickly was a testament to his hard work and talent at running a business.

At least that's what Erin wanted to believe. Her mother liked to remind Erin that she too often assumed the best about people, which allowed them to regularly take advantage of her.

But David McCay hadn't taken advantage of her, even though it was the stuff of her fantasies. Even though his nephew, Rhett, was now in her kindergarten class and David had been with the boy and his mother for back-to-school night. Erin had barely been able to put a sentence together with David towering over the other adults in the back of her classroom, but he hadn't bothered to acknowledge her. Heck, it was doubtful he even knew she existed.

Except when she blinked and looked up, he was staring straight at her. Sparks of awareness flamed through her body, setting every inch of her skin on fire. He lifted one thick brow as if he could read her thoughts. Which might be impossible since it felt like all of her brain cells had spontaneously combusted under the weight of his stare.

She heard Melody giggle behind her, and Suzie gave her a little shove forward. David now stood at the edge of the bar, only a short distance from her, with movement all around him. Customers in groups laughed and talked. A waitress set her tray on the rich wood bar top. A group of women near the edge of the bar vied for his attention. But his focus remained on Erin.

Then something—someone—suddenly blocked her vision. Cole Bennett, Crimson's recently elected sheriff, was talking to David. Cole was also tall and broad, and to use one of her mom's favorite expressions, made a better door than a window.

Erin shifted to the right as she overheard Cole mention Rhett, David's nephew. David's gaze hardened and his jaw clenched. Unable to stop herself, she moved forward, sidestepping a couple heading toward the back of the bar and a group of twentysomething guys who looked like they'd just come off a hiking trail, until she stood directly behind the sheriff.

She was five feet four inches tall in the clogs she favored for work, so both men towered over her and were completely unaware she was listening to their conversation. Invisibility was Erin's unintentional superpower. She knew much more than she should about her coworkers and neighbors, simply because people didn't notice she was there.

"Rhett is safe," Cole told David. "But they can't get him to come out."

"What the hell was Jenna thinking?" David asked, then scrubbed a hand over his jaw. "No, don't answer that."

"She's in trouble, David. The crowd she's running with—"

"I'll handle it." He pulled a set of keys out of one of the pockets in his tan cargo pants. "I just need to tell Tracie I'm leaving for the night. I'll be over for Rhett."

"I have to call Social Services," Cole said softly, and Erin felt the tension ratchet up a notch.

"Give me some time with him first, okay?"

"Can you—"

"I'll handle it," David repeated. He moved behind the bar and spoke to the woman filling two pint glasses from the tap.

The sheriff walked out of the bar, patrons instinctively clearing a path for him although he wasn't in uniform tonight.

When she looked up, David McCay stood toe-to-toe with her. She realized she'd moved forward to block his path from behind the bar.

In her daydreams, she'd compared his eyes to the brilliant summer sky above the ragged peak of Crimson Mountain or the iridescent cobalt of a tropical lagoon.

But now his frosty stare was more like the ice blue of a glacier, so cold a shiver passed through her.

"I don't have time for this, sweetheart. You and your friends are going to have to play your liquid courage bar games with someone else."

"It's not a game," Erin said.

"Darlin', you ordered a froofy drink in my bar. It's either a game or a joke."

This close to David, the heat and frustration radiating off him made her feel different from the woman she knew herself to be. She was aware of her body in a way that was new and exhilarating. She wanted more. She wanted…something she couldn't name. Still, the promise of it made her weak with longing.

Also braver than she'd ever been. Or maybe *crazy* was a better word, because when he moved to step around her, she placed a hand on his arm.

"I can help with your nephew."

His sleeves were rolled up to the elbow. His skin burned hers, and the rough hair on his forearm tickled her fingers. A current passed through him, the force jolting Erin like she'd been struck by lightning. He stilled and the power it took to rein in all the things she imagined he was feeling right now made an answering strength bubble up inside her.

"Let me help, David." It was the first time she'd spoken his name out loud. To her friends, he was simply "the hottie brewmaster."

"You're drunk," he said, his gaze focused on where her fingers wrapped around his arm.

"No. I only had one drink. I'm fine now. Promise." She lifted her hand. "Rhett is in my class," she said, in case this enormous, angry man truly had no idea who she was.

"I know." One side of his mouth almost quirked. "I came to back-to-school night."

So she wasn't quite invisible to David McCay. A little thrill tickled down her spine. "I've connected with him. He responds to me."

David's cool blue gaze met hers again, and he gave a brief nod. "Let's go then."

Erin swallowed. This was really happening. "I just need to tell my friends I'm leaving."

"My truck is out front," he said, his voice a low rumble. Then he turned and walked away. Erin had the distinct impression if she didn't get her butt in gear, he'd readily leave her behind.

No chance she was letting that happen.

"I've got to go," she said as she rushed to where Melody and Suzie stood gawking. She grabbed her purse from the tabletop.

"With the hottie brewmaster?" Melody asked, her voice a high squeak.

Suzie pumped a fist. "No beating around the bush tonight."

"It's not like that." Erin glanced over her shoulder but David was already out the door. "I can't explain now. I'll see you at school tomorrow."

Before her friends could respond, she hurried toward the brewpub's entrance. The young, flawlessly mountain-chic brunette at the hostess stand gave her the once-over and arched a brow, wordlessly communicating that a woman like Erin had no business following David McCay out into the night.

Normally Erin would agree, but this was more than

her hidden crush on the man. It was about helping a troubled five-year-old boy. Erin's students were family to her, and she took her responsibility to heart. She had a Spidey sense for the ones who needed a little extra; whether it was the child or their family circumstances, Erin made it her mission to connect with every student in her care.

From the moment Rhett McCay had slunk into her classroom clutching his beautiful mother's arm, Erin's radar had been on high alert. Jenna McCay clearly loved her son, yet the woman seemed high-strung and flighty. Erin had the impression Rhett's home life was anything but stable.

She might not have the guts to talk to David on her own, but she was fearless when it came to one of her kids.

A huge black Chevy truck idled near the curb, and she knew David was behind the wheel. Not that she was a stalker or anything, but Crimson was a small town and she'd seen him drop off and pick up Rhett at school several times.

"I'm fearless," she whispered to herself when her legs wanted to stop on the sidewalk. It was late September and the evening air was crisp, the changing season scenting the breeze.

If Erin were an ice cream flavor, she would be straight-up vanilla. Everything about her life was ordinary, ordered and infinitely normal. Somehow she knew getting into David's truck was going to add a whole slew of strange toppings to the mix. She might long for adventure, but this wasn't what she had in mind.

She conjured up Rhett's sweet face, with his shaggy blond bowl cut and mischievous blue eyes. With a calming breath she moved forward, opened the passenger-side door and climbed in.

"You ready?" David asked in that deep, hot-caramel-syrup voice of his.

Absolutely not, Erin thought.

"I'm ready," she answered.

David was going to kill his little sister, if she didn't manage the task on her own first.

He concentrated on navigating the route from the bar to Jenna's small apartment complex on the outskirts of Crimson as fast as he could without breaking any laws. He took slow breaths in and out to calm himself. Of course any thoughts of doing her harm were a joke, although she seemed hell-bent on getting into as much trouble as she could find.

Which had been one thing when they were teenagers, but Jenna had Rhett now. The constant stream of dead-end jobs, loser boyfriends and wild partying wasn't only hurting her. The thought that Rhett would end up somehow irreparably scarred kept David up more nights than he cared to admit.

He'd moved to Crimson from Pittsburgh almost two years ago to watch out for them. But between the hours he'd put in opening the brewery and Jenna's resentment over what she saw as his attempts to control her life, he hadn't spent nearly as much time with them as he wanted.

His greatest fear was that he would fail his nephew the same way he'd failed Jenna.

"I'm guessing you and your sister are pretty close?"

David blinked and glanced at the woman sitting next to him in the truck's cab. Lost in his own thoughts, he'd almost forgotten about his uninvited passenger. What the hell had possessed him to allow Rhett's kindergarten teacher to come along on this mission anyway?

David was a master at keeping everyone in his life at arm's length, even Jenna and Rhett. How had this tiny woman with the thick ponytail the color of maple syrup and big eyes to match managed to slip through his defenses?

"We're Irish twins," he offered as an answer. "Ten months apart."

"That must have been fun growing up," she said, her voice gentle. The exact kind of voice that could lull a classroom of restless kids into sitting in a quiet circle to learn. Most kids anyway. He still had trouble believing Rhett could calm his squirmy body enough to sit still.

"Not for our mom."

She gave a small laugh. "If Rhett takes after the two of you, your mother had her hands full."

"Yeah," he agreed, and felt the knot in his chest loosen slightly at the affection in her voice. David had no problem with his nephew's rambunctious personality, but he was normally in the minority.

He didn't say anything more, and Erin didn't speak for a few minutes. David liked quiet, but other than Tracie at the bar, most women he knew couldn't tolerate it. The silence that filled his truck now was strangely comforting, like an extra blanket thrown over the bed on a cold winter night. Like all good things, it didn't last.

"What happened tonight? Is your sister in trouble? Is Rhett okay?"

David sighed. He knew the questions were coming, and he owed the soft-spoken teacher an explanation before they reached the apartment. "How much did you overhear from Cole?"

"No details. Just that there was a problem and Rhett wasn't cooperating."

"He's hiding," he said, trying in vain to stop the anger and frustration from trickling into his voice. He could feel it seeping through his pores, making his blood run hot and raging. "Apparently he's wedged under the kitchen sink. Jenna had a party, and things got out of hand. The cops busted it up and found drugs."

Erin gave a sharp intake of breath, rousing his temper even further, like a backdraft making a fire blaze out of control. "Jenna loves that boy with all her heart, but she's in a bad way. It's why I moved to Crimson in the first place."

"To help your sister?"

To save her, he wanted to answer, but he only nodded. David knew his limitations better than anyone, and he was nobody's hero.

"She's been clean for almost two years," he said without emotion. "It's been tough, but I thought she had her demons under control. Cole took everyone to the station. They didn't realize Rhett was there until the place was empty and he made a noise. The deputies tried to get him out, but he freaked and scratched one of the officers. I know Cole so he called me before the social worker."

He bit the inside of his cheek and waited for the recrimination he deserved. He should have seen the signs that Jenna was teetering on the edge. He knew her better than anyone. Why the hell couldn't he keep her safe?

He pulled into the parking lot of the shabby apartment complex. There were two buildings, both with faded siding and balconies that looked like they wouldn't hold the weight of a litter of kittens. He'd begged Jenna to let him help her move to a better place, but his sister was stubborn and resented any time he tried to "take control" of her life.

"We'll make sure he's safe," Erin said as he turned off the truck's engine.

Safe. The word had haunted him—and tainted every relationship in his life—for over a decade. Now this too-sweet-for-her-own-good woman offered it to his nephew like she had that kind of power. Damn if David didn't want to believe it was true.

He shifted to face her, the dim light of the parking lot illuminating her face so that her creamy skin looked like something out of a dream. Unable to resist, he ran the pad of his thumb over the ridge of her cheekbone, marveling at how soft her skin felt.

The inherent goodness radiating from her drew him in at the same time he knew he should push her away. Someone like Erin MacDonald had no business knowing the ugly details of his sister's struggles. She was Rhett's teacher and nothing more. But he couldn't let her go quite yet. Tonight she was his talisman. He had to believe having her close would keep the darkness always skirting the edges of his life at bay.

He dropped his hand and they got out of the truck and started toward Jenna's apartment. Toward the little boy David was determined to keep safe, by any means necessary.

Chapter 2

"Come on, buddy. You've got to come out."

The muscles bunched in David's broad shoulders as he shifted his weight to one arm and leaned closer, reaching into the open cabinet under the kitchen sink.

A high-pitched scream split the air and several bottles of household cleaners tumbled out onto the scuffed linoleum floor.

David sat back on his knees with a muttered curse. "He bit me," he said, examining the back of his hand where a semicircle of angry red teeth marks was clearly visible.

"Same thing happened to me," Cole Bennett whispered. Cole had been waiting at Jenna McCay's cramped apartment, clearing out the other officers when David and Erin arrived. "I didn't want to force him out because I was worried he'd get hurt banging his head on the pipes if he struggled."

The two men, both so strong, looked absolutely baffled at how to lure the young boy from his hiding spot. Erin glanced around the apartment and suppressed a shudder. On every surface, abandoned beer bottles and red plastic cups competed for space with fast-food wrappers and empty chip bags. It looked like a college fraternity house the morning after a huge party. The colorful drawings stuck to the front of the refrigerator were the only hint that a kindergartner lived here.

One of the crayoned pieces of art gave Erin an idea. She moved toward the narrow hallway, stepping over trash until she got to a half-open bedroom door. The space was neat and clean, untouched by the mess in the rest of the apartment. Toys lined one wall and the small bed was covered with a football-themed comforter. She grabbed the stuffed blue dog sitting on top of the pillow and hurried back to the kitchen.

David was once again on all fours in front of the cabinet, speaking so softly she couldn't make out his words, only the rough yet surprisingly gentle timbre of his voice.

She crouched low next to him and tilted her head until she could see Rhett's eyes, wide and still terrified. "Rhett," she said, "It's Ms. MacDonald. I found your stuffed dog and wanted to let you know he's okay."

A faint whimper came from the cabinet. "Ruffie," the boy whispered.

"Ruffie is safe," Erin said, using the same tone she would when soothing a child scared of letting go of his mother's leg on the first day of school. "You're safe, too. Your uncle David is going to take care of you. But we need you to come out now."

The boy wedged himself farther into the corner, as

if he could make himself invisible. God, Erin did *not* want this child to feel like he needed to be invisible. David's large hand settled on the small of her back, and the steady pressure and warmth of his skin were more of a comfort than she would have guessed.

"Ruffie needs you." She placed the small dog in front of her, just on the edge of the cabinet. "He's scared and needs a hug. Can you do that for him?"

She held her breath for what felt like an eternity, then released it as the boy slowly unfolded his body and climbed out. Her fingers remained wrapped around the stuffed animal's back leg to make sure Rhett wouldn't try to grab it and retreat again.

Once he was in the light, she could see the smudge of dirt on his chin and the tearstains on his ruddy cheeks. Her heart broke for what this young boy had already seen in his life. David made a sound low in his throat and scooped up his nephew and the raggedy blue dog. It was as if a dam broke in Rhett and his whole body began to shake as he burrowed into David's embrace.

She straightened and stepped away, closer to the sheriff. Somehow it felt wrong to bear witness to the moment between David and Rhett, both tender and raw. It was obvious David was trying to keep his emotions hidden, but pain and guilt were bright on his handsome features, like a stoplight in the dark.

"Nice work," Cole Bennett said and put a hand on her elbow to lead her to the apartment door. "You're like a kindergartner whisperer." She started to turn but stopped at the sound of David's voice.

"Stay."

One word, but the intensity of it rocked her to her core. She glanced up at Cole, who arched a brow.

"I'll stay," she told him.

He nodded. "Someone from Social Services will be here soon. I can let them in. They'll want to talk to David and the boy."

"We'll be ready," she said with more confidence than she felt.

She turned back and followed David to the couch, quickly cleaning off the coffee table and dumping everything into the trash before lowering herself next to him.

Rhett still clung to him, chubby fingers holding fistfuls of flannel shirt in a death grip. "Where's Mommy?" he asked in a tiny voice.

"She's..." David paused and his gaze slammed into hers. The pain in his eyes made her want to wrap her arms around both him and Rhett and make this whole night go away. "She's safe. Sheriff Bennett is taking care of her."

Erin wondered exactly how Jenna McCay was being cared for, and she hoped that whatever was happening Jenna was coherent enough to feel horrible about the situation she'd created for her son.

"It was loud," Rhett said. "Mommy's friends woke me up. I came out to tell her, but there were so many grown-ups and I couldn't find her. Then everyone started yelling and I got scared and hid under the sink."

"That was real smart of you," David told the boy, his hand smoothing Rhett's sleep-tousled hair.

After a moment Rhett tipped up his head to look at David. "When is Mommy coming home?"

"I'm not sure, buddy. But I'll stay with you until she does, okay?"

Rhett chewed on his bottom lip for a few seconds, then nodded. After a knock at the door, Cole let in a gray-haired woman who appeared to be in her midfifties. She wore a plain white button-down shirt and dark pants and looked about as no-nonsense as they came.

The woman spoke to Cole in hushed tones for a few minutes, then they both approached.

"This is Becky Cramer from the county Human Services department," Cole said.

Becky gave David a small nod, then bent to look at Rhett. "You've had quite a night," she said gently.

"It was loud," Rhett said, turning in David's lap but not releasing his shirtfront.

"I'm David McCay." David offered the woman his hand. "Rhett's uncle. He'll stay with me while we sort out things with Jenna."

Becky shook his hand, then glanced at Erin.

"I'm Rhett's kindergarten teacher, Erin MacDonald." She saw a flash of surprise pass over Becky's sharp features.

Right. How was she supposed to explain why she'd ended up on the couch with David and Rhett, caught up in the middle of family drama that had started long past regular school hours?

"Erin is a friend of mine," David answered. Becky seemed to have no issue with that response, whereas Erin had trouble keeping her jaw from hitting the floor. Friends with David McCay? In what lifetime?

Men like David didn't have boring kindergarten teachers as friends. Before he came to Crimson, he'd been a major-league baseball pitcher. He must be used to drop-dead gorgeous women who were exciting and sexy.

Erin knew she was boring. And ordinary. Not at all David's type. She'd had a boyfriend last year—an accountant at a firm in town. He was quiet, average and exactly her type. Greg had broken up with her to date someone who was better than average, but that didn't mean Erin could change the person she was on the inside. No matter how much she wanted to try.

David had been her unrequited crush since the moment she'd first seen him. It was a harmless fantasy with no chance of rejection. Never had she expected to get to know him, let alone be part of his life in this kind of personal way.

Her mind drifted to that moment in the car when he'd traced his thumb over her cheekbone. The simple touch had sent shock waves rippling through her and ignited a kind of flash-point desire Erin hadn't realized she was capable of feeling.

"It's important the school and the family work together," Becky said, bringing Erin back to the current conversation with a jolt, "to keep the boy's life as stable as possible during this time."

She looked at Rhett, who had fallen asleep in David's arms. "Let me put him to bed," she whispered, "while you two finish talking."

David relaxed his grip, allowing her to lift the boy into her arms. She made sure to take the stuffed dog, too. Rhett remained asleep as she tucked him back into bed, sighing when his head hit the pillow. Erin sat on the mattress for several minutes, rubbing the boy's back to make sure he didn't wake again. She couldn't imagine how scared he must have been earlier, unable to find his mother and with the wild party in full swing.

She made a silent vow. She *would* keep him safe, no matter how far out of her comfort zone—and tangled up with David McCay—that led her.

* * *

It was almost two in the morning before David let himself into the apartment, exhausted and emotionally drained. Erin had agreed to stay while he went to see Jenna. Cole was keeping her overnight on possession charges but had agreed to drop them if she entered a rehab program.

David had helped his sister get clean once before, and it was a rough road. She swore that tonight's tumble off the wagon was a onetime occurrence. David wanted to believe her, yet he'd heard so many excuses over the years. All he knew was he had to protect his nephew. There could be no repeats of what Rhett had gone through tonight.

It never should have happened in the first place, and he couldn't stop blaming himself.

The apartment was quiet when he entered, and he found Erin asleep on the couch, curled on her side as if she didn't want to take up too much space. It blew his mind that the buttoned-up schoolteacher had so willingly pitched in to help with his hot mess of a life. He understood that Rhett was her student. But David had never encountered a teacher like her.

Hell, he would have paid a lot more attention in school if he'd had someone like Erin MacDonald in his corner.

If possible, she looked more luminously beautiful asleep than she did awake. She was like a damn fairy-tale princess with her creamy skin, straight nose, rosy cheeks and the long, dark hair that fell over her face. It was easier to study her now than when those too-knowing bourbon-colored eyes were staring back at him.

He covered her with a blanket and went to check on Rhett. Unlike Erin, the boy was sprawled across the bed, arms and legs reaching out like a starfish. Jenna claimed she'd meant to have only her new boyfriend and a few of his buddies to the house to watch the Broncos play, but things had gotten out of hand. According to Cole, the boyfriend was serious bad news, having had more than a few run-ins with law enforcement over the years.

How the hell did Jenna manage to attract the biggest scumbags on the planet every time she found a new man? He would have asked her, wanted to rail and shout, but she'd looked so defeated sitting alone in the holding cell. She understood she'd messed up and he knew from experience that heaping on more condemnation would only put her on the defensive.

Fear and guilt had warred in his sister's pale blue eyes, along with the remnants of a long-ago pain that she could hide from most of the world, but not from him. She'd agreed to check into a treatment program, so finding a place for her would be the first thing on his to-do list after getting Rhett to school in a few hours.

He lowered himself into the recliner next to the couch. Erin had cleaned the messy apartment, another debt of thanks he owed her. David hated owing people anything, had learned the hard way to only depend on himself. Yet he couldn't help but be grateful for the chance to simply sit and rest for a few minutes.

His eyes drifted shut, although he didn't intend to fall asleep. The next thing he knew, someone was shaking him awake. He blinked and found himself staring into Erin's huge brown eyes.

"I have to go," she whispered. "I need to shower and change before school."

David blinked and tried to look more with-it than he felt. "What time is it?"

"Almost six in the morning." She moved away and he had the ridiculous urge to pull her down against him. These past few hours had been the soundest he'd slept in years. Something about having this woman close soothed the demons that waited for him in the dark.

"I'll give you a ride," he told her, rising from the chair. His lower back ached, and as he looked around the small apartment, reality came crashing over him like a tidal wave. Today was going to be awful. "I'll need to wake Rhett and—"

"One of my girlfriends is on her way." Erin shoved a thick lock of hair behind one ear. "Rhett needs all the sleep he can get. He's coming to school today, right?"

"Yes," David answered, mentally listing all the things he had to get done. "He needs a routine now more than ever."

"How's your sister?"

"She feels terrible and says she's committed to straightening out her life once and for all. I need to pick her up this morning and then make arrangements to get her to a treatment facility."

"So Rhett will be staying with you while she's in rehab?"

"Yes. Not here. I live in a loft above the brewery."

"How long is the program?"

He sighed. "A month. Rhett doesn't know she'll be gone. I'll tell him when he wakes up, but she won't leave until tomorrow afternoon. I want him to spend time with her—to know that she's okay."

"It could be traumatic," Erin said with a nod. "But we'll get him through."

He didn't want to admit how much her words reso-nated with him. When had he suddenly become afraid of dealing with things on his own? David prided himself on never being dependent on anyone, let alone a woman who'd been a stranger only twelve hours ago.

She worried her bottom lip between her teeth, a nervous habit he'd seen her do several times since they'd left the bar. That moment when he'd caught her staring at his ass felt like a lifetime ago.

He ran a finger across the seam of her lips. "You need to give that lip a break. It's too pretty to take so much abuse."

"Oh," she breathed, pink rushing into her cheeks. He wasn't sure what had surprised her more—his touch or the fact that he thought her mouth was pretty. Pretty and far too kissable to be good for either of them.

"I appreciate your help," he said, the words rusty and unfamiliar on his tongue. "I'm going to make sure Rhett has a stable home life, but having a teacher who understands what he's going through will be important."

She inclined her head to study him. After everything she'd witnessed and what she'd clearly inferred about the dysfunctional McCay family, it must seem odd for him to suddenly be speaking so formally.

"Of course." Her brows knit together, causing a small crease to appear on her forehead. He resisted the urge to smooth it away…barely. "I should go. Melody doesn't live far from here. She'll be waiting."

She moved across the small space, and he didn't say anything until the door to the apartment had almost closed.

"Erin."

She turned, one hand on the doorknob. "Yes?"

"I'd like to repay you for last night." The thought of

remaining in debt to her—to anyone—chafed his skin like an itch he couldn't quite reach.

"There's no need—"

"There *is* a need." The need pounding through him to claim her. He tried to convince himself the longing would be quenched if he could do a favor to repay her for—in large part—rescuing him last night. "I could make a donation to your class or host the school's Christmas party at the bar, free of charge. What do you want?"

She stared at him for several long moments, the air between them growing thick and hot. She cleared her throat and said clearly, "I'd like to have an affair with you."

Then she was gone, the door clicking shut behind her.

And David was left staring after her, wondering if the whole thing had been some kind of bizarre dream.

Chapter 3

"You asked him to hit the sheets?" Melody let out a hoot of laughter. "Who are you and what have you done with my friend Erin?"

Erin kept her palms pressed tight against her cheeks, willing her face to stop burning. "Oh my gosh," she repeated for the tenth time since she'd climbed in Melody's minivan and told her friend how she'd left things with David. "I'm nobody. I'm delusional. He's going to think I'm crazy. Maybe I *am* crazy."

"You're not crazy." Melody reached out and gently pulled Erin's hands away from her face. "But did you ever think of asking him out on a date?"

"Clearly I wasn't thinking at all." Erin shook her head. "And of course I didn't ask him for a date. David McCay would never go out with someone like me."

"Bargaining for sex seemed like a better idea?"

Erin groaned. "Oh my gosh."

"Why wouldn't he go out with you? You're cute. You're nice. You have decent teeth."

"Decent teeth? My best friend thinks one of my top three selling points is decent teeth? This is even worse than I thought."

Melody laughed softly. "Suzie and I saw the way he looked at you at the bar last night. It was kind of hot."

"The way he looks at a parking meter is hot. That's David. He's not for me. We both know he's not for me."

Her friend didn't deny it, and Erin wasn't sure whether to feel justified or hurt by the silent validation.

"Then why make your little request?"

Erin thought about how she'd felt with David watching her across the small apartment. The way she'd seemed to come alive when he'd placed his hand on the small of her back. The longing for something more in her life.

"He asked me what I wanted and my mouth formed the words before my brain could catch up. He *is* what I want. Not forever. Not for real. But the chance to be with him…"

Melody sighed. "Can you imagine?"

For Erin, fantasizing about David was akin to fangirling over a comic book superhero played by some hot Australian actor on the big screen—larger than life. He was so handsome he took her breath away, but was a whole galaxy out of her league.

He'd probably even look darn good in tights. Erin giggled at the thought, and the fact that she *had* asked him for an affair. What had she been thinking?

"I want to be seen," she said softly. "I'm tired of being invisible."

"We see you," Melody answered. "The kids see you."

"They see Ms. MacDonald. For a school year. Then we have kindergarten graduation and they move on. They grow up. They aren't *mine*." She took another breath. "It's the same reason I'm working with Olivia Travers at the community center on the Crimson Kidzone project."

"You're comparing starting an after-school program for at-risk kids to sleeping with the town hottie?"

"Yes." Erin shook her head. "No. I mean, not when you put it like that. But Kidzone will belong to me. I can make a lasting difference in this community."

"You do that already. That's what being a good teacher is all about. Elaina loves you."

"She's a great kid, but you know that already." Melody's daughter, Elaina, was in Erin's class this year and was the same mix of sweet and spunky as her mother.

"Takes after her dad," Melody said with a wink. Melody had two young kids and a husband who worked long hours as one of Cole Bennett's deputies to provide for his family.

She pulled to a stop at the curb in front of Erin's apartment building. Erin had lived in her apartment in the converted redbrick Victorian since she'd moved back to Crimson after college. All of her furniture was hand-me-downs from her mother. She had white walls and a shower that never got hot enough and it was all… adequate.

"I want to do more, Mel. I want to *be* more. Average has always been enough for me, but sometimes I want more than an ordinary life."

"David McCay sure isn't average."

Erin smiled. "It was a stupid request, and I'll have

to apologize. Or maybe he'll pretend it never happened and save us both a lot of embarrassment."

"Is that what you want?"

"It's what I *should* want. I didn't help him last night because I expected anything in return. Rhett's a special kid, but it's clear his life hasn't been easy. He definitely has some behavioral issues, but we were making progress in class. He was responding to me. I don't want him to slip through the cracks."

"Don't take it back, Erin. How many women like us get a chance with someone who looks like that?"

"Says the woman with a ridiculously handsome husband."

"I love Grant to distraction, but we're already a boring married couple. Let me live vicariously through you and your little adventure. I vaguely remember what it was like to be single and playing the field."

"You and Grant started dating when we were juniors in high school."

Melody rolled her eyes. "I said vaguely."

"I need to shower and get ready." Erin opened the car door, the morning breeze tickling the hair that had come loose from the ponytail she wore almost every day. "It's going to be a long one. I'm meeting Olivia at the community center after school to finalize the details on the outreach program."

Melody leaned over the console as Erin hopped out of the car. "At least reassure me that this business with your hottie brewer has nothing to do with the jerk exboyfriend."

"Nothing at all," Erin confirmed, and shut the door behind her, never revealing that the fingers of her other hand were tightly crossed behind her back.

* * *

Erin parked around the corner from the Crimson Community Center later that afternoon and kept her head down as she moved along the bustling sidewalk. Growing up, Crimson had been nothing more than a sleepy mountain town, always in the shadow of nearby Aspen, which felt to Erin like the more glamorous and showy older sister.

But in recent years, Crimson had come into its own, attracting new residents and an influx of visitors who appreciated the town's laid-back vibe and the myriad outdoor fun available in the mountains surrounding it.

Now the town was busy most weekends, even though the summer crowds had dispersed and they had a good two months before ski season kicked off.

She'd managed to avoid David at both drop-off and pickup today, although she'd pulled Rhett aside during reading groups after she'd watched the boy purposely knock a bin of markers to the floor, then blame the mess on Elaina Cross, who sat next to him. At first he'd refused to speak or even make eye contact when she'd brought him into the hallway. Eventually he blinked away tears and told her his mommy was going away to a place that would make her better and he had to stay with his uncle David.

Wrapping Rhett in a tight hug, Erin had reassured him that both his mother and his uncle loved him. She'd cautiously brought up the previous night and they'd talked a little about his fears and how important it was for him to feel safe.

While she couldn't avoid David forever, a little distance might work to Erin's advantage. A fierce war was raging between her brain, which wanted the whole embarrassing situation to disappear, and the rest of her body, which was singing the "Hallelujah" chorus at the mere thought that David might agree to her outrageous request.

Erin had been with one and a half men in her lifetime. Well, two men to be exact, but she only counted the first as a half because he'd gotten so drunk during their date that he'd fallen asleep kissing her. Talk about a blow to the ego, and her ego hadn't been much of a force in the first place. But the jerk ex-boyfriend Melody had referred to was the final nail in Erin's confidence coffin.

She and Greg Dellinger had dated for six months, and their relationship was fine. *Fine*. That should have been her clue to run away as fast as she could. She'd watched enough rom-coms to know that falling in love was supposed to be better than *fine*.

It had been Greg who'd broken up with her, blissfully explaining that he'd fallen in love with a woman who was beautiful, sexy and exciting. Tacitly implying that Erin was none of those things. Not a big shock, but it stung.

Maybe she owed Greg a thank-you, though, because it had been while reevaluating her life—halfway through a carton of Chunky Monkey—that Erin decided she wanted more.

Deserved more.

Changing up her love life was a daunting project, so she'd started her be-more-than-ordinary makeover by contacting Olivia Travers. Ever since she was a girl, Erin had wanted to be a teacher—to help kids learn but also give them a chance to discover all their potential and coax it out.

The same way she'd wished for someone in her life to notice her. With Crimson's ever-expanding population and changing demographics, she was afraid that the neediest kids in the community were getting overlooked. Lost in the shuffle or with families that didn't want the stigma of coming forward for assistance.

Olivia, who'd founded the community center two years ago, had the best of intentions but funding was often difficult to come by for free programming. Erin had outlined her plan for Crimson Kidzone, scheduled a meeting and pitched her idea, offering to volunteer her time to start the program and also work on grant writing to gain additional support.

Her friends at school had encouraged her, while her mom wondered why she'd want to spend more time with children than she already had to for her job. Maureen MacDonald was a quiet, keep-to-herself type of woman. She loved Erin and had done her best after Erin's father died of a sudden heart attack when she was in kindergarten. But Maureen dedicated more of her time to her psychology practice than she did to motherhood, and she and Erin had little other than genetics in common. Her mother was content to remain in her introverted bubble and that's how she'd raised her only daughter.

Erin was stepping out of that bubble, even if the encounter with David made her want to jump right back into it.

Her nerves disappeared as soon as she walked into the community center. Her personal life might be a hot mess, but she knew in her heart that the after-school project would be a success. She wouldn't settle for anything less.

Olivia was waiting at the reception desk for her, a chubby-cheeked baby cradled in her arms.

"I hope you don't mind an audience for our meeting," she said apologetically. "The babysitter called in sick."

"Any opportunity to get my dose of snuggles." Erin shifted her backpack so she could reach for baby Molly, who was the most scrumptious five-month-old she'd ever seen.

The little girl was a perfect mix of her mom and dad. She had eyes the same striking green as her mother's. But instead of Olivia's dark hair, she was a towheaded baby with wispy blond hair the same color as Logan Travers's, Molly's doting daddy. Erin wasn't part of the Traverses' wide social circle, but she'd seen the group of friends around town enough to know that Logan, while big and brawny on the outside, was absolute putty in his daughter's hands.

"You're a natural with kindergartners *and* babies," Olivia said as she transferred her daughter to Erin. Coming from Olivia, who was naturally beautiful and had the gentle spirit to match, Erin was grateful to receive the compliment. "Did you grow up in a big family?"

A little pang of disappointment passed through Erin as she shook her head and pressed a kiss to the baby's soft forehead. "I'm an only child, but I always thought it would be fun to have a big family. I love babies."

"You were meant to be a mother."

The other woman's words made something go soft and melty in Erin's heart. She wanted to be a mother, to have someone—or even better, multiple someones—to call her own. The thought of a baby with David McCay's big blue eyes made her chest flutter.

"I have a gut feeling," Olivia continued, "just like I did when you contacted me about the after-school program." She leaned in closer. "Any potential suitors or shall I put the word out? I've learned to trust my instincts."

"Praise the Lord for your instincts," a deep voice said, "or you never would have taken a chance on me." Erin glanced over her shoulder to see Olivia's husband, Logan, standing right behind her. And next to him… David McCay.

Molly let out a little squeak as Erin squeezed a bit too tightly. She rocked the baby and Molly immediately grinned and tugged on the ends of Erin's hair.

"That's right," Olivia said, leaning into her husband when he moved around Erin and draped an arm across her shoulders. "Can you blame me for wanting everyone to be as happy?"

"I'm happy," Erin whispered, even though it wasn't quite the truth. She could feel David's eyes on her, and although she didn't meet his gaze, the intensity of his stare made the hair stand up on the back of her neck.

"How about you, David?" Olivia lifted a brow. "You're single, right?"

"Yep," came the rumbly answer.

Olivia smiled. "Crimson is the perfect place to find true love."

"David is here to talk about the beer for Oktoberfest," Logan said, dropping a kiss on the top of Olivia's head. "Although I'm sure he appreciates your matchmaking efforts."

Erin risked a glance at David, who shrugged. Suddenly she was terrified he might reveal what she'd asked him. It was crazy, but she couldn't stop the fear coursing through her. He opened his mouth but before he could answer, she blurted out the first thing that came to mind, even though it was an obvious lie. "I've got a boyfriend."

Olivia looked disappointed. "Well, I guess I wasn't meant to be a matchmaker after all."

"We'll have to find other ways to keep you busy," Logan said.

"Right now, Erin and I need to go over the last-minute details for her after-school outreach project. The program starts Monday." She scooped the baby out of Erin's arms and handed her to Logan. Molly gurgled happily, curling a fist in the soft denim of her daddy's shirt.

Olivia moved toward the hallway that led to the community center's classrooms. "You coming, Erin?"

Erin realized she was staring at the baby, her arms strangely empty without the lotion-scented bundle. "Right." She darted a glance at David, who arched a brow in response.

One small brow arch she felt all the way to her toes.

An imaginary boyfriend. That should end things before they even got started.

Forcing a smile, she looked from David to Logan. "See you both later," she called, and hurried after Olivia, ignoring the regret that surged through her as she walked away.

Chapter 4

David waited outside the community center's front door, watching groups of people take to the streets of Crimson on this beautiful fall Friday night. The temperature was quickly cooling, typical at altitude once the sun dipped behind the majestic peak of Crimson Mountain to the town's west.

He imagined the crowds heading toward Elevation for a drink with friends, a reminder that he should be tending bar tonight. He'd been lucky with the brewery, opening just as the picturesque mountain town was hitting a resurgence and having a knack with brewing the ever-popular craft beers.

But he didn't take his success for granted. After destroying his baseball career thanks to one night of reckless stupidity, he'd learned to work hard for what he wanted. He should be working now. Or checking in with

Jenna, who was spending the night with Rhett in his loft before they drove to Denver tomorrow to put her on the plane headed for the rehab center in Arizona.

He should be a dozen places that didn't involve standing in the shadows waiting for Erin. David was long past the days of making stupid choices when it came to women, and he'd never had any interest in the type who looked as wholesome as a tall glass of milk.

The door opened and Erin walked out, and all the reasons David shouldn't be waiting for her disappeared under the relentless drumming of need pulsing through his body. He might not understand his reaction to the beautiful schoolteacher, but neither could he ignore it.

"Tell me about the boyfriend," he said, stepping out to block her path.

She stumbled back a step, pressing her hand to her cheek. "Holy cow! You scared the pants off me."

David felt his mouth curve at that. If only.

"No one says *holy cow* in real life," he muttered, reaching out a hand to steady her.

She shrugged off his touch. "Clearly people do say *holy cow*," she countered. "Because I just did." She crossed her arms over a chest that could benefit from a low-cut blouse. Oh, yes. David would definitely like to see this woman in something far more revealing than the conservative pastel-colored shirts she seemed to favor.

The thought of undoing a few of her buttons made his blood run alarmingly hot.

"Why are you skulking around out here?"

"I'm not skulking," he told her. "I'm waiting for you. You were just about to explain why you asked me for sex when you have a boyfriend."

Her delicate brows winged up. "No, I wasn't." She

glanced over her shoulder. "Keep your voice down. I don't want anyone to hear…" Even in the waning light he could see color flood her cheeks. When was the last time he'd been around a woman who actually blushed?

"That you propositioned me?" he supplied.

"Stop," she said on a hiss of breath. "It wasn't like that."

"It sure sounded like that to me. But I guess you need to keep me your dirty little secret since there's a *boyfriend* in the picture." He tapped a finger on his chin, as if pondering the concept. "I've never been a kept man before. I'll admit it has a certain appeal."

Her eyes narrowed. "You're teasing me."

He didn't bother to hide his grin. "You seem unfamiliar with the concept."

She stared at him a moment longer, then gave a small sigh. He could almost feel on his skin the puff of breath that left her lips. Damn, but he wanted to feel it. He wanted to taste her to gauge for himself whether she was as sweet as she looked. He eased closer to her, slowly, as if she might spook if he moved too fast.

He'd meant to confront her, demand what the hell she'd been thinking when she'd made that shocking request. But he liked the easy banter they fell into far too much. His life had never been easy, and a bit of innocent flirting with Erin gave him a few minutes' reprieve from all the things he couldn't control.

She bit down on her lip but didn't shy away. He liked that, too. "I don't have a boyfriend," she mumbled.

"Really?" he asked, even though he'd guessed as much.

"Olivia was intent on playing matchmaker, and I didn't want you to be forced into asking me out or anything. That's a horrible feeling and I'm not…"

"Interested?" He chuckled. "We both know that's not true."

A shadow clouded her gaze, and he wasn't sure what he'd said wrong, but he wanted to kick himself for it.

"I'm not your type," she said through clenched teeth, coming up on her toes and tipping back her head so that he got his wish and felt her breath tickle his chin. Her scent was a mix of cinnamon and sugar, like he imagined a kitchen might smell with a batch of cookies baking in the oven. Warm, inviting and the exact opposite of the cramped galley kitchen in the apartment where he'd grown up.

He was so caught up in his reaction that he almost missed the words she spoke. As it was, by the time he opened his mouth to correct her, she'd brushed past him and was around the corner of the building.

"Erin, wait," he called, but instead of slowing she moved faster. It only took a few strides to catch up to her.

"I need to go," she said, keeping her gaze on the ground in front of her when he blocked her path.

"Why do you think you're not my type?" He was curious to know whether her reasons matched his.

She gave a little shake of her head.

"Erin."

"Am I your type?" she asked suddenly, her honey-colored gaze slamming into his.

He opened his mouth, shut it again. How was he supposed to answer that? When she made to move around him again, he settled for the truth.

"You're way too good for me."

The comment earned him an eye roll. "If you say the words *it's me, not you*, I'm going to punch you."

"I'm guessing you don't go around punching people."

"You make me want to start."

He laughed again. "How is it that I'm the bad guy right now?"

"You're not," she whispered. "I should never have made the request. I was tired, and it was stupid and embarrassing. Can we just forget about it?"

He wished he could. Getting involved with this woman—in any capacity other than as his nephew's teacher—was sure to be trouble for both of them. Why couldn't he make himself walk away?

"No one," he said softly, unable to resist stepping into her space again, "would have to force a man to ask you out."

It was her turn to laugh, but there was no humor in it. All the light was gone from her golden eyes, and he wanted nothing more in life at that moment than to reignite it. "I know who I am, David."

He lifted his hands to cup her cheeks and felt a slight shiver pass through her. It drove him crazy with need. "Take another look," he said, and touched his lips to hers.

Erin's eyes drifted closed even as her body opened like the petals of a flower unfurling in the warm sunshine. Take another look? She'd planned to hold on to this moment like a priceless piece of art. If she could she'd frame it and hang it on her wall so she could always remember.

David McCay was kissing her, and quite thoroughly at that. His lips were soft but firm as they glided over hers and she couldn't resist darting her tongue into his mouth. He rewarded that bit of bravery with a small groan, which made sparks dance across her skin. She leaned into him, her breath hitching when his fingers laced through her hair and tugged gently.

A whistle from a passing car made her wrest away from his embrace. She squeezed her hands into fists and pressed them to her sides when all she wanted was to wrap herself around him and hang on for dear life.

"Women like you don't do PDAs on the sidewalk," he said, his voice rougher than normal.

She bit down on the inside of her cheek and looked up at him through her lashes. "I don't make it a habit," she admitted. The truth was she'd never before had the opportunity. But it was Friday night and it wouldn't be good for one of her students or another teacher to catch her in a full-blown make-out session on a public sidewalk.

"Too good for me," David repeated, and Erin realized he'd actually meant the words when he'd said them earlier.

Her ex had said something similar when he'd broken up with her, but the insinuation behind the comment had been quite different. *Good* had been another way of saying *boring*. But if the heat in David's gaze was any indication, he didn't find her the least bit boring.

Erin's long-suffering ego broke out into a little happy dance, but she quickly pulled the plug on the music. "That isn't true," she said, pressing a hand to lips still tingling from his kiss.

"You asked me for an affair, sweetheart." He smoothed a loose strand of hair away from her face. "Not a date. We both know what that means."

"Would you have gone out on a date if I'd asked?"

He shook his head, and she tried to ignore the pang of disappointment that snaked through her.

"You're a white-picket-fence girl. America and apple pie. What you saw at my sister's apartment pretty much sums up how I was raised. I come from that world. It's what I know."

Right now that didn't matter. This man had flirted with her, then kissed her senseless. Twenty minutes with David had been more exciting than the sum total of the rest of her life. Heck no, she couldn't have an affair with him, even if he was willing. She was liable to spontaneously combust. It was time to get the subject back to safer ground.

"How's Rhett doing?" she asked, reaching into her purse for her keys. She moved to the edge of the sidewalk where her Subaru hatchback was parked at the curb.

"He's with his mom tonight. They're staying at my loft."

"Is your sister okay with going into treatment?"

He nodded. "Deep in her heart she doesn't want to repeat the mistakes our mother made. I have to believe last night was a wake-up call for her."

"Then maybe it was a blessing in disguise. I hope she gets the help she needs." She hit the remote start on her key fob.

"I hope Rhett and I survive the next month together." He ran a hand over his jaw and the scratching sound made her want to whimper. She was truly pathetic.

"He's welcome at Crimson Kidzone in the afternoon. It starts Monday at four. Sign him up if you need a break."

When he stared at her, she held out a hand. "No strings attached or indecent proposals from me. Promise."

He took her hand but instead of shaking it, pressed a

lingering kiss on her knuckles. "That would be a huge disappointment."

Erin sighed. Cue the weak knees. "You don't mean that," she whispered.

"I might have enough willpower to leave you alone, but that doesn't mean I won't be thinking about how good we could be together."

He released her hand and she clutched it against her stomach, feeling ridiculously like a teenage girl who wanted to hold on to the imprint of that kiss. "Good to know," she told him.

He winked at her. "Night, Erin. Sweet dreams."

"Seriously, McCay? Your nephew's kindergarten teacher?"

David blew out a breath at the annoyance in the feminine voice behind him.

He hoisted a bushel of hops over his shoulder and turned. "I don't know what you're talking about, Tracie, but I promised Rhett I'd take him fishing after thirty minutes of screen time so I need to make the most of my electronic babysitter."

It was early Sunday morning—too early considering David hadn't gotten to sleep until after 3:00 a.m. He'd paid one of the waitresses to babysit his nephew last night, which had left him short-staffed since his best— if mouthiest—bartender Tracie Sheldon had taken the evening off for a date with the local orthopedic surgeon who'd been asking her out for months.

Tracie stood behind him now, wearing running shorts and a long-sleeved athletic shirt. Her short blond hair stuck out from under a bright pink headband and he guessed she'd stopped into the bar in the middle of her daily five-mile run.

"Besides, shouldn't you be busy basking in post-date glow or doing the walk of shame or something?"

"I'm not that kind of girl," she shot back, then added softly, "anymore. Besides, it wasn't a good match."

With a quiet sigh, David dropped the heavy bag to the floor. "Why not? Your doctor has bellied up to the bar several nights a week for the past month, even when he's on call and drinking root beer. We might serve up a helluva plate of chicken wings and some crazy good nachos, but there's only so much bar food a man can take."

He leaned in closer. "Unless he has another compelling reason for becoming a regular."

"Compelling." Tracie snorted. "Right. He's a surgeon, Davey, my boy. I'm a high-school dropout bartender. We have nothing in common."

"I've spent some time talking to Luke Baylor. He's a decent guy, Tracie. Worked his way through med school. You work hard, and you're not a high-school dropout anymore. It won't be long until you graduate nursing school. You should hold your head high."

"So tell me about the schoolteacher," she countered, placing her hands on her hips.

"I don't know what you've heard, but there's nothing to tell."

"Do you like her?"

"Do you like Doc Luke?"

She arched a brow. "We had dinner at Carlo's Bistro last night. Remember Lance who washed dishes here for a while?"

"Yeah." David nodded. "Punk kid."

"That's the one. He's a busboy at Carlo's and was all

too happy to stop me on the way to the restroom and report he saw you and a dark-haired librarian type sucking face on the street."

David felt a headache begin to pulse behind one temple. "No one was sucking face."

"I figured it was the teacher after seeing the way she looked at you Thursday night. Like she was a kid in a candy store and you were her favorite flavor."

He didn't want to admit how much he liked the idea of that. "You're changing the subject."

"You started it."

"We're quite a pair." He wrapped an arm around the tiny blonde's shoulders—she barely came to his chest—and pulled her in for a hug. "I'm not going to stop trying to make you believe you deserve some happiness."

"Goes both ways," she said, and gently elbowed him in the ribs.

He grunted and squeezed her shoulders. "Rhett's happiness is what matters to me now."

At that moment, Rhett gave a small shout. "Ms. Mac-Donald," he yelled, and scrambled out of the booth, his iPad forgotten on the table.

Tracie took a step away from him as David turned to see Erin, backlit in the doorway of the bar by the morning sunlight. Her dark jeans hugged her curves and a cranberry-colored sweater with a scooped neckline made her skin look even more luminous. It was difficult to read her expression, but her gaze was bouncing between him and Tracie in a way David didn't like one bit.

"Don't just stand there staring," Tracie muttered. "Go to her. I'm going to slip out through the kitchen."

"Tracie, you don't need to…" David started, but he was talking to her back.

"Ms. MacDonald, I live in a bar now." David cringed as Rhett's voice carried across the empty space.

"We don't live in the bar," David corrected as he moved forward. *Go to her*, Tracie had said. What he wanted to do was swing her into his arms and bury his nose against the crook of her neck. Her thick hair was pulled back into another ponytail.

Did she ever wear it down? Right now he would give just about anything to see it falling in waves over her shoulders. He'd been too long without a woman if he was now obsessing over Erin's hair.

"I know," she answered. "You have a loft upstairs. I didn't mean to interrupt." Her gaze traveled past him to where Tracie had disappeared. "I was heading to the bakery and your door was open…"

"You're not interrupting," he said quickly, coming to stand behind his nephew. "Tracie works here, and she stopped by after her run. She had a date last night." She bit down on her lip and he quickly added, "With some-one else. Not me. We're not…" He raked a hand through his hair. "She's a friend. The guy she went out with is a doctor. A surgeon. He—"

"Uncle David, why are you talking so fast?" He glanced down to find Rhett staring up at him, then raised his gaze to Erin's. He was babbling. He'd never babbled in his entire life.

She flashed a shy smile. "I'm going to grab breakfast at Life Is Sweet, then head over to the community cen-ter to set up a few things for tomorrow. I thought Rhett might like to help me if it's okay with you."

He felt Rhett fidget against his legs. "What do you think, buddy? We can head to the river a little later if you want to help Ms. MacDonald."

"I might mess things up," Rhett said, kicking the toe of one ratty sneaker against the scuffed wood floor. "I have to stay out of the way around here."

David sighed. He'd said those words this morning—pre-coffee—when he'd set up Rhett with the iPad.

"You won't mess up anything." Erin crouched down in front of the boy. "In fact, some of the supplies I'm using are way back in a closet and I need someone small enough to crawl in and push them out to me."

Rhett nodded. "I can do that."

"Then we've got a deal." She straightened, and David expected to see censure in her big eyes, but instead they were gentle in a way that made his heart hammer in his chest.

"Can I go in my pj's?" Rhett asked.

Erin smiled. "This might be a good time to get dressed for the day. Can you do that?"

"Me and Ruffie have a bedroom upstairs." He pointed to the raggedy blue dog sitting on the booth where he'd been playing a video game. "He gets nervous when we're not together."

"He's welcome to come with us," Erin offered.

"Yeah," Rhett agreed. "He'd like that."

He ran to the table, grabbed the dog and then headed for the hallway leading to the staircase that accessed the upper floor. There was also an entrance off the street, but David used the one that led directly into his office in the back of the bar when things weren't busy.

"I suck at this," he mumbled when Rhett was out of sight. "Jenna hasn't even been gone twenty-four hours and Rhett feels like he's in the way."

"It's a big change for both of you. How did it go yesterday?"

"Jenna cried. Rhett cried. He was sullen all day yesterday, and the first thing he asked this morning is when she's coming home. I felt like a total ass for arranging her stay in rehab. Maybe she could get clean and still be here, you know?"

"It's not long in the grand scheme of things and could make a real difference. That would make everything worth it. A kid deserves to grow up feeling safe. Your sister is lucky to have you to step in and help her. You're giving both of them another chance."

He blew out a breath. "How did you know exactly what I needed to hear this morning?"

Color rose to her cheeks. "It's the truth."

It wasn't just the words she spoke that made him feel better. It was the fact that she'd come to check on him. Okay, maybe she'd come to check on Rhett, but David still reaped the benefit. *She* was exactly what he needed. "Thank you."

They stared at each other for several long moments, and the spark of awareness that connected them seemed to shimmer and thrum in the air. It made him want to pull her in and kiss her again, but then he thought of Tracie and the kid who'd reported him Friday night. Normally, David didn't care who saw him doing what, but Erin was different. She was too good to be dragged through any sort of gossip mill, especially when she was starting her new program at the community center.

He crossed his arms over his chest to resist the urge to touch her. "Rhett won't be long." He made his tone purposefully chilly.

Disappointment flashed in her brown eyes before she cocked her head and studied him, as if she was trying to riddle out secrets. "This place is different during the day," she said, moving away from him and trailing her long fingers over the polished mahogany of the bar. He could imagine a lot of other places those fingers should be traveling. Namely all over his damn body.

"The architecture is beautiful." She pointed to the vaulted ceiling, where rough-hewn beams stretched across the open space.

"Logan helped me design it," David said, following her as she moved through the high tables. Following her like a puppy on a leash. Never had he felt so under a woman's spell as he did with Erin. The crazy part was she had no idea the power she had over him.

"Did he do the renovations, too? When I was growing up, this place was a grocery store, then it stood vacant for a number of years."

He'd forgotten that she was a Crimson native. The town was a tight-knit community and everyone seemed to know their neighbors and their neighbors' business. But before Rhett started school, David had never heard of Erin MacDonald. "The building was bank-owned when I bought it. I got a great deal."

She smiled at him over her shoulder. "You must have had a clear vision."

"I went to college on a baseball scholarship, but only lasted a couple of years. It sounds crazy now, but I took a brewing lab sciences class freshman year and got hooked on the process. I was good at it, but baseball came first. When I got drafted, the beer brewing moved to the back burner for a few years. I stopped playing ball, but then Jenna needed me out here. I needed a job and had enough money to make the business work."

"Why did you give up baseball?"

He gave a harsh laugh. "Not exactly my choice. I

screwed things up pretty good. Not worth rehashing the details, but suffice it to say it was totally my fault."

"You do that too much," she said, moving toward him until she was directly in front of him. "You take the blame for anything that goes bad."

David felt his eyes narrow. "Only when I deserve it."

She poked him in the chest. "It seems like you're of the opinion that you always deserve it."

He clamped his mouth shut and stared down at her. There was no right way to respond to that. He didn't always do the wrong thing, but the times he'd messed up in his life had resulted in grim consequences for the people around him.

"You can't control everything. Sometimes bad stuff happens no matter what you do to prevent it."

He wrapped his hand around her finger and lowered it. "Other times it can be prevented, and I've often failed at that."

He expected her to wrench out of his grasp, but she surprised him by gently squeezing his hand. "I wish you saw yourself the way I see you."

David felt her words like a vise clamping around his heart. The ways this woman could wreck him boggled his mind. Pulling away from her, he took several long steps toward the back hallway. "Rhett, you almost ready?" he called up the stairs.

"Coming," the boy shouted as his small feet pounded down the steps. He bounded into the hallway, the ever-present blue dog tucked against his side.

"Shoes, buddy," David said softly. His nephew had a habit of putting his shoes on the wrong feet.

With a sigh, Rhett dropped to the floor and undid the Velcro straps of his superhero sneakers and switched them to the correct feet. David's heart squeezed even harder as Rhett's tongue darted out the corner of his mouth. It meant he was concentrating hard and was the same quirk Jenna'd had as a girl.

David ruffled Rhett's hair as he stood. "Listen to Ms. MacDonald and do what she says," he told the boy. "No trouble."

"Okay."

He turned and looked at Erin, but her attention was focused on Rhett. "I'm glad you're coming with me this morning," she said.

Rhett gave a sharp nod and inched forward.

"I need another hour or so to get things settled here," David told her. "I'll pick him up after that."

"No rush," she answered, but still didn't look at him. "We'll stay busy."

He'd been the one to pull away a few minutes ago, but now the distance separating them seemed wider than simply physical space. It felt like he was losing something that had never belonged to him in the first place. The sensation made him want to throw a tantrum, like a baby whose favorite toy was taken away.

Erin held out her hand to Rhett, and the boy placed his smaller one in it. They walked out the open door and disappeared into the cool autumn morning.

David stood in his empty bar, staring at the dust motes that floated through the rays of sun shining in from the bar's front windows. He'd never minded being alone before. Why did it feel so damn uncomfortable now?

Chapter 5

"I owe you for this morning."

Erin almost stumbled off the end of the fishing dock at the sound of David's voice directly behind her.

He reached out a hand to steady her, but as much as she wanted to lean into his touch, she shrugged it off. Not going there, she reminded herself.

"You don't owe me. I told you I wanted to help with Rhett."

One side of his mouth quirked as he stared at her from behind dark sunglasses. "You also told me—"

"Don't say it." She held up a hand. "We've agreed that request was a moment of sleep-deprived stupidity on my part."

"I haven't agreed to anything." His deep voice once again set off tremors inside her.

"I thought you and Rhett were going to look for rocks to skip."

David gestured to where the boy was busily digging in the sand and gravel that made up the shoreline of Crimson Reservoir. "He got distracted."

She smiled as she watched Rhett, crouched low and with his too-long hair hanging over one eye, his attention completely focused on his task. "This is good for him, David. He needs some time to just be a kid in nature."

"This place can make anyone feel better."

She lifted her gaze to take in the awe-inspiring scenery around them. They were standing on the east side of the seven-mile-wide reservoir situated about thirty minutes outside of town. Rhett had insisted she accompany them on their planned fishing trip when David came to pick him up at the community center.

She should have said no. It had been a spontaneous decision to make the boy part of her morning on her way to the bakery earlier. A good decision, she thought, because both Rhett and David had looked grateful and relieved at her offer. But spending too much time with David was dangerous for her emotional health.

She'd spent far too much time since Friday replaying their kiss in her head. Instead of satisfying her, it had made her want more, even though she knew she shouldn't.

This afternoon only heightened her need. Having a crush on David was one thing, but watching his patience with Rhett and how hard he was trying to connect with the boy made Erin like him on an entirely different level. Once Rhett got tired of fishing, he'd gone to play on the shore, leaving David and Erin together on the dock.

Sunlight sparkled on the water, and a breeze made the changing aspen leaves flutter and sing around them. The breathtaking view of Crimson Mountain on the far side of the water made the reservoir one of the most beautiful places she'd ever seen. It seemed funny now that she'd never come out here before.

Her mom hadn't been much for outdoor activities. Erin knew kids came to the lake to hang out in high school, big groups or on dates. She was pretty sure the scenic overlook they'd passed on the way to the parking lot was still a popular make-out spot for teens in town. But she'd never been part of that crowd.

Now she wished she had been.

"I'd give way more than a penny to read your thoughts right now." David bent and picked up the fishing pole that he'd left next to her on the dock.

"I was thinking about what I still need to do to be ready for tomorrow," she lied.

"That makes you blush?"

She pressed her hands to her cheeks. "I'm not blushing."

He chuckled. "Want to throw in a line yourself? All you've gotten to do so far is watch me teach Rhett to fish."

"He likes it out here. Outside. Sitting in a classroom all day is tough for boys, and a lot of them go home and spend the rest of the day playing video games or watching TV."

"Like my nephew?"

She shrugged. "I'm sorry. I'm not trying to criticize your sister."

"It's fine," David answered, his voice tight. "Just because I moved to Crimson to help doesn't mean I knew how to or that Jenna wanted me involved. I should have been paying more attention. She was hiding things from me. Turns out Rhett was alone a lot more than I realized. He's pretty addicted to his screen time."

"Then today is even more of a treat for him."

David stepped closer, and she could see the shadow across his jaw that meant he hadn't shaved that morning. He wore faded jeans and an olive-colored T-shirt with the Elevation Brewery logo across the front. Everything about him fascinated her.

"So you gonna do some fishing?"

"I don't know how," she answered, but took the thin pole he held out to her. "I mean, I was listening when you showed Rhett but…"

"I'll give you a lesson, too." He grasped her shoulders and turned her so she was facing the water. Then he moved to stand behind her, his body touching hers from chest to thigh. A crazy buzzing started in her head, and she swallowed back the little whimper that rose in her throat.

"Hold the pole so your two middle fingers are on either side of the reel," he said, his breath warm against her neck.

She tightened her grasp on the fishing pole and heard him chuckle. "Not in a death grip. Firm but not too tight."

She choked back a laugh because it sounded a lot like he was instructing her on something other than fishing. "Okay," she whispered.

"Hold the line against the rod with your index finger and flip the bail with your other hand." He guided her hand to the narrow piece of metal. "Give the line some slack and we're going to bring the rod back and cast."

Her mind was reeling, but she tried to follow his directions. With a shaking finger, she flipped the bail, drew the pole over her head and cast. The line spun, then the bobber dropped with a *plop* into the water only a foot in front of the dock.

"I can't do this," she whispered, trying to hand the pole back to David and move away.

"You can," he said, and tightened his hold on her. He took the rod from her, his arms reaching around her, and reeled in the line. "The motion comes from your wrist and hand, not your shoulder. Now take a breath."

She did and was immediately overwhelmed by the scent of soap and mint gum with the irresistible essence of David thrown in for good measure. It was different from kissing him, of course, but no less intimate. Erin struggled to keep her reaction to him hidden. "I've lived my whole life without learning to fish," she told him. "I can probably manage without the skill."

"Not on my watch," he said, and wrapped her hand around the pole once again. "You're going to catch a fish today."

Erin forced another breath and concentrated on not freaking out any more than she already was. Her goal for the year had been stepping out of her comfort zone, and today definitely counted. She glanced over her shoulder to see Rhett still focused on his rock and stone collection on the bank. "I don't know about a fish," she murmured. "I'll be satisfied if I throw this thing in the water without embarrassing myself."

"It's called casting a line," David said against her ear. His lips brushed the sensitive skin just below her earlobe.

A shiver ran through her in response, and she gripped the fishing pole more tightly. "I can't focus when you do that."

"Then you should stop being so sexy."

She grunted out a laugh at that. Erin was a lot of things, but sexy had never been one of them. The reminder was enough to help her rein in her foolish desire for this man. She couldn't help but think this was another part of his thank-you to her for helping with Rhett. Have a little flirtatious pity on the boring schoolteacher.

She squeezed her eyes shut for a moment and tried to compose herself. He was a man. She was a woman. They were fishing while his nephew—her student—played nearby. A casual afternoon. No need to read more into it than that.

"Tell me what to do again," she told him when she'd pulled herself together.

He repeated the instructions and she followed them, letting out a small cry of delight when the fishing line sailed through the air to land a respectable fifty feet out in the lake.

"I did it," she whispered.

"Now reel it in again," David said.

She did and the zip of the spinning reel was the best thing she'd heard in a long time. She cast twice more, the feel of the rod in her hand more natural with every moment.

"I think you've got it."

She realized David was still standing directly behind her only when he moved away. Her body wanted to protest, but she was too excited about her newfound skill at casting.

"I like it," she told him.

"We'll move to fly-fishing next," he answered with a slow smile. "I'd like to see you in a pair of waders."

Before she could react, the orange bobber floating

on top of the water disappeared and she felt a hard tug on the line.

"A fish!" Rhett yelled at the top of his lungs as he ran toward them.

"Reel it in," David shouted as the line made a fast whirring sound.

With a squeak, Erin grabbed the spinning handle of the reel and began to turn it counterclockwise toward her body.

David was behind her again a moment later, his hand steadying her arm.

"Pull the rod against your body," he commanded. "You'll get more leverage."

"Take it," she said in a rush of breath. "I can't—"

"Yes, you can."

"You're doing it, Ms. MacDonald," Rhett said excitedly when he got to her side. He tugged on the hem of her shirt. "Don't let it get away."

"Keep going," David told her, his voice gentler. "You've got this."

Erin felt a grin split her face as she continued to bring the fish closer to the dock. David disappeared for a moment, then reappeared a minute later with a net in one hand.

"Bring him in, sweetheart," he said as he knelt at the edge of the dock.

The fish surfaced and struggled in the water, fighting hard against the hook that tethered him to her line. The sound of splashing broke the quiet of the lake as the water rippled and churned around the fish.

"He's so cute." Rhett crouched down next to David. "He's a boy, right?"

"Hard to tell right now." David grabbed the line, then

scooped the net into the water. When it emerged again, the fish was in it, its gills opening and closing in the unfamiliar air.

"I don't want to kill him," Erin said, suddenly having a rush of sympathy for the little creature.

"It'll be fine," David assured her. "Hold the net, Rhett."

"Got it." The boy grabbed the handle with two hands while David removed the fish from the net. He pulled a tool out of his pocket and stuck it into the fish's mouth, extracting the hook.

Then he turned and presented the creature to Erin. "Here you go."

She placed the rod onto the dock and stepped forward. "It's so pretty." She traced one finger over the fish's pink-tinged side.

"It's a rainbow trout," David told her. "Hand Rhett your phone and take the fish. We'll get a photo before we throw him back."

"Or her," Erin said. "He could be a she."

"Yeah, but I don't think you want to cut her open and look for an egg sack."

"No." Erin made a face at the same time Rhett shouted, "Yes!"

She took her phone from her pocket, flipped it to camera mode and handed it to Rhett.

"Hold on tight," David advised as he passed the fish to her.

She didn't have time to think about whether she actually wanted her hands on the slimy, slippery creature before it was in them.

Despite the fact that she was slightly grossed out by

holding a fish, she smiled when David took the phone from the boy and snapped her photo.

"Now throw it back," he told her and she flipped the fish into the reservoir. There was a splash, and the fish shimmered on the surface for a few seconds before swimming off.

"Bye, fish," Rhett called, then glanced up at David. "Can we skip stones now?"

"Sure, buddy. We'll collect the fishing gear and head over to you."

"I'll get more ready." Rhett smiled, then walked back toward his rock pile.

"I held a fish," Erin murmured, still holding her arms out in front of her.

"Like a pro," David confirmed. He pulled a bandanna out of the pocket of his cargo pants and took her hand in his, gently wiping each of her fingers.

"I'm going to need to shower for days to get the fish smell off me."

"One hot shower should do the trick," he said with a smile. "If you're looking for a volunteer to scrub your back…"

She yanked her hands away from his. "You shouldn't tease me."

He leaned in and brushed a quick kiss across her lips. "Who says I'm teasing?"

Heat spiked through her, and her whole body flooded with need. As if unaware of her reaction, David simply grabbed the fishing pole and net and walked off the dock toward Rhett on the shore.

She followed, trying to keep her focus on the boy. That's why she was here—to help with Rhett. Anything more would surely end in emotional disaster.

* * *

David climbed the front steps of Crimson Elementary the following Wednesday afternoon, cursing himself for believing he finally had his life under control.

After Sunday's fishing excursion, something had changed with Rhett. His nephew had always been a bit distant, as if Jenna had warned him about coming to rely on Uncle David. Although he understood the sentiment, the tacit rejection still stung. But between the fishing lessons and skipping stones across the placid surface of the reservoir, the boy had started to relax and engage with David in a way he hadn't before.

David gave a lot of the credit to Erin. Her presence seemed to bridge the gap that he couldn't manage on his own. Rhett clearly loved having the attention of his teacher outside the classroom. Her easy smile and gentle encouragement softened the boy, and he was far more connected when she was around.

The funny thing was, David felt the exact same way. Despite a long string of girlfriends, he'd never been one for domestication. He was used to tumultuous relationships—loud arguments and intense make-up sessions that he'd assumed were normal given how he was raised.

Everything in his life had been emotional crisis and big scenes. But Erin made the ordinary bits feel just as exciting as the adrenaline rush that came from being swept along in a drama-filled haze.

He hadn't seen much of her since Sunday, despite dropping off and picking Rhett up from school every day and the fact that the boy had spent two afternoons in her after-school program.

It was a relief to have a safe place for Rhett to be in the hours before David could break away from work.

He'd hired another bartender so he didn't have to deal with late nights, but with the plans for Oktoberfest and the festival's highly anticipated beer competition well under way, this wasn't a time he could take an extended vacation from the bar.

Between school, Erin and a couple trusted babysitters, David thought he was successfully managing his newfound role of single parent. Then he'd gotten the call from the school's principal, alerting him that Rhett had been in a fight with another boy during recess, the result of which would be a one-day suspension.

Hell, even David had made it to third grade before he'd been suspended for the first time. So much for having things under control.

He was buzzed into the building and headed for the reception desk. The woman behind it glanced up as he approached. She took him in head to toe and he saw her eyes widen. That's when he remembered the T-shirt he was wearing, which had the words I'd Tap That emblazoned across the front.

Way to make an impression.

Rhett's principal was going to love him. David did a mental eye roll as he wondered what Erin would think.

Probably that she'd dodged a bullet when he hadn't immediately taken her up on her offer to have an affair.

A moment later, an older woman with a sleek brown bob and wire-framed glasses came out of the office to greet him.

"Mr. McCay, I'm Karen Henderson, Crimson Elementary's principal."

"Call me David," he said as he shook her hand.

"Thank you for coming in today. I'm sorry we're meeting under these circumstances. I understand from

Ms. MacDonald that there have been some disruptions in Rhett's home life recently."

David gritted his teeth as he followed the woman into her office. "Is Rhett okay? Where is he?"

"He'll be along shortly," she said, moving behind her desk and taking a seat. "He's with the school counselor at the moment. I wanted a chance to speak to you first."

The office was just as he remembered the principal's office at the three different elementary schools he'd attended as a kid. His mom had a habit of moving frequently, taking short-term leases on whatever cheap apartment she could get near her latest boyfriend.

"There's no need to sugarcoat it," he told her. "My sister is getting help for her problems. Rhett and I are coping as best we can. You can be sure nothing like today will repeat itself."

She nodded and opened a file on her desk. "I appreciate that, Mr. McCay."

"David."

"The other boy—the one he fought with—is also being disciplined. He's a second grader at the school."

David felt his temper flare. How had Rhett managed to get in a fight with a second grader?

"Why did it happen?" he demanded. "Rhett's only been at the school a month."

She shook her head, her already-thin lips pressing into a tight line. "From what the teachers and I were able to get out of them, the other boy made a disparaging remark about Rhett's mother."

Everything in David went still—only for a second. Then memories from his childhood, of his mother and the fights he got in defending her honor, crashed through him.

"I want to see Rhett," he said through clenched teeth. "And Erin. Where's Erin?"

The principal's shoulders stiffened. "Ms. MacDonald," she said, placing an emphasis on the name as if to remind him of his place, "is out of the building today."

"Out where?"

"At a district-wide training. Rhett's class had a substitute teacher. Mrs. Mills has been a sub at the school for quite a few years, longer than Ms. MacDonald has been here. She's quite capable."

"She's not Erin," he said. At the woman's frown, he added, "Ms. MacDonald. Rhett has a special bond with Ms. MacDonald."

The woman's frown deepened. "Be that as it may, she's his *teacher*, Mr. McCay. Nothing more. Whether it's with Ms. MacDonald or another member of our staff, your nephew is in good hands at our school."

There was a knock at the door, and it opened to reveal another woman who looked to be about ten years younger than the principal. She was petite, with bright red hair and a kind face. "Rhett would like to see his uncle."

Karen Henderson nodded and the door opened wider to reveal Rhett standing next to the redhead.

David stood, not sure where to start with the conflicting emotions simmering inside him.

To his surprise, Rhett launched himself forward and covered the space between them in a few hurried steps. The boy reached out, and David automatically lifted him into his arms. Rhett held tight, his small body shaking as he clung to David.

"It's okay," David whispered, even though it was a lie for both of them. "You're okay."

"We need to talk about the situation," the principal said softly, and Rhett's hold on David tightened even more. "He has to understand—"

"I'll make sure he understands," David said. "Right now, I'm taking him home."

"Mr. McCay—"

"A one-day suspension." David glanced over his shoulder as he moved toward the door. "He'll be back in class on Friday."

He didn't bother to wait for a response. Settling Rhett's weight on his hip, he walked out of the school and toward his truck, which was parked at the curb. "Let's get you buckled in," he said gently, and after a moment Rhett's arms went slack.

"Are you hurt?"

The boy gave a slight shake of his head.

David settled him in the booster seat Jenna had helped him install and strapped him in, the buckle clicking shut.

Rhett kept his head lowered, and David didn't say anything else. He needed to get away from the school and also wanted some time to rein in his emotions. Anger was part of it—some of it aimed at Rhett for getting into the fight in the first place. But most of it was leveled at Jenna, for putting all of them in this situation.

He flipped on the radio as he pulled onto the road, and a raucous country song about whiskey and women who broke a cowboy's heart filled the cab.

It fit his mood perfectly.

Not that his heart was broken. He wasn't fool enough to open himself up to that kind of trouble. But betrayal swept through him nonetheless. He'd so quickly come to rely on Erin—her sweetness and the kindness she'd shown toward Rhett. He'd wanted to believe…that it was more than a sense of duty. Of course she had other responsibilities, and caring for Rhett was part of her job.

He glanced in the rearview mirror and saw Rhett with his head still down, wringing his small hands together in his lap. His chest rose and fell in shallow breaths, as though he was also struggling to hold it together.

David's anger melted away. He still wanted answers from his nephew, and for the boy to understand that fighting at school wouldn't be tolerated. But the kid was hurting and probably felt totally alone in the world. David knew a lot about being alone.

He didn't want that for Rhett.

Downtown Crimson was bustling as he turned the truck onto Main Street. The weather was perfect for the first week of October, still warm with just a hint of cool to the air. High on the mountain, the aspen leaves were changing from green to gold. Soon the riot of color would extend down into town, and the weekends would be busy with fall tourists and a few hunters on their way to higher elevations.

He pulled the truck to a stop against the curb and punched in a quick text to Tracie. He was supposed to have a meeting this afternoon with the head of a regional bottling company to ensure that everything was on track for the Oktoberfest celebration. He was going to have to delegate, even though it killed him to relinquish that kind of control.

He'd catch up later, he told himself. Right now, the more important work was with his nephew.

"This isn't your parking spot." David undid the buckle of the booster seat, and Rhett climbed out of the truck to the sidewalk.

"I thought we'd stop at Life Is Sweet for a cookie on

the way home," David told him, pointing to the sign above the bakery a few doors down.

As they walked, Rhett said quietly, "I got in trouble today."

"I know, buddy. That's why I was at the school."

"Do you still want to get me a cookie?" There was a hitch in his voice that made David's chest ache.

"I sure do." David ruffled his hair. "We're going to need to talk about what happened, but I think a snack will make both of us feel better."

"Yeah," Rhett agreed after a moment, and slipped his hand into David's.

The chimes above the door jingled as they walked in. Despite living in Crimson for almost three years, David had only been in the bakery a handful of times. He wasn't much for sweets and didn't drink coffee. Besides, there was something about the cozy feel of the space that made his skin itch with a need he couldn't quite identify.

The woman who owned Life Is Sweet, Katie Crawford, was always friendly and he'd met her husband, Noah, on several occasions.

But a bakery was different from a brewpub. There was a sense of community that radiated from it, and David had never had a desire to be part of any community.

Yet somehow he knew it was the right thing for Rhett.

Maybe for both of them.

He ordered two chocolate chip cookies and a milk for Rhett, then they took a seat in the small café area at a wrought iron table. There was a young couple at the table next to them, both with steaming coffee mugs in front of them and both tapping away on their phones. David had seen the same thing happen with people in the bar. They came in groups but instead of talking, they spent their time scrolling through social media or dating sites.

It made him feel old at twenty-nine that he wanted no part of online dating. He hadn't even thought about dating since his move to Crimson—at least until he'd met Erin.

With a sigh, he put her out of his mind as best he could and focused on Rhett.

The boy was nibbling the edge of his cookie and had a tiny smear of chocolate at the corner of his mouth.

"A second grader?" David asked casually, figuring the best way to deal with today was to get straight to the point.

Rhett shrugged. "He was only a little bigger than me."

"That's not really the point."

Rhett paused midbite and glanced up. "Mommy said you got in lots of trouble when you were a kid. She told me not to be like you."

David sighed. *Thanks, Jenna.*

"That was probably good advice, but here we are. Want to tell me about the fight?"

Rhett shook his head, his shaggy hair falling across one eye. Add a kid's haircut to the to-do list, David thought.

"We have to talk about it, unless you'd rather go back to the school and talk to Ms. Henderson and your teacher."

"Ms. MacDonald was gone today," Rhett said glumly. "I can't tell her."

Right. Erin hadn't been there to run interference. David knew he had no right to be angry but couldn't seem to stop the feeling of betrayal that washed through him. Erin made him believe he wasn't alone in caring for Rhett. That he had things under control. It was somehow easier to direct his frustration toward her than to any of the other things in his life that seemed beyond his control. "Then tell me."

"He called Mommy a bad word," the boy said, breaking the remainder of his cookie in half. "Real bad."

"What word?"

Rhett scrunched up his nose, as if he'd smelled something rotten. Then he climbed off the chair and moved to David's side. He stood on tiptoe and when David bent toward him, whispered the word *slut* in his ear.

Blood roared in David's head as he stared down at his *five-year-old* nephew. "Do you know what that word means?"

"Isaac said Mommy's boyfriend is his daddy, and she stole him from Isaac's mommy."

David didn't know much about the man his sister had been dating for the past few months. She'd told him he had a good job and they were just having fun together. Either she didn't know or had forgotten to mention that he also had another family. One that was targeting Rhett.

"What's Isaac's last name?"

"I don't know," Rhett answered, climbing back into his seat. "He came up to me when I was on the monkey bars and pushed me and said mean things about Mommy." He gripped the milk bottle tightly. "I got really mad. I didn't mean to get into a fight, Uncle David. Then the teacher came and yelled at me and he cried and she yelled more." He shook his head. "Ms. MacDonald never yells no matter how mad we make her."

"Ms. MacDonald won't always be there for you,

Rhett." David didn't mean for his words to come out harshly, but the boy's bottom lip quivered.

"He shouldn't have said what he did about your mom." David gentled his voice and leaned forward. "Did you explain it to your teacher and the principal?"

Rhett shook his head, and by the set of his jaw David understood why. Rhett was young but still old enough to understand there could be some truth in the other boy's accusations. Not the name-calling. That was inexcusable. But Jenna had a history of making poor choices in men.

Just like David's mother. He'd spent too much of his childhood trying to protect his mom without even realizing he was doing it. Making excuses for why she missed parent-teacher conferences, pretending she was picking him up around the block when in reality he walked home, forging signatures on forms and permission slips every year.

He'd tried to protect Jenna, but in the end he'd failed her.

He wouldn't fail Rhett.

"I'm going to make sure it doesn't happen again," he promised the boy. "But if anyone gives you trouble, talk to a teacher instead of fighting. Talk to me. I'm here to help you, Rhett. It's my job."

"I thought your job was making beer."

David smiled, but the muscles of his face felt stiff. "I do that, too, but nothing is more important to me than you. Nothing."

Chapter 6

Erin walked into Elevation later that night, her eyes scanning the bar for David.

Instead, the gorgeous bartender who'd given her the once-over last Sunday met her gaze.

"He's got the night off," she said as Erin approached.

"I went upstairs and rang the bell," Erin admitted, "but he didn't answer."

"Maybe he doesn't want to talk," the woman said and turned her back on Erin to grab two pint glasses from underneath the shelf behind her. "To you," she added over her shoulder.

Erin felt color rush to her cheeks. She was well aware that David didn't want to talk to her. She'd been trying to get in touch with him since she stopped at the school after her district meeting and Karen Henderson told her what had happened with Rhett on the playground.

The principal had made it quite clear that Erin should keep her relationship with both Rhett and David professional and not allow herself to become involved in their personal lives.

Smart advice, but Erin's heart was already involved. It killed her to think of the boy in trouble and afraid when she hadn't been there to smooth things over for him.

She stepped up to the bar and waited for the bartender to serve the two beers to the men sitting next to where Erin stood.

"Why don't you pull up a seat and talk to us, darlin'," one of the men, a scruffy-looking guy in a Broncos jersey, said.

Erin swallowed. The only time she'd come to a bar before tonight had been with a group of girlfriends, and no one had paid much attention to her. "Thank you for the offer, but I don't think so." She leaned toward the bar and caught the petite blonde's eye. "I need to see David," she whispered.

"He's no fun anymore," the second man said. "Doesn't live up to his baseball reputation at all."

"Shut up, Donnie," the bartender snapped.

"You know it's true, Tracie," the man shot back. "If half the stories about Dave are true, he got more action than a fox in a chicken coop back in the day."

"Now all he does is work." The first man darted a look at Erin. "No matter how many hot chicks throw themselves at him. We need some excitement around here."

Tracie rolled her eyes, and Erin wasn't sure whether it was in response to the man's complaint about David or the implication that Erin was a "hot chick."

"You'd better not let your wives hear you talking like that," Tracie said.

"Why do you think we want Davey to get some action?" Donnie took a long pull on his beer. "I don't want trouble at home. But I'm not dead, just married."

The bartender huffed out a laugh and turned away without bothering to acknowledge Erin again.

Erin should give up. David didn't want her, and she could talk to Rhett when he returned to school after the suspension.

Somehow she couldn't force herself to walk away. That was what she'd ordinarily do, but she was done being ordinary.

She stepped behind the bar and followed Tracie down the length of it, tapping the tiny woman on the shoulder when she got close.

"Seriously?" the woman asked as she whirled around. "You can't be back here."

"I need to see him."

"He's used to handling things on his own." Tracie crossed her arms over her chest and glared at Erin. "It's easier that way. No one gets hurt."

Erin was pretty sure the gorgeous bartender wasn't only talking about David. "He doesn't have to do this alone." She made her voice purposefully gentle. "I'm not going to hurt him. I promise."

Tracie studied her for a few seconds, then reached in her pocket and pulled out a set of keys. "The silver one unlocks the office and the staircase inside that leads up to the loft. You'd better make this right. David and Rhett both need that."

Erin had no idea how to make anything right at the

moment, but she nodded and took the key ring. "Thank you."

"You're different than you look," Tracie said. "Stronger."

A bit of happiness trickled through Erin at the reluctant compliment. "You're not quite as scary."

Tracie laughed softly. "Don't tell anyone."

Erin closed her hand around the keys and headed through the brewpub. She unlocked the office door and flipped on the light, taking a moment to gather her courage before moving to the wood panel door on the far side. Away from the noise of the bar, every sound seemed amplified and the *click* of the lock as she turned the key reverberated in her ears.

She let herself into the narrow staircase and locked the door behind her, as she had in the office, as well. Before she made it halfway up the stairs, the door at the top opened.

David stared down at her, his expression unreadable with his face concealed by shadows.

"Do you pick locks in your spare time?" he asked.

"Tracie gave me the key," she said, proud that her voice didn't shake. She forced herself to keep moving toward him, even though her knees were practically knocking. As silly as it sounded, it felt like she was going into battle. "You wouldn't return my calls and texts or answer when I knocked."

"Rhett was in the bath."

"I wanted to check on him." She was on the step below him now, gazing up into the hard planes of his face.

"You'll see him when he goes back to school," he said tightly. "Unless there's another sub in his class."

"That's not fair. What happened today isn't my fault."

For a moment she thought he might slam the door in her face, and she wondered what had possessed her to come here in the first place. Maybe her fantasy life had truly taken over and she'd imagined the connection between them. Maybe she was so desperate to be needed by someone that she'd read more into the situation than was really there.

Then he reached out and hauled her against him. His arms wrapped tight around her, and he rested his cheek on the top of her head. She could feel the tension coiled in him, electric and barely contained. And she knew she hadn't imagined any of it. This man needed her, and that understanding made her heart sing.

"You're right. I'm angry at Jenna for putting all of us in this position. I don't mean to take it out on you. I'm sorry."

"Me, too," she answered, speaking into the soft fabric of his shirt. She turned her head so she could feel the warm skin of his throat against the tip of her nose.

He drew back, smoothed his thumbs over her cheeks.

"No. I'm a jerk, Erin. You're right. None of this is your fault. It's easier to be angry at the school and you than to admit how badly Jenna has screwed things up. To admit that I stood by and let her."

"You didn't—"

"I should have known more about her new guy. Should have realized he was bad news and protected her and Rhett. Hell, the whole reason I moved to Colorado was to take care of things, and I let myself believe that just my mere presence here would make everything fine. I was a fool."

"You're here and you're trying. Give yourself a break."

He shook his head. "I can't. The stakes are too high."

She wanted to wipe the pain from his eyes, to take some of that burden and carry it for him. He'd uprooted his life to take care of his sister and nephew. He moved halfway across the country and had become a successful business owner and part of this town. There had never even been a question that he would step in for Rhett and get Jenna the help she needed. David was a good man, but he refused to see that in himself. Erin wished she could find a way to show him.

"I'd like to talk to Rhett." She forced herself to step out of David's embrace. It was too easy to forget that their relationship wasn't actually a relationship. He needed her help with his nephew, and she'd made the commitment to give it.

His attention wasn't about her—not really. She'd had a crush on him for far too long and he hadn't even known she existed. If it wasn't for the fact that she'd inserted herself into his life, he'd still be nothing more than her fantasy man and she'd be…nothing to him.

"We were watching a few minutes of television," he said, then glanced at his watch. "It's almost bedtime." He reached around her to shut the door to the staircase, then led her down the hall toward the main section of the apartment. They passed through the kitchen, which looked like a cozier version of the pub decor. The cabinets were dark wood with dark gray concrete countertops. Four chairs were tucked against the long island, exact copies of the bar stools downstairs.

"Dinner?" she asked, pointing to a half loaf of bread and jar of peanut butter sitting on the cluttered countertop.

David shrugged. "I tried to make grilled cheese sandwiches but burned the hell out of them. PB&J was the best I could do."

"Grilled cheese can be complicated," she said gently, earning a small laugh from David.

"It's better when I bring up food from downstairs," he admitted.

The far end of the kitchen opened to a family room, with wide-plank wood floors and oversize furniture. She could see *The Lego Movie* playing on the flat-screen TV that hung on one wall, and Rhett glanced up as they approached, then did a double take when he saw her.

"I got aspended," he announced, his voice solemn. "I can't come to school tomorrow."

"I know," she said, lowering herself to the cushion next to him. "That's why I stopped by tonight. I wanted to tell you that I'm sorry I wasn't at school today to help you on the playground."

"Uncle David said I can't hit people," Rhett told her, "even when they're mean."

"That's good advice." She reached out and gently smoothed away the hair that was falling across Rhett's eyes. "You can always talk to another teacher or Ms. Henderson if I'm not there."

"I hate Isaac." Rhett held his hands tight in his lap. "He called Mommy a bad word. It's not her fault his daddy wants to be her boyfriend. Lots of people want to be her boyfriend."

Erin heard a sound from David that sounded like a growl but focused her attention on the boy. "You love your mommy very much," she told him. "She's lucky to have you and I bet she's working hard to feel better and misses you so much."

"I miss her," Rhett whispered.

"I know you won't be at school tomorrow, but I hope your uncle will bring you to the community center in the afternoon. You can draw a picture for your mommy that shows how much you love her to give to her when she comes home."

Rhett looked from Erin to David. "Can I go, Uncle David?"

"Sure, buddy," came the rumbly response. "As long as you promise no more fights."

The boy nodded, then yawned. "I promise," he said sleepily.

"Time for bed," David announced.

"Can Ms. MacDonald read me a story?" Rhett asked, scooting off the couch.

David cleared his throat and Erin glanced back at him. He lifted one brow, silently leaving the decision up to her. Her life before last week had been so simple and straightforward. And boring.

"I'd love to," she told Rhett, and her heart melted a little when he grabbed her hand to lead her out of the family room.

She loved the hugs and hand-holding from her students, but there were always some who remained physically distant and she tried to respect that, too. Rhett had been one of those this year, which made the fact that he was reaching out to her mean so much more.

Glancing over her shoulder, she saw David watching them with an unreadable expression. Maybe she'd overstayed her welcome, but it felt right to be part of their lives.

"Are you okay if I check in downstairs for a minute?" he asked. "I'll be back up to tuck him in."

"Take your time." She handed him Tracie's keys and turned back to Rhett.

The boy led her down the hall to a small bedroom with a bathroom connected to it. It was clearly a guest room, with just a bed and nondescript chest of drawers against one wall. Rhett's stuffed blue dog sat on top of the plain beige comforter and there was a basket filled with random toys shoved in the corner.

Rhett grabbed the same pair of football-themed pajamas he'd been wearing the night of his mother's party from a pile of clothes stuffed into a laundry basket and spilling over onto the floor. "I need to get my pj's on and brush my teeth before we read."

"Is it okay if I fold some of your laundry while you do that?" she asked.

"I guess. Uncle David washes my clothes but says there's no point in putting anything away when I'm just going to wear them again."

Erin tried to keep her smile from showing. That was exactly something a single man would say. "Is that what you did with your mommy?"

Rhett shook his head. "Mommy and me folded laundry after dinner. I did the socks."

"Then I'll save the socks for you," Erin said.

"I'm good at them," Rhett confirmed, and disappeared into the bathroom.

She heard the sound of water running and then Rhett brushing his teeth. She folded the clothes and put them away in drawers, hoping that small thing would help him feel more settled.

It made her feel like she was contributing something, making up for how she hadn't been there for him earlier. Rationally she knew it wasn't her fault. Her work on the district planning committee had taken her out of the building for a day of training. Teachers got subs all the time for a variety of reasons. But it didn't change the fact that the boy had needed her, and she'd failed him.

She couldn't let it happen again.

After a few minutes, Rhett returned to the bedroom.

"Dirty clothes in the laundry hamper," she said, pointing to a wicker basket next to the dresser.

"You sound like Mommy," he told her as he went back to retrieve his discarded clothes. But he was smiling as he climbed on the bed next to her. The first smile she'd seen from him tonight.

He rolled the socks into balls, then handed her a Magic Tree House book from the nightstand. She made sure he was snuggled in tight, then started to read about ninjas and two time-traveling kids.

She finished a chapter, then glanced down at Rhett to see his eyes had drifted shut, Ruffie tucked under his arm. She stood slowly and smoothed the covers over both the boy and the stuffed dog. Erin had so much in her life—a great job, good friends, a mom who loved her. But there was nothing she could truly call her own, and spending time with Rhett made it clear how much she wanted that.

The relentless pounding in her chest sounded strangely like her ovaries stomping their tiny reproductive feet, as if to say, "it's about time you remembered we were withering away here." Well, not exactly withering. She had plenty of time to settle down. The scary truth was that she was already settled but seemed destined to be stuck alone.

She wanted to change her life, but maybe it had been a mistake to focus on her professional life when her personal world was so sorely lacking any excitement. David McCay would be an adventure—the kind that could ruin her for any other man. It might just be worth the risk. She shook her head and commanded her ovaries to shut down the party. This was the kind of thinking that had led to her outrageous request, and she didn't need to revisit that moment.

After returning the book to the nightstand, she turned to find David watching her from the doorway. Color rushed to her cheeks as if he could read her thoughts.

He stepped back just enough to let her out, then moved forward to place a gentle kiss on Rhett's forehead and tuck the sheets around him.

When Rhett was settled, David pulled the door shut and motioned her down the hall. "Did I hear you tell your ovaries to shut up?" he asked when they reached the kitchen.

She clasped a hand over her mouth to stifle a hysterical giggle. "Of course not," she said in a rush of air. "That would be crazy. Do I seem crazy to you?"

"At this point," he said after studying her for several moments, "you seem like a gift from heaven."

Oh. Well, that was unexpected. And lovely.

"I'm doing my job," she answered automatically.

"How does finagling the key to my apartment from Tracie fall under a teacher's job description?"

"I wanted to check on Rhett."

He moved closer, crowding her a little. But she didn't step back even though that was her inclination. She stood her ground. "That's not all you want," he whispered.

There weren't enough words in the English language to cover all the things she wanted from David. From life. From this moment.

"Ask me again," he told her, threading his fingers through her hair. The desire she saw in his blue eyes mesmerized her. A longing that matched her own, making her need grow that much more intense. "Ask me to have an affair with you."

"Kiss me," she said instead. Those two words were the only ones she could force her mouth to form at the moment.

He lowered his mouth to hers, claiming her lips with a force she felt all the way to her toes. How could the way he touched her feel both infinitely gentle and demanding at the same time? She wound her arms around his neck and gave herself over to the sensation. It was too much and not enough, and she whispered the one word that pounded through her whole body. "More."

Chapter 7

It was like the Fourth of July inside David's brain. He'd kissed plenty of women—taken some of them to his bed—girlfriends and baseball groupies who made it their mission to snag a professional athlete. None of them had affected him the way Erin did.

He wanted to blame it on his basically celibate lifestyle since settling in Crimson, but he knew it was more than that. It was the woman in his arms.

A shiver passed through her when he sucked her sensitive earlobe into his mouth. He lifted her onto the edge of the counter and positioned himself against the sweet V of her body, even as he did his best to keep his raging lust under control.

She deserved more than he could ever offer her in life, but the least he could do was refrain from mauling her like some sort of randy teenager. He wanted to savor each moment they spent together, to get down on his knees and worship every inch of her—to beg her to stay with him.

His hands trembled as he undid the buttons of her crisp linen blouse, revealing a pale blue bra covering the most beautiful breasts he'd ever seen. His mouth went dry and all he could do was stare at the creamy skin, flushed with pink.

He traced one finger over the edge of the fabric, earning a whispered moan from Erin.

"Amazing," he murmured, and she shook her head.

"You don't have to say that. My body is average at best." He'd heard plenty of women disparage themselves, mostly fishing for more compliments, but Erin made the statement like it was a well-known fact.

"Nothing about you is average."

She flashed a self-deprecating smile. "Everything about me is average."

"No." He placed a finger to her lips when she would have argued. "You have a gorgeous face and the most kissable skin." He trailed his mouth down the long column of her throat, and it almost drove him over the edge when she dropped back onto her elbows, pressing her breasts high into the air.

"The best part is that the way you look is only part of what makes you beautiful. When we're together, I feel things I didn't know were a possibility for a guy like me." He swirled his tongue around the tip of her breast through the fabric of her bra.

She moaned and he gathered her close, kissing her with all of his pent-up desire, letting her feel exactly how much he wanted her. She tugged on his T-shirt and he pulled it over his head and let it drop to the floor. Her hands smoothed up his chest, making his breath catch. His whole body pounded with need.

He wanted to strip off her clothes and feast on her. He wanted to lose himself in the moment and take her, make her his.

No.

A woman like Erin would never be his. Reality came crashing down around him, and he jerked back.

She stared at him, her gaze hazy with lust. Her breasts rose and fell as she struggled to make her breathing normal again. She sat on the edge of his counter, soft and sexy and ready for him. Hell, she had no idea how sexy she was.

"I'm sorry," he said, and wanted to punch his own face as her gaze clouded with doubt and then embarrassment.

She scrambled off the counter and turned away, quickly buttoning up her blouse. "Do I thank you now?" she asked quietly, the ice in her tone cutting across his skin. "Are we even? I came to see Rhett and you gave me a little taste—" she waved her hand toward the counter "—of that. I should be grateful, right?"

"Don't say that." He spun her around to face him. "Don't make this into something it isn't."

"I have a pretty good idea of exactly what this is and isn't," she said, her tone miserable.

"You have no idea." He ran a hand through his hair, trying to figure out how kissing this woman had become so complicated. Sex had always been simple. Straightforward. Meaningless. The fact that he wanted it to be so much more with Erin scared the hell out of him.

But the last thing he wanted was for her to believe he didn't want her.

"You mean something," he said. "To Rhett." He cleared his throat. "To me."

She bit down on her lip and he had to stifle a groan.

"I'm his teacher," she said without emotion. "I'm helping you manage these weeks without your sister."

"It's more than that," he said. "I like you, Erin."

"Enough to kiss me," she said through clenched teeth, "but not enough for sex."

"That isn't what this is about. You're not the kind of woman I want to sleep with—"

"I get it," she said, blinking rapidly.

Damn. He hoped like hell she wasn't going to cry. He was making a total mess of everything.

"We're obviously done here." She offered him a stiff little wave. "I assume it's okay if I let myself out the front door?"

He wrapped his fingers around her wrist and pulled her close. "I'm trying to give you a compliment. You deserve more than a quick roll in the sheets after an exhausting day. You're the kind of woman who men take on dates and home to meet their parents. I told you, you're apple pie and white picket fences. I'm late nights wrangling drunk tourists at a bar."

She tugged her wrist out of his grasp. "You're a baseball player," she said, spitting out the words like an accusation.

"Not anymore."

That earned him an eye roll. "You were a famous pitcher for a major-league team. Talk about the American ideal. It's our national pastime."

"I'm not good for you."

She threw up her hands. "Why does everyone think they know what I want more clearly than I do? My mom thinks my expectations of life are too high. My ex thinks I can't be adventurous in the bedroom because I don't have the body of a stripper. You want me up on some holier-than-thou pedestal."

"Your body is perfect," he said, wishing he could punch whatever idiot boyfriend had made her believe otherwise.

"Yeah," she said on a derisive laugh. "Really hard for you to resist. But someone in this town is going to want me." Her voice cracked a tiny bit and she sucked in a breath. "Even for one night. Hey, we're standing above a bar. I bet I can find a guy downstairs willing to be with me."

She turned on her heel and stalked toward the door to his loft. "Bring Rhett to the community center tomorrow at four," she called over her shoulder.

As angry as she was with David, she was still looking after Rhett. Taking care of both of them, really. And David was watching her walk away to find another man.

How big of an idiot could he be?

He caught up to her just as she reached for the door handle.

"Go on a date with me," he said, pressing his hand to the door to keep it shut.

She stilled, but it took her a minute to lift her gaze to his. "What?"

"We can go to dinner or on a hike or whatever you want."

Her eyes narrowed. "Why are you asking me out? Is this more payback for helping with Rhett? I care about him. You don't have to—"

He brushed his lips across hers. "Do you always argue when a man asks you on a date?" he asked against her mouth, then leaned in to press his forehead to hers, the tips of their noses touching.

She inhaled, her warm breath tickling his skin. "I'm not your type," she said.

"No," he countered. "I'm not *your* type. You deserve way better than me. But I'm asking anyway. Go out with me."

She didn't answer for so long he thought she might decline the invitation. He didn't blame her. He knew what he had to offer someone like her. A whole lot of drama and baggage. It would have been smarter to have just taken what she offered earlier. Maybe he could have gotten her out of his system.

But he wanted more.

"Okay," she said when he started to pull back.

He grinned, feeling like he'd just purchased a winning lottery ticket. "I'll call you," he said.

"Really?" She laughed softly. "We could just grab dinner after you pick up Rhett tomorrow night."

"Nope. I'm going to call you, and we'll make a plan and it will be like…"

"A date?"

"Like we're courting," he answered, the sound and connotation of the old-fashioned word appealing to him. Thanks to the baseball groupies who had hung around the fields since high school, David had never had to try hard with women. They fell into his lap—sometimes literally.

The idea of actually making an effort was new and strangely exciting. The thought of earning his place at Erin's side made nerves flutter through his chest.

"Courting," she repeated. "Are you sure?"

"Absolutely," he said, and kissed her again.

Then he opened the door. "I'll talk to you soon."

She looked slightly puzzled, which he found adorable. He wanted to keep her guessing.

She'd just started down the stairs when he called her name.

"Um…" He ran a hand through his hair, uncharacteristically anxious. "I hope this means you aren't heading downstairs to look for a guy. I know you don't owe me anything but—"

"I'm going home. Good night, David."

He blew out a breath as he closed the door. What the hell was he so nervous about? And possessive? He'd never cared before about being exclusive with the women he dated.

But it made him ridiculously happy to consider the possibility of Erin becoming his. He rubbed his shoulder as he moved through the apartment, turning off lights. It was still early compared to his normal hours, but David was tired as hell. All he wanted was to drop into his bed and dream of Erin.

Rhett tugged on Erin's arm as she handed Mari Clayton, the program director for the Aspen Foundation, her grant paperwork the following afternoon. It was just after six, and the other kids who'd come for tutoring and after-school activities had been picked up already. David was running a few minutes late so Rhett had been playing with Lego blocks while Erin began the meeting with the woman she hoped would fund Crimson Kidzone so it could be expanded. Erin needed the money to hire a part-time staff person.

There was so much she wanted to do for kids in the Crimson community now that she'd started, but all of it took money. Mari seemed receptive to her ideas, so

Erin had high hopes that the grant request she was submitting would be approved.

"Excuse me for a moment," she said to Mari, and turned to Rhett. "What do you need, Rhett?"

"Isaac is here." The boy gave her a pained look. "And Mommy's boyfriend."

She turned to where he was pointing. Another boy with dark hair and eyes stood in the doorway to the community center's makeshift classroom.

She recognized Isaac Martin, the boy Rhett had fought with at school, although his family had moved to Crimson last year so she'd never had him in class.

He wore baggy sweatpants and a Denver Broncos jersey. Next to him stood a tall, lean man close to Erin's age whom she recognized as Joel Martin, Jenna McCay's boyfriend and Isaac's father. His black hair was slicked back from his face and, although his features were classically handsome, his eyes had a hard edge to them.

He met her gaze and gave her a quick once-over. Goose bumps shivered across her skin, and not the kind she got when David looked at her. This man's stare made her feel uncomfortable and strangely nervous. She saw his gaze switch to Mari for a second before dismissing her just as quickly as he had Erin.

"The lady at the desk said this is where I sign my kid up for day care," the man said, arms crossed over his chest.

Isaac glared at Rhett, who moved behind Erin's legs, holding tight to the denim of the dark-washed jeans she wore.

"I'd be happy to get you an enrollment form," she answered. "Although it's not exactly day care." She threw

Mari an apologetic glance. "I offer an after-school enrichment program three days a week and—"

"Whatever," the man said. "Can I leave him now? His mom don't get off work until seven and I have things to do. His sisters are with their dad tonight and he don't want to stay by himself."

Erin had spoken to Melody after the fight about Isaac's family situation. According to her friend, the boy had two older stepsisters but his mother was single and struggling to keep her household together.

"Isaac is welcome to be part of the program," she said, keeping her voice steady, "but it only goes until six and he can't start until the paperwork is completed."

"*He's* still here." The man pointed at Rhett. "Isaac and him can play."

Rhett dug his fingers into her legs, and she wanted to wrap him in her arms. Isaac glared at them both. His father shifted to get a better look at Rhett, then did a double take.

"That's Jenna's kid," he muttered, then swatted Isaac on the back of the head. "He's the one that hit you, right?"

"Mr. Martin, what happened between the boys is a matter for the school to deal with. Rhett is going to be picked up in a few minutes, and I can get you an enrollment form but—"

"How's your mama doing, boy? It was a shame the crap got out of hand that night. I'm looking forward to her getting back so—"

Suddenly Joel jerked back as David spun him around and slammed him against the wall, pressing his forearm to the other man's throat. "You won't see my sister again. You won't look at her. You won't acknowledge her existence. Are we clear?"

Mari Clayton gasped and Erin peeled Rhett's hands off her legs and hurried forward. What kind of example were these two grown men showing boys who had just been disciplined for fighting? Not to mention the fact that the last thing Erin needed was a scene in the middle of her meeting with a potential donor.

Joel coughed and fought, but David had at least thirty pounds on him and showed no sign of backing down.

"Get the hell off me," Joel bit out, his voice hoarse. "Jenna can make her own damn decisions."

"Tell me you're going to leave my sister alone."

Erin didn't recognize this version of David. Gone was the laid-back bar owner or the caring—if sometimes clueless—uncle. Anger and violence radiated from him, making him seem like the man he'd warned her about.

Isaac had moved back into the hall, his small body shrinking against the door frame.

"David." She placed a hand on his arm. "Stop. This isn't the place. You're scaring the boys."

"Listen to the lady," Joel said, but as soon as David loosened his grip, the other man struck out, his fist connecting with David's jaw.

Erin heard a scream and realized it came from her throat. David shoved Joel again, and the tall man stumbled into the wall.

"Enough," she shouted.

Both men stilled at her tone. She might be shaking with nerves, but she had enough experience as a teacher to take command of the situation.

"The community center," she said slowly, as if settling a dispute over a favorite crayon, "is not the place for you two to have this…" She searched for the right word and settled on "conversation. You both have boys watching your every move."

David pressed a hand to his jaw and glanced over his shoulder to where Rhett was staring, wide-eyed, at the scene playing out in front of him.

"Dude grabbed me," Joel muttered. "I got to defend myself."

"Mr. Martin," she said firmly, "you can request a Kid-zone enrollment form at the community center's front desk." She turned to Isaac and gentled her voice. "We'd love to have you in the program, but there is no fighting or name-calling here. It's a safe place for everyone. Do you understand?"

The boy's brows lowered but he nodded. His father muttered under his breath a string of expletives so explicit it made her breath catch in her throat. David moved forward again with a growl, and she stepped between the two men.

"It would be a good idea for you to leave now," she told Joel. "Isaac, I hope to see you next week."

Joel's upper lip curled into an ugly sneer as he narrowed his gaze on David. "A real man don't let no woman push him around. Your sister knows what it's like to be with a baller." His mean brown eyes shifted to Erin. "Maybe Ms. Teacher wants something more in her life, too. What you say, baby?"

David snarled and tried pushing around Erin. "I'm going to—"

"No." She took a step to the side so she was still blocking him. "Mr. Martin, you need to go."

With a sickeningly sweet smile and a salute, the man turned away. "Come on, Isaac. Let's blow this place."

Erin stood watching them walk down the hall for

several moments, willing her breathing back to a normal pace.

"Erin." David's voice was gentle, but when he went to place a hand on her shoulder, she swatted away his touch.

"I'll deal with you in a minute," she said through teeth clenched tightly so no one would notice how much they were chattering. "Take care of Rhett. I have a meeting to finish."

Nervous laughter sounded from behind her. "I think we're finished here for tonight."

Mari Clayton had gathered her bag and purse and was staring at Erin and David, her cheeks flushed and a hand pressed flat to her chest.

"Uncle David," Rhett called. "You got in a fight just like me."

She heard David sigh as he moved toward his nephew. "I'm sorry about that," he said to Mari. "There was some history there but this wasn't the time or place for us to play it out."

The woman swallowed and nodded. "I understand."

He turned back to Erin, but she gave him a quelling glare, then focused her attention on Mari. "You can't possibly understand."

"You're right. This felt more like *Fight Club* than an after-school program for kids. I applaud what you're trying to do, Erin, and it's clear the community needs a safe place for kids to go. Still, I'm not sure your program and the Aspen Foundation are a good fit."

Tears stung the back of Erin's eyes. It was adrenaline, she knew, but this was not how the meeting with Mari was supposed to end. "I apologize for the scene. But I hope you'll change your mind. I think this demonstrates just how important a community outreach program that brings kids together is for Crimson."

"But can you keep the children safe?"

There was a slight hint of accusation in Mari's tone; Erin's doubts crashed around her like a thousand ocean waves. Her mother's refrain of "be happy with good enough" rang through her mind. Kidzone had been in place one week and already there was a question about whether she could manage it.

"I firmly believe I can," she lied to her potential donor. She wanted to make a safe place for kids to come after school, but Erin knew better than most that wanting something and getting it weren't always the same thing.

"Let's touch base in a few weeks," Mari said noncommittally. "The decisions about our fall funding cycle will be made by the end of October. It may be better to wait until your program is more established."

Biting down on the inside of her cheek to keep from crying, Erin nodded. A moment after Mari walked away, Olivia appeared in the doorway. "Is everything all right? Rita said a guy just stormed by the front desk, dragging a boy along with him."

"A potential client," Erin said, shaking her head.

"Isaac's daddy is mean," Rhett whispered.

"No way are you going to let that kid in here."

She turned from Olivia to see David staring at her, hands on hips, his features hard as granite.

Olivia stepped forward. "Rhett, I was about to box up the cupcakes someone brought in today. Would you help me, and you can take a couple home for you and your uncle?"

"It's fine, buddy," David said when the boy looked up at him. "Ms. MacDonald and I will work things out in here."

Rhett moved toward Olivia.

"I'm going to ask Mommy," he told Erin as he passed, "not to be his girlfriend anymore when she gets back."

"I'm sorry he scared you," she said, reaching out to ruffle his hair. "You know you're always safe with me."

He nodded. "Can I bring a cupcake for Ms. MacDonald, too?" he asked Olivia.

"You bet," she answered and took his hand to lead him away.

As soon as the boy was gone, all of the adrenaline that had kept Erin together through that ugly scene drained from her body. She dropped her head into her hands and drew in a deep breath.

"Erin."

She glanced up to see David taking a step closer. "Don't," she whispered, and automatically moved back. "You don't get to tell me how to run this program. You certainly don't get to make a scene in front of the foundation representative I was hoping would give me the money to hire additional staff and really make this thing work."

"I didn't realize who she was," he said, rubbing a hand over the shadow of stubble across his jaw.

She hated that even now, as angry as she was with him, the scratchy sound still made her tingle all the way to her toes.

"It doesn't matter," she said, crossing her arms over her chest. "You were out of line."

His head snapped back as if she'd struck him. "You heard what he was saying about Jenna. The things he insinuated toward you. I'm not going to stand by and let a creep like that get away with—"

"You're Rhett's guardian now, David. His role model. How can you expect him to work out his problems without violence when you set that kind of example?" She knew she was being harsh, but her emotions wouldn't let her back down. "Joel Martin is awful but there are better ways to deal with him."

"What ways?" he countered. "Watching the guy get away with whatever he wants? Letting his kid bully my nephew and disrespect you and my sister?"

"I don't need you to protect me."

He barked out a laugh. "It sounds like you don't need me at all."

She bit down on her lip, unsure of how to respond. She didn't want to need him but couldn't resist the current of awareness pulsing between them, despite their differences and her anger.

"Thank you for keeping Rhett today," he said quietly, smoothing a finger over the furrow she knew formed between her brows when she was upset. "I'm sorry I screwed things up with your meeting. I wasn't joking when I told you I was bad news, Erin. This afternoon proves my point."

"David."

He dropped his finger to her lip. "You've gone out of your way to help me, and I'm grateful. What happened here was a crappy way to show it."

Before she could respond, he dropped his hand and walked out of the room, presumably to collect Rhett from Olivia.

Erin wanted to rush after him, to launch herself at his big frame and hold on tight. David didn't belong to her, but her chest ached at the thought of losing him. She'd managed to carve out a decent life for herself, and she should be satisfied with that. It was easier and a lot less pain in the long run.

Chapter 8

When the doorbell rang that night, David's heart leaped. He rubbed at his chest as he went to answer it, hope rising like a bird on a current of air that Erin was paying him a visit.

He hated himself for hurting her, then walking away. He'd sat on the couch since putting Rhett to bed with his phone in his hand, typing out a half dozen texts but deleting each one.

She'd seen his true colors, although it might be better that it happened now instead of down the road. If he'd actually had the opportunity to truly claim her as his own, he wasn't sure he'd ever be able to let her go.

But hope was a painfully resilient emotion, unwilling to let go of even the briefest glimpse of happiness. If Erin had come to him, maybe he still had a chance. With a deep breath, he opened the door.

"Hello, David. It's been a while."

Without his hand gripping the door handle, David would have stumbled back a step. His mouth went dry and it felt like someone had dropped a lead balloon on his chest. "Mom."

"Are you going to invite me in?" Angela McCay peered around him into the apartment. "Kind of a fancy place you've set yourself up in, even if you're living over a bar."

"Mom, why are you here?"

She smoothed a hand over her hair and flashed him a sad smile. "Isn't it obvious? I'm making things right."

He hadn't seen his mother in over five years, but she looked the same as ever. It was as if Angela drank from the fountain of youth and never aged. Her blond hair was shorter than he remembered, a simple cut that fell to just above her shoulders. Maybe there were a few thin lines etched into the skin around her vivid blue eyes.

But she remained as beautiful as she'd been when he was a boy. At Rhett's age, David would sit on one of the chairs in the kitchen and watch her move about the room—on the rare occasions when she cooked a real dinner—and think how lucky he was to have Angela as his mother. It took him a while to learn that a person's outward beauty wasn't always an accurate measure of who they were on the inside.

Too much had happened in their small family, terrible things and small mistreatments that his mother had either been responsible for or turned a blind eye to as they unfolded. He wished he could recapture some of his unconditional love from childhood, but he was an adult and had spent too long nursing old wounds to let them go so easily.

Yet she was still his mother, so he stepped back to let her into his apartment and, he supposed, his life.

"Did Jenna call you?"

"Yes, and it's about time," his mom answered as she moved past him. "My bags are in the hall. Be a good boy and bring them in for me."

"Bags?" he asked even as he pulled in the two suitcases and closed the door. "How long do you plan to be here?"

She turned to him. "As long as it takes. Your sister wants me here. She thinks you need help."

"I'm not the one in rehab," he muttered.

"That might have been a bit of overkill," she said, arching one brow. "Jenna could have recovered on her own."

"We've tried that before. It didn't take, and Rhett is old enough now to be affected. She needs to get healthy, and it has to stick this time."

She studied him for a moment, then sighed. "You always were her knight in shining armor." She stepped closer and raised a hand to his cheek. "You took care of both of us."

The scent of her shampoo, honey and almond, drifted up to him, taking him back to sharing a bathroom in their tiny apartment growing up. He'd taken countless lukewarm showers as a kid after his mom and sister used up their limited supply of hot water, but he'd always loved the way the bathroom smelled after his mother got ready.

"I did a sucky job at it," he said, letting his eyes drift closed and losing himself in the familiar touch and scent.

She patted his cheek. "You tried, and that's what counts."

If someone had asked, David would have claimed he didn't need anything from his mother. Not her help, not her approval and certainly not her blessing. Yet those words of absolution seemed to loosen the chains that were locked tight around his heart. They didn't eliminate his guilt and regret, but somehow they made him feel better.

"You tried, too," he told her, his way of offering an olive branch after so many years of animosity between them.

"We both know I didn't," she said quietly. "I was a hot mess, and you and your sister got pulled into it. I thought baseball was your ticket out until the accident…"

"It wasn't an accident." He took a step away and crossed his arms over his chest. "It was a stupid bar fight, and I never should have been there in the first place."

She gave him a speculative look. "And now you own a bar."

"It's a brewpub, Mom. I'm good at making beer." He laughed softly. "Maybe better than I was at pitching."

"How's your shoulder?"

"Fine."

"Do you ever think about going back?"

A familiar tension pulsed through his body, making his blood feel like it was tinged with acid. He'd spent months rehabbing his shoulder with grueling exercise and physical therapy. He refused to believe that stupidity had ended his baseball career in a matter of minutes. Guys came back from injuries and surgeries—sometimes better than they'd been in the first place.

Not David.

He paced to the edge of the living room, glancing out at the view of Main Street from his front window. If it weren't for Jenna's move to Colorado and his frustration over a shoulder that wouldn't return to its normal strength, this town would mean nothing to him. But Crimson had been the best thing to happen to him. It made the ache of losing baseball—his escape and sanctuary—tolerable. Even from his place on the periphery, this community had helped him to stop looking back to what could have been and focus on the life he had.

"Not anymore," he told his mother. "My life is good now. Healthy. I want that for Rhett and Jenna." He moved toward her. "I need help, and if you're willing to give it you can stay. But we're doing things my way. There are rules and structure."

Angela made a face. "I've never been much for structure, honey. You know that. I'm here to bring some fun and sunshine into that boy's life."

Which sounded like his mother blowing sunshine. But if Jenna had called her, he would make it work. "Fun is fine," he said, resisting the urge to roll his eyes. "But he needs a routine. We're giving him that, and we're going to do the same for Jenna when she gets back. She's got to clean up her life, whether she likes it or not."

His mother rose to her tiptoes and kissed his cheek. "Your sister is lucky to have you. It's not too late for our family, David."

He hoped she was right. "You can stay in my bedroom. I'll take the couch."

"I don't want to be an imposition," his mother said, even as she shrugged out of her brightly colored cardigan and draped it over the back of the couch. "Will you be a dear and bring my bags? Do I have my own bathroom?"

Before David could answer, a small voice called his name. "Uncle David?"

He turned see Rhett standing at the edge of the hallway, wiping the back of his hand across his eyes.

"Is Mommy here? I woke up and heard her voice."

David heard a tiny gasp behind him. He was used to
how much Jenna and their mother looked alike but hadn't
realized they sounded similar, as well.

"Your mom isn't here," he said gently. "But your
grandma has come to visit." He moved to reveal Angela standing behind him.

"Hi, sweetie boy," she cooed. "Do you remember your
grandma?"

Rhett shook his head.

Angela made a sound of distress, then pasted a bright
smile on her face. "You were a baby the last time I saw
you. It was before you and your mommy moved to Colorado." She stepped forward. "I'm going to help Uncle
David look after you until she comes home, okay? We're
going to have lots of fun together."

Rhett slanted his head, studying Angela. "You don't
look like a grandma," he said.

David gave a small snort of laughter, earning a nar-
row-eyed glare from his mother. She reached for the
sweater and quickly put it on over the silky tank top
she wore underneath. Angela had never dressed like a
typical mother, either.

"Doesn't change the fact that I'm yours," she said.
"You good with that?"

Rhett's sleepy blue gaze met David's. "Your mom
called your grandmother," David told the boy. "So she
could stay with us."

After a moment Rhett nodded. "Okay."

"Time to go back to bed," David told the boy.

"I can tuck you in," Angela offered.

"I want Uncle David," Rhett whispered.

David felt his heart clutch, but heard his mother sigh. "You bet, buddy." He put a hand on his mother's shoulder. Although he'd never had much sympathy for her, he understood what it was like to be unsure how to do what was right.

"Give it time," he whispered, and took Rhett's hand.

He led the boy back to his bedroom, retrieved Ruffie from the far side of the bed and settled Rhett under the covers again.

By the time he came out, his mother had moved her bags into his bedroom. She'd taken his clothes out of the dresser and filled a laundry basket.

"I hope you don't mind if I unpack," she said, folding a stack of more tank tops. "I hate living out of a suitcase."

He thought about asking her about her current life and if she had a home base now. Other than a monthly bank transfer into her checking account, David wasn't exactly up to date on his mother's life. But he could save that for another night. Apparently, they'd have plenty if she was here until Jenna returned.

"Rhett doesn't normally wake during the night," he told her. "Since you're here, I'm going to go downstairs and check on the bar."

She raised one finely penciled cyebrow. "Are *you* drinking, David?"

"Mom, I brew beer for a living. I drink, but it's not a problem."

She tsked softly.

He sighed. "I haven't been drunk since the night of the bar fight."

"At least I would have understood if you'd been drinking when you gave that woman and her boyfriend most of your money. I'm not so sure about your decision-making when you're sober."

"I put that man in the hospital for almost a month. Everything changed in one moment. I owed them."

"He fell and knocked his head on the corner of the table."

"Because I punched him."

"After he knifed you."

"I'm not having this discussion again," he said through gritted teeth. "Jenna wants you here, and I'll honor that. But I'm not rehashing old history. I don't get drunk anymore, and I watch my temper. Things are good in Crimson, and I intend to keep it that way."

She studied him a long moment, then nodded. "Fine. Go do what you need to do. I'll be here if my grandson needs me."

David nodded and headed for Elevation. Halfway down his private staircase, he stopped. His chest rose and fell and it felt like someone had lobbed a grenade at him. How the hell had his life spun so out of control? He was the temporary guardian for his five-year-old nephew and his mother—who had the maternal instincts of a feral cat—was now his child-rearing partner?

He turned and took the steps back to his apartment two at a time. Grabbing his jacket and the set of keys off the hook on the wall, he let himself out the front door and walked toward his truck parked in the alley behind the building.

He had plenty to take care of at both the bar and the brewery, but there was other business that called to him in his current mood.

Erin looked out the peephole of her apartment's front door and sucked in a breath.

"I know you're in there," David said softly, sounding like a man who had the patience to wait all night for her if that's how she played it. "Talk to me, Erin. Please."

Damn her weakness for good manners. A well-timed "please" got her every time.

She opened the door a few inches and tried not to notice how gorgeous he looked standing on the other side. He wore dark jeans, engineer boots and a heavy canvas jacket to ward against the crisp evening temperatures that signaled fall in the mountains. His hair was disheveled, like the wind was blowing or he'd been running his hands through it.

The way she wanted to run her hands through it.

"Can I come in?" he asked in that same quiet tone that made his already low voice sound like a growl.

"Where's Rhett?"

"Asleep," he answered automatically. "My mom is at the apartment in case he wakes up."

"You have a mom?" Erin was so shocked she stepped back and the door opened a little wider.

One side of David's mouth quirked up. "Would you like to see my belly button to prove I'm not an alien?"

Her mouth went dry as she glanced at the edge of his jacket. *Heck, yes*, her body screamed. *Take off your clothes, hottie brewmaster.*

"No," she said, her voice coming out a chirp. "I know you're human, but I didn't realize your mom was coming to visit."

She wanted to smack herself on the head. Of course she didn't know anything about his mother. The intimacy between her and David had developed too quickly and under such strange circumstances.

"If you invite me in, I'll tell you about it." He leaned

closer. "Your neighbor's front curtains are fluttering like mad. I swear she's going to call the cops, and the last thing I need is Cole coming after me."

"That's Ms. Kronkowski," Erin said without even having to look at which apartment he was talking about. "Because I'm single she thinks I must be a wild party girl."

David chuckled.

"Hey," she said, pushing at his chest. "That's not funny."

"Yes, it is." His eyes grazed up and down her body and she realized she'd let the door open enough that her Hello Kitty pajamas were on full display. "It's not even ten and you're ready for bed."

"I was reading," she countered.

"Let me guess," he said. "A romance novel."

She narrowed her eyes, not sure how she felt about him pegging her reading tastes so easily. "What do you have against heroes?"

"I don't trust 'em," he said with a shrug. "If a guy seems too good to be true, he probably is."

"Not on my e-reader," she answered, but gestured him into the apartment, both because she didn't want Ms. Kronkowski to go apoplectic and because Erin's ex-boyfriend had seemed too good to be true. And he'd turned out to be a first-class jerk.

"Tell me about the guy who hurt you," David said, pulling the door shut and coming to stand in front of her.

Could he read her mind? She gave a strangled laugh and asked, "Is that why you're here?"

He shook his head. "I'm here to apologize, but I want to know about you."

"There's nothing to know. If you don't believe me, talk to my mother. She'll be happy to tell you how ordinary I am."

When his gaze turned sympathetic, Erin closed her eyes and sighed. "I didn't mean that. I don't want to talk about my ex-boyfriend or my mother with you."

He laced his fingers with hers when she opened her eyes, then led her to the couch, taking a seat and tugging her down next to him.

"I'll start," he told her, using his thumb to trace circles around the center of her palm. The featherlight touch made her skin tingle. "I'm sorry I lost it today at the community center. I was out of line, and the last thing I want to do is jeopardize your program. You've been a lifesaver for me, and you deserve better in return."

"Every kid gets a chance," she told him, "even the ones with awful parents. I can't turn away a child because you have a personal issue with his father."

"I get that," he said, "even if I don't like it. Hell, maybe if Jenna and I had a teacher like you back in the day, things could have been different for us." He dropped his head to the back of the couch, staring up at the white ceiling in her apartment. "Which brings me to my mother. She showed up tonight because my sister called her to help. She seems sincere, but things have never been great with us. Motherhood wasn't really her thing, so Jenna and I did a lot of raising ourselves."

"You took care of your sister," Erin said quietly.

"Not very well," he told her, pulling his hand away. "I was obsessed with playing baseball. The funny thing was that one of Mom's boyfriends actually bought me my first ball and bat. He was a third baseman in the minor leagues, a decent guy." He gave a half-hearted chuckle. "Of course, that meant he and my mom didn't last long. She was a magnet for losers, just like Jenna. But I kept playing ball."

"And you were good," she said. "I Googled you."

"You Googled me," he repeated softly. "I can't even imagine the crap you found about me online."

She shrugged. "You've had an exciting life."

"Hardly." He shook his head. "I screwed the whole thing up."

"Because of your injury," she prompted.

"I don't talk about it."

"You can with me."

He studied her a moment, then nodded. "It was a stupid bar fight. I'd met a woman after one of our home games and we started hooking up. It wasn't love or dating. I didn't know anything about her other than she was hot. I was twenty-five and stupid as the day is long. I had an ego to match my pitching talent. The woman had a jealous husband."

"She was married?"

He gave a sharp nod. "I swear I didn't know that, but it doesn't matter. We were out and her husband came busting into the bar, hell-bent on beating me to a pulp. He was a big guy."

"You're a big guy."

"I was also drunk and sloppy. But I'm a decent fighter. Just not against a knife."

"David," she whispered, noticing that he'd moved his hand to massage his shoulder.

"In retrospect," he said quietly, "that guy did me a favor."

"He ended your career."

"My reckless behavior ended it, and who knows where I'd be if it hadn't happened. I wouldn't have moved to Crimson to help Jenna." He gave her a lop-sided smile. "I wouldn't have met you."

"Oh," she breathed, because somewhere in his words was the nicest compliment she'd ever received.

"From my perspective, ordinary is the most exciting thing going." He draped an arm across the couch cushions, his fingers just grazing her back. The gentle touch made her body come alive.

"There's nothing exciting about my life," she said, shaking her head.

"Come on," he prompted. "Give me more than that. Help me understand you, Erin. I know you're a great teacher, but I also know the program at the community center means more to you than just another way to help kids."

She bit down on her bottom lip, then sucked in a breath when he ran the pad of his thumb over the same spot.

"I want something that belongs to me," she said after a moment. "I want to do something that my mom can be proud of—"

"She should be proud that her daughter is one of the best teachers around."

If only it were that simple. "We moved to Crimson after my dad died when I was just a little older than Rhett. They were older when I was born." She cleared her throat and added, "I was definitely a surprise. Dad was a college professor and my mom is a psychiatrist. It was clear from the time I was little that I wasn't like them. They loved me, but I didn't quite fit. They were both so smart."

"You're smart."

"My mom is a legitimate genius and I'm—" she shrugged "—average."

"Don't say that."

"It's true. I wasn't the kid she expected to get. After

Dad died, I'm not sure she knew what to do with me. I
wanted to do things like Girl Scouts and slumber parties,
and she thought I should be spending more time with my
head in the books. When it became clear I wasn't going
to live up to her high standards, she kind of lost interest."

"How could anyone lose interest in you?" He shifted
closer, cupped her cheeks in his warm palms. "You're
smart and beautiful, and you have the biggest heart of
anyone I know."

"Apparently," she muttered, "big hearts aren't as valuable as big breasts."

He blinked and dropped his hands. "Come again."

"Have you heard of Brazen Peaks?"

"The restaurant outside of Carbondale?"

"I think the correct term is 'breastaurant,'" she told him.

"Right. So what?"

"Have you been there?"

He shook his head. "Not my scene."

"My ex met his new girlfriend there. According to him,
she's sexy, adventurous and exciting." She made a face.
"I'm pretty sure that means I'm none of those things."

"Or it means your ex is an idiot." He leaned and brushed
his lips across hers. "Trust me. Your ex is an idiot."

She couldn't stop the smile that tugged at the corners
of her mouth. It felt like the door to the cage she'd been
living in her whole life had just been thrown open. When
her friends told her that Greg was a fool for dumping
her, she'd assumed they were just being kind. Her mother
certainly hadn't bothered with that sentiment. She'd simply shaken her head and said that until Erin lowered her
standards, she was bound to be disappointed by men.

But David made the comment with so much convic-
tion, she believed every word of it. If a man like him

found her attractive, what did the opinion of her two-timing ex-boyfriend matter anyway?

"Show me your scar," she said suddenly, then felt her eyes grow wide.

David looked as surprised at her request as she was at making it.

"I'm not sure that's such a grand plan, darlin'," he told her, his voice husky.

"Please," she whispered, hoping the magic word would have the same effect on him as it did on her. "I want to understand what happened to you."

"Isn't it enough to know I'm damaged goods?"

"You're not, and neither am I."

He lifted a brow. "Does that mean I get to see your breasts?"

Her mouth dropped open.

"I'm joking," he said, shrugging out of his jacket. "Although it's not such a bad idea now that I think about it. Best way to prove without a doubt that your ex-boyfriend was a total loser, don't you think?"

Erin swallowed. "I actually can't think right now."

David chuckled. "Then let's do this thing while your brain is jumbled." He grabbed the hem of his dark gray henley and pulled it over his head.

If Erin hadn't been able to think a moment ago, looking at David's gorgeous body made her feel like her mind had just been put in a blender. Every single one of her brain cells chose that moment to go on sabbatical, a fact that made the rest of her body sing with glee.

Because her body wanted things from this man that her brain couldn't handle. She knew David was big and broad, but she hadn't expected the golden skin or the darker hair that covered his chest. His body was all muscle, lean and toned and more delicious than anything she'd ever seen.

He moved, turning so she could see his beautiful back. The hard planes were just as pronounced, but at the top of his left shoulder was a pink scar about three inches long. It had clearly healed, but the color hadn't faded as much as she would have expected. The skin was raised where it had been sewn together.

"It's not pretty," he said over his shoulder. "They call it a keloid scar."

"That's why it's raised?"

"Yeah. They can do therapy to flatten it, but I never bothered. It's a reminder of how stupid and reckless I was."

Holding her breath, she reached out to run her fingertips along the ridge. His skin was warm, and she felt him stiffen under her touch.

"It's a good reminder that you're human," she told him. "Because otherwise you're a little too perfect."

"I'm far from perfect."

The feel of him mesmerized her. The fact that she was actually touching the man she'd had a crush on for months had sparks flying all through her body. "Hate to break it to you, but your body didn't get that message."

"You like my body?"

She snorted. "A ninety-year-old grandma would like your body."

"I've changed my mind." He moved so quickly all she had time to do was yelp, then she was in his arms with his heat enveloping her. "If I take off my clothes, you have to take off yours."

It was even more difficult to form a coherent thought

with his chest hair tickling her cheek. She glanced to one side and—oh my—nipple at eye level.

She didn't even realize she'd licked her lips until David let out a soft groan. "Killing me here, darlin'. I can't even imagine what you're thinking, but I'm guessing it's dirty and I know I'd like it."

"Nothing I want to do to you is dirty," she said, trying to control her breathing. "People do it all the time. It's completely natural."

He lowered his head until his mouth skimmed hers. "What I want to do to you, Erin, is hot and dirty and no one can do it like me."

A volcano erupted inside her body. With just his words, David had her more aroused than she'd ever felt in her life. She brought a hand to her face and patted her cheek.

David smiled against her lips. "What are you doing?"

"Just making sure I didn't spontaneously combust."

He pulled back to gaze at her, his blue eyes warm and full of equal amounts of desire and amusement. "You're something special."

She opened her mouth to automatically correct him. No, she wasn't special. She was average. Ordinary. Boring.

But the way he looked at her made her *feel* special, so who was she to argue? "Fake it 'til you make it" had been her mantra during her first year of teaching, when she wasn't confident in her ability to handle a roomful of kindergartners.

The same principle applied now.

She reached up and fused her mouth to his, sliding her tongue along the seam of his lips. He rewarded her with a groan, and she felt it all the way to her toes. He lifted her until she was straddling him, her knees digging into the soft cushions of the couch.

She draped her arms around his neck and ran her fingers through his hair, every inch of her front plastered to the front of him. He deepened the kiss, making her senses reel. She wanted David with a thundering need that surpassed anything she'd felt before.

Her desire was so all-encompassing that she didn't even hesitate when he tugged at the hem of her cotton pajama top. She raised her arms and allowed him to pull it over her head, then gasped as his jaw grazed her breast.

"I'm not wearing a bra," she murmured, more to herself than him, suddenly remembering that she'd been tucked in bed reading when he'd knocked on her door.

"It's my lucky night," he said against her skin. His mouth closed around one nipple and Erin's body sang with joy. She gave herself over to the sensation of it, the gentle pressure and the sweet words he whispered as he held her.

He claimed her mouth again as his hand trailed under the waistband of her pants and into her panties. She whimpered when he dipped his fingers into her, the fire banking deep within her suddenly bursting into a million flames. He continued to kiss her, his tongue mimicking the motion of his fingers, and she exploded around him on a sharp cry.

It was like nothing she'd ever experienced and more than she would have guessed was possible, and she wanted the moment to last forever.

Chapter 9

The sensation of Erin coming apart in his arms was pure bliss to David. From the tiny gasps of pleasure to her flushed skin to the way she cried out his name at the end, she was absolute perfection. It beat out the moment he was drafted by the Pirates, the first time he pitched a major-league game and so many wild nights with women he'd lost count. Which only made it that much more difficult to pull away.

Erin had gone pliant in his arms, soft and a little sleepy. He wanted nothing more than to finish what they'd started, to carry her to the bedroom and worship her body from head to toe. But she deserved better than an unplanned roll in the sheets.

She was worth more than she believed, and he was certain that taking her now was something they'd both come to regret.

He picked up her shirt and dropped it over her head.

She automatically pushed her arms through the sleeves, then frowned.

"What's going on?"

Her dark eyes were big and lovely and full of so much trust that he was sure to screw up in the end.

"I'm tucking you in," he said, grabbing his shirt from the floor, then moving one arm around her back and the other under her knees. He lifted her off the couch and started for the narrow hallway he assumed led to her bedroom.

She splayed her hand across his chest, her thumb just brushing one nipple, and he almost stumbled a step. "I'm not sleepy," she told him.

"It's late, Erin, and I didn't mean for things to go so far."

"So this was an accident?" Her eyes narrowed. "Or a mistake?"

He moved into the bedroom, where a lamp on the nightstand illuminated the space in a golden glow. She had a wrought iron bed frame with a patchwork quilt on top—both feminine and classic. Perfect for Erin.

As he lowered her onto the bed, which was unmade only on the side where she slept, he couldn't help but smile at the array of things spread across the quilt on the other side. There was an e-reader with a polka-dot cover, several paperback books, a box of tissues and…

"You have a cat?"

She darted a glance to the ball of fur that didn't so much as offer a tail flick to acknowledge that people had entered its space. "That's Sugar. She's kind of standoff-ish until she gets to know you."

"See," he said, dropping a kiss on the top of her head, "there's no room for me in the bed anyway." He gestured to the stack of books as he pulled on his henley. "You have too many heroes already."

"You're placating me," she told him, "and I don't like it. That was—" she pointed toward the family room "—pretty darn awesome for me. Beyond awesome. I'm grateful, but I also understand if I don't do it for you. Just man up and tell me."

He grabbed her wrists, pinned them above her head and leaned in to take her mouth, allowing all the frustration and need pounding through his body to transfer to the kiss.

Maybe he was trying to freak her out, to prove that what he wanted was surely more than she was willing to give. Instead, she met his desire with her own, and it tore through him like a brush fire, igniting every part of him until he had to force himself to release her again.

"I want you, Erin. I want us. I want to start with all night, and keep going for as long as you'll let me."

She drew in a breath, pressed her fingertips to lips swollen from his kiss. "Then why…"

"I'm not exactly a stand-up guy, but I know when a woman deserves more than I can give. When I told you I wanted to court you, it wasn't a joke. I want you to feel special—"

"Mission accomplished on the couch."

"I want you to understand how special you are. I wish you saw yourself the way I see you." He straightened, shook his head. "I have to admit I didn't think you'd accept my apology tonight, and I wouldn't have blamed you in the least."

"I'll find another way to get funding," she said, but he could hear the hesitation in her voice. He wanted to kick himself for how he'd acted earlier. He'd spent his whole life dealing with losers like Joel Martin, and had been in more than his share of fights to defend his sister. But he was older now, and he should be smarter. He had Rhett to think about.

And now Erin.

More than anything, David wanted to be the type of man who would deserve her.

"I'll help you," he told her.

"You don't have to—"

"Let me help you."

She gave him a shy smile. "Okay."

"And let me take you out on a real date." When she didn't respond immediately, he added a soft, "Please."

"You're pretty good with manners," she told him, rolling her eyes.

"I'm good with a lot of things." He leaned in and gave her one last lingering kiss. "I plan to demonstrate every one of my skills for you."

To his surprise, she laughed. The sound loosened the invisible band that stretched tight around his heart. "Are you sure you don't read romance novels? Because that sounds like the perfect hero line to me."

"No hero here," he told her. "But I hope you have some sweet dreams tonight."

"Good night, David," she whispered.

"Good night, Erin."

By the beginning of the following week, Erin wondered if she'd dreamed her whole encounter with David.

A sweet dream, indeed, but disappointing to think she'd made the whole thing up in her head.

What other explanation could there be for the fact that she hadn't seen or heard from him in five days?

She might not be an expert on courting, but there was no doubt that's not how it typically went.

Each day, regret plagued her. The more plausible explanations for David's silence were a lot harder to take. Maybe she shouldn't have let things go so far on her couch. It felt like he put her up on some pedestal she wasn't interested in standing on, so could it be possible that he'd lost respect for her? The more logical reason was simply that he wasn't interested yet didn't want to hurt her feelings.

Which hurt her more than if he'd been honest in the first place.

She'd thought he might ask her out for the previous weekend, and she'd been fool enough to check her cell phone compulsively most of Saturday, waiting for a call that never came. In the end, she'd ordered pizza and binge-watched *Pride and Prejudice*—both the BBC and Hollywood versions. Then she'd thrown in *Bridget Jones's Diary* for an extra Colin Firth fix.

She told herself she should get in the habit of keeping her books on her nightstand instead of the other side of the bed. But really, why bother when Sugar was the one sharing it?

Rhett had been making progress with his social skills, playing with Elaina during recess and interacting with the other kids in the after-school program.

Joel Martin hadn't been back to see her, but Isaac's mother, Danielle, had signed him up for the program on the two days when she worked until five at the Hair Nation salon outside of town. Other than a subtle side-eye toward Rhett, the woman had been polite and grateful to have a place for her son to go after school.

Isaac and Rhett had seemed to silently agree to a truce. The funny thing was the boys had a lot in common. Both were slow to make friends but craved social interactions. They liked building things and games of any sort. She'd managed to engage them both in a puzzle Monday afternoon and wished their parents could handle things so maturely.

It was nearly five on Tuesday when an older woman with thick blond hair piled high on her head and makeup applied to make her look ten years younger sauntered into the room.

"Rhett, baby," she called, "get your things. Nana's taking you out for a special treat."

Rhett looked up from where he was making a race car out of modeling clay. "I'm 'posed to stay here until Uncle David comes to get me. He's picking me up."

"Change of plans," the woman said. She moved forward and adjusted her oversize purse on her shoulder. "I'm Angela McCay, Rhett's grandma."

Erin felt color rush to her face at the way Angela's gaze seemed to take her in and automatically dismiss her. "David mentioned you arrived in town."

Angela's blue eyes turned assessing. "Oh, did he now?" She shrugged. "I don't think he talked about you. Are you and my son close?"

"Um…we know each other because of Rhett." If David hadn't mentioned her, she wasn't going to give this woman any details of her relationship—if she could even call it that.

Rhett came to stand next to Erin. "I told you Ms. MacDonald is my favorite teacher."

"You're in kindergarten," Angela said, reaching out a hand to tousle Rhett's blond hair. "There isn't a lot to compare her to."

"She's still my favorite," Rhett said, his small chin jutting out.

Erin felt a flood of gratitude for the boy and his innocent loyalty.

"Do I need to sign something to check him out?" Angela asked, ignoring Rhett's comment.

"Each parent or guardian submits a form naming the people approved to pick up their child from the program." Erin tried not to fidget under Angela's stare. She could see where David and his sister got their looks.

Angela might be a little rough around the edges, but it was clear she must have been a traffic-stopping beauty in her day. Lines snaked out from the edges of her eyes and around her mouth, but she still had high cheekbones, bee-stung lips and the kind of figure that seemed out of place on a woman with a five-year-old grandson.

She wore a long-sleeved white T-shirt, low-slung jeans and boots. Around her neck were several strands of turquoise layered on top of a couple of heavy silver chains.

"I'm his nana," the woman said, her tone icy. "Of course I have permission to pick him up."

Erin pressed her fingers to the place on her chest where a knot of nerves was forming. "If you'd wait a minute, I'll call David to confirm."

Just then one of the third-grade boys lobbed a purple crayon across the table at one of his friends. Instead of its intended target, the crayon hit the water cup a threesome of girls was sharing as they painted. The dirty water spilled across the table, sending the girls into a screaming panic.

"It's okay, girls," Erin said, holding up a finger to ask Rhett's grandmother to wait a moment. "We can clean things up."

"Are you in charge of all these kids?" Angela asked over the din.

"I have help," Erin answered, trying not to sound defensive, "but she went down to the office to make copies."

"Looks like you've bitten off a little more than you can chew."

Embarrassment rushed through Erin. The old adage was one of her mother's favorite reminders from when Erin was a girl. Every time Erin wanted to sign up for a new activity or try out for a team, her mother had said, "Don't bite off more than you can chew."

She hurried over to the side table and grabbed a roll of paper towels. "I've got it under control."

"While you deal with—" Angela waved her hands at the mess "—I'm going to take Rhett."

"I really need to talk to—"

"My new shirt," one of the girls screeched. "Paint water's ruining my new shirt."

"Honey, let me make this easy on you." Angela reached out and took Rhett's hand. "I'll text my son and let him know the boy's with me. You take care of your mess."

"It's not a mess," Erin muttered at the same moment one of the girls, Ava Elliott, punched the boy who'd thrown the crayon in the stomach.

Erin hurried to them as the boy doubled over in pain.

By the time she looked up again, Angela and Rhett were gone.

Claire Travers, the teenager who was assisting her with the program, came back in the room, her eyes growing wide at the chaos and commotion. "I was gone for like five minutes," she said.

"It's fine," Erin called. "Get Ava and Paige cleaned up, okay?"

She helped the boy who'd been punched, Fletcher, to a seat on the beanbag.

"Can't breathe," he whispered on a gasp.

"She knocked the wind out of you." Erin smoothed his hair away from his face. "Look at me and concentrate on moving air in—" she took a breath "—and out," she said on an exhale.

Fletcher swiped a hand over his eyes and did what she said. After a few minutes he was breathing normally.

Claire managed to calm the girls and soon everything was back under control. Erin grabbed her phone to text David about his mother just at the same time parents started arriving to pick up kids. She meant to get back to the text, but as the last child walked out with her mother, Sara Travers poked her head into the room.

"So this is where the child-wrangling magic happens?" she asked.

"I helped manage a full-blown meltdown today with a couple of the girls," Claire proudly told her stepmother.

"She was brilliant," Erin confirmed, feeling slightly awkward under Sara's gorgeous blue gaze. Sara had been a famous child actor before her career got derailed in her teens. She'd come to Crimson a few years ago, fallen in love with Josh Travers and helped him open the Crimson Ranch guest ranch. Since then, her career had made a resurgence and now she balanced her Hollywood life with her life in the mountains.

Although Erin didn't know her personally, she'd seen Sara around town quite a bit. With Crimson's proximity to Aspen, she should be used to movie star sightings, but it felt different with Sara. She was an integral part of the community after having lived in Crimson only a few years. Erin was still skirting the sidelines even though she'd spent most of her life in town.

Olivia, who was Claire's aunt by marriage, had arranged for the girl to assist Erin in the afternoons. Erin still hoped to receive funding to expand the program and her staff. Until then, Claire was a huge help. The girl was only fifteen but already had an instinctive talent for connecting with young kids.

"Way to go, Claire-bear," Sara said, giving the girl a quick hug. Although she wore a casual pair of distressed jeans with an oversize sweater, she still managed to project a look of subtle glamour. "You're amazing."

The girl rolled her eyes like a typical teenager, but Erin could tell the simple praise meant a lot to her. It seemed to come so easily, and not for the first time Erin wondered what it would have been like to grow up in a household where she'd been valued instead of constantly found lacking.

"Your dad is waiting downstairs," Sara told Claire. "The truck is parked at the curb. We thought we'd grab dinner in town. Why don't you head on down?"

Claire smiled at Erin. "I'll see you tomorrow?"

"I count on it," Erin answered. "I really appreciate your help, Claire."

The girl disappeared through the open doorway.

"She's special," Erin said to Sara.

"I wanted to tell you how much Josh and I appreciate you giving her this opportunity. She loves kids, and has plenty of experience babysitting, but this is different."

Erin gave a small laugh. "Not too different some days."

Sara inclined her head. "When did you know you wanted to be a teacher?"

Erin thought about how to answer the question. She'd played school with her stuffed animals as a young girl, then been the one to ask teachers if she could help with the younger kids at recess as she'd gotten older. But she'd also known being a teacher wouldn't be enough to satisfy her mom, so she'd feigned interest in a variety of more high-profile careers until she'd gone to college and immediately switched her major from premed to elementary education.

"My mother," she said, keeping her tone neutral, "was very much of the belief that 'those who can, do, and those who can't, teach.'"

Sara groaned softly.

"I think I knew—or at least recognized that I liked working with kids—for most of my life. All of my pretend play centered around setting up classrooms for my dolls and stuffed animals."

"I didn't have much of a childhood," Sara said, surprising Erin with her candor. "I was the breadwinner in the family, and whether or not I wanted to act, that was what I had to do."

"Would you have chosen something else if you'd had the chance?" Erin couldn't help but ask.

"Maybe," Sara said with a shrug. "Something normal where I could just be a regular person."

Erin blinked. She'd spent her whole life wanting to be something other than regular. Now a famous actress stood in front of her wishing for normal.

"I've got the best of both worlds now. But I don't want Claire to go through what I did…" Sara paused, then added, "Or what you did as she tries to figure out her path in life."

"She's young and obviously quite intelligent." Erin

straightened a stack of papers on the desk, then pulled her purse out of a drawer. "She's lucky to have people in her life who want to support her. She'd be an excellent teacher, and I'm sure she'll succeed in whatever she chooses to do with her life."

Sara drew in an audible breath. "Will you record that so I can play it back to her when the teenage drama and doubts get to be too much?"

"Keep her engaged and stay involved in her life. I know you're busy and have plenty of important things to take care of, but if you ever want to come with Claire, I can always use more hands on deck."

Sara's already huge eyes widened further. She looked around the room, then back to Erin. "Would that be weird? I'm not great with kids. I mean, I was one and I have Claire and Emery, but she's a baby. She can't talk."

"My kids like to talk," Erin said with a smile. "Especially when they have people to listen to them. You're an actress. I'm sure you can fake it."

"I faked it for a lot of years," Sara said, then laughed. "I'm an expert."

"Tell me about it," Erin muttered. It was strange to feel this camaraderie with a woman whose life was so different, but comforting at the same time.

"I'll let you get on with your evening," Sara said, stepping forward to envelop Erin in a quick hug. Sara's fragrance was subtle and earthy but clearly expensive, and Erin couldn't wait to tell her friends she'd been hugged by the A-list actress. "We should get together some time. A bunch of us have regular get-togethers—mostly for Mexican and margaritas but sometimes coffee or yoga. I'll call you before the next one and you can join us."

"Thank you," Erin whispered, feeling better than she had in a long time.

As Sara turned to leave, David rushed into the room. "Sorry I'm late. We were having trouble with fermenting the most recent batch of the wheat beer."

"Hey, David." Sara smiled. "I'm looking forward to watching you win the big prize in a couple of weeks."

"If we sort through the problems with this latest batch, maybe I'll actually have a beer to enter."

"Good luck," Sara said with a grin, and walked out of the room.

"Thanks." He ran a hand through his hair, then turned to Erin. "Where's Rhett?"

"With your mother," she said, her stomach dropping at the way his brows drew down. "She was supposed to call you."

Pulling his phone out of his pocket, he shook his head. "No texts or calls."

"She told me—"

"I thought you weren't supposed to send him home with random people. Isn't that why I filled out the paperwork?"

"His grandmother isn't random," Erin insisted, even though she'd given the same argument to Angela. "She wanted to take him out for a fun afternoon."

David muttered a curse under his breath then said, "You don't want to know my mother's definition of fun."

"I thought she was here helping," Erin said, throwing up her hands. "She's staying with you. You don't trust her with Rhett?"

"I trust her." David paced to the edge of the room. "Sort of. But she's been talking about taking him up the mountain to see the leaves changing. I told her she had to stay in town with him, and we got in an argument about it. My mom is flighty and reckless. For all I know, she'll start a hike with him and lose him in the woods."

"No," Erin whispered. "That's not possible."

"She took Jenna and me to downtown Pittsburgh one year for a Christmas parade. She got sidetracked by some sale at a department store and left us on the street with instructions not to move. Apparently, she forgot that she was doing more than a shopping trip and went home. The police finally picked us up after a street sweeper called them. According to my mom, she thought we were playing in the backyard."

"David."

"It was below freezing," he said, almost as an afterthought. "Just like it gets cold up on the mountain at night this time of year."

Erin shook her head. "That can't be what's happened. I bet she went for an ice cream. If you said not to leave—"

"My mom doesn't give a—" He clamped his mouth shut. "She means well and she's been fine this time around, but she's not always reliable. Not when it counts."

"David, I'm—"

He held up a hand. "It's not your fault. I believed she'd changed. I needed to believe because it's what Jenna wanted and I have no clue what I'm doing with a five-year-old boy."

"You're handling things like a pro," she said, reaching out a hand to squeeze his arm and trying not to take it personally when he shrugged off her touch.

"Clearly, this night is a great example of that." He hit a button on his phone. "Maybe I'll get lucky and she'll pick up."

Erin waited, hoping with every fiber of her being Angela answered. A moment later, David took the phone away from his ear and shook his head. "Straight to voice mail. She's either ignoring me or out of cell range."

"A text might go through," Erin suggested quietly.

He punched in a message, hit Send, and they waited again. David's full mouth pressed into a thin line. "I've got to call Cole and see if he has any deputies up on the mountain. It's going to get dark soon, and I need to know Rhett is okay."

"I'm sorry," she whispered, feeling miserable.

"It's not your problem," he answered even as he continued to stare at the phone. "You're just the teacher."

Erin swallowed. She knew he hadn't meant the words as an insult. He was stressed and worried. But just as he'd wanted to believe in his mother, Erin had wanted to believe in him. In the two of them. He'd said he'd wanted her. Wanted "us."

But once again, she wasn't enough.

He turned away when Cole picked up, and she could hear him explaining the situation to the sheriff. After a minute, he faced her again. "He's going to check out some of the more popular driving routes for viewing the changing leaves. I'm going to look around town to see if they're down here, then head up myself."

"Will you text me when you find them?"

He studied her as if weighing his answer, then finally nodded.

"How can I help?"

"You can't," he whispered, then walked away.

Chapter 10

The sun had set over the craggy peak of Crimson Mountain, and the sky was aflame in shades of pink and orange as Erin took a curve on the two-lane highway that led up the mountain. Within a half hour, the whole mountainside would be cast in shadow, so there wasn't much time for an effective search.

Her heart felt like it was breaking when David said he didn't need her, but she refused to let that stop her from trying to find Rhett and Angela.

It had been almost an hour since he'd walked away from her, so maybe David had tracked them down by now and hadn't bothered to text her. Erin couldn't take the chance. She was done sitting on the sidelines letting life pass her by, especially when she'd been the cause of the mess they were in.

There were so many service roads and gravel offshoots of the main highway it was difficult to know where to start. Obviously, Cole Bennett and his team of deputies were experts, and she hadn't even thought to ask David what kind of car his mother drove. But Erin had some experience on these roads. She'd always loved the changing colors that swathed the mountains. For a few weeks, the brilliant patches of bright yellow aspens and a few orange and red clumps of scrub oak made the whole valley look like it was on fire.

She turned her car onto a dirt road that led to one of the most picturesque vistas overlooking the valley. It wasn't quite as popular as some of the well-known leaf-viewing drives in the area but remained a favorite with locals.

Angela wasn't a local, but if she'd stopped at the hardware store or the gas station on the west side of town, this was where they would have sent her.

Erin ignored the gorgeous scenery surrounding her and concentrated on scanning the edges of the road and the myriad pull-offs that led to private cabins or trailhead access for hiking.

It was a little bit like searching for a needle in a haystack. When she darted a quick glance at her phone she realized she was out of service range. So even if David had tracked down Rhett and texted her, she wouldn't get the message.

The car climbed almost to tree-line level, Erin growing more frustrated by the second. Why had she allowed Angela to take Rhett? The answer was clear—Erin didn't have enough faith in herself or her authority to stop the other woman. Which was stupid, because of all the things Erin had been too scared of failing at to try, working with kids had never been one of them.

She was a great teacher, and her after-school program was already making a difference. Two of the teachers at school had reported that their students—the ones who'd been identified as troublemakers—were less disruptive and more responsible in class. The kids had cited some of the self-directed exercises for regulating behavior Erin had taught them for the changes.

No matter what her mother thought…or Angela…or David…or her ex…she had value. Maybe if she started believing that about herself, other people would, too.

She was about to turn the car around and head down the hillside when she caught sight of an older-model sedan parked on the side of the road about two hundred yards in front of her.

Adrenaline spiked through her when she noticed the Pennsylvania license plate. As she approached, the driver's-side door opened and Angela stepped out, her pale blond hair shining in the waning light.

Erin breathed a huge sigh of relief as she pulled her Subaru to a stop behind Angela's car. She checked her phone—still no service, but as soon as they got back into cell range she could let David know Rhett was safe.

"Stupid car battery gave out," Angela said sullenly. "And I've got no service up here. We've got satellite radio that can play music anywhere in the dang world. Don't you think they could get some decent coverage for phones?"

Rhett jumped out of the car through the open door. "Ms. MacDonald, you found us."

"Your uncle is worried," Erin said, crouching down to wrap her arms around the boy's shoulders as he ran to her.

"Since when did my son become a worrywart?" Angela retrieved her purse from the front seat of the car and slammed the door shut. "I texted him a message that Rhett and I were getting ice cream and going to look at leaves."

"He never got a message from you," Erin said, feeling

defensive on David's behalf. "You promised you'd get in touch with him if I let you take Rhett today."

"Let me?" Angela scoffed. "I'm his grandma and I'll take him—"

"No." Holding tight to Rhett's hand, Erin stepped forward. "When Rhett is at school or with me in the afternoon, he's my responsibility. Unless you have permission from David, I won't allow you to pick him up again."

Angela studied her through narrowed eyes. "Is that so? You do realize my daughter is the one who called and asked me to drive halfway across the country to look out for her boy?"

Erin felt Rhett stiffen beside her. "Rhett," she said, gently taking him by the shoulders, "you should get in my car. It's cold out here. We'll take the booster seat from your grandma's—"

"Nana doesn't have a booster," he interrupted quietly.

"We'll make sure she gets one," she told him. "Your nana and I have a few things to work out and then we'll go find Uncle David."

Biting his lip, the boy looked between Angela and Erin, then headed for the car.

"I'm his grandmother," the older woman repeated as Rhett shut the door.

"I appreciate that." Erin forced her shoulders back and her hands at her side. "I know Jenna is working through her issues, and I understand you're here to help. David does, as well. But he's in charge, Angela. He's balancing so much and trying to do his best by Rhett."

"Sounds like you know my son pretty well." Angela gave her another once-over but before she could continue, Erin held up a hand.

"I hope David and I are friends, but even if we're not,

I care about Rhett. He's a great kid and I want to see him through this. We all do." She stepped forward. "I'm not the enemy, Angela. Neither is David."

She saw the woman's shoulders deflate slightly. "Do you know what happened to Jenna when they were in high school?"

Erin shook her head. "I don't, and it's none of my business if David doesn't want to tell me." As much as she wanted to know.

"You should ask him before you get too close."

At Angela's words, a sinking feeling rippled through Erin. Whatever had happened to his sister in high school clearly formed the man David was today. Erin might not know any details, but she understood it must have been traumatic.

"My son is not the type of man who's good for a woman like you." Angela reached out and, to Erin's surprise, patted her softly on the arm. "Rhett is lucky to have you in his life." She took a deep breath, then added, "He's lucky to have David, too. I'm freezing my fanny off up here now that the sun is gone. Let's get back to town so I can make this right with my son."

Erin nodded and they headed to the car. The drive was quiet until they got into cell phone range. Angela's phone was still dead, but Erin's gave several insistent chirps. She took the phone from the console and handed it to David's mother. "You call since I'm driving."

Out of the corner of her eye, Erin saw Angela smile as she looked at the phone.

"What's so funny?"

"You have my son in your contacts."

"Yes."

"His occupation is listed as 'hottie brewmaster.' Is that an official title?"

Erin suppressed a groan. Melody had entered that into her phone, and Erin had forgotten to change it.

"You're stalling," she said as an answer. "Call him."

With a small laugh, Angela hit the button to dial David. After a minute she said, "This is your mother. We're on our way back to town. I left you…" She was quiet for a moment. Erin could hear the muffled rumble of David's voice through the phone but couldn't make out what he was saying. Based on the furrow between Angela's brows, it wasn't good.

"She drove up the mountain and found us," Angela said. Another pause. "It's not my fault the wreck of a car I drive died. Rhett is fine."

"I'm hungry," Rhett called from the back seat.

"He's hungry," Angela repeated, then went silent again as David said something else. "What's that?" She made the sound of static. "Sorry, you're breaking up. We'll see you at home in a bit."

Erin arched a brow as Angela disconnected the call. "Faking a bad connection?"

The older woman shrugged. "He has all night to rip me a new one. I'd like a few minutes of quiet to gather my wits." She pressed her hands to her cheeks. "For the record, my plan was to get a treat and see the leaves, not to get stuck up on the mountain in the cold at dusk."

A rush of emotion flooded Erin when Angela's voice cracked. Despite the attitude, Erin realized David's mother had been more scared than she'd let on to be stranded with Rhett. Erin reached across the console and patted the woman's leg. "It all turned out okay in the end."

"Thank you," Angela whispered and squeezed Erin's fingers.

"Wonder what Uncle David will make for dinner," Rhett said from the back seat. "I'm so hungry even his cooking will taste good tonight."

Erin laughed and was once again reminded how resilient kids could be. "We'll soon find out," she told Rhett, and concentrated on getting them home safely.

David's heart clamored in his chest as he waited on the sidewalk in front of Elevation, and the unfamiliar feeling sent shock waves through him. When was the last time he'd been so worried? The past hour had been the longest of his life. After talking to his mother, he'd gotten in touch with Cole, who had been on the mountain searching for Rhett.

As much as it killed him, David had kept close to town, wanting to remain reachable by his mother if she called. He'd never expected Erin to be conducting her own search, let alone to find his mother and Rhett—especially not after how he'd treated her.

He massaged the back of his neck with one hand. He had the uncanny ability to continuously push away the one person who was quickly coming to mean the most to him.

A small Subaru hatchback pulled to the curb in front of the bar. His mother opened the passenger door at the same time Rhett bounded out from the back seat. David opened his arms, catching the boy and spinning him around.

"Nana's car broke," Rhett said into his neck. "And I'm hungry. Did you make dinner?"

"Even better." David kissed the top of the boy's head and dropped him back down to the ground. "The cook at Elevation made you mac and cheese."

"Mac and cheese," Rhett shouted happily. "Nana, did you hear? Uncle David didn't cook!"

His mother smiled at Rhett. "It's your lucky night." She held out her hand. "Come on. Let's go upstairs."

"I got to get my backpack," Rhett said and turned for the car again.

It was then David realized Erin had also gotten out of the car and now stood at the edge of the sidewalk. His knees almost gave way from the feeling of longing that charged through him. He wanted to rush forward and enfold her in his arms, somehow knowing that if he held her, his world would fall into place.

Her dark hair was uncharacteristically down, curling over her shoulders and the light jacket she wore. The coat wasn't enough to stave off the cold, and he saw her shiver as a gust of wind whipped down the street. She held out the small Ninja Turtles backpack to Rhett. "Here you go, sweetie."

"Thanks for rescuing us, Ms. MacDonald," Rhett said as he grabbed the pack.

"I'm glad you're safe. See you tomorrow at school."

"Thank you," his mother added, and Erin gave her a little wave. Then Angela and Rhett disappeared through the door that led up to the apartment.

"Erin." David stepped forward, but she held up a hand. "Go take care of Rhett."

"You found them."

"I know you didn't want me involved, but I couldn't just walk away. Don't be too hard on your mother. She's more shaken up by this than she lets on."

He blinked. "Are you defending my mother?"

"I guess I am. She's trying, David. We're all trying. Tonight was my fault for letting her take him without your permission." She laughed softly, then added, "But you know that already."

"No." He reached for her wrist and spun her to him when she turned away. "I'm sorry about the things I said." He brushed his fingers across her cheek. Darkness had officially fallen and her skin glowed under the light of the streetlamps. "I'm sorry my go-to emotion is anger. It's been that way for a long time, Erin. I don't know how to change it."

She looked up at him through her lashes. "Do you want it to change?"

"For Rhett, yes." He pressed his forehead to hers and whispered. "For you, yes." There was no way to put into words all the things he'd change for this woman if he could. "Why couldn't we have met when my life was simple?"

He felt rather than saw her smile. "Exactly when was your life simple?"

"Third grade," he answered without hesitation. "I had a crush on Brandi Doerger. I chased her around the playground until she agreed to be my girlfriend. Then I kissed her under the flagpole."

She pulled back enough to look at him. "Where is Brandi now?"

"Ours was a short-lived romance."

"And why is that?"

He shrugged. "She wanted me to meet at the candy store across from school and buy her favorite candy bar to prove I was her boyfriend."

"You didn't have the money for a gift?"

"I had a baseball game to get to with my friends."

"So you stood the poor girl up?"

"I was the pitcher," he said, hoping that explained everything. When he was nine, it seemed like a good enough excuse, but as something like disappointment flashed in Erin's gaze, he realized that nothing in his life had ever been simple.

"You don't have anything to prove to me." She untangled herself from his embrace and walked to her car.

He glanced up to his apartment windows and knew he had to see to Rhett and talk to his mother. But he couldn't let Erin leave like this. Not again.

"Give me another chance," he called.

She stilled in the midst of opening her door and turned to face him. "Why do you even want one?"

A group of twentysomethings was walking toward Elevation and a couple of them hooted with laughter at her question. "She's gonna roast you, dude," one of the taller guys said, slapping David on the arm as he walked by and into the restaurant.

Had he ever been that young and carefree? No, he'd been young and disastrously stupid.

"Because," he said, ignoring everything except Erin's brown eyes, "nothing in my life makes sense right now except you."

He stepped closer but still respected the space she'd put between them. As much as he wanted to push her to let him in despite what a jerk he'd been. It had to be her choice. Never in his life had he wanted a woman to choose him as much as he did now. "Even though I keep finding ways to screw it up, I want you."

Her fingers tightened on her purse strap, as if there was a debate raging inside her brain. It would be the smart thing to walk away from him right now. He sure as hell hoped she wasn't going to do the smart thing.

"Can you define another chance?"

He wanted to pump his fist in the air. She was watching out for herself, but she hadn't said a straight-up *no*. He had a chance, but he had to work for it. David might have made a lot of mistakes in his life, but he could work for something he wanted.

"A real date."

"I've heard that offer before," she countered. "Yet here we are."

Right.

Although he knew how to work, he'd never needed to try to get a woman. "Saturday," he continued. "All day. I'll pick you up at noon."

"What about Rhett?"

David must be more out of practice with women than he even realized. The fact that her first question was about his nephew made his heart clench in ways he didn't want to examine.

"I'll work it out."

She bit down on her lip as her gaze skittered away. "I don't want to force you to take me out. I wasn't lying when I said you have nothing to prove to me. You don't owe me a—"

"I do have something to prove. I need to prove that I'm not the guy I keep showing myself to be. Go out with me, Erin. Please."

She took a deep breath, then met his gaze again. "Do you know I'm a sucker for the word *please*?" she asked, her tone almost annoyed.

He laughed softly. "I didn't before now, but you can bet I'm going to use it to my advantage."

"I'll see you at noon on Saturday," she whispered.

"You'll see me this week," he corrected, "with Rhett. But Saturday is going to be special."

"Can I ask what we're doing?"

"You can ask, but I won't tell. I'm going to wow you. Just wait."

She rolled her eyes and muttered something that sounded like, "If you only knew."

With a small wave, she got in her car and pulled out of her parking spot and down the street.

David glanced up at the apartment windows again but before he went upstairs, took a quick detour into Elevation.

Tracie was tending bar, and he grabbed her shoulders and spun her to face him. "I need to impress a woman," he said. "With a date."

"Take off your shirt," one of the women sitting at the bar told him. He turned to see three women who looked vaguely familiar staring at him. He thought he recognized them from dropping off Rhett at school. Great. Now he was going to be known as the incompetent guardian who couldn't handle women.

Had he really just asked Tracie for dating advice in the middle of his bar?

Two of the women giggled, then the blonde with a short bob leaned forward. "My divorce was final last week." She winked. "I think you're damn impressive just standing there so—"

"Enough," Tracie interrupted the woman, and waved over the new bartender she'd hired to work evenings while David was with Rhett. "Hey, Mark, will you pour these three lovelies a round on the house? No need for the ego-stroking, ladies. I'll take it from here."

She pushed David toward the end of the bar. "What in the hell are you talking about? From the stories I've heard, you went out with half the single women in Pennsylvania in your day. Why do you suddenly need dating advice?"

David gripped the edge of the bar, almost wishing he was still the hot-tempered young baseball phenom who could get away with throwing a fist through the wall. "I asked Erin out."

Tracie stared at him for several moments, then prompted, "And..."

"I told her it was going to be special."

"So make reservations at some swanky place in Aspen," Tracie told him. "I know beer is your thing, but you do remember how to pay for expensive food and wine, right?"

"I need to wow her."

She held up her hands. "Dude, if you're looking for bedroom advice—"

"No," he said quickly. "But Erin is a...a..."

"A woman?"

He blew out a breath. "A lady. I'm not trying to wine and dine her to get into her pants."

One side of Tracie's mouth curved. "You don't want in her pants?"

"Of course I want—" He stopped, growled under his breath. "She's special. I don't want to screw it up. Any guy with a phone and credit card can make a reservation. I need it to be something more."

"I've never seen you like this, boss." She shook her head. "Thank God."

"Forget it."

She laughed, then chucked him on the arm. "I've got an idea. But your prim and proper teacher lady is into you. You know that. I know that. It's a small town, and the school district set likes Elevation. I've seen the way she looks at you when she's here with her friends, and that was before Rhett."

"I never noticed her."

"Because men are idiots." Tracie tsked. "My point is that she's kind of…a sure thing. She crushed on you hard."

"I still need to earn it." He leaned in closer. "Help me. Please."

Tracie rolled her blue eyes to the ceiling. "I bet that sad puppy-dog face and the *please* work on her every time."

"Kind of," he admitted.

"That girl and I need to spend some time together." The new bartender called to Tracie as a line formed in front of the bar. "I've got to get back to work," Tracie said, giving him one of her patented smirks. "Don't want the boss to catch me slacking. I'll come in tomorrow after my run and we can plan world domination—or at least kindergarten teacher domination."

"That sounds kinky."

"You never know," she called over her shoulder as she headed back to the bar. "That might be how she likes it."

David's mind started to wander to an image of Erin dressed in nothing but—

He slapped his palm against his forehead several times. That kind of daydreaming wasn't going to get the five-year-old boy waiting upstairs bathed and ready for bed or his mother dealt with in any sort of productive way.

After scanning the interior of the bar one more time to make sure things were under control, he headed for his apartment. He had to keep things on track this week. He had one more chance with Erin, and he wasn't going to blow it.

Chapter 11

"I've never heard of a therapy rabbit." Erin watched in wonder as her Kidzone students took turns petting the bunny that happily hopped up to each of them on the activity rug.

"Fritzi is special." She glanced at Caden Sharpe, the local rancher who also ran an animal rescue center out of his property, his hard features suddenly surprisingly gentle.

Emily Whitaker Crenshaw, the mom of one of Erin's former students, had suggested she call Caden. His manner was gruff, and Erin had been certain he'd refuse her request to bring the kids to his ranch. Instead, he not only set up a time for them to visit but also offered to stop by the community center with a couple of the animals he'd trained as therapy pets.

Caden had been a few years ahead of her in school

and had been so surly and mean as a boy she'd barely had the nerve to make eye contact with him. She'd heard rumors that his early life had been tough and wealthy rancher Garrett Sharpe had adopted him when he was ten years old. But even the stable home and the brothers he'd gained in his new family hadn't seemed to settle his restless spirit.

He reminded her of some of the kids she worked with and hoped that meeting Caden, who was also an army vet, would help them realize they had other paths available to them.

Although right now Fritzi the bunny and Otis, the yellow Lab enjoying belly rubs from a group of girls, were the real stars of the show.

"You're doing good work here," Caden told her. Erin realized those were the most words she'd heard the man string together in a sentence.

"I sometimes think I'm in over my head," she admitted. "But as amazing as this community is, there was a need for these kids that wasn't being filled. There are too many who have the potential to get into trouble if no one is watching out for them."

He shifted slightly and she colored under his intense gaze. "I wasn't talking about you."

A noise came from him that might have been a laugh, but it was rough like it had been closed in a drawer and forgotten for too long. "I remember you now," he said. "You were always smiling."

Erin felt her blush deepen. "Did you know that smiling can reduce your blood pressure? Plus it's an easy gift to offer another person."

"People used to be afraid to smile at me."

She raised a brow. "I think that's how you liked it."

He laughed again. "Maybe. The animals help with that."

She gave him her brightest smile. "Thank you for bringing them here and the invitation to visit the ranch. It will mean a lot to the kids."

He studied her for another long moment. "Would you want—"

A flash of movement over his shoulder caught her eye and she realized David was standing in the door watching the exchange.

"Come on in," she called, glancing at her watch. "I didn't realize it had gotten so late."

"I'm a few minutes early," David said. As he walked toward her, his hand came around from behind his back and she realized he held a bouquet of roses. "These are for you."

"Oh." She pressed a hand to her chest. "No one has ever brought me flowers who wasn't one of my students." She wrapped her hand around the stems, her fingers brushing his. The current of awareness between them zinged to life and she had to fight to remember they were standing in front of ten kids, as well as Caden Sharpe.

"You should have them all the time," David told her.

She heard a sound that might have been a growl come from Caden, but when she turned he was simply watching the kids and the animals.

"Do you two know each other?" she asked, lowering her nose close to the flower petals and inhaling the fresh scent.

"We've met," David answered. "I get all my beef from Sharpe Pointe Ranch."

"Yep," was Caden's only response.

"Great." She glanced between the two men and wondered why it felt like there was some invisible sword-play going on. "Caden brought his animals to visit with the kids."

"I brought flowers," David said immediately.

She nodded slowly. "Um, yes, you did. And I love them."

David leaned a little closer to Caden. "She loves them."

A muscle ticked in Caden's jaw. "I'm going to round up Fritzi and Otis," he told her. "I'll see you when you bring the kids to the ranch. You're welcome any time."

"I definitely will. Thank you."

She watched him turn to David. "She's going to call me," he said under his breath.

David's shoulders stiffened but before he could respond, Erin placed the flowers on her desk and clapped her hands to get the kids' attention. The noise level was surprisingly low given how excited the kids had been to see the bunny and dog. But she had to admit there was something inherently relaxing about the energy of the two animals. She sensed that with Caden as well, despite his gruff demeanor, and was happy he'd found a purpose in life.

"It's time for the animals to go," she announced to a round of groans. "But Mr. Sharpe has invited us out to his ranch for a longer visit." That got some cheers from the kids. "Can you give him a big thank-you for coming to see us today?"

Caden seemed embarrassed by the attention, and left quickly after packing up the bunny and putting Otis on a leash. Parents started to arrive soon after for pickup, and she waved as David led Rhett from the room.

Soon only Isaac remained, and he sat at one of the small craft tables, his head bent forward.

"Your mom will be here soon, sweetie," Erin told him, bending to clean up a few crayons that had been knocked to the floor.

As she straightened, a tear dropped to the desk in front of the boy. He quickly wiped at his cheeks and turned away from her.

Isaac had been a tough nut to crack. He rarely interacted with the other kids and usually stayed in the corner pretending to read a book that was far above his basic reading level or doing a puzzle. She'd talked to his classroom teacher and the school counselor, but both women had seemed at a loss for how to reach him. Phone calls to Joel and his mother, Danielle, had gone unanswered and voice mails not returned. Both mom and dad shut Erin down when she tried to speak to them at pickup.

It sometimes felt like the only emotion the boy could access was anger, so to see him embarrassed by his tears broke her heart.

"Do you want to talk about it?" she asked softly, resting her hip on the desk across from where he sat.

He shook his head and refused to meet her gaze.

"Fritzi and Otis were really cool. I noticed Otis seemed to like you a lot." What Erin had witnessed was Isaac planting himself at the dog's side and refusing to give up his spot. He'd spent the entire visit gently stroking Otis's furry head and bending down to whisper in his ear. Thanks to his training as a therapy dog, Otis had been patient with the attention. The other kids had seemed to take it as Isaac's due that he got the prime real estate to love on the animal.

"My dad gave away Jack," he whispered, his voice cracking on the last word.

"Was Jack your dog?"

Isaac looked up, tears shining in his eyes. "The best dog ever. But sometimes he got scared when dad yelled and it made him pee on the floor."

"Some dogs get nervous with loud noises," Erin agreed. Like Caden, Isaac rarely spoke more than monosyllabic responses to the direct questions she asked. It both thrilled her and hurt her heart that he was sharing this small piece of his life with her now.

"He barked, too, but never at me. He loved me best of all."

She fisted her hands at her side, every part of her wanting to reach out and hug the boy but afraid of scaring him away if she did. "I can understand why. You were great with Otis."

"We'll get another dog," a soft voice said from behind Erin.

She whirled around to see Isaac's mother standing in the doorway, not bothering to wipe away the tears that stained her cheeks. Danielle Rodriguez was petite, with beautiful dark hair that fell to the middle of her back and wide-set eyes. Erin guessed they were about the same age, although Danielle's features had a weariness and worldliness stamped across them that came from too many years of hard work, hard living and struggling to raise three kids on her own.

"Your father is not living in my house anymore," she said, switching her gaze to Erin, then back to her son. "And that two-timing jerk isn't invited back. We'll start looking for a dog when I get off work tomorrow. I promise."

Isaac was out of his chair in an instant, hurtling toward his mother and wrapping his arms tight around her waist.

She bent to hug him close, and a lump formed in Erin's throat at the tenderness of the moment. Maybe her program was having the impact she'd hoped for after all.

After a few minutes, Danielle straightened. "Get your backpack and lunch box, Isaac," she told her son, dropping a kiss on the top of his head. "Your sister has dinner going at home." Isaac moved toward the row of backpacks, and Danielle turned to Erin. "I know Joel sees this program as a way to get out of spending time with him on the days when I work late."

Erin acknowledged that truth with a small nod. "Whatever the reason, I'm glad he's here."

"Me, too," Danielle said, squaring her shoulders. "We've got a long way to go, but kicking Joel to the curb was a good start."

"Will he still be a part of Isaac's life?"

Danielle shrugged. "If he gets his act together. My boy wants his father in his life. But I'm done with Joel, and he's mad as hell. Thinks being my baby daddy gives him a right to whatever he wants from me. He's a cheater and a liar. I deserve better than that."

"You do," Erin agreed instantly.

Isaac came over with his backpack. Although the scowl was back on his face, his little shoulders seemed to carry less of a weight than they did minutes earlier.

"We're going to get another dog," he said quietly, leaning in close to his mother and glancing up at Erin.

"I promise," Danielle whispered, ruffling his hair.

"I'll text you Caden Sharpe's number," Erin told her. "He's the man who brought the therapy pets to visit us today. He runs a small rescue organization out of one of the barns on his ranch. Maybe he can help you find a new dog."

"Thank you," Danielle said. "For everything."

Erin nodded and spent another twenty minutes cleaning up and preparing for Friday's class. She trimmed the stems of the flowers David had given her and put them in a vase before leaving the community center. Most nights classes ran past the time she finished, so there was always someone at the reception desk.

She waved goodbye and walked out into the darkening night. The crisp breeze made her pull in a sharp breath. The change of seasons was a fickle time in Crimson. Summer could linger for weeks, then disappear within a day. Sometimes fall would last just as long, but more often winter inserted an icy blast of cold to remind everyone what to expect over the next several months.

Colder weather made Erin wish for things she didn't have, like someone to cuddle up to on a frosty winter night. Sugar was a great cat, but not much of a snuggler. It was time to put the heavier comforter on her bed and get out her cold-weather clothes. Maybe she needed to give Caden a call and adopt another furry friend.

She knocked her closed fist against her forehead several times to stop pathetic internal ramblings. In her mind, she'd already skimmed past the date with David to when he inevitably lost interest in her. She'd become one of those single women whose only emotionally intimate relationships were with her pets.

"I don't know what you're thinking," a voice said from the shadows, "but I like that head of yours way too much to watch you abuse it."

She looked up to see David standing a few feet away,

hands shoved deep in the front pockets of his jeans. He'd put a heavy canvas jacket on over the flannel shirt he'd worn earlier to pick up Rhett. The bulk of it made him look even broader than normal.

His hair was, as usual, casually tousled, and a hint of stubble shadowed his jaw. He was every one of Erin's fantasies come to life, and it positively terrified her.

"Silly thoughts," she mumbled. "What are you doing here? Is everything okay with Rhett?"

"He's fine. The bar is slow tonight so I had Tracie come up to stay with him and my mom for a few minutes." He took a step closer. "I wanted to see you."

"Hi," she whispered as he drew her forward, wrapping his arms around her. She shivered as he nuzzled his nose against her throat. "You're cold."

"I was waiting for you to keep me warm," he said into her skin, and it was like he'd read her mind.

"Thank you again for the flowers," she said, then lifted onto her toes and kissed him. It was the first time she'd initiated a kiss, and he seemed happy to let her take the lead.

Despite the chilly air, Erin's whole body ignited in flames. She was so lost to this man. While it might be her downfall, she couldn't bring herself to care.

"Tell me about Caden Sharpe," he said when she finally pulled back.

It was difficult to remember her own name, let alone anything else, so it took Erin a few moments to answer. "He's a way nicer guy than people give him credit for. I think he's just misunderstood because of his past and the trouble he got into as a kid."

He studied her face as if trying to decipher some sort

of complicated puzzle, which was crazy because Erin had always been an open book.

"Do you always see the best in people?" he asked finally.

"I try to. Is that a bad thing?"

"No. It's one of the things I—" He coughed and cleared his throat. "One of the things that makes you special. You realize Sharpe likes you."

"Because he was kind enough to bring a couple of therapy pets to visit the kids?" She rolled her eyes. "He was doing a favor for a friend and I benefited from it."

"I saw how he looked at you and—"

"Are you jealous?" Erin felt her mouth drop open. "Oh my gosh, I got flowers and a man is jealous over me. Those are two firsts in one day." She pulled away and did a little two-step dance routine in front of him.

"I'm not jealous," David muttered through his teeth. "But don't go out with him, okay?"

She stopped dancing and moved closer. "Of course I'm not going to go out with him. I'm going on a date with you."

He blinked several times. "Some women date more than one man at a time."

"I'm not one of those," she assured him, then wound her arms around his neck and kissed him again. She knew her reaction made her seem like the biggest dork in the world, but she didn't care. This man, who made her heart sing, had brought her flowers *and* wanted her for himself. "I only want you. But I'm flattered that you're jealous."

"Flattered?" He gave a small laugh. "You should tell me to mind my own damn business."

"I like being your business, as long as you know I'm

going to continue to see Caden. He and the animals help with the kids."

He inclined his head. "I'd never tell you who you can or can't see. I just want to be sure *you* know you're mine."

Erin's mouth went dry. She'd never had anyone claim her before, and the thought of it was both exhilarating and terrifying.

Then a movement behind David distracted her. A man with a dark hoodie seemed to be watching them from the shadows of the nearby alley. "Um, okay… I think."

David looked over his shoulder, following her gaze, and the man quickly walked down the street away from them.

"Did you know him?" David asked gently.

"I don't think so."

"Where's your car?"

"It's fine," she assured him. "This is Crimson."

"Humor me," he insisted. He kissed the tip of her nose, then walked her to her car.

After a few more kisses, she drove home, tingling from the ends of her hair to her toes. She'd been *claimed* and could barely wait to see what that meant for Saturday.

Chapter 12

An unfamiliar lightness bubbled up in David at the sight of Erin waiting for him outside her apartment building Saturday morning. It was as if he'd taken a big swig of champagne and the bubbles were rioting around his stomach. His feelings for her were different from anything he'd experienced before. Today was his chance to make her understand how much she meant to him.

But he had no plan to blurt out that he loved her, as he'd almost done when she was in his arms. Hell, he'd known her for only a few weeks and he wasn't built for love in the first place.

Longing was a different story. The yearning he felt for her pulsed through him like blood in his veins. She gave him hope and made him happy in a way he hadn't even thought possible.

It had seemed like a joke when she'd asked him for

an affair. Physical desire was one thing, but his need for Erin transcended what his body wanted. In such a short time she'd become like the air he breathed, necessary for his very survival.

So he had to make this day count.

As soon as he pulled to a stop, she opened the truck's passenger-side door and climbed in.

"I'm ready for our adventure," she said, tossing her tote bag into the back seat.

He grinned and flipped his sunglasses onto his forehead. "I can see that. You know, I would have come to pick you up at your door." He reached into the back seat and handed her another bouquet of flowers. "I brought these for you."

Color rushed into her cheeks as she gazed at them. "I must seem like a total fool," she said, biting down on her lip. "I know the woman is supposed to wait for the man, but I was so excited and it's a gorgeous day and—"

He leaned in and kissed her, breathing in to capture her scent and the sweetness that always seemed to surround her. "I've been watching the clock all morning," he admitted. "I couldn't wait for this date to begin."

"Let me run and put these in water." She opened the door, then looked back at him over her shoulder. "You don't have to bring me flowers."

"I'm courting you," he reminded her.

She flashed a shy smile. "I don't think I've ever been courted before."

"It's a first for me, too."

"You're doing pretty darn well," she said, and hopped out of the truck.

His cell phone rang as he watched her enter the building. Pulling it out of his pocket, he said a silent prayer everything was okay with Rhett. His nephew had been invited to a birthday party for one of his friends from school, and David's mother had promised she'd get him there safely and follow all the house rules David had set.

He'd asked Tracie, who was working all day, to keep an eye on them this morning. Later this afternoon, David's friend Jase Crenshaw, who had a stepson only a year older than Rhett, was going to take the boys to the park and out for ice cream. He'd also asked Olivia Travers to stop by, trying to cover all his bases to make sure Rhett was safe.

Angela seemed to take it all in stride. Since the fiasco on the mountain, she'd been on her best behavior and David had to admit he was grateful to his mother for her help.

It wasn't a local number flashing on his screen, and he recognized the Phoenix area code from where Jenna was doing her stint in rehab. His stomach in knots, he accepted the call, only to have his sister immediately lay into him.

"I can't believe you're messing around with Rhett's teacher," she said, her voice a low hiss.

"Jenna," he said, breathing out a sigh. "Is everything okay?"

"Do I sound okay? I had to trade three packs of Skittles to be able to make this phone call. You know how I love Skittles."

One side of his mouth curved. "I know. Exactly why are you calling?"

"To tell you to leave Ms. MacDonald alone."

"How do you even—"

"Mom told me. She said you've got the hots for Rhett's teacher and you're even taking her out on a date.

As far as I know, you haven't dated anyone since you moved to Crimson and you can't start with the teacher. She's off-limits."

"Why?" he asked, trying to keep his temper under wraps. His sister was doing great in her program, but he knew she was still fragile. The last thing he needed was to set her off.

She blew an agitated breath into the phone. "Rhett loves that woman and whatever program of hers he's going to in the afternoons. It's all he talks about when he calls."

"She's great with him."

"Yeah, so if you piss her off by treating her like crap, she could take it out on him."

"She'd never do that," he answered automatically, then added, "Besides, I'm not going to hurt her."

"You hurt everybody."

The words were like a knife to his gut, because coming from his sister they meant so much more. Unwanted memories flooded through him. He swallowed against the bile rising in his throat, trying to forget. Willing himself to forget.

"I know I've messed things up royally," Jenna said in a quieter tone, "and I appreciate you stepping in to help with Rhett. I need his world to be stable, David. I need to believe he's going to get through this. She's a big part of that."

So am I, he wanted to argue, but only repeated, "I'm not going to hurt her."

At that moment Erin emerged from the apartment building, smiling as she walked toward him. If his sister was right, he should throw the truck into Reverse and drive away before this went any further. Because there was no doubt in his mind how far he'd take it if Erin got in next to him.

All the way.

"Promise me you'll leave her alone," his sister whispered.

"I've got to go," he said as an answer. "You take care of you, Jenna. I've got things under control."

He ended the call before she could argue, and he had no doubt she would if given the chance. His sister had seen him at his worst, just like he had with her. How could either of them believe the other had things under control?

Erin climbed into the truck. "I'm ready." She turned to him and her smile disappeared. "What's wrong? I saw you on the phone. Is it Rhett?"

"My sister called." He tapped his fingers on the steering wheel, wishing he hadn't talked to Jenna. All of his happiness from earlier had been colored by her doubts, which mingled with his into some sort of poison that seeped into every cell.

Erin placed a hand on his arm, and the gentle touch felt like a brand through the fabric of his shirt. "Is she okay?"

"She told me not to go out with you," he said quietly. As much as he didn't want to share Jenna's warning with Erin, it was the only way through this.

"She doesn't even know me." Erin drew back her hand. "Is it the mercy date thing?"

He shifted to face her. "What 'mercy date thing'?"

"You taking me out as a thank-you for helping with Rhett." She made a face. "Because of that stupid comment I made about the affair."

David raked a hand through his hair. He hated the

doubt that now shadowed Erin's dark eyes. He'd done his best to plan a perfect day, and now it was tainted before they even started.

"She doesn't want me to go out with you because you're too good for me. She thinks I'm going to hurt you."

When Erin didn't immediately refute his sister's claim, David slammed a hand against the steering wheel. "Damn it," he muttered. "You agree. We haven't even started and you think I'm going to hurt you."

He stared out the front of the truck, unable to look at her and see the truth on her face. This was his chance. *She* was his chance to finally get something wholly right in his life. And not one person believed he could do it.

"David."

"We should end this now," he told her. "I don't want to hurt you."

"There are no guarantees in life." He felt her press closer. "Please look at me."

He gave a small laugh, then turned. "I can't resist a 'please,' either." Her face was only inches away from his and, once again, her beauty slayed him. He focused on the tiny flecks of gold at the edges of her dark eyes and tried not to think about losing her before she was even his.

"My life has been safe for as long as I can remember. I didn't risk anything and had little to lose. My job is stable, my boyfriend bored me to tears. Typically, the most excitement I have is when a new book from one of my favorite authors comes out."

He smiled. "I'm going to read one of those romance novels so I know what all the hype is about."

She rolled her eyes. "My point is that with you, I feel like I'm living the adventure I've always wanted."

"You're doing that on your own," he countered. "You're helping with Rhett. You've made a difference in the lives of the kids in your program. It's you, Erin."

"Then I'm happy to share it with you." She sat back and arched a brow at him. "You know, I could be the one to hurt you. I could break your heart."

David opened his mouth to tell her his heart was too closed off to be in any danger of breaking. But at that moment a flash of pain pierced his chest so sharply it made his breath catch. "Anything is possible," he answered instead, struggling to keep his voice neutral.

"That's right," she agreed, thankfully oblivious to the strange things going on inside him. "Anything is possible. Life is a gamble. I want to take a risk with you, David. No matter what the outcome."

Despite his reckless youth, all his life, David had made decisions based on keeping himself or the people in his life safe. Baseball gave him a way out of his tumultuous childhood. Moving to Crimson had made it easier to watch out for Jenna and Rhett. The brewery gave him a stable income doing something he was good at. He'd always chosen women who wanted nothing more from him than a good time. Being with Erin wasn't safe—for either of them.

But she was worth the risk.

He leaned in and kissed her deeply, realizing he'd quickly become addicted to the taste of her. The more time he spent with her, the more he wanted.

How could he consider pushing her away? She was too important, and he wasn't going to hurt her. He wouldn't let himself.

"Are you ready for the best day of your life?" he asked, finally pulling back and shifting the truck into gear.

She laughed. "Pretty confident in yourself."

"I'm confident in us," he corrected and turned the truck toward the highway.

Butterflies danced through Erin's stomach as David drove out of town. It had been easy enough to toss off the comment about either of them getting hurt, but she had no doubt her heart was on the line.

As much as she'd tried to stop her feelings from spiraling out of control, Erin was falling for this man. Hard. If this day was half as good as he promised, she'd be a goner for sure.

But she hadn't been lying when she told him he was worth the risk. Her life had been spent taking the safe path, but the only things that had gotten her were frustration and discontent.

Even if she lost her heart, at least she could say she tried.

They headed up the mountain, and he turned off at the sign for Cloud Cabin.

"This is private land," she said, even as she leaned forward to gaze up at the tall pines arching over the road.

"I know," he answered.

"Crimson Ranch owns Cloud Cabin. Josh and Sara opened it last year for their guests. I guess a lot of family reunions and corporate events are held there in the summer."

One side of his mouth crooked. "Yep."

She figured David must know what he was doing, but curiosity niggled at her. "Are we trespassing?"

"Nope."

"Are you going to tell me anything?"

"You look beautiful."

Erin sat back in her seat and didn't bother to hide her smile. Even if David had doubts and his sister had doubts and everyone around them had doubts, this day felt perfect to Erin. "It's an adventure," she whispered.

A couple of miles in, a driveway split off to the right. David took the turn and within a few minutes they arrived at Cloud Cabin. The house was magnificent, large without being ostentatious and made completely out of hewn logs. A patio wrapped around two sides of the cabin on the second floor, and she could see a fire pit and several pieces of outdoor furniture arranged at the far end.

"It's amazing," she whispered.

David parked the car in front of one of the three garage bays on the lower level. "Some famous architect Sara knows designed it. They brought in the timber from Montana, but sourced the rock locally from the quarry near Meeker."

"What's that?" She pointed to the small cabin that sat at the other side of the clearing.

"Caretaker's cabin," David told her. "When they have big groups at Cloud Cabin, the staff stays there."

"Is anyone up here now?"

"You and me." He bussed her cheek.

She found herself unable to move even as he got out of the truck and came around to open her door.

"You okay, honey?"

She bit down on her lip. "I've lived in this town most of my life, so I'm used to seeing rich people. I've had wealthy students and walked the streets of Aspen, but I've never… I've never actually been in a place like this."

He leaned in and whispered in her ear, "You have to get out of the truck if you're going to make it to the cabin today."

She laughed and pushed him away. "You make fun, but that's because you were a rich and famous baseball player. You probably hung out on yachts and stuff."

"A few speedboats in Miami, but no yachts." He took her hand and tugged until she stepped out onto the gravel driveway. "Money makes things easier, but it's not important beyond that."

"What people do with it is important," she corrected. "Like fund an after-school program."

"And that," he agreed. "This place is ours for the day. Let's go explore it."

He laced his fingers with hers as they walked up the flagstone path that led to the front door. David produced a key from his pocket and unlocked the door, holding it open for Erin to walk in.

She wasn't sure what she expected, but it wasn't a space that immediately seemed to wrap around her and make her feel at home. The foyer was cozy and bright, with framed paintings of mountain vistas on each wall. The family room was situated to one side. Rich, colorful rugs covered the hardwood floor, and overstuffed furniture had been arranged to make a cozy sitting area in front of the massive stone fireplace.

"What do you want to do first?" he asked. "There are ATVs in the garage, a hot tub out back." He led her into the kitchen, where wood cabinets and gorgeous marble countertops balanced the industrial feel of gleaming stainless steel appliances.

"I could make us something to eat."

She glanced up at him. "You're going to cook?"

"Let me rephrase that," he said. "I could heat up the food that the head chef at the brewery prepared for us."

She grinned. "You've thought of everything."

He turned to her fully, wrapped his arms around her waist. "I wanted this day to be about you and me. No distractions. No real life butting its ugly head in. You and me."

"You and me," she repeated, and held on tight as he claimed her mouth. It was like they were the only two people in the world, and she let all her worries and doubts drift away. He lifted her into his arms, then sat her on the edge of the counter, pressing himself into the V of her legs.

Her body tingled with need and awareness, and she could feel that he wanted her, too. It made her want to forget everything else and beg him to take her to the bedroom. What would it be like to spend an entire day in bed with this man?

The air seemed to get caught in her throat at the thought, because what if she ruined everything by not knowing what she was doing. Kissing was one thing, but the rest...

"ATVs," she blurted, wrenching herself away from him.

He stared at her as if she were speaking a foreign language, then laughed softly. "ATVs it is."

Chapter 13

David breathed in the pine-scented air and tried to keep his focus on the path in front of him, and not on Erin's body pressed tight against his on the back of the ATV.

Once again, his desire for her had almost gotten the best of him. If she hadn't stopped it, he would have taken her right on the counter...or the floor...or wherever she would have him. He'd arranged with Josh to borrow the cabin so he could give Erin a day away from the responsibilities of life but still remain close to town if Rhett needed him.

It was becoming more and more difficult to keep his mind on anything except what she would feel like under him and how much he wanted to explore every inch of her beautiful body.

She shifted behind him, and he slowed the powerful machine, not wanting to scare her. Instead, she leaned in closer and shouted, "Faster." That was all the encouragement David needed to hit the throttle.

He tightened his grip on the ATV's handles and maneuvered through the pine forest and out into a clearing that overlooked the valley below them. As soon as he pulled to a stop and cut the motor, Erin jumped off the back.

"That was so cool," she cried, bouncing up and down on her toes. "We were flying."

He grinned at her happiness. Everything with Erin felt new and made him want to shake off his typical attitude and see the world through her eyes.

"Can I drive on the way back?"

"Of course." He gestured to the meadow behind them. "The trail loops around this field. You can use it like a practice course."

"On my own?" she asked, her eyes bright with excitement.

He laughed. "Ditching me already? Yes, I brought picnic supplies. I'll lay everything out while you take this baby for a ride."

He unloaded the soft-sided cooler and blanket he'd packed in the ATV's cargo area. Despite the fact that it was early October, they'd been blessed with a summer-like day. The sun shone brightly in the clear blue sky, and even the breeze that whispered through the trees felt warm.

"Climb on," he told her, then stifled a groan at the way her eyes widened. "The ATV," he clarified, wishing he'd locked her in the cabin and had his wicked way with her when he had the chance.

Instead he watched her position herself on the ATV. He gave instructions on how to put it into gear, braking and steering around turns. Erin's fingers trembled slightly as she gripped the handlebars. He wrapped his hand around hers. "Don't be nervous."

"I've never even driven a stick shift," she admitted.

"We'll put that on the list," he assured her, "and this is way easier. Just don't make sharp turns going fast."

"Because I'll flip it?" she asked, biting down on her lip.

He couldn't resist the urge to brush a quick kiss across her mouth. "You're not going to flip it. Go get 'em, Erin Earnhardt."

She turned the key, then shifted the machine into gear. He gave her a thumbs-up when she glanced over at him, and with a nod she hit the gas and took off down the path.

The ATV lurched forward several times as she got used to driving it. But after a few minutes, she was moving at a steady pace around the perimeter of the meadow. Slow but steady.

She pulled to a stop in front of him when she'd circled the entire path and clapped her hands together. "How'd I do?"

"Great. But you can go a little faster if you want."

She scrunched up her nose. "That was boring, right?"

"Watching you is never boring, but trust yourself. You can handle the machine." He reached out and tugged on the end of her ponytail. "You can handle anything."

Determination seeped into her gaze, lighting her eyes with a fire that made him want to shout for joy. This was the woman he knew and...

Once again, not going there.

She steered the ATV down the path once more. Within minutes, David regretted his words as the ATV went faster and faster around the dirt trail. He motioned for her to slow down as she sped past him, but she either didn't see or chose to ignore the warning. Her hair came undone and flew out behind her, like she was some ancient Amazon warrior racing into battle.

He held his breath as the ATV suddenly veered sharply to the right, and two of the wheels lifted from the ground.

"No," he shouted, already running toward her.

At the last second, Erin shifted her weight and the machine straightened on the path once more.

David bent forward, placing his palms on his knees as he struggled to pull air in and out of his lungs. The ATV was at his side a moment later, and he quickly turned the key, then hauled her into his arms.

"What the hell happened?" He hugged her close, then gripped the sides of her head with his hands, moving her away enough that he could examine her face. "Are you okay?"

She grinned up at him. "Did you see me go up on two wheels?"

"See you," he shouted. "I almost had a heart attack watching you. I thought I said no sharp turns."

"A chipmunk ran across the trail."

He couldn't understand how she remained so calm when his heart was rioting in his chest. "I didn't want to hurt him."

"So flipping the machine seemed like a better alternative?"

She laughed and smoothed the hair from his forehead. "I didn't flip. I had the whole thing under control. Remember, I can handle anything."

He stared at her for a moment, taking in the pure joy on her face. "You're really okay?"

"Maybe your mom was onto something when she said you were a worrywart."

"My mom has no idea what she's talking about."

Erin reached up and covered his hands with hers, a frown pulling on the corners of her mouth. "You're shaking," she whispered.

"You scared the hell out of me." He closed his eyes and leaned in to place a kiss on her forehead. "Adventure is fun, but it would kill me if I couldn't keep you safe."

He touched his lips to each of her eyelids, then trailed kisses down her cheek and along her jawline. It was as if he needed to touch every part of her to reassure himself she was okay.

"I'm fine," she assured him. "I'm sorry I scared you." She tilted her head so that her mouth met his, and the kiss quickly turned molten. He couldn't wait anymore. His body still shook from fear of her being hurt, and he channeled his thundering emotions into the kiss. Scooping her into his arms, he strode across the field to the place he'd spread out the blanket and lowered her to it.

The sun remained warm on his back and he buried his nose in the crook of Erin's neck, breathing in her scent mixed with the smell of pine trees and fresh mountain air. It was intoxicating in a way not even the finest liquor or the most powerful drug could be, and he was an instant addict.

His body trembled as he tried to control his need, to take things slow, to allow this to be her choice. More than anything, he wanted her to choose him.

"I want you," she whispered into his ear, and it was like every prayer he'd never had the guts to say had been answered.

* * *

For a moment Erin wondered if she'd said the wrong thing. David stilled above her, the muscles of his back going rigid under her hands.

He lifted his head, the intensity in his blue eyes stoking the fire inside her almost as much as his kisses had.

"I had a plan for this," he told her, his voice rough. "Champagne and rose petals and—"

"Actual rose petals?" she asked on a hoarse laugh.

To her surprise, pink tinged his cheeks. Who knew she could make David McCay blush?

"It seemed like something one of your romance heroes would do," he told her.

"You're the only man I want." She ran her hands down his back and up under the hem of his sweater. He gritted his teeth as she drew her nails along the bare skin of his back. "And I've waited long enough, David. Please don't make me wait anymore."

"I guess I can't refuse since you said please," he whispered against her lips.

Then he kissed her again and all her senses began to sing, a choir of desire and lust building in her body. After a few minutes he sat back, straddling her legs as he knelt. He slowly unbuttoned her denim shirt, his gaze fierce as inch by inch, her skin was revealed to him.

She shrugged the shirt off her shoulders, any wariness she had about being with a man so much more experienced than she was forgotten because of the longing reflected in his eyes. Longing for her.

The sun was like a warm bath on her skin, and she reached forward and tugged his sweater up and over his head.

She'd seen his chest before, but the sunlight casting

his body in silhouette was perfection. He rolled to one side and quickly toed off his boots and undid his jeans, pushing them down over his lean hips.

Reaching behind her back, she unhooked the clasp of her bra and let the soft satin material fall away from her body, then shimmied out of her jeans and panties. David let out a small groan as he knelt at her side again, a condom packet held between two fingers.

"You make me want to lose myself," he said, covering her body with his. "You make me forget everything except this moment."

"I think that's the point," she said, then gasped as he filled her. She wound her arms around his neck and kissed him, arching up so that every part of her touched every part of him.

He groaned in response and she felt an unfamiliar surge of power lick through her. She could feel that he was holding himself back, trying to take it slow because that's what a woman like Erin would want. But she wanted *more*. She wanted everything, and David was the man she wanted to give it to her.

Or even better, she'd take it from him. She moved her hips at the same time she raked her nails over his muscled shoulders. "Let go," she whispered, and without even having to add "please," he gave her exactly what she wanted.

They found a rhythm all their own, deep and intense and exactly what Erin craved. Her pleasure built in thick waves and she lost herself in the sensation of it and the fact that David seemed as overwhelmed by desire as she felt. He whispered her name like a prayer and buried his face in her neck. Then he nipped at the sensitive flesh of her ear and Erin spun out of control, gripping him tighter as she hurtled over the edge of passion.

He followed a moment later and Erin wasn't sure if it was her own heartbeat or his she heard pounding through her head. He continued to kiss her throat as she came back down, humming soothing little sounds against her skin.

"That was incredible," David whispered into her hair. "You were incredible."

Erin still felt like she was floating through the air, and the only thing that tethered her to earth was his deep voice. It was as if she'd shrugged off the old, boring version of herself and had begun to step into becoming the person she was meant to be.

"*We* were incredible," she corrected him, because she knew that nothing in her life would ever compare to this moment. Whether they lasted another week or for an eternity—and how she longed for an eternity— he would always hold her heart.

Even though he hadn't said the words *I love you*, she had to believe he felt something for her. It was in the way he looked at her, the intensity of his touch, the way her body came alive as he moved inside her.

"Are you hungry?" He trailed his fingers over her stomach in small figure-eight patterns. "You distracted me with your race car ATV driving and I never got the food unpacked."

She kissed his shoulder. "I think you distracted me by getting naked," she said, earning a rumbling laugh from him. "But now I'm starving."

After several long, lingering kisses, he rolled away from her and she grabbed her clothes. As she dressed, Erin looked around in wonder. She'd just had the most amazing sex she could ever imagine in the woods. Outside. She almost giggled at the thought of it. Talk about an adventure.

They ate the lunch he'd packed, sandwiches, fresh fruit and the best chocolate chip cookies she'd ever tasted. After repacking everything into the ATV, they took a short hike up to another overlook. Erin told him more about her relationship with her mother and her friends at school. While David peppered her with questions, he offered little about his life in return.

"What happened to Jenna?" she asked finally, as they stood together gazing out over the valley.

"You were there that night," he said casually. "You saw her apartment and—"

"I'm not talking about recently." She made her voice level, even though nerves tumbled through her. "I mean years ago. Something happened, and I don't know what it was, but it's clear you feel responsible for it."

He dropped her hand and stalked toward the path that led to the ATV. For a moment she thought he was going to leave her standing by herself in the woods. How was it possible he'd willingly shared his body with her but not whatever it was that so obviously burdened him about his sister?

Just before disappearing around the bend, he turned and walked back to her, his gaze fierce.

"I've never talked to anyone about Jenna," he said.

"Let me be the first."

He was silent for so long she thought he might refuse. Then he gave a jerky nod. "I started playing for a club baseball team in high school. Kids from the area, but no one from my neighborhood. These were boys whose parents could afford to sponsor the team, buy us the best equipment and make sure college scouts took notice. I knew my only chance of getting out of our crappy neighborhood was a scholarship." He shook his head. "Jenna didn't like the team because it took me away from home. We were on the road a lot during the summer."

"It was your dream," Erin said softly.

"Yeah," he agreed, his voice filled with bitterness. "My dream. Mom had started dating a new guy around that time and it got serious real quick. I didn't mind the guy—he wasn't as bad as some of her boyfriends—but Jenna didn't like him. He got too into the 'father' role, trying to impose house rules and curfews."

"This man lived with your family?"

David shrugged. "Not officially, but he stayed over a lot. Mom definitely knew how to pick the losers. Jenna asked me to kick him out or talk to Mom about kicking him out, but I was too busy with baseball to even care. The dude left me alone. It was Jenna he wanted to fall into line. Her wild streak had always been blatant and she was mouthy with anyone who gave her grief about it."

"She sounds like a lot to handle."

"We mostly raised ourselves, so she wasn't much into being 'handled.'" He gave a small laugh. "She still isn't. But it doesn't excuse what happened to her."

His shoulders rose and fell, as if he was struggling to catch his breath. Suddenly all of it came together. His protective instinct around his sister while holding tight to the belief that he'd failed her. The ambivalence toward his mother. Her mouth went dry but she forced out the words, "Did your mother's boyfriend—"

"He tried but Jenna fought him off." His hands fisted at his sides. "He knocked her around pretty good, but my mom came home from work. He went after her, too, but a neighbor called the cops and he was arrested." He turned to her, his eyes bleak. "I should have been home that day after school. We didn't even have baseball practice, but some of the guys were hanging out so I went with them instead."

She grabbed his hand and forced open his fist, lacing her fingers with his. "It wasn't your fault, David. You were a teenage boy. How were you supposed to know something like that would happen?"

"Jenna asked me to walk home with her," he whispered. "She didn't like being alone in the apartment with Mom's boyfriends. I told her she'd watched too many after-school movies and she was just trying to get attention." He blew out a breath. "She never forgave me."

Erin moved so she stood directly in front of him and waited until he finally looked down at her.

"She hasn't forgiven you? Or you haven't forgiven yourself?"

Chapter 14

David stared down into Erin's luminous brown eyes, unable to speak. To his knowledge, Jenna and their mother were the only people in the world who knew about what had happened that afternoon. They were the only ones who truly understood how badly he'd failed them.

Until now.

He'd been reluctant to share the memory with Erin, terrified it would change things between them. How could she not despise him after how much his selfish choice had cost his family?

But instead of judgment, her gaze was filled with sympathy and...could that possibly be understanding he saw when she looked at him?

"What's the difference?" he asked when he finally found his voice. "I failed her. I failed my mother."

"Your mother's boyfriend was at fault. You were a kid."

"I was the man of the house," he insisted, because that was the truth he knew. A tear spilled from the corner of her eye, and he caught it with his thumb. "Why are you crying? The last thing I want to do is make you cry."

She gently pushed at his chest, but when he started to take a step back, she leaned in and wrapped her arms around his waist. "You big oaf," she said into his jacket. "I'm crying *for* you. For all the years you've carried that guilt around inside you and punished yourself for something that was *not* your fault."

Her words stunned him. He'd never cared about anyone's opinion of him. David made his own luck in life—good or bad—and he told himself that's how he liked it. But something unfurled in his chest as he held Erin, looking out to the town that had become his true home. She still wanted him despite his failures, and the realization made him almost dizzy with relief.

"Don't cry, sweetheart," he whispered, resting his chin on the top of her head and rubbing her back. "I'm not worth a single one of your tears."

"You are," she insisted, sniffing loudly. "You're worth a lot more than you believe. I hate that you can't see the man that I do when I look at you."

He closed his eyes and breathed in the scent of her, let it wash away all the bad things he believed about himself—if only for a short time. Hell, it was good to feel truly happy. "I think that makes us even," he told her, "because I hate that you think you're ordinary."

She gave a soft laugh and wiped her face on his jacket. "That's different."

He tipped up her face and kissed her. "You are beautiful, extraordinary and special to me."

Her lips curved into a smile against his. "This is the best date ever."

"And we haven't even hit the hot tub," he said, earning another laugh.

Feeling lighter than he had in years, David led her back down the trail to the ATV. He insisted she drive back to the cabin, a fact he was pretty certain thrilled her given how many times she let out whoops of delight as she maneuvered through the trees.

They changed into bathing suits kept at the cabin for guests, and he opened a bottle of wine before climbing into the bubbling hot tub with a breathtaking view of the surrounding peaks.

The wine lasted longer than the bathing suits, and it wasn't long before he carried Erin into the cabin's master bedroom and made love to her again.

He'd assumed being with her would make the pounding need inside him lessen, but every touch and whisper that crossed her lips only made him want her more. There had never been anyone like her in his life. For the first time ever, he wanted to claim a woman as his and never let go.

The sun dipped over the mountain far too soon and they made their way back down to town.

He'd called both his mother and Tracie from the cabin's landline to check on Rhett and how the day was going. The boy had been thrilled with all the attention he was getting during the day, but when he heard his uncle was with Erin, he begged David to bring her home to have dinner with them.

"Is your mother going to be okay with that?" Erin took his hand as they drove down the mountain road.

"My guess is she'd rather have you there than me," he told her.

"That's not true. She loves you." Erin squeezed his fingers. "She's your mother, David."

"Right. And when do I get to meet your mom?"

Immediately she tried to pull her hand away from his, but he quickly interlaced their fingers.

"My mom and dad wouldn't believe we're together," she told him.

He felt embarrassment wash through him and struggled to keep his voice even. "Because I didn't graduate from college?"

"No," she insisted. "Not at all. You're a former baseball star and you own the hottest bar in Crimson. She's even been to Elevation. My mom likes the honey wheat beer and the artichoke dip."

"It's a real crowd pleaser, but I think you've got it all wrong. I could throw a ball and now I make beer. It's not the same as what you do, Erin. You change kids' lives."

"Kindergarten is just colors and shapes and noise control according to her."

"It's a big deal," David told her, willing her to believe him. To recognize how amazing she was and all she'd accomplished. "How long have you been a teacher?"

"Seven years."

"So your first class of students is in sixth grade?"

She nodded. "Their last year at the elementary school before junior high."

"I bet more than a few of them still visit you."

"Of course. They come in at recess or help me during my planning session."

"Do they do that for all the teachers?"

He studied her face as he waited for an answer. He

could see her mulling over the question and how to respond. "It's just that I'm the most accessible," she said finally.

"Crimson Elementary is one building. All the teachers are accessible. You make an impression, Erin. How many famous people have you heard refer to teachers who made a difference in their lives?"

She rolled her eyes. "They're talking about college professors like my father was or acting teachers or vocal coaches. Not kindergarten."

"You're making a difference to Rhett."

"Because he's a great kid."

"Jase Crenshaw told me his stepson with Asperger's still asks for you to be his teacher."

"Davey is really special, too."

"Which kids aren't special to you?"

He turned down the alley behind Elevation and parked in his spot in back of the kitchen.

"They're all special," she answered immediately.

"You have to admit some of them are little pains in the neck. I know I was." He turned off the ignition and braced himself for her response.

"Don't say that. I'm sure you were adorable at five."

"I was a hellion."

"The kids I have are amazing."

"What about Isaac Martin?"

She hesitated, then said, "Well, I never had him as a student because they moved to Crimson last year. But I've been getting to know him in the after-school program and he's actually quite sensitive. I think the trouble between his parents caused him to act out, but his mom changing things around will help."

"You proved my point." He hopped out of the truck

and walked around to her door. When she climbed out, he took her hand. "You're the kind of teacher who believes in the potential of each of her kids."

"Kindergarten is all about potential."

"Tapping into that potential is all about you."

She opened her mouth, as if to argue with him, then snapped it shut. Her eyes widened and a smile lit up her entire face. "I'm good at what I do," she said softly, as if it were a new revelation to her. "I'm really good."

"The best," he agreed. "Don't let anyone make you feel like you don't matter. You do."

They walked through the narrow space between the buildings, and David unlocked the door leading up to the apartment.

"This day was perfect." Erin leaned in to kiss him.

"You're perfect," he said. And for the first time in forever, David felt totally at peace with his world.

The following week, preparations were well under way for the town's Oktoberfest celebration, although that meant Erin hadn't seen as much of David as she would have liked.

She'd had dinner with him, as well as Angela and Rhett, most evenings and last night he'd knocked on her apartment door at nearly midnight. He'd clearly been exhausted but showed up holding a small bouquet of flowers, which had become his calling card.

"Courting," he whispered into her hair as he wrapped her in a tight hug. "I hope I didn't wake you. I know I should have called or texted first, but I had to see you." He kissed her, then stifled a yawn.

"If this is the kind of energy you put into a booty

call," she said with a laugh, leading him into the apartment, "you need to work on your skills."

He nuzzled his face into the crook of her neck. "I have mad skills."

"Trust me, I know." She set the flowers on the counter and turned in his arms. "But you also have dark circles under your eyes."

"Are you offering mc makeup?"

"I'm offering," she said, tugging him toward the bedroom, "a few hours of decent sleep. In a real bed, not the couch."

He let out a soft moan. "I hate to admit how good that sounds. I came here with every intention of having my wicked way with you."

"Save your energy for Oktoberfest."

"Only if you promise to wear a dirndl to the competition."

"To match your lederhosen?" she asked, pushing him down onto the bed.

"You know you love my lederhosen," he said sleepily, bending forward to take off his boots.

Erin's heart swelled as she watched him undress. There were so many things about this man that she loved. The way he tried so hard at everything he did—from the brewery to taking care of Rhett to repairing his relationship with his mother. The way he made Erin feel both cherished and challenged—as if he had no doubt she could handle everything life threw at her.

She would have never guessed that the crush she'd had on him for months could so quickly turn into a much deeper connection. But somehow they fit together perfectly. She softened some of his rough edges and he'd helped her unlock her confidence. His belief in her helped her realize she needed to believe in herself.

She'd even gone to see Mari Clayton from the Aspen Foundation, asking the woman to reconsider funding Erin's after-school program. Before David, Erin would have simply accepted the foundation's declining her request. But the program with the kids was too important to give up and she had no doubt any longer that she was the one meant to lead it.

Sugar rose from her place on the pillow next to Erin's and slowly walked over to rub against David's back. He'd even won over Erin's cantankerous cat.

The past month hadn't been easy, and they were both being pulled in a hundred different directions. But the time they spent together was precious, and Erin wanted to believe they had the basis for something strong and lasting.

She was already in her pajamas, so had no issue crawling into bed next to him when he held up the sheet and comforter. He pulled her in close so her back was against his chest, then draped an arm around her.

"I really did mean to ravish you," he said, dropping a featherlight kiss at the base of her neck.

"Sleep," she whispered, and within seconds felt him relax and heard his breathing slow.

She snuggled in tighter and closed her eyes, happy to fall asleep in David's arms and even happier when she awoke an hour later to find him unbuttoning her pajama top.

"I got my second wind," he told her, and proceeded to make good on all his promises about ravishing and wicked ways.

They made love deep into the night, but he left at dawn, wanting to be back at his place before Rhett woke up.

"Jenna will be out of rehab soon," he told her as he put on his jeans and boots. "She's doing well and can't wait to get back to her son."

"Do you think she's going to be able to stay healthy this time?"

A shadow passed over his face. "She loves Rhett more than anything." He sighed. "I definitely hope she loves him enough to make the alcohol and drugs a thing of the past. My mom is going to stay in town for a while, and I plan to be more involved in Jenna's life, whether she wants it or not."

"You're bringing your family back together." She sat up in the bed, tucking the sheet under her arms. "I'm proud of you."

He stilled as color crept into his cheeks. "Thanks."

"I like making you blush."

"I don't blush," he said, sounding offended, which made her smile.

"You're definitely blushing," she told him with a wink.

Pulling his sweater over his head, he moved toward her, then tugged on the sheet.

Erin yelped and held it tight to her body, but let it slip when he kissed her deeply. "First you hint that I need a nap and now you accuse me of blushing. What's next?"

"Next is you go home before *I* have *my* wicked way with you," she said, squealing when he tickled her.

"So tempting," he whispered. "When my life gets back to normal, I'm taking you away for the weekend. You and me and a hotel room all weekend long."

"I think I'd like that."

"I think you'd love that."

She had to bite her tongue to keep from whispering, *I think I love you.*

But he must have read something in her eyes, because he pulled back suddenly, like she'd scalded him. Definitely too soon for *I love you,* but he was planning weekend trips, which meant something.

He brushed her hair away from her face. "Thank you for tonight."

"Literally my pleasure."

He flashed a lopsided grin, then walked out of her bedroom. She waited until she heard the apartment door close then threw on her robe and went to lock the door. She parted the front curtains and watched him drive away, wondering if she'd ever get used to the thought of David McCay belonging to her.

Chapter 15

"Stop messing with your hair," Melody told Erin Friday night as the two women walked toward the park at the center of downtown Crimson. "You look beautiful."

Erin immediately pressed her hand to her side. "I wasn't messing with my hair. I'm just not used to wearing it down and styled."

"It looks pretty," Melody's daughter, Elaina, told her. "Like you're a princess."

Erin felt a bit like a princess tonight, the first evening of Crimson's Oktoberfest celebration. Melody had convinced her to have her hair done at a local salon and buy a new outfit for the event. Although it was out of her comfort zone, Erin had chosen a chic but casual fitted sweaterdress from the small boutique they'd gone to in Aspen. It had been over her budget but too perfect to pass up. Paired with her vintage cowboy boots and some chunky jewelry she'd borrowed from Melody, she felt amazing and couldn't wait to see David's reaction.

"Thank you, sweetie," Erin said, and smoothed a hand down the girl's blond braid. She nudged Melody, who was pushing her son, Lane, in the stroller. "Do I look like the kind of woman who could attract the town's hottie brewmaster?" she whispered.

"I don't think you need to worry about that," Melody answered with a laugh. "You've already caught him— hook, line and sinker."

"That's right." Erin took a deep breath and whispered, "David McCay is mine." A tiny bubble of happiness floated up inside her. She'd done it. In the space of a month, she'd turned her ordinary life into something extraordinary. It wasn't just David. Karen Henderson, the elementary school's principal, had called Erin into her office the previous afternoon. Apparently she'd fielded calls from several families requesting to be put on a Kidzone waiting list.

While Karen admitted she'd been skeptical at the beginning, Erin's program was turning out to be a valuable asset to the community and great PR for the school district. Mari at the Aspen Foundation had agreed to do another site visit and allowed Erin to resubmit her grant proposal along with letters of recommendation from eight of the ten families who had kids enrolled in the program.

"Where's Daddy?" Elaina asked, gripping Melody's leg. "There are lots of people here."

"He's keeping everyone safe," Melody said gently. "We'll see him when he gets off duty in a little while."

Erin looked around the streets of Crimson, with the shops still brightly lit to take advantage of the Oktoberfest crowds. She hadn't seen so many people converge on downtown since last year's Christmas festival. "It's huge," she said, clapping her hands. "I knew it would be, but I'm so happy for David. He worked hard to make this event a success."

"Apparently lots of people like beer and German food." Melody smiled. "When are the beer contest winners announced?"

Erin glanced at her watch. "In about ten minutes. Let's head to the grandstand. I want to be there when his name is called."

"The supportive girlfriend," Melody said, gently elbowing Erin in the ribs. "It's a good look on you."

Suddenly there was a commotion on the sidewalk in front of them. Melody gripped the stroller as Erin grabbed Elaina's hand, pulling the girl toward the side of the brick building.

A moment later, Joel Martin stood directly in front of her, and she gasped as she saw the flash of a blade in his hand.

"You did this to me," he said, his voice an angry snarl.

Erin's throat went dry even as her heart pounded in her chest. "I don't know what you're talking about," she whispered as she pushed Elaina behind her. "Please put away the knife."

"The hell you don't," he said, his eyes narrowing. "My old lady kicked me out because of you. My kid don't want to talk to me. Your boyfriend made sure I lost my job at the tire store, and now I got nothin'."

She could see a crowd beginning to form in a wide circle around them, and met Melody's gaze behind Joel's shoulder. "Elaina," she whispered. "Go to your Mommy, okay?" She started to give the girl a gentle push but Joel stepped forward.

"Don't move," he shouted. "You don't get to tell no one what to do tonight. Not until I'm done with you."

The little girl buried her face against Erin's leg with a whimper, and Erin saw Melody's face turn white as ash.

"I can't talk to you when you're waving a knife at me," she said, willing her voice to be calm. "Please let the girl go to her mom. She has nothing to do with this."

"You and your damn kids," he muttered. "You think you're so great, like you rule the school."

She shook her head. "I don't think—"

"All this started with that stupid McCay boy. His mama was a hot little piece, but I didn't want nothin' to do with the kid. Now I've got the sheriff breathing down my neck every time I turn around, and my life is in the toilet."

"I'm sorry," she said automatically. Was there anything she could say to this man that would stop his tirade?

"I'm going to make your boyfriend sorry for messing with my life. You'll all be sorry if you don't help me fix it."

Erin swallowed. She hadn't realized David had been in contact with Joel since that day at the community center. What had he done to make this man so angry?

"What can I do?"

She could see more people beginning to gather around them. One man called for Joel to set down the knife, but Joel only brandished it more erratically. Where was Cole Bennett or Melody's husband, Grant, when she needed him?

"You gotta talk to Danielle. Get her to take me back. Tell her I'm a good daddy and I got a right to see my son."

"I don't think—"

"Tell her," he shouted, taking a menacing step forward. At the same time, the crowd parted and Grant Cross muscled his way into their small circle.

"Drop the knife," he commanded, his gaze white-hot.

"Back off," Joel answered, slashing at the air with the weapon.

Elaina let out another little cry and whispered, "Daddy."

Before Erin could stop her, the girl tore away from Erin's embrace and ran toward her father. Grant's attention switched from Joel to his daughter as he moved forward.

Joel thrust out the knife again, just as Elaina ran past. The girl screamed as the blade sliced into her side. Then she crumpled to the ground.

Erin heard another scream that she recognized as Melody's.

Joel was momentarily still, clearly shocked by what he'd done. In those few seconds, Grant made his move, grabbing Joel's wrist and twisting it away from his body. Although Joel struggled, the knife clattered to the ground, and Erin kicked it out of reach. Cole came through the crowd and slapped cuffs on Joel, reading him his rights as Grant bent to his daughter, calling for an ambulance.

Erin rushed toward Melody, who had pulled Lane out of the stroller and was elbowing her way through the crowd to get to Grant and Elaina.

The next few minutes were a blur. Erin took the boy from Melody, who maintained more composure than Erin could have ever imagined. Joel was taken away by another deputy, and Cole turned his attention to crowd control, instructing onlookers to give the Cross family space. Two EMTs were on the scene soon after, and Elaina was placed on a stretcher, then into an ambulance.

Erin handed Lane to a tearful Melody and promised to call Melody's parents and come to the hospital.

As the ambulance disappeared around the corner, Erin felt her knees start to buckle. A strong hand wrapped around her shoulders, and Cole led her to a bench outside one of the nearby shops.

"Is Elaina going to be okay?" she asked, fighting back tears. The EMTs had loaded the girl into the ambulance, but she'd looked so pale against the bright streak of blood staining the front of her unicorn T-shirt.

"The blade penetrated high," Cole said, rubbing a hand over his face. "We've got to hope it didn't hit a lung or major artery."

Nausea washed through Erin, forcing her to bend forward and swallow hard to keep from throwing up all over Cole's shiny black work boots.

"I should have never let her dash away from me," she whispered.

"Don't blame yourself." Cole reached out a hand and squeezed her shoulder. "Joel Martin might be pissed about his life, but he had no business with that knife."

"He reeked of liquor."

"Probably high on something, too." Cole sighed. "I know you want to get to the hospital, but I need to ask you a few questions first."

"Of course. Let me call Melody's parents, then I'll talk to you."

Cole nodded. "I've got to do some crowd control and make an announcement to keep everyone down here calm." He looked out toward the center of the park. "I can already see the news moving through the crowd. Are you going to be okay?"

Erin wanted to scream that she wouldn't be okay until she knew Elaina would recover, but nodded instead.

Cole studied her a moment longer. "My squad car is parked at the curb. If you want to avoid talking to people, I can put you in there for some privacy."

"I'm fine. Go on, Cole." As he walked away, she managed to get her phone out of her purse. Unfortunately, her hands were shaking so badly she couldn't hold them steady enough to access Melody's parents' number in her contacts. Tears spilled onto the phone's screen, and she tried to blink them back. Now was not the time to lose it.

She finally made the call, her heart breaking as Melody's mother began to sob loudly on the other end of the line. She spoke to Melody's father, who remained calmer and promised to get his wife to the hospital.

She'd just returned her phone to her purse when David raced up to her and hauled her into his arms. "Did that scumbag hurt you?" he asked, breathless as he held her tight against him. "I'll kill him if he hurt you."

She wanted so much to sink into him and take the comfort that he offered. Instead, she pulled back. "Did you get Joel fired from his job?"

"What?" David seemed confused by the question.

"Joel said we'd ruined his life and that you made him lose his job."

His gaze turned steely. "Yeah, I talked to the guy who owns the tire store—told him he needs to pay attention to the sort of people he hired."

She moved away, out of the warmth and safety of his embrace. "Why would you do that?"

"You're kidding, right? I did it because the guy

screwed with my sister, then his son bullied my nephew."
He held out his hands. "Clearly tonight is evidence that
Joel is a loose cannon. I figured he'd move on if he
didn't have a job. You'd already told me his girlfriend
had kicked him to the curb. I didn't like the idea of
him being anywhere near Rhett or you during the after-
school program or still in town when Jenna returns."

It felt like her heart had taken a direct hit. "I shared
the information about Danielle Rodriguez in confidence.
If you had concerns about Rhett's safety while under my
care, you should have come to me about it."

"What would you have done?"

"Assured you that I had things under control," she answered, trying to ignore the fact that he hadn't denied
having doubts about her ability to keep his nephew safe.

"Like things were under control tonight and a little
girl ended up in the hospital?"

"That wasn't my fault," she insisted, even though
she'd said almost the same thing to Cole minutes earlier.

His blue eyes turned hard. "Are you saying it's mine?"

"I'm saying that by trying to control everything without talking to me, you put me at risk."

"I was trying to protect you," he said, his voice tight.

There had been a time when Erin believed she needed
a man to take care of things for her, and she still wanted
someone to rely on in her life. But not like this. She'd
just come to realize her self-worth and wasn't about to
let anyone, even David, diminish it now.

"I don't need you to protect me," she whispered. "I
need—"

"Join the club," he muttered, walking away several
steps before stalking back to her. "My sister didn't want

my help. My mother thinks she can handle everything just fine without me. I thought you were different."

"I thought *you* believed in me," she countered.

"I do."

She shook her head. "Not if you're going behind my back to handle things that involve me. That isn't trust."

"It's how I take care of the people I love."

Silence stretched between them, fraught with tension.

Was she included in the people he loved? Was he actually trying to say the words she longed to hear? She shook off her curiosity because the whole thing was twisted now.

"You didn't think I could handle it." Her voice shook as she said the words, but she tipped up her chin, refusing to ignore the crux of the problem.

"You're a kindergarten teacher," he said, as if that explained everything.

She felt her eyes widen and he quickly added, "You have no experience dealing with people like Joel Martin."

"Really?" She stepped forward and jabbed her finger into his chest. "You think I don't see bullies working at an elementary school?"

"He's more than a bully, and we both know it."

"And apparently because I'm *just* a kindergarten teacher, you don't have to share things with me."

"I never said *just.*"

"I know what you meant." She shook her head. "I've got to give a statement to Cole so I can get to the hospital."

"I'll drive you."

"No. Tonight is important to you."

"Not as important as you."

She studied him for a moment, willing those words to be true. But everything he'd said to her earlier seemed to refute that. Even the way he'd used the word *love* seemed wrong.

"I thought you were different," she whispered. "I thought you believed I could handle anything. That I was strong and capable." She gave a quiet laugh. "You made *me* believe in myself. And now…"

"Now what?" He moved closer, but she didn't back away.

"Now I can't go back to who I was before. I want more, David. I deserve more."

"I thought I could give you that."

She lifted her hand and trailed her fingers over the rough stubble that shadowed his jaw. "I did, too. We were both wrong."

Then she turned and hurried to where Cole Bennett waited next to his patrol car.

"Everything okay?" the sheriff asked, one brow raised as he watched the place she knew David stood behind her.

"No," she answered honestly. "But it will be. I'm ready to answer your questions."

"You won!" Tracie raced from behind the bar and threw her arms around David when he finally made it back to Elevation after Oktoberfest ended for the evening.

There was a loud round of applause from the bar's patrons, many of whom had come to Elevation to celebrate after the event.

He gave them a half-hearted wave and tried to muster a smile, but his insides were churning with a mix of guilt and regret. He'd beat out two dozen other breweries to win top honors at the festival and a nationally known distribution company had approached him about bottling not only his Altitude IPA, the award-winning beer, but two of his other more popular selections.

He couldn't care less.

"What's wrong?" Tracie asked when she took in his expression. "Did you hear an update on the Cross girl?"

"As far as I know, she's still in surgery." Bile rose in David's throat as he spoke the words. The knife blade had nicked Elaina's right lung, and she'd been rushed into the OR as soon as she arrived at the hospital. Cole Bennett had driven Erin to the hospital, then come back downtown to oversee the end of Oktoberfest, but David knew the sheriff would be back with the family and the Crosses' friends now, waiting for word on the little girl.

"She's going to be okay," Tracie whispered, with more confidence than David felt.

"It was my fault." He rubbed a hand over his face. "If I hadn't antagonized him…"

"You didn't put the knife in his hand or tell him to come after Erin."

"I knew he was unstable and a drug user. I wanted to mess with his life, to make him angry for his role in Jenna's relapse and how he'd treated Erin. I should have let it go."

"You couldn't have known how he'd go off."

"No," David agreed, "but it doesn't change that he did."

He'd told Erin he wanted to protect her, and that was true, but it had been anger fueling him when he'd interfered with Joel Martin's life. Now an innocent girl was paying the price for David's mistake.

Elaina was the same age as Rhett. His nephew had talked about the girl several times, and David couldn't imagine what that family was going through right now because of him.

"David."

"I'm fine, Tracie," he said when the bartender continued to study him. "Don't worry about me. Get back to work. I need to go upstairs and check on Rhett."

She watched him a few more moments. "I'm still happy for your success tonight," she said, squeezing his arm as she moved past him. "You've worked hard for it."

One of his regular customers walked by and patted him on the back. "Nice work tonight, McCay. Why don't you come to the back room and have a celebratory drink with us? One of the ladies is asking about you."

"Thanks, Brad." David forced a smile. "I'll be over in a minute."

This had been his life before Rhett and Erin, and up until a few weeks ago, he'd been happy with it. Or at least he hadn't realized what he was missing. He'd been given a taste of how much better his life could be, but somehow he'd managed to muck up the whole thing before he'd even had a chance to truly claim it.

Maybe this was all he was meant to be. The local brewery owner who'd share a couple drinks with patrons or a few hours with a willing woman before retreating to his solitary existence.

No harm, no foul. Nobody got hurt.

Which didn't explain the searing pain that burned across his chest, refusing to ease.

Brad turned and gestured to him, hitching his thumb at the cute blonde standing at his right side. The woman offered David a slow, sexy smile full of promise. The exact kind of promise he needed to numb his brain and his body and forget about the things he couldn't control and what he'd lost because of it.

David slipped into his apartment later that night—or in the early morning hours of the following day, to be exact. He'd stayed at Elevation until closing but had refused the lovely blonde's offer of a nightcap in her hotel room.

His life might be in the toilet, but he was no longer the man he used to be—the one who would flush it away with no thought of the consequences.

Cole had texted to say Elaina was still in surgery, so David grabbed a pillow and blanket from the side table and started to make up his temporary bed on the couch.

Once Jenna returned, he'd have his apartment to himself again. He had visions of Erin spending the night here in his big bed and the thought of waking up after a full night's sleep wrapped around her body still made his heart clench. After tonight, he wasn't sure his fantasies would ever become a reality.

"Uncle David?"

Rhett stood in the doorway to the hall, sleepily rubbing his eyes.

"Hey, buddy, why aren't you asleep?"

"Is Elaina going to be okay?"

"The doctors are doing everything they can for her," he answered, moving toward the boy. He crouched down until they were at eye level. "I know she's a friend of yours."

Rhett nodded. "She was my girlfriend but then she started dating Micah from the other class. We're still friends, though. Her favorite color is purple."

"Then let's go out tomorrow and buy her a get-well gift that's purple." He lifted the boy into his arms and walked toward the bedroom. "Do you have a different girlfriend?"

"No, I still like Elaina. She got mad when Isaac and I got in a fight."

"You're definitely my nephew," David muttered. "Sorry to tell you this, but you're in for a lifetime of girl troubles if you take after me. So don't, okay?"

"Is Ms. MacDonald your girlfriend?" Rhett asked as David lowered him to the bed.

"I don't know," David answered honestly. "I think I messed it up."

"By fighting?"

"Sort of," David admitted.

He pulled the sheet around the boy and leaned in to drop a kiss on Rhett's forehead.

"Will you stay with me until I fall asleep?"

The nightlight plugged into an outlet on the far wall cast a soft glow across the room. Rhett looked so small and innocent tucked into bed, and it killed David how much the boy had seen and experienced during his young life. Childhood was supposed to be about building forts and sneaking an extra cookie after dinner, not having a mother taken to rehab and a friend stabbed on a busy street.

When bad things had happened to David as a kid, he'd had Jenna to lean on. He couldn't even count the number of nights he'd dragged his pillow and blanket into her tiny room and slept on the floor next to her bed so neither of them had to be alone.

But even though he might not be the world's best role model, David was the person Rhett had as his own.

He toed off his boots, then drew back the covers. "Scoot over," he told the boy, and got into the bed. His feet hung over the edge and Rhett had left him only a small corner of the pillow, but when the boy reached out in the dark and wrapped his small hand around David's larger one, there was no place in the world David would have rather been.

He closed his eyes and tried to control the emotions pummeling him from every angle. In the dark, listening to Rhett's steady breathing, it was difficult to tamp down the regret and pain coursing through him at the knowledge that he'd very likely lost Erin.

Maybe he could find some stupid late-night movie on TV and try to forget—or at least ignore—the mess he'd made. His plan was to leave as soon as Rhett fell back to sleep, but the next time he opened his eyes, light streamed through the curtains.

"You snore," Rhett told him matter-of-factly.

David blinked at the boy, whose face was directly in front of his on the pillow. "I don't snore," he said, his voice rough. How had he managed to sleep the whole night in this tiny bed? "And you kicked me."

Rhett grinned. "I know. Mommy says I sleep like a starfish."

"You remember she's coming back in a week, right?"

"She said we can move into our new house."

"Yep." David pulled in a deep breath. He'd finally convinced Jenna to let him help her with rent on a cozy duplex on the south end of town. The three-bedroom house had a small fenced yard in the back and was in a neighborhood of young families, stable professionals and a few older couples who had been there for decades.

Angela was going to stay with them until Jenna was

ready to handle life on her own again. They had a lot of work to do to keep his sister on the right path, and David hoped a decent rental house was a good first step. At least it was something he could control, unlike everything else in his life.

"There's a yard and a park at the end of the block," he told Rhett. "The last time I drove by I saw kids playing soccer on one of the fields."

Rhett scrunched up his nose. "I'm not good at soccer."

"Says who?"

The boy shrugged. "I never played."

"Well, you can learn." David sat up and stretched his legs. His back ached and there was a kink in his neck, but it was worth it because Rhett seemed happy. "We'll buy a ball today."

"You play baseball."

"I can play soccer, too." He moved to the edge of the bed. "At least I played when I was your age. I must remember something."

Rhett looked unconvinced. "That was a long time ago."

"Thanks for the reminder." David grabbed his phone from where he'd left it on the dresser. Several texts had come through overnight, but the one that made his heart lighten was from Cole. He turned back to Rhett. "Elaina made it through surgery and is resting now."

"She's okay?"

"She's going to be fine."

"We can get her a purple soccer ball," Rhett announced as he placed Ruffie on top of the pillow. "Me and her can both learn to play."

"She and I," David said automatically, then swallowed. He was correcting the boy's grammar like a parent would do.

"I thought I heard voices," his mother said from the doorway.

Rhett pointed at David. "We had a sleepover."

A smile tugged at the corner of Angela's mouth. "Your Uncle David snores."

Rhett laughed. "I told you so," he said to David.

David bent and gathered the boy in his arms, lifting him high in the air then pretending to let go before catching him again. "I'll teach you to make fun of me."

Rhett squirmed and giggled and finally shouted, "I got to pee."

David immediately set him on the ground. "Well played, buddy."

"Go to the bathroom and get dressed," Angela told the boy. "I'm going to take you and your uncle out to breakfast."

"Pancakes," Rhett yelled, then grabbed a wad of clothes from the floor and ran toward the bathroom.

"Clean clothes," Angela called after him.

David smiled. "I don't think I cared about clean clothes until—"

"You cared about girls," his mother supplied.

"True enough." He massaged a hand along the back of his neck and turned to make Rhett's bed. "I can't believe I slept the night in here."

"You'll be glad to get us out of your hair when Jenna comes back."

"It hasn't been so bad," he said, surprised to find he meant the words. "But living above the bar isn't the best for a five-year-old boy."

"You've taken good care of him," his mother said gently.

David's chest pinched as he thought of the price an innocent girl had paid for him trying to protect his nephew.

He turned to find that his mother had stepped farther into the room. "Last night wasn't your fault."

"She's going to be okay," David said, not addressing her comment directly. "She made it out of surgery."

Angela nodded. "Still doesn't make it your fault."

"I wanted to hurt Joel Martin." He swallowed to stave off the anger that rose in his throat at the thought of the man. "I purposely messed with his life to get back at him for giving Jenna the drugs."

"She took them," Angela said. "Your sister has to work out her demons on her own, David."

"Demons that are there because I didn't protect her," he countered, then added softly, "Because I didn't protect either of you."

Tears shone in his mother's pale blue eyes, still so striking after all these years. "How do you think I feel? I was the one who trusted that creep around my daughter. I let him into my home and—"

"You didn't know."

"I should have." She gave a humorless laugh. "Jenna knew. She hated him from the start."

"You did the best you could at the time."

"How is it you can forgive me but not yourself?"

Her voice was like a caress, the gentle motherly tone he'd always wanted to hear when he'd been a kid. The way he heard Jenna talk to Rhett. For all of his sister's problems, she loved her son. David hoped for all their sakes it would be enough to help her vanquish her issues once and for all.

But he couldn't release the belief that he'd failed his sister and his mother. Just like he'd failed Erin last night. No matter what his intention had been, the outcome was what mattered.

"I'm going to take a quick shower," he told his mother without answering her question.

He started to walk past her, but she threw her arms around his waist and hugged him tight. "You're a good man, David. I love you."

Emotion rushed through him like a tidal wave, turning him into the vulnerable boy he'd been so many years ago. He couldn't remember ever hearing his mother say she loved him, and so he'd convinced himself he didn't need the words.

One more delusion shattered.

He hugged her back and whispered, "I love you, too," then broke free of the embrace and left the room. If he allowed himself to feel anything, there was a good chance he'd have to feel everything.

And an even better chance he'd never recover.

Chapter 16

A week after the accident, Erin parked her car outside the Crosses' two-story house in a newer subdivision west of Crimson. She opened the back of her car and pulled out gifts from the staff and students at Crimson Elementary that she'd offered to bring to the family.

Elaina had been released from the hospital the previous afternoon but still had a few more days of rest at home before she could return to school.

Erin had canceled Kidzone for the week, and quite possibly for good. She couldn't bear the idea that Elaina had been injured because Erin had angered a parent and he'd come looking for revenge.

What if she couldn't keep them safe? There were district-sponsored security measures in place at school, but the responsibility for her students during the after-school program was completely hers.

She wanted to believe she could handle anything,

but Friday night's tragedy had rocked her confidence to its core. Her mother had always told her to be satisfied with good enough, but Erin hadn't listened. She'd wanted more from life—to be more.

But not at the cost of a child's life.

She had two big boxes filled with stuffed animals and games plus several trays of meals to deliver. Instead of making two trips, she piled everything into her arms, trying to distribute the weight as best she could. A few steps up the front walk she realized her mistake. One of the boxes began to teeter, and she tried to adjust her hold so everything would fall back into balance.

Instead, the lasagna she'd placed on top of her load started to slide and would have splattered to the ground if a set of strong hands hadn't stopped it.

"Whoa, there," David said against her ear, his arms coming around her to steady the pile. "You may have bitten off more than you can chew with this one, darlin'."

Erin gritted her teeth. Didn't that just about sum up her life at the moment?

"I've got it under control," she said, even though it was obvious she didn't have anything under control.

"I know you do," he agreed, "but can I help anyway?"

She wanted to turn down his offer, to prove that she could handle this one tiny task. But a homemade lasagna would inevitably end up all over the concrete.

"Thanks," she muttered as he took three boxes off her pile.

"We got Elaina a purple soccer ball," Rhett said as he skipped up the walkway next to her. "'Cause Uncle David is going to teach her like he taught me."

"He taught you," Erin corrected with a smile. "I saw you playing at recess today."

"I made a goal." He held up an oversize gift bag. "I

bringed her a pink baseball bat, too, so we can learn to play baseball."

"Brought," both Erin and David said at the same time. One small word, yet Erin felt the connection between them zing to life and did her best to ignore it.

David had made his choice by not believing in her, and she'd made hers as a result. There was no going back now.

She knocked to announce their arrival, then they walked into the house together. Lane toddled down the hall toward them, followed by Grant.

"Whett, Whett, Whett," the boy called.

"I don't know who's more excited for your visit," Grant told Rhett. "Elaina or her brother." He glanced at Erin. "Thanks for bringing all of Elaina's stuff. Did you guys come together?"

"No." Erin and David answered simultaneously once more, and Erin felt a blush creep up her cheeks.

Grant looked between them with raised eyebrows. "Okay, then. Elaina's on the couch in the family room," he said to Rhett. "Lane can lead you back there."

"Come on," Lane shouted at the top of his lungs, because he seemed to have no volume control. Rhett followed the boy, leaving Erin standing with David and Grant in the small foyer.

"I'm going to put everything in the kitchen," she said, feeling suddenly self-conscious. She'd spent a lot of time at the hospital with Melody but hadn't talked to Grant since the night Elaina was hurt. Not since he'd watched Erin let his daughter run past the man holding a knife.

One glance at David showed he looked as uncomfortable as she felt. Instead of taking solace in that, Erin wanted to reach out and comfort him.

"I have something to say to both of you." Grant moved to block her way down the narrow hall.

"You don't need to do this." David shifted slightly to stand between her and Grant, as if shielding her from whatever the stoic deputy might tell them.

"I don't blame either of you for Elaina's injury," he said, ignoring David. "And it's obvious you each blame yourself or each other. I can't tell which it is, but I want you to stop."

"I should never have let go of her," Erin blurted, fresh tears clogging her throat. She'd already cried so much since Friday night but her heart was a bottomless reservoir of guilt.

"No one would have been in that situation if I hadn't antagonized Martin," David said, more to her than Grant. "If anyone is at fault—"

"Someone is at fault." Grant's voice was firm. "Joel Martin. We're going to make sure he pays for what he did to my little girl. But the blame is solely his, and I want you both to understand that. I've had the worst couple of days of my life and I'm not going to stand here and argue. Do I make myself clear?"

Grant might not be in uniform at the moment, but he still commanded respect. Erin knew it was pointless to argue with him.

"Thank you," she whispered. Trying to discreetly wipe her eyes on her sleeve, she moved past him to the kitchen.

As she placed the packages on the counter, she felt David at her side.

"Listen to Grant," he said, setting the boxes he carried next to hers.

"I could tell you the same thing."

"But you won't," he countered, "because we both know I set off that guy. I only wanted to—"

"Don't say 'protect me.'" Fists clenched at her sides, Erin turned to him. "I can't do this with you again, David."

His lips pressed together in a firm line, but he nodded. "When are you going to reopen the program?"

The question caught her off guard.

"Rhett keeps asking," he added. "I guess he's been working on something for Jenna when she comes back."

Erin smiled even as a band of emotion tightened around her chest. "It's an adventure book—pictures of all the things he wants them to do together. He's been putting a lot of time into it."

"He's worried about finishing before she returns."

There were so many things unfinished right now. Erin hated letting go of Kidzone, but panic pounded through her every time she thought of Joel Martin and what could have happened if he'd chosen to confront her during her program hours at the community center. "I'll bring it to school, and he can work on it there."

"You didn't answer the question," he said softly.

"I'm a kindergarten teacher." She cleared her throat when her voice cracked. "You said it yourself. I'm not a social worker or someone trained to work with families in crisis. I had an idea for a way to help but…"

"It was a great idea." He leaned in so they were at eye level. "It still is."

"Maybe Olivia can find a person better qualified—"

"Kidzone belongs to you."

Her heart squeezed at the tenderness in his tone. She'd wanted the program to be hers, just like she'd wanted to believe David belonged to her. But in the last few days she'd never felt more alone.

"I've got to go," she whispered, turning from him. It was too hard to pretend she was fine when her heart wouldn't stop breaking. "Tell Melody I'll talk to her later."

"Erin," he called as she hurried away, but she didn't stop. Couldn't stop. Not when she might crumble into a million sad pieces if she did.

"You turn your foot just a little," Rhett shouted, "then look up and kick!"

Elaina Cross clapped as Rhett shot the soccer ball toward the goal David had set up on the far end of the backyard. She sat bundled up on a patio chair watching Rhett teach Lane how to kick the ball. Both boys ran across the yard, Rhett slowing his pace to match the toddler's. David's stomach tightened when Lane stumbled, but Rhett took the boy's hand and they continued together.

"He's sweet with Lane," Melody said gently.

"Yeah," David agreed, pride creeping into his tone. "He's a good kid. Thanks for letting him visit Elaina."

"She's thrilled. Now that she feels better it's difficult to rest all day."

"She looks good." David glanced at Melody. "She'll make a hundred percent recovery, right?"

"According to the doctor," Melody answered.

David nodded. "I have to tell you how sorry—"

"Grant spoke to you," Melody interrupted.

"He did."

"Then no apologies. There's only one person responsible for Elaina's injury, and it isn't you."

"Or Erin," David added automatically.

"Of course not," Melody agreed with a sigh. "Although I can't get her to believe that."

"You have to convince her to reopen the Kidzone program."

"What are you talking about?" Melody turned fully to face him, shock and concern warring in her tone.

"She isn't running the program. You didn't know?"

Melody shook her head. "I've been kind of preoccupied."

"I thought it was temporary, but the way she sounded today…"

"We can't let her do that."

Lane shouted for his mommy to watch him kick, and Melody called out a few words of encouragement. When the boys were occupied again, her gaze swung back to David. "Crimson needs that program. *Erin* needs that program."

David rubbed a hand against the back of his neck. "I said some things Friday night," he admitted.

"I'm guessing they were stupid things?" Melody crossed her arms over her chest.

"Really stupid," he agreed.

"Fix it," she told him.

"I can't. Erin ended—"

"Do you love her?"

"I don't… I mean…she deserves more than—"

"Simple question. Do you love her?"

David felt himself shift uncomfortably under Melody's steely gaze. The woman barely reached his chest, but she was a force to be reckoned with nonetheless.

"I love her," he whispered.

"Then fix it," she repeated.

He opened his mouth to argue, then shut it again. He was used to working hard but had never had to put himself on the line emotionally. Hard work and commitment, he was quickly discovering, were two different things.

Yes, he loved Erin. She was the best thing that had ever happened to him, like winning the relationship lottery—unexpected and wholly life-changing. But what if he tried to make things right and she still said no?

What if he wasn't enough?

He started to shake his head, but Rhett looked over at that moment, flashing a wide grin as he dribbled the ball toward Elaina. Joy radiated from the boy with such intensity it stole David's breath. A month ago he would have never guessed Rhett could look that happy. David might not have known what he was doing when he stepped in to care for his nephew, but that hadn't stopped him from trying.

And he sure as hell had no idea how to be a man worthy of Erin's love, but he knew for certain he couldn't win her back if he didn't try.

He glanced down at Melody, already feeling a strange sense of accomplishment, and grinned when she gave him an approving nod.

"I have an idea," he told her. "But I'm going to need a lot of help to pull it off."

"You've got it," she answered immediately. "Anything for Erin."

David took a deep breath, resolve filling him. *Anything* to win back Erin.

"Any place but Elevation." Erin refused to budge from where she stood on the sidewalk as Melody and Suzie tried to tug her forward.

"I'm craving artichoke dip," Melody insisted. "You can't deny me after what I've been through."

"Seriously?" Erin glared at her best friend. "You're using Elaina's injury as a ploy to force me to see David? That's shameless."

It was Friday night, exactly two weeks after the confrontation with Joel Martin, and her girlfriends had wrangled Erin into agreeing to a happy hour downtown. The truth was she needed a night out and away from her lonely apartment.

Even the promise of a BBC movie marathon had done little to lift her spirits. All she could think of was the nights she'd spent with David and how much comfier her bed was with his arms wrapped around her.

She hadn't seen him since the afternoon at Melody's house, although Rhett and a few of the other kids continued to ask when Kidzone was going to open again. Even Erin's principal had gently suggested she continue the program, but Erin couldn't bring herself to take that chance again.

How could she expect parents to trust their kids with her when she didn't trust herself?

"I'm not forcing you to talk to him," Melody argued.

"Even though," Suzie added, "you're clearly miserable without him."

"I'm not miserable." Erin bit down on the inside of her cheek to keep from saying more. She was *beyond* miserable, brokenhearted in a way she hadn't known existed. How had she ever believed falling in love was worth this kind of pain?

"Artichoke dip will make you feel better," Melody said, wrapping an arm around Erin's waist.

Erin gave a small laugh. There was no sense arguing, and she couldn't avoid David forever. Crimson was too small a town for that kind of blessing. "Fine. He might not even be here. His sister is home now. They're probably out as a family."

"Probably," Melody said, her voice uncharacteristically high-pitched.

"What's the matter?" Erin asked. "You sound strange."

"I'm hungry," Melody said. "For—"

"Artichoke dip," Erin said, then stopped outside the brewery's front door. "Are you pregnant again? I've never seen you with such a strong craving."

"Just go in already," Suzie muttered.

"Fine," Erin agreed, throwing open the heavy walnut door and striding through. "Are you both happy now?"

"Yes," Melody whispered over her shoulder. "And I hope you will be, too."

Erin didn't have a chance to ask what her friend meant because a loud chorus of cheers rang out from the crowd filling the bar.

She glanced around and saw people she knew from every facet of her life. Teachers, parents and kids from the elementary school; Karen Henderson, the school's principal; as well as Sara and Josh Travers and their group of friends. There were people she'd gone to high school with and even her mother waved to her from a seat at one of the high-top tables in front of the bar.

"What is this?" She automatically took a step back, but Melody pushed her forward.

"You finally taking center stage," her friend whispered as David came out from behind the bar.

"It's a fund-raiser," he said, moving closer. "For you and Crimson Kidzone."

"But the program isn't—"

"Going to start up again until next week," he said loudly. "That's what I told Ms. Clayton from the foundation."

He gestured over his shoulder to where Mari Clayton from the Aspen Foundation stood at the edge of the crowd. The woman gave Erin the thumbs-up and Erin waved in return before her gaze slammed into David's once more.

"This town needs Kidzone," David continued, taking another step toward her, "and the program needs you, darlin'. Everyone in Crimson agrees." He lifted his hands. "Don't we, everyone?"

There was another round of applause and shouts of support. Erin's heart thudded and she pressed her fingers to her wet cheeks as a hush fell over the room. "I don't know what to say," she whispered.

"Say you won't give up." David reached out and covered her hands with his, wiping away her tears with the pads of his thumbs. "On yourself or on me."

A woman's voice cut through the quiet. "Even though he sometimes acts like an idiot."

"Thanks, Mom," David muttered, lacing his fingers with Erin's.

Erin tried not to laugh as she met Angela's brilliant blue gaze across the bar. The older woman stood next to her daughter, who was holding tight to Rhett's hand and looking somewhat uncomfortable as people turned to stare at their small group.

"Mommy's back," Rhett shouted to Erin.

Erin saw color flood Jenna's cheeks, but the woman stepped forward. "I'm very grateful to you and your program," she said, clearing her throat when her voice cracked. "I'm grateful for the support you gave Rhett while I was getting help. This community needs more people like you."

There was another round of applause, and Erin felt her face grow hot. "Everyone is staring at me," she said quietly.

"Because you're amazing," David said. "This town needs you." He pressed a gentle kiss to her knuckles. "But not as much as I need you."

She sucked in a breath at his words. "David."

"Don't say no yet." He squeezed her fingers. "I know I've said stupid things and done stupid things, but please give me another chance. I love you, Erin. I love who you are— your heart and your beauty. I love that you make me want to try harder than I ever have. You make me believe that I can be the type of man you deserve. Let me prove it to you."

She swallowed against the sob that rose in her throat. "You don't have to prove anything to me, David. I love you just the way you are."

"I'm not perfect," he told her.

"You're perfect for me," she countered.

"I know you want a hero."

She lifted up on tiptoe and kissed the corner of his lips. "I want *you*," she whispered, then laughed as he enveloped her in a hug so tight she knew he'd never let her go.

There were more cheers but Erin barely heard them over the wild beating of her own heart. David kissed her deeply.

"Forever," he said when he finally pulled back to look at her. His blue eyes shone with so much love. The intensity of it made her breath catch.

"Forever," she agreed, knowing this moment was just the start to the grandest adventure she could ever imagine.

* * * * *